Fortuné Du Boisgobey

**The Steel Necklace and Cécile's Fortune**

Fortuné Du Boisgobey

**The Steel Necklace and Cécile's Fortune**

ISBN/EAN: 9783337267940

Printed in Europe, USA, Canada, Australia, Japan

Cover: Foto ©Andreas Hilbeck / pixelio.de

More available books at **www.hansebooks.com**

# THE STEEL NECKLACE

AND

# CÉCILE'S FORTUNE.

# VIZETELLY'S HALF-CROWN SERIES.

*DU BOISGOBEY'S SENSATIONAL NOVELS.*

XXI.

# THE STEEL NECKLACE

## AND

# CÉCILE'S FORTUNE.

By FORTUNÉ DU BOISGOBEY.

FIFTEENTH THOUSAND.

LONDON:

*VIZETELLY & CO., 42 CATHERINE STREET, STRAND.*

1888.

THE GABORIAU & DU BOISGOBEY

# SENSATIONAL NOVELS.

UNIFORM WITH THE PRESENT VOLUME.

THE STANDARD says:—"The romances of Gaboriau and Du Boisgobey picture the marvellous Lecoq and other wonders of shrewdness, who piece together the elaborate details of the most complicated crimes, as Professor Owen, with the smallest bone as a foundation, could re-construct the most extraordinary animals."

*The following Volumes are already Published.*

## By ÉMILE GABORIAU.

| | |
|---|---|
| IN PERIL OF HIS LIFE. | DOSSIER, NO. 113. |
| THE LEROUGE CASE. | THE MYSTERY OF ORCIVAL. |
| LECOQ, THE DETECTIVE. 2 Vols. | THE COUNT'S MILLIONS. 2 Vols. |
| THE GILDED CLIQUE. | LITTLE OLD MAN OF BATIGNOLLES. |
| OTHER PEOPLE'S MONEY. | INTRIGUES OF A POISONER. |
| THE SLAVES OF PARIS. 2 Vols. | THE CATASTROPHE. 2 Vols. |

## By FORTUNÉ DU BOISGOBEY.

THE TIMES says:—"M. Du Boisgobey gives us no tiresome descriptions of laboured analysis of character: under his facile pen plots full of incident are quickly opened and unwound. He does not stop to moralize; all his art consists in creating intricacies which shall keep the reader's curiosity on the stretch, and offer a full scope to his own really wonderful ingenuity for unravelling.

| | |
|---|---|
| THE OLD AGE OF LECOQ, THE DETECTIVE. 2 Vols. | THE MATAPAN AFFAIR. |
| THE SEVERED HAND. | THE CRIME OF THE OPERA HOUSE. 2 Vols. |
| IN THE SERPENTS' COILS. | A FIGHT FOR A FORTUNE. |
| THE DAY OF RECKONING. 2 Vols. | THE GOLDEN PIG. 2 Vols. |
| BERTHA'S SECRET. | THE THUMB STROKE. |
| WHO DIED LAST? | THE CORAL PIN. 2 Vols. |
| THE JAILER'S PRETTY WIFE. | PRETTY BABIOLE. |
| THE ANGEL OF THE CHIMES. | HIS GREAT REVENGE. 2 Vols. |
| THE CONVICT COLONEL. | THE NAMELESS MAN. |
| THIEVING FINGERS. | FERNANDE'S CHOICE. |
| A RAILWAY TRAGEDY. | THE PHANTOM LEG. |
| THE STEEL NECKLACE AND CECILE'S FORTUNE. | THE DETECTIVE'S EYE AND THE RED LOTTERY TICKET. |
| THE RED BAND. 2 Vols. | THE GOLDEN TRESS. |

# THE STEEL NECKLACE.

## I.

IT was neither an aristocratic wedding nor one of work people, where each person present settles his own score. There were no private carriages at the door of the restaurant, but the bride and bridegroom had come with their friends in hired landaus, drawn by horses bedecked with ribbons, and driven by coachmen with white gloves. The dinner had been ordered in the suburbs, as in Paris itself rooms where a hundred persons can sit down to table are rather scarce ; but the establishment kept by old Cabassol, at Boulogne-sur-Seine, is not a common tavern. It makes a speciality of furnishing wedding-breakfasts and dinners for the wealthy middle classes at a fair price. More than one well-to-do merchant, who is now high up in the world, feasted there on the happiest day of his life, when he made his beginning in business, and thought himself extremely fortunate in having married the daughter of a shop-keeper, with a dowry of a hundred thousand francs.

On this occasion the wedding was that of a physician's daughter and the cashier of a banking-house. The physician had died two years previously, and had left a handsome fortune to his only daughter. The bridegroom merely possessed his salary and a small sum of money he had saved up ; but his prospects for the future were bright enough. The banker, in whose employ he was, had promised to take him into partnership, and intended to make him his successor. Edmond Trémentin, the husband, was thirty years of age, and Élise Aubrac, his bride, was nineteen. Edmond was a tall, handsome, and very intelligent fellow ; Élise was adorably pretty, good, and amiable. Everything augured well for their happiness. There were no mothers-in-law nor fathers-in-law to disturb their conjugal felicity, as they both happened to be orphans. Élise was seated beside M. Verdalenc, the banker by whom her husband was employed, while Edmond, who sat opposite to her, was placed between Madame Verdalenc and Madame Aubrac, a widow and aunt by marriage to his wife. These respectable ladies and this honourable financier had arranged the marriage, which was not entirely a love-match, and they appeared overjoyed at their success.

All the friends and acquaintances from far and near had been invited. The dinner was a capital one, and the wines excellent. There was to be a dance afterwards, and it promised to be a very gay one—at least, judging of the conversation which became more and more animated, as toast succeeded toast. The moment had come when, in accordance with old traditions, it is the custom to sing over the dessert ; but the banker Verdalenc, who prided himself on his good manners, did not give the signal. All his clerks were there, and some of them would have gladly indulged in appropriate ditties, but they did not dare to. As for the young ladies, who were impatient to waltz, they were beginning to find the dinner too long.

This was also the opinion of two guests, seated side by side at the further end of the long table—two guests who belonged neither to the banking nor to the medical profession. They had been invited somewhat by chance. One of them was a dramatic author, whose pieces had met with some success, and who often gave boxes to Madame Verdalenc, knowing that she was very fond of the theatre, but did not like to pay for her seats. His companion was a painter of talent, who had formerly been intimate with Dr. Aubrac, and had painted the portraits of the father and the daughter. They had come to this family gathering out of politeness, but as they were not wonderfully amused by the toasts and speeches, they exchanged whispered observations upon the wedding-guests, including, of course, the newly married couple. "I say," said the painter, whose name was Alfred Caussade, "when you write a part for Geoffroy, of the Palais Royal, you ought to take Verdalenc for a model. He's Joseph Prud'homme all over, with his gold eye-glasses and his bass voice."

"I'm not such a fool! He is too useful to me," replied the dramatist, George Darès. "He sings my praises to all the merchants of the Rue du Sentier. Besides, without taking him, there is no lack of types here. The bridegroom is far more worth studying than Verdalenc."

"He has the head of a model. He would make a capital shop-walker no doubt, but I don't see anything peculiar about him."

"Because you haven't seen much of him. But I've seen him at work, and, I assure you, he is well worth studying. He began by sweeping out Verdalenc's office, and you will acknowledge that he must have possessed great energy and cleverness to become the gentleman you see. The fact is he has succeeded by ingratiating himself with the women also. He was once Madame Verdalenc's lover."

"What ! She is fifty-five at least."

"She was only forty-five when he succeeded in pleasing her. He also gained the good graces of the husband, and he has retained the friendship of the wife since it is she who has made this match."

"With poor Élise. Ah ! I pity her, for what you tell me shews that the fellow is a schemer of the worst sort. By Jove ! if my

old friend, the doctor, had lived, this would never have happened. Unfortunately, his sister-in-law, who has had charge of the
girl, is quite destitute of common-sense. What can you expect
from an old fool who calls herself the Baroness Aubrac, on the pretext that the father of her late husband was a colonel and baron of
the First Empire? What surprises me is, that Elise consented to
marry that insipid dandy."

"That insipid dandy knows how to keep his secrets. He has
had three or four intrigues in good society, and no one has ever
known who the ladies were, although they have been useful to him.
It is said that Madame Verdalenc was jealous of the last one, and
to spite her rival, she induced Edmond to marry, and talked to
Mademoiselle Aubrac, till the latter ended by consenting, although
she had a previous attachment."

"Where the devil did you learn all this?"

"I am intimate with a young man whom you must have met,
and I know he was in love with this very girl. He is so still, and
I fear that the sorrow of losing her will drive him nearly crazy.
He is a poet, so it won't be very remarkable."

"A poet?"

"Yes. Louis Mareuil, who has published a volume of verses,
and who writes for newspapers in his leisure moments."

"I know him. He is a very good-looking fellow and he has some
talent. And Élise preferred that cashier to him! But I've had
enough of all this and I'm going to take my departure as soon as
they rise from the table."

"I'm going to leave, too. But the question is to find a vehicle
to take us back to Paris. It is ten o'clock, and here we are at
Boulogne, where cabs are not plentiful after sunset. There is no
room for us in the carriages of the wedding-party, and the weather
is frightful—"

"That's true; it's raining pitchforks," said Caussade, glancing
at the windows against which the rain was beating. The dining-
room was on the first floor of old Cabassol's establishment, but
this first floor was only raised a few feet from the ground. The
night was dark, and the wind blew furiously.

"Well," remarked Darès, "we had better take the tramway at
Saint-Cloud. We have only to cross the bridge. Ah! Edmond
is getting up to reply to the speech of his benefactor, Verdalenc.
See how the bride is blushing. She suspects—"

But at this moment, a crash of falling glass interrupted the dramatic author. A pane of one of the windows had been shivered to
pieces, and the bridegroom, who was facing the window, staggered
and then fell to the ground. A bomb bursting on the table would
not have more dismayed the guests than this sudden fall of the
bridegroom, who had risen to drink a glass of champagne to their
health. Some thought that he was tipsy, and, to tell the truth, he
had drunk a good deal. However, those who were nearest hastened
to his side, and succeeded in raising him in their arms. Then a

cry of horror resounded on all sides. Blood was flowing in streams from a wound in his breast, coursing down his shirt and staining the hands of those who upheld him. He was dead, plainly enough ! he had been shot through the heart !

The bride fainted, while the baroness fled to the other end of the room, and Madame Verdalenc sank down on to the floor. M. Verdalenc, in his deep bass voice, called for a doctor, and as there were three or four present—old friends of Élise's father—there was no lack of medical assistance. But the guests, filled with terror and consternation, did not dream of asking whence the murderous bullet had come. They had only heard the crash of the broken glass. The wind had no doubt deadened the report, and yet the shot must have been fired from near by.

The only person fully cognisant of what had happened was George Darès, who at the very moment when M. Trémentin fell, was observing Élise, seated with her back to the window which her husband faced. Not only had George witnessed the breaking of the pane of glass, but he had also seen a flash outside. A glance at the victim of this abominable crime was enough to show that all the care lavished upon him would never restore him to life, and so Darès, who was very clear-headed, at once thought of the murderer. " They will let him escape if we don't take care," he said, quickly, to his friend Caussade. " But he hasn't had time to go far as yet. Will you help me to catch him ? "

" Willingly," answered the painter, who was never astonished at anything. And, thereupon, instead of joining the group around the murdered man, they hastened to the door.

" Some one is certain to have arrested him," said Caussade, as they descended the stairs. " There must be plenty of people in the streets."

" You forget the rain," replied Darès, and he was right, for they had no sooner crossed the threshold of the house than they saw that the street was absolutely deserted. Adjoining the Cabassol restaurant there is an inn with sheds and stables, and the coachmen of the wedding-party, having placed their horses and carriages under cover, were now supping there together. They evidently had no knowledge of what had happened, for they were still at table. " I see no one," growled George Darès, glancing right and left. " The rascal has already decamped. But which way has he gone ? I have no idea ; have you ? "

The street was neither broad nor long. It joined on one side the highway which leads from Auteuil to the bridge of Saint-Cloud, while, on the other hand, it conducted to the road bordering Baron Rothschild's property and leading to the Bois de Boulogne. Over the way in front of the restaurant, the only building was a wooden hut, which some workman had probably used as a storehouse for his tools, for it did not appear to have ever been inhabited. George Darès, however, fancied that the murderer might have taken refuge there, and he was walking towards the cabin, which was perched on a little hillock, when Caussade exclaimed : "I see him ! He is running towards the wood."

The dramatist turned, and, by the uncertain light of a distant street lamp, he perceived a man running with all his speed and carrying an object resembling a gun. This man was at least fifty yards in advance, and he was proceeding at a pace which left the two friends little hope of overtaking him. "At all events, let us try," said Darès.

Caussade assented, and they started off in pursuit of the fugitive, crying out : "Stop him !"

Unfortunately, there was no one there to do so, and they could only rely upon themselves. The chase commenced under bad conditions for the pursuers, for the man perceived and heard them, and the fear of being caught lent him wings. He was short and slender ; from a distance, indeed, he looked ..ne a child. He was now making for the Bois de Boulogne where the darkness would hide him from the eyes of those who were trying to overtake him. They might have succeeded in an open country, for they probably possessed more staying power ; but they could not run as fast, and the murderer soon disappeared under the trees. They remarked, however, that, instead of taking to the bushes, where they could never have found him, he followed a winding path which must lead to the Longchamps race-course, and so they were not discouraged. They entered the wood two minutes after he did ; but in the darkness, Caussade stumbled in a rut and fell. He rose with an oath, but as Darès had stopped to help him, they had lost some seconds, and the object of their pursuit had escaped. "I have had enough of it," growled the painter.

"I haven't," replied the playwright, "but it is no use going on. We are distanced."

"Besides, if we chanced to catch him up he might fire upon us. His gun must have a couple of barrels. He has a second bullet at our service, and we haven't even a cane—"

"Hush ! Listen !" interrupted Darès. "Don't you hear the sound of wheels below there, in front of us ? He is driving away, I'm sure."

"What ? Do you imagine he has a vehicle at his orders ? Murderers don't generally ride about in carriages."

"True, but everything connected with this affair is extraordinary. And, besides, this man is evidently not a professional murderer. He didn't kill Trémentin to rob him. So there must be some vengeance in all this ; and rich people who revenge themselves are still to be found in the world. But the noise has ceased. In half an hour the fellow will be in Paris, and there is nothing to prevent him from walking about the boulevards. No one will recognise him, for no one has seen his face. But let us go back ; I'm wet through, and I want to get dry."

"So do I. We are in full dress, without overcoats or hats. The bride can boast of having made me commit a pretty piece of folly.

I started on this fine expedition on account of her husband, and I shall be lucky if I escape without a chest complaint."

"By-the-way, Alfred, the charming Élise is a widow. Louis Mareuil can marry her now."

"Widow before being a wife," muttered Caussade. "There's a fine situation for you to utilize in a comedy."

"I only write vaudevilles and burlesques," replied George Darès, "and there is nothing funny in this affair. It is decidedly a tragedy."

"It will end in an exciting trial if the man who got away from us is found. I doubt it very strongly, though. But let's return. I'm shivering all over, and, besides, I should like to know what the wedding-party have been doing, while we were pursuing the assassin."

"So should I. Come on, let's run. It will warm us."

They now retraced their steps. The storm had increased in violence, and the wind blew in their faces—unfavourable circumstances for conversation, so that they proceeded in silence. Still Darès, as he hastened along, examined both sides of the road. On the right hand rose the wall of Baron Rothschild's park, and on the left there was a barren tract of land. The street or road where the restaurant was situated had houses only on one side, for the wooden hut which was opposite Father Cabassol's establishment could scarcely pass for a tenement. Thus the murderer had had every facility to fire and escape without being seen. He must have chosen his position in advance, and have fully calculated his chances.

"George," began Caussade, tired of keeping his thoughts to himself, "I think, like you, that Trémentin was the victim of revenge ; but I can't imagine who killed him. In such cases it is often said : 'Look for the woman.'"

"Yes ; and in the present instance the saying is peculiarly appropriate. The fellow we have been pursuing may have acted under orders."

"You mean for some woman, eh ? But what woman ? Has some forsaken inamorata, furious with him for marrying, had him murdered at his wedding dinner ? That would be a thoroughly feminine vengeance ; but what woman could it be ? It seems that M. Trémentin had had several love affairs."

"Yes, but I don't know who the women were. I only know one of them, the one I spoke to you about at dinner."

"Madame Verdalenc ! it's impossible that she can have had a hand in it for she desired this marriage. Wasn't it she who arranged it ? "

"She, at least, strongly contributed to it. So she can have had no reason for resentment against Trémentin ; and, besides, she was seated beside him when he was struck. Had she promoted the murder, she would have chosen a less dangerous place : the bullet might have glanced aside."

"Then it must be her rival—the woman who, for the last six months, has engrossed the handsome cashier's attention, and I suppose that Madame Verdalenc will denounce her."

"Yes, if she knows her name, which I am not at all sure of. Trémentin was very discreet."

"Then this death will remain inexplicable. How I pity Élise Aubrac."

"She is not so much to be pitied. She didn't love Trémentin, and she is free to marry again, and according to the dictates of her heart."

"By-the-way, may not the shot have been fired by the jilted lover?"

"Louis Mareuil? He is incapable of such an action, I assure you. He would gladly have killed Trémentin in a duel. In fact he insulted him recently, and it was not his fault if nothing came of it. But to assassinate him, never!"

"I suppose, too, that he hasn't the slight figure of that rascal who ran off?"

"He is not very tall nor very stout," answered Darès, with a little hesitation; "but that proves nothing. Besides I would willingly bet that at this moment he is quietly engaged in writing an article for to-morrow morning's newspaper. He must live, you know, and poetry doesn't support poets, whereas a reporter has a salary. Here we are, however. It seems to me there is a crowd before Cabassol's."

"Yes, a dozen people, more or less; and I see some servants, too; and some gentlemen coming out of the restaurant."

"They are going for the commissary of police, probably. They don't seem to be in much of a hurry, and the magistrate will arrive rather late to solve the mystery. I have a great mind to make my investigation before he commences his."

"What, do you mean to encroach upon the province of the police?"

"Yes, you have worried me by suggesting that Louis might be suspected. I am going to try to obtain proofs of his innocence, in that cabin yonder; I am convinced that the shot was fired from there."

"That's probable; but even were it certain, what do you expect to find."

"Why, the murderer may have left some traces. At all events, come on!"

"But suppose we are found in that cabin; we might be taken for accomplices."

"That would be a good joke. Why, all the wedding-party would testify that we were sitting at the table when Trémentin was shot. So come on."

"What the deuce is the matter with you?" fumed Caussade. "Will you at least promise me that after this silly inspection, you will let me return for my hat and overcoat?"

"Of course I shall; I don't want you to return to Paris bareheaded."

As George said this, he hastened up the slope on his right hand,
and Caussade followed, reluctantly enough.  The hillock on which
the cabin was perched was full of holes, and strewn with refuse
and *débris*, of all kinds, piled up by neighbouring villagers,
so that in the darkness, the two friends constantly risked
their necks by falling into a ditch or stumbling over a pile of
stones.   At the first false step Caussade began to swear like a
pirate, and so loud that Darès implored him to be silent.   The
visit to the hut had to be made with as little noise as possible, for
fear of attracting the attention of the people gathered around the
door of the restaurant, and Darès was very desirous not to be
interrupted in his work.   On the side by which the two friends
approached, the hut had no opening, but Darès darted round to
the other side, where he perceived a door standing wide open, and
swinging to and fro in the wind.  "I was sure of it," he cried.
"The scoundrel was hidden here.   And he was in such a hurry to
be off, that he did not take the time to close the door."

"Of course not.   He was afraid this cabin would be searched
the first thing, and he didn't dare to delay.   But how do you explain why he took the road to reach the Bois de Boulogne, when
he could so easily have cut across the waste ground ?"

"He knew all about the ditches and ruts and so on.   So he preferred to take an easier road at the risk of being perceived, and he
was quite right, since no one saw him except ourselves.   But that
is of no consequence.   I want to see if he has forgotten anything
inside the hut.   Cleverness isn't everything when a man is going
to commit a murder, especially when he is not accustomed to it ;
he is always a little nervous, and does not think of everything.
The proof of it is that he forgot to close the door and take away the
key : see, it is still in the lock.   If he had taken the precaution to
remove it, we could not have made sure that anyone had been in
here."

"Well, we are sure of it," sneered Caussade.   "What then ?"

"Come inside with me, if you care to know any more."

Darès entered first, followed by Caussade, who had had quite
enough talking in the storm ; and, on crossing the threshold, they
found themselves in complete darkness, although George had not
closed the door behind them.   "I've some matches in my pocket,"
said Caussade, "and I'll strike a light."

"No : I object to that," exclaimed Darès.   "The light would be
seen, and in a moment all those fools, who are in front of Cabassol's, would be here.   There is a window facing the street, in
front of us."

"Ah ! that will be useful to see what the wedding-party is
doing !"

"And to examine the inside of the hut.   There is a street-lamp
below there, not to speak of the lights of the restaurant.   Let us go
further in, unless you prefer to mount guard here while I inspect
the place."

"No, indeed! As I have been foolish enough to let you drag me into this ridiculous enterprise, I'll go on to the end."

They advanced, and in the first place ascertained that the wooden hut was not, as they had thought, a mere storehouse for workmen's materials and tools. It was divided by a partition into two rooms, in which there was neither fire-place nor furniture, but which could have been used to live in by some unexacting tenant. Darès did not fail to call his companion's attention to these details. Nothing escaped his notice, and he drew deductions from everything. The door between the two rooms was open, like the outer one, and they passed into the second apartment, where it was lighter, thanks to the street lamp standing under the window. This window was furnished with wooden shutters, which the murderer had neglected to close after firing, and Caussade started forward to see what was going on outside. But Darès caught him by his sleeve, saying: "I hope you don't intend to show yourself! You can see quite as well by standing back a little. We are just on a level with the windows of Cabassol's dining-room."

"That's true, and there are no shutters. We can see as well as if we were in the room itself. Yes, I can see everything. The unfortunate Trémentin is still in an arm-chair with the four doctors about him. Verdalenc is talking to his clerks, but his wife isn't there, nor Élise either; they have been taken away."

"Well, as one of them has lost her husband and the other her lover, it is natural enough that they shouldn't care to remain in the presence of the dead body. What astonishes me the most is, that I do not see the slightest sign of the police. The guests, however, haven't budged from the dining-room. Upon my word, I should say that they haven't yet realised that Trémentin has been killed by a bullet, and that the shot was fired from here. As for myself, I mean to know who fired it. The scoundrel chose his position well. It isn't fifty feet from here to the spot where the bridegroom was seated, and a horizontal shot is the easiest of all. He must have thrown open the shutters, knelt down, rested his weapon on the window-sill, and, as that poor devil of a Trémentin was exactly on a line with his gun, his aim was an easy one, and only a very poor marksman could have missed."

"On the contrary, it seems to me that he must have been very skilful, for Élise was seated opposite her husband, and if he had fired a little too low, he would have killed her. And, indeed, nothing proves that the shot was not intended for *her*. That would be queer, eh?" sneered Caussade; "and it would rather upset your ideas."

"No. And, if by chance your guess is a correct one, it would be overwhelming proof that my friend Mareuil isn't guilty. There might be reasons for his killing the husband, but Élise, whom he adores—it's absurd! Besides, I'm sure that he had nothing to do with this affair; and he doesn't even suspect that Trémentin has been sent into a better world. The mystery will be promptly cleared up. There will be no difficulty in discovering the owner of this cabin, and when that is known, the rest will be easy. If he proves that he was not the murderer, he will have to say whom he gave the key to."

"Exactly; and I suppose we shall be summoned as witnesses. I shall say that I've seen nothing, and the truth is, I haven't seen much. But hallo! here is a piece of paper," said Caussade, stooping down to pick up something on which he had stepped.

"Let me see," said Darès, quickly. "Ah! this is singular. These are some leaves torn out of a book; and the man must have used them for wadding; so his gun was a muzzle-loader. That is a point to guide us already, and when I know what book these leaves come from, I shall have another indication. Give them to me."

"I don't want them, I'm sure. Here they are." Darès then took the leaves and placed them in his pocket. "Ah!" said the painter, "there is some disturbance in the dining-room, and I see a person all in black. Unless I'm mistaken, the commissary has arrived."

"Yes, it's he. Let us be off, my friend. The search is about to commence, and I don't care to be surprised here."

"All right; let us try to reach the cloak-room before our absence is noticed, for if we were asked where we had been, we should have to tell."

They approached the door of the hut, when it seemed to them that they heard footsteps outside. They stopped and listened. The steps approached, slow and uncertain, like those of a man groping his way in the darkness. "Suppose it were the murderer returning for his wadding," thought Darès.

Caussade had the same idea, and was cursing his friend in his heart, when a human form appeared on the threshold. Darès caught Caussade by the arm and drew him quickly on one side, so as to leave the entrance free to the intruder. The playwright did not wish to be seen, but he wished to see, and he stationed himself with Caussade against the partition near the door. The new comer, after hesitating a moment, decided to enter, and, without thinking of looking to see if anyone was hidden in the first room, he made his way slowly towards the open window which overlooked the street. When he had crossed the threshold of the inner room, Darès glided out, followed by Caussade, who asked nothing better than to retreat as soon as possible. The painter thought the adventure was ended, but the headstrong playwright, who kept hold of him, stopped, after a few paces, near a depression in the ground, a sort of ditch two or three feet wide, and exactly opposite the entrance to the cabin. From this point he could observe the movements of the individual he was watching, for the latter, in coming out, must pass quite near the two friends. "This time," whispered Darès, "I think we have him. I was right. It is the murderer. He has got rid of his gun and has come back for the leaves he used as wadding. You can look, my good fellow, but you won't find them, for they are in my pocket."

"That the murderer?" murmured Caussade, shrugging his shoulders. "You forget, he got into a vehicle, and is now on his way to Paris. You yourself said so just now."

"I said so, it's true, but I may have been mistaken; he may have left his vehicle, after escaping from us, or his driver, who must be in league with him, must have driven him near here."

"I will never believe that. This fellow is simply some inquisitive person like ourselves, who has entered to see what is going on in the dining-room. The proof of it is, that he is looking out of the window instead of searching for the leaves you set such a great value upon."

"You have no eyes; he has exactly the height and figure of the rascal we pursued to the edge of the wood."

"There is a certain resemblance, but this one is taller."

"We shall see him close by in an instant; he won't stay long in that hut, where he might be caught at any moment."

"The danger of being caught doesn't seem to trouble him much, for he takes no precautions to conceal himself. He is quietly standing at the window where all the people in the street can see him. Ah! he draws back. It seems he has had enough of it. If you think of arresting him, don't expect any help from me. I'm not charged with arresting criminals."

"Hush, and don't stir! I want to know who it is, that's all."

Caussade, calmed by this promise, complied. The man soon came out of the hut. The night was too dark to distinguish his features, but Darès noticed that he wore a low soft hat, and remembered, at once, that the fugitive he had given chase to had worn one exactly like it. He fancied that the man would, at once, make for the wood again, and he was not a little surprised to see him skirt the summit of the hillock, evidently seeking a good place to descend to the street. He had taken no notice of the two friends, who had kept perfectly motionless, and he soon found what he was looking for—a kind of path which the street-boys had made in going up the embankment to fly their kites.

As Caussade saw him disappear, he remarked, sarcastically, "If that is Trémentin's murderer, it must be confessed that he has plenty of assurance. There he goes to mingle in the crowd, in front of Cassabol's."

"Well, what of it? That's a scheme, and the best of all," replied Darès, without being disconcerted; "no one will dream of accusing a man sauntering about in the crowd. I shall be soon satisfied, however, for I am going to look him in the face. Let us join him."

The street was now full of people, and as the rain still fell, nothing could be seen but a conglomeration of open umbrellas. The man in the soft hat had nothing to shield him, but he did not seem to mind the downpour. He approached the most compact group, and listened to what was being said, as if anxious for information.

The crowd was watching the door of the restaurant, in front of which two policemen, who had doubtless come with the commissary, were on guard. No one paid any attention to the stranger, who kept himself a little in the background, and who did not dare to question his neighbours, although he doubtless longed to do so. Darès guessed this, and hastened towards him so as to speak to him about what had taken place. He glided softly behind him, and then unceremoniously asked : " Well, have they arrested the blackguard who committed the deed ? "

The stranger turned at once, so that he and the playwright found themselves face to face. " Marcuil ! "—" Darès ! " These two exclamations burst forth just as Caussade joined his friend. " Ah, how glad I am to see you ! " said the young man addressed by the playwright. " You will be able to tell me what has taken place. I have heard them speaking of a murder."

" What are you doing here ? " interrupted Darès, stupefied.

" A sentiment stronger than my will impelled me here—a sentiment you probably guess."

" I guess it, perhaps, but I can't understand it. So you have come to Boulogne expressly for the pleasure of contemplating the windows where Mademoiselle Aubrac's wedding dinner is taking place ? A singular idea, my dear Marcuil, you must confess."

" I had lost my head. I didn't reflect what I was doing."

" And have you been here long ? "

" No ; twenty minutes ; half an hour, at the most. I came from Auteuil on foot. I asked where the Cabassol restaurant was, and I was told in the street. As I approached, I perceived some people running from the opposite side, and, on advancing, I saw some others come out of the house. Then I heard some cries, and thinking that an accident had happened, I approached. Need I tell you that I did not dare to enter ? "

" And you haven't had the curiosity to ask for information ? "

" I spoke to a servant I met, but he scarcely answered me, though I gathered that some one had been killed. Then I thought that, from the bank over the way, I could see into the room where they were dining, and I went up there. The door of that hut was open, so I went in ; and as the window was open also, I looked out."

" What did you see ? "

" The wedding guests surrounding a person seated on a chair—a person either wounded, or dead perhaps, but I couldn't see. I hadn't the patience to wait, so I came down to the street again, and I was about to make inquiries when you spoke to me. So it is really true that a crime has been committed ? "

" An abominable crime. A shot, fired from that cabin you were in just now, killed—"

" Whom ? " asked Louis Marcuil, in a tone of anguish.

Darès, whose suspicions were increasing, wished to put Mademoiselle Aubrac's rejected lover to the proof. " The bride," he said, regarding him fixedly.

"She! it is she who is killed! Unhappy man that I am, I hoped it was he!"

This cry, which came from Mareuil's heart, made Darès tremble. Others than he had heard it, and two or three people turned to see who it was that had spoken such singular words; in truth, the speech was of a nature to attract attention from the least inquisitive and most indifferent person. Caussade, who was already prejudiced against Mareuil, took this exclamation for a confession of guilt, and nudged his friend Darès, who, feeling the full import of these imprudent words, said roughly enough to the young poet, "Great heavens, man! you should reflect before speaking. If there were an agent of police here, he would fancy that *you* had shot M. Trémentin."

"Well, what does it matter to me what they think?" exclaimed the young man in despair. "She is dead; I would like to die as well!"

Darès began to repent of having set a trap for Mareuil, for he perceived that a crowd was beginning to gather about him, and he noticed an individual leave the group, no doubt to go and report to the commissary what he had heard. "Are you mad?" said the playwright in a low voice, drawing Mareuil aside. "If you wish to be arrested, please yourself, but don't compromise others." And, as Mareuil did not seem to understand, he added: "I was jesting with you. Élise Aubrac is not even wounded. The bullet must have passed two inches above her head."

"And he?" cried the lover, who had lost all control of himself.

"He was struck, and instantly killed. I can imagine that you don't regret him, but I implore you, don't show so much joy. We are observed. Follow me a little further off. I want to speak to you. This is not the first time you have met Caussade; he won't be in the way."

The poet turned towards the hillock, but Caussade made some objections. From the moment of recognising Louis Mareuil, whom he had met occasionally, the suspicions he had expressed to Darès had returned to him, and the unfortunate words spoken by the young man had confirmed them to such a point that he was strongly tempted to believe him to be the assassin. However, Darès insisted so strongly that the painter decided to follow him, although determined to take no part in the conversation. "My dear Louis," said the playwright, placing his hand on Mareuil's shoulder, "I expect an explanation from you, and you can give it to me to-morrow. But just now, I advise you to leave here as soon as possible. We will accompany you to the end of the street. Take advantage of the opportunity to disappear."

"Why?" asked Mareuil. "What have I to fear?"

"I will tell you when you come to see me. This is no place for you, and I don't want any one but ourselves to know that you have been here, for, if others learned it, it might cause you some trouble."

"No, don't go," said Caussade, ill-humouredly. "It is too late. Some one is coming towards us ; and if you were seen running off, it would be much worse."

The painter was right. Two men were advancing, sheltered under the same umbrella, and escorted by three individuals of common appearance, one of whom pointed with his finger towards the little group formed by Darès, Caussade and Louis Mareuil. "It is the commissary of police," muttered Darès. "I might have guessed it. For Heaven's sake, don't open your mouth, except to confirm what I say." And thereupon he went deliberately forward to meet the approaching party.

"What, is it you, my dear fellow ?" cried M. Verdalene, who was with the commissary. "They told us—"

"I can imagine it ! We are in such a muddy condition that the commissary's attention has been directed to us. Well, we have rather important information to give him. We have been chasing the murderer, who escaped us by entering the Bois de Boulogne. But, in the first place, please declare that you answer for us, and that we were at table with you when the shot was fired."

"Certainly, that is quite true," said Verdalene, decisively ; "and your names are so well known that you do not need my guarantee. Commissary, I have the honour to present to you my friend, M. George Darès, the playwright, and M. Alfred Caussade an historical painter. They were dining with us, and were the only persons who did not lose their heads, for they thought of pursuing the scoundrel who has killed poor Trémentin."

"We accept the compliment," replied Darès, "for we deserve it. It is not precisely pleasant to run after a rascal in a beating rain, especially in evening dress. We look like pickpockets, and I am not surprised that we have been denounced to the police. No great harm is done, however, since you are here to bear witness that we are honest men. The scamp had good legs, and at least fifty yards' start—"

"But you saw him ?" asked the commissary.

"Yes, at a distance, and from behind. He still carried the gun he had used, and I should not be surprised if he had hidden it in the bushes."

"I don't believe, however, that he himself has remained there, and I must first visit the hut where he posted himself to fire. Hold yourselves in readiness, gentlemen, to be summoned before the examining magistrate," said the commisary.

"We shall be at his orders," said Darès, who had done his best to prevent the commissary from addressing Louis Mareuil. Caussade did not say a word, but he was inwardly raging at having to give his testimony before a magistrate. The poet meanwhile kept in the background, and seemed to have nothing to do with the interview, although he was no doubt thinking of Elise Aubrac, whom he had believed dead, and who was now a widow. But commissaries have good eyes, and the one who was questioning the dramatist, suddenly pointed to Louis Mareuil, and asked : "This gentleman is with you?"

"Yes," answered Darès, "we met him here. I have known him for a long time, and he was asking me what had happened when you came up. I told him of M. Trémentin's death." And as he perceived that the commissary did not consider this explanation sufficient, he hastened to add : "M. Mareuil is engaged in literary work, and we are neighbours. I live in the Rue Condorcet, and he lives in the Rue Frochot. He has not, however, the honour of knowing M. Verdalenc, and he was not a guest at the wedding, but he had dined at Saint-Cloud, and was waiting for the tramway at the corner of the street when he saw a crowd assemble before the restaurant. He wished to know what was the matter."

"That is very natural," said the commissary, coldly. "But the gentleman can give his own explanation, for he will be summoned also. I will take down his name and address. Now, gentlemen, I will detain you no longer." And he made a sign to his men behind him. Two of them carried lanterns and went on ahead to light the way—while the third received an order, given in a low voice, and disappeared in the crowd. M. Verdalenc then followed with the commissary, after pompously shaking Darès by the hand, and exclaiming, by way of farewell : "If such a crime remains unpunished, I shall despair of justice ; but the head of the guilty party shall fall, I swear it by the broken-hearted widow of the unfortunate Trémentin ! "

On any other occasion, the playwright would have laughed at this grotesque vow ; but he was not in a good humour, and he simply turned his back on the banker with a shrug of the shoulders. Then, addressing Mareuil, who was still absorbed in his reflections, he curtly said : "I have helped you out of this business, and you must now take care of yourself. Return home and remain there. Watch your actions and measure your words, if you don't want to be annoyed by this business. Go now, and come and see me when you are calmer."

Then, without waiting for an answer, Darès pushed his way through the group in front of the restaurant. Caussade followed, and they reached the door just as a landau was driving away. They had barely time to leap aside, to avoid being knocked down by the horses, who started off as gaily as if they had been taking the newly married couple home. But inside the vehicle, the two friends perceived poor Élise, supported by her aunt, the dignified Baroness Aubrac, who was overwhelming her with sympathy. The poor child was horribly pale, and her contracted features showed her suffering ; but she was not weeping. Her sorrow must have been all the keener as she did not allow it to burst forth. Tears relieve, but her eyes were dry. It was heart-rending to see her, still in her white robe, and crowned with orange-blossoms, the bride of a day, suddenly plunged into mourning. The landau turned down the street, scattering the crowd right and left, and started off for

Paris through the Bois de Boulogne, along the same road that the
murderer had taken in his flight. "Oh, that's outrageous!" cried
Caussade suddenly. "Look at your friend Mareuil running after
the carriage! He certainly wants to be arrested."

"I can do nothing," said Darès. "I warned him; and if the
commissary arrests him, it won't be my fault."

"I think that you went altogether too far, in answering for him,
for I shouldn't be at all surprised if he were guilty. His conduct
is very strange, and his being here is extremely suspicious, not to
speak of that exclamation that escaped him."

"If he is accused, he will be able to prove his innocence. You
know as well as I do that the shot was fired by another. We will
bear witness to that, if we are questioned."

"I shall bear witness to nothing at all. Let us get our overcoats
and try to obtain a conveyance to take us back to Paris."

Entering a corridor, at the end of which there was a servant who
had charge of the overcoats, hats, wraps, and other objects belonging to the wedding guests of both sexes, they elbowed their way
towards him. The entire house was in confusion. The women
were sobbing, the men were excited, and the servants increased the
disorder by running aimlessly up and down the stairs. Darès came
across one of Verdalenc's clerks, who told him that his employer's
wife had been attacked with a violent fit of hysterics, and that one
of the bridesmaids was in no better condition. The unfortunate
Trémentin had not given the least sign of life, and he had been
laid upon old Cabassol's bed, until the commissary returned
and gave his instructions. There was nothing for the two friends
to do at the restaurant. At last they succeeded in obtaining their
hats and overcoats, but they found it impossible to procure a vehicle
of any description. The wedding-carriages were reserved for the
bridal party and the nearest relatives. And the young clerks were
running about the streets of Boulogne in search of a passing cab, or
trying to induce some market gardeners to harness a cart.

"Well," said Darès, "the simplest means are always the best.
Let us take the tramway at Saint-Cloud."

"All right!" rejoined Caussade, in a peevish tone. "We shall
have another tramp through the mud; but never mind. Ah!
you'll never catch me again mixing myself up in what doesn't concern me at all."

"You see the dark side of everything just now, Caussade, because
you are wet through; and I acknowledge that our position isn't a
pleasant one. So I forgive you, and won't argue with you until we
are more comfortable. Meanwhile, be calm. Our trials are nearly
over; we shall soon be home again."

They were near the Rond Point de Boulogne where there is a
tramway office, and in the distance they could distinguish the red
light of an approaching tramcar. "There is no use going further,"
said Darès. "Let us wait in the office till it comes along, and if
there is room, we can get in." So saying he entered the office and

spoke to the clerk, who did not appear to know anything of the murder committed at Cabassol's, and who declared that at that time of night the cars were not full one day in the week. " Well, I was right," said the playwright, turning to his friend. " Thank Heavens, in an hour we shall be home, and able to put on some dry clothes. I'm like a wet rag. And, dear me, where have I put my handkerchief ? " Then as he began searching his pockets, he suddenly drew out a roll of printed paper.

" Ha ! there is your wonderful find ! " sneered Caussade. " Let me see it." And he took the roll in his hand.

" No folly now," said Darès, lowering his voice. " Examine it, if you like, but return it to me afterwards. If the officials should accuse Mareuil, those leaves might help to find the real criminal."

" Well, I advise you not to produce them, for they are torn out of a volume of poetry."

" Impossible ! " cried Darès, approaching nearer to see the leaves which his friend was trying to read by the dim light of a lamp fixed to the wall of the tramway office.

" It is perfectly true, my friend. These are verses, and M. Mareuil is a poet."

" He is not the only one ; and this book can't be his."

" When I find the title, you will be able to tell. Unfortunately the assassin tore the leaves across, and has left only imperfect fragments. Here, however, is the top of a page. ' Songs of the Sea-shore.' That's the title ! Are you satisfied now ? "

" Only too well ! " murmured Darès, in consternation.

" Then I was not mistaken. The book is his. Do you still wish to keep this ? "

" Come, gentlemen, make haste ! " cried the office clerk. " Here's the car ! "

" More than ever ! " brusquely replied Darès to his friend. " Give it to me, and let us go. I will talk with you about it to-morrow."

## II

M. Pierre Mornas was the last representative of an old family of magistrates. His great-grandfather, his grandfather, and his father had been judges , he was one himself, and his son would have been one if he had had a son, but his wife had not yet given him a child. She had, however, brought him a very large fortune. In fact, Mademoiselle Berthe d'Arlempe had a million of francs when he married her. The house where they lived in the Rue de Turenne, belonged to her in her own right. She was the daughter of a man who had made a great deal of money by speculating in land under the last empire, and who had commenced to sign his name with an apostrophe after the " d " as soon as chance had made him a land-owner.

Berthe was wonderfully handsome. She was about thirty-five, and she possessed remarkable intelligence and great amiability. Society appreciated her, as she deserved, and the poor of the neighbourhood blessed her. She had chosen M. Mornas because she liked him, and, during the fifteen years they had been married, their happiness had known no cloud. They were, indeed, quoted as models to the hard-hearted bachelors who did not believe in conjugal felicity. Pierre Mornas was devoted to his wife and the judicial profession, which he had entered three months before his marriage. He had made good progress, and he hoped to obtain a still better position, for he was ambitious. He was a hard-worker, and quiet in his tastes. He divided his time between his duties and his home, where his beloved Berthe made his life a happy one. The rooms they occupied on the first floor of their house were charming, and Mornas gladly returned there after long sittings passed in examining prisoners and listening to witnesses. He had at one time gone a good deal into society ; but now his wife almost always went alone, when she went out at all, which was very seldom. She preferred to receive at home some intimate friends, a few women of her own age, and half a dozen agreeable men. She had artistic tastes, and gave musical or literary evenings. Being above reproach herself, she had a right to be severe on others, and so she never admitted women who had allowed themselves to be talked about. She also managed her property and the servants with surprising wisdom. Pierre Mornas reigned, but did not govern, and he found that the system which allowed him to devote himself entirely to his duties, worked marvellously well, for he was always admirably served, and his fortune increased every year. He had nothing to desire—nothing, except the opportunity of showing his capacity for the difficult position of an examining magistrate. He longed to be intrusted with one of those startling cases which throw the whole country into a commotion, but up to the present time he had not had such luck. Meanwhile, he contented himself with what was given him and the affection of his wife, which had never been greater, showing itself in constant attentions of all kinds.

It was noon, and they were finishing breakfast alone, as was their usual custom, for they always had so many things to say to each other that monsieur's valet and madame's maid would have been in the way. On this particular morning they were talking of business matters which Berthe ordinarily managed alone, though she never failed to consult her husband when there was need of it. Such was indeed the case now, although Pierre was little disposed to treat of money matters. "My dear," she said, in her sweet voice, "you know that I am the advocate of the poor; and it is absolutely necessary for me to tell you about the position of one of our tenants."

"You are going to speak of old Gigondès," said M. Mornas, gaily. "But don't be so serious. We are not at a grand ball, or with the Verdalencs, who pride themselves on their dignified manners."

"You are right. If I see the Verdalencs too often, I shall fall into their grandiloquent ways. I did right not to go to the wedding of their cashier yesterday."

"Especially as you were not well; you would have been laid up to-day if you had not remained at home. But, plead your case; the court is listening."

"Very well; you have guessed correctly. M. Gigondès has not paid his rent again. He now owes us four quarters. Besides, he is sued for his taxes, for which we are responsible, as you know."

"Then turn him out. That will prevent him from being behindhand again."

"But if we send him away, it would be his ruin."

"Is that so? I don't want to ruin any one. But—why doesn't he pay? He is a doctor, and he must have some patients."

"He did have some. He is a homeopathist you know, and he was considerably patronised. But, for a year past or more, he has abandoned his practice to undertake scientific researches. He makes experiments upon animals, and his rooms are full of those he tortures."

"That explains to me why I stepped upon a guinea-pig at the foot of the staircase on coming home the other evening. It was very aggravating, and we must certainly turn the man out. I don't at all like the idea of having a menagerie in my house."

"The menagerie is on the fourth floor, and we live on the first. It doesn't annoy us much.

" What ! you, Berthe, who are so kind-hearted, do you under-take the defence of an old idiot who probably dissects live rabbits ? "

" M. Gigondês is a very learned man, my dear. He has sent an essay to the Academy of Medicine, and he hopes to obtain a prize of fifty thousand francs, as a reward for some discovery he has made. I believe it is a way of killing people with a millionth part of a drop of blood."

" And you wish me—a magistrate—to encourage such things ? " exclaimed M. Mornas, laughing heartily. " Come, my dear Berthe, your charity goes too far."

" But this poor man won't kill any one, I assure you, and I—"

Madame Mornas paused in the middle of her sentence. Her husband's valet was entering the dining-room, carrying a letter upon a silver salver. The judge took it, and when the servant had retired. "Ah ! ah !" he said, "this comes from the public prosecutor. Some new affair, probably, and important too, for otherwise this note wouldn't have been sent here. Who knows if it is not to tell me that I am charged with an investigation which will finally lead to my advancement ? "

" A great crime, then ? " said Madame Mornas, sadly. "I can't share your satisfaction. Are you so very anxious to send some great criminal to the scaffold ? "

" Well," replied the magistrate, tearing the letter open, "if a crime is committed, some one must try it, and I might as well have the honour as any one else. But let us see, in the first place, if I am nursing a vain hope." And he read aloud : "My dear Mornas—You know all the interest I take in you—so you will not be surprised if I write to tell you privately, of a piece of news which you will soon be officially acquainted with. You have been appointed to take charge of a difficult and mysterious affair, and you will have an opportunity to win your spurs ; for I am sure you will discover the criminal concerning whose identity we at present have scarcely any clue."

" Yes, yes ; I shall discover him," cried M. Mornas, enthusiasti-cally, as he paused in his perusal. " At last, I hold my advance-ment in my hands ! "

" What need have you of that? I warn you, I sha'n't love you any better than I love you now."

" But you will not love me less, Berthe," said the magistrate, smiling ; " and you will see more of me, for I sha'n't be obliged to stay all day at the Palais examining knaves and fools."

" Ah ! now you are more sensible ; but, all the same, remember the fable of the milkmaid and her pail. You are making some fine plans and building great hopes upon an affair you know nothing about, for your friend has forgotten to give you any details."

" Wait. I haven't finished his letter. Listen to the remainder : ' Hasten to the Palais, where you will find your instructions on your desk. I will tell you, however, that a murder was committed last

evening, under singular circumstances.' Ah! good heavens!'"
cried M. Mornas, instead of finishing his reading. "Do you know
that the bridegroom was killed during the wedding-dinner to which
you were invited—killed by a bullet in the midst of the guests—"

"What! Élise Aubrac's husband? Ah! that is horrible!'"

"Yes; for all my dreams are over. I cannot investigate an
affair in which so many people I know are mixed up."

"Really, Pierre, I don't understand you. How can you think
of your own interests in presence of such a calamity? It isn't you
that I pity, but that young girl. What will become of her?"

"I pity her too, although I have only seen her once, at Madame
Verdalenc's ball."

"But I have spoken to her very often and I like her very much.
She is charming, and she deserved a better husband than they
gave her."

"Ah! I shall never again have such an opportunity. The
victim and the witnesses are all in good society, the murderer as
well, perhaps, and a mystery to boot! Such a thing doesn't happen
once in ten years. Ah! I certainly have no luck!"

"What, my dear, you worry about your career, when two
families are plunged in mourning! Ought you not rather to think
of the cause? But this young man must have had some enemies,
for Mademoiselle Aubrac certainly had none. I will go and see
her, and tell her how much I sympathize with her in her sorrow."

"Go as much as you like, since I can have nothing to do with
the affair," answered M. Mornas, rather bitterly.

"The Public Prosecutor says nothing more?" asked Madame
Mornas, after a pause.

"Absolutely nothing."

"So that you have no idea who is suspected?"

"How could I have an idea? I know nothing of Trémentin's
antecedents or habits. As for the bride, I have heard that she was
the daughter of a physician, and lived with her aunt, a certain
Baroness Aubrac, who is, so people say, an absurd sort of woman."

"But with your experience in criminal matters you must already see in what direction one ought to look for the murderer."

"Before doing that it would be needful for me to study the
papers in the case and hear the testimony. However, one of my
colleagues will have charge of the business, and will gain all the
honour."

"Listen, Pierre," said Madame Mornas timidly. "You will do
me this justice that I have never interfered with your duties as a
magistrate—"

"Not enough, my dear. I should have liked to see you more
interested in them."

"Well, will you allow me to advise you to accept the charge now
offered you?"

"I should like nothing better, but I really can't."

"Because you have occasionally met the persons whose names will figure in the case? The scruple does you honour, but do you think that the public prosecutor did not inform himself before entrusting the affair to you? I am confident that he is aware that these persons are known to you and that he chose you, because he relies upon your acquaintance with their characters as well as upon your intelligence and impartiality."

" That is possible, after all," muttered M. Mornas.

" He was aware also," continued Berthe, "that to discover the truth in certain exceptional matters, a man must have seen the world, and have learned to know the human heart. Many of your colleagues are not in that position, and would not direct the inquiry with the delicacy which is needful, when it is a question of discovering a criminal among people of social standing. A magistrate, accustomed to track professional ruffians, would, perhaps, proceed brutally, and Heaven knows whom he would accuse ! "

" Any magistrate, worthy of the name, would first attempt to find out if M. Trémentin had any enemies, or if anyone would be benefited by his death. It is evident the whole case lies there."

" Well then, a magistrate, who was liable to fall into error, and judge by appearances, might imagine that the person most interested in getting rid of M. Trémentin was—his wife. I should not say this if I were not sure that Élise is quite incapable of committing a crime, or even thinking of such a thing. Still, it is true that she was married somewhat against her will. She was in love with a young man, who was not in a position to marry her, and she ended by yielding to the entreaties of her aunt, who pleaded the cause of Verdalenc's cashier. Élise contracted a *mariage de convenance*, and among those who know the truth, some might make evil insinuations against her. However absurd a calumny may be, it makes its way, and if it reaches the ears of a magistrate, liable to unjust suspicions, the consequences are sometimes terrible. Do you understand now, why I should like the affair to remain in your hands? "

" You go too far in your suppositions, and you have too bad an opinion of my colleagues ; but you are right, perhaps, in advising me to accept ; for I am sure of myself, and my superiors know me. I can, besides, consult them, tell them the peculiar situation I am in, and if they bid me go on, well, I won't throw up an investigation which will certainly procure me a high rank."

" I shall be glad for that young girl's sake—and for yours," rejoined Madame Mornas, extending her hand to her husband, who pressed a kiss upon it. "Poor Élise's only mistake was in listening to her aunt's advice. If she had had the courage to resist her, and marry according to her heart, she would not be a widow to-day, for, to my mind, M. Trémentin has been assassinated by some jealous woman. People said that he was a regular Don Juan."

" Then that gives us an idea where to look for the murderer," said the magistrate, quickly, raising his head like a war-horse who hears the sound of the trumpet.

"Oh ! I only remember the rumours which were current in the society he moved in, and I should not like you to attach any importance to my words. You will know how to find the criminal without my interference."

"You would manage the case better than I ; and if I undertake it, I shall often appeal to you for advice. Besides, if it is true that Trémentin was such a man as you say, you will have guessed correctly at the very beginning, my dear Berthe."

"I repeat that I have only heard rumours, and nothing more. His conquests have been spoken of, but no names were ever given. He was a tall, strong-looking fellow ; and I suppose he would be called handsome by some people. But he lacked distinction, and I never understood how he could fascinate a woman, for his appearance was highly displeasing to me, almost as much as yours is pleasing."

"He did not resemble me, indeed," said M. Mornas, who was neither tall nor broad-shouldered, and who, without being ugly, had a sort of hatchet face, more calculated to intimidate a witness than to charm the fair sex.

"Fortunately," murmured Berthe, giving her husband a look which would have made the heart of a septuagenarian beat.

"Don't look at me like that, or I shall never go," said M. Mornas.

"Oh, go, I won't detain you," laughed Berthe. "The brougham is ready, and in a quarter of an hour you will be at the Palais. I sha'n't see you again till this evening ; but during your absence, to bring you luck, I am going to do a good action."

"By consoling M. Trémentin's widow ? Well, I don't suppose she receives anyone as yet. Besides, if I am to take charge of this case, I beg you to be careful. The wife of a magistrate must do nothing open to suspicion."

"Fear nothing, Pierre ; I will be prudent. I shall see Élise, if you don't forbid my doing so, but later on. To-day I am simply going up to see that poor M. Gigondès, and tell him we will not worry him for his rent."

"You are the genius of charity," exclaimed M. Mornas. "Go and reassure the old fellow, and we'll agree to give him a receipt in full for all he owes us, when I have discovered the murderer of your friend's husband."

"I should like nothing better, and I can tell our lodger this news in advance, for I am sure you will find the criminal."

A long kiss concluded this conjugal interview. The magistrate was dressed in black, with a white cravat, as becomes a judicial magnate of the old school. He was quite ready to go to his office, and so he went off to begin the fight against M. Trémentin's murderer. On her side, Madame Mornas gave her maid orders not to admit any visitors, and then she tripped up the three flights of stairs which led to M. Gigondès' apartments. She was in a hurry to ease his mind as to the negligence he had shown for a year past respecting his rent, and she rang the bell with a sharp jerk. A sound of footsteps answered the peal ; the door half opened, and a strange figure appeared. M. Gigondès, who was sixty, had the head of an octogenarian, with a face as creased and as wrinkled as a dried-up apple. He had a fur cap on his head, and he was enveloped in a dressing-gown of a colour impossible to define. At sight of Madame Mornas, he started back in surprise, and faltered out a few words of excuse for the past and promises for the future ; but the magistrate's wife interrupted him, saying, in her silvery voice : " I have not come about your rent, my dear sir ; I have come to call upon you."

" You do me great honour, madame," murmured the old man, without opening the door any wider ; " but my apartment is rather in disorder, and I don't dare to ask you to come in."

" Why not ? I know that your scientific work absorbs you entirely, and a savant has a right not to trouble himself about household matters. We are very proud, both my husband and myself, to have you in our house, and please receive me, for I am greatly interested in your discoveries, and it is a desire to know something about them which has brought me here."

" Is it possible ? " exclaimed M. Gigondès, stepping quickly aside so as to allow his landlady to enter.

" Yes, indeed," she said gaily. " I am very ignorant, but I want to be taught ; and then, you know that curiosity is woman's great fault."

" Come in, madame, come in," said the old man, eagerly. " I shall be only too happy to explain my work to you, all the more happy as I think I am likely to succeed in my purpose ; and if I do so, as I am almost certain I shall, I shall be able to pay the debt which troubles me. You have been kind enough to give me time, and—"

" Oh, my dear sir," interrupted Madame Mornas, while the old man closed the door behind her, " don't speak any more about that, or rather, let us discuss it and have done with it. My husband agrees with me in giving you all the time you want. Our *concierge* will receive orders to wait till you are ready, and I beg of you not to be uneasy on the matter."

M. Gigondès broke into protestations of gratitude, to which Madame Mornas listened with a smile. She examined the room into which she had been introduced, and saw that the furniture was covered with a thick layer of dust, while the floor looked as if it had never been swept. A portrait of Hahnemann, the inventor of homeopathy, hung upon the wall, and was draped with cobwebs. " You see, madame, that my rooms are not very well kept," sighed the old man. " I was obliged to send my servant away, as he was of no use to me, since I no longer have any patients, and, besides, I pass all my time in my laboratory."

" Let us go in there," said Madame Mornas, who had decided to go on to the end, so as to give a flattering pretext to her charitable visit.

In the so-called "laboratory" matters were even worse. There were piles of papers and multitudes of broken vials on an old worm-eaten table, and on one side stood a huge case divided into various compartments, which were occupied by rabbits and guinea-pigs. Straw and vegetable leaves were scattered over the floor of the room, and on the mantelshelf, instead of a clock, there was an immense cabbage. "So those are the poor animals which you experiment upon?" asked Berthe. "My husband told me that your apartment resembled Noah's Ark. Oh! he was only in jest," she added, seeing the piteous expression on M. Gigondès' face. "He knows that you are working for science, and he would have come with me to see you this morning, if he had not been summoned to the Palais on a very serious matter, and a sad one too, for it has cast a young lady I know into mourning. Yes," continued Madame Mornas, "Élise Aubrac's husband has been murdered. You must have heard of her father. He was a physician."

"A physician!" repeated M. Gigondès. "Why, she must be the daughter of that scoundrel Aubrac, my persecutor!"

"What do you say, sir?" cried Madame Mornas. "Élise Aubrac's father was a very skilful physician and a very honest man."

"Neither the one nor the other, madame," replied Gigondès, in a passion. "He was an ass, like all allopaths, and he was a lying, envious knave. Ah! you who have such a kind heart would scarcely believe the cruelty that man displayed. He swore an implacable hatred against me, although I had never done him any harm. But he was jealous of my success."

"Really? That's strange. You cannot have had the same class of patients, since you belonged, I believe, to two opposing schools."

"That is the very reason why he declared war against me. He commenced by publicly attacking homeopathy. But he did not stop there. He attacked me personally and my work. He published libels in which he pretended that my experiments were idiotic, that I myself did not believe in the great discovery I announced to the Academy. It was as if he had said that I was only an impostor. In a word, madame, he ridiculed me, scoffed at me, and finally ruined me; for his slanders produced their effect. The Academy refused to listen to me, and all my patients left me."

The old fellow grew animated as he spoke, and anger transfigured him. His stooping figure became erect again, the colour mounted to his parchment-like cheeks, and his little grey eyes sparkled like stars. Madame Mornas observed him with curiosity, and wondered at the violence of a scientific passion, which can stifle all human sentiments, and rejuvenate an old man. Assuredly, M. Gigondès, however much he may have loved in his youthful days, had never favoured any woman with such transports of affection, as the transports of rage he now showed against his detractor. Berthe pitied him,

and tried to calm him. "Every misfortune has its bright side,'
she said, gently. "By giving up the practise of your profession,
you have been able to devote yourself, exclusively, to your researches. Sufferers have lost by it, no doubt, but science will
profit by it, since you are on the point of finding what you have
sought after with so much patience and perseverance."

"I have found it," cried the irascible savant. "I only want to
make one last experiment, to prove, victoriously, the accuracy of
my theory upon blood-poisoning. I shall make this final experiment, even if I have to make it upon myself, and when the whole
world has admitted that I am right, that miserable Aubrac will be
shown in his true light ; for I shall prove that he was only a
brute and a liar, and, what is worse, a thoroughly bad man."

"I don't know if he was as wicked as you paint him," remarked
Madame Mornas, quietly ; "but death effaces everything, and he
is no longer here to defend himself. You ought to forget your
grievances."

"Never !" exclaimed Gigondès, energetically. "I cannot treat
him as he deserved, as he is dead, but I should like to visit his sins
upon his children, even unto the third and fourth generation."

At this declaration, Madame Mornas burst out into a merry peal
of laughter. "Do you know," said she, "that it is very fortunate
for you that you are not acquainted with his daughter ? His son-
in-law has been killed by a bullet, and, if you were heard to speak
as you just did, you might be accused of having committed that
abominable crime. You might vainly say that you knew nothing
of the use of fire-arms—"

"I know surer means !" hissed the old man.

"Ah, yes ! the poison you have discovered ; but I don't believe
you would operate upon anything but animals," said the magistrate's wife.

"Unfortunately, I can't," growled Gigondès.

"What ! do you regret not trying it upon human beings ? "

"From a scientific point of view, I do, for the objection may be
raised, that rabbits and guinea-pigs have not enough vital strength
to resist the inoculation of tainted blood. But a prick of a pin to
an adult would completely demonstrate my discovery. However, I
know that the laws forbid such a thing."

"I should say they did. If they allowed it, savants like you
would depopulate the world."

"Oh, no," replied the old man, calmly. "It would suffice to
hand us over all the criminals condemned to death. Science should
be thought of before everything."

"I fear that you would not succeed in converting the magistrates
to your ideas," said Berthe, coldly. "But you are right ; science is
a fine thing, and I deplore my ignorance. So I should feel flattered if you would be kind enough to explain to me your great
discovery. I will not swear I shall understand, but I will try to."

"A child would understand, and, if you will deign to give me a little attention, you shall know as much about it as I do. In the first place, I introduce into a rabbit's neck or paw, a mere drop of carbuncled blood, that is to say, blood which comes from an animal which has died of a carbuncle. The rabbit dies on the fourth or fifth day afterwards. With its blood, I prick a second rabbit, which dies in three days' time, a third, pricked with the blood of the second, dies in forty-eight hours. With the seventh, I obtain death as quick as lightning ; and, note this point—always by diminishing the dose. So I finally kill with a trillionth of a drop. The more the dose is diminished, the more the strength of the poison is increased. Isn't that magnificent ? "

" It is wonderful," said Madame Mornas, as seriously as possible. " So you can kill any one on the spot or after a long interval as you please."

" Certainly, after a very long interval even ; for, after the seventh rabbit, the violence of the poison diminishes. Look ! I pricked that brown one yesterday with the blood of the eleventh edition. He has still three weeks to live, but he will surely die on the twentieth or twenty-second day."

" I fear, however, that the propagation of your astonishing discovery will not be favoured. When I think that I have only to dip one of my hairpins into the blood of one of your rabbits, and that my maid, in dressing my hair, might prick me, it makes me shudder and I shall forbid her to come up here."

"No one comes in here, madame, and you alone know my secret. My report to the Institute is not yet finished."

" Keep your dangerous secret to yourself, then, I beg. Those who possessed it could rid themselves only too easily of those they did not like."

" And with impunity, too. The poison leaves no traces."

" Indeed ? Well, I sha'n't repeat what I have learned to my husband. He would be capable of giving you notice to quit. He is not a savant, but a judge, and from constantly examining criminals he sees them everywhere."

" But, madame, I swear to you that I haven't committed any crime and I never shall commit one. You must not take what I said just now as serious."

, " About your desire to experiment on your fellow creatures ? Oh, I am sure you did not mean that, my dear Monsieur Gigondès ; and now that I have reassured you on all points, I will leave you to your work. I must go and inquire about that poor woman whose husband was killed on the very day of her marriage."

" The murderer made a poor job of it," murmured the old man ; " to use a gun, when he could have— At all events, homeopathy is avenged for Aubrac's outrageous attacks."

" Do you excuse the murderer ? " cried Madame Mornas.

" No," said M. Gigondès, glumly. " A crime is a crime, after all ; and, besides, it was an innocent man who suffered. But when Aubrac was persecuting me I should have liked to try upon him the discovery he persisted in denying : he would then have been forced to acknowledge the power of infinitesimal doses."

"Yes, the trillionth of a drop and the seventh rabbit," murmured Berthe, looking with mingled astonishment and pity at the old monomaniac, who spoke with so much coolness of poisoning a man in order to demonstrate a scientific truth. "It is frightful, and I congratulate myself on being one of your friends, for it would not be wise for any one to offend you : he would simply risk his life."

"Good Heavens, madame, I have been a little hasty, perhaps ; but when I hear the name of my persecutor spoken, I lose all self-control. I have too strong a memory. I never forget injuries I have received, but I do not forget kindnesses either ; and I promise you, madame, if you ever have need of me—"

"I understand," said Madame Mornas, laughing ; "the first time I wish to get rid of any one, I will come and ask for your receipt. Meanwhile, calm yourself, my dear sir, and think no more of what you owe us."

The old man was profuse in his thanks, and conducted his indulgent landlady to the top of the stairs. She shook hands with him, although he inspired her with a certain amount of repugnance, and she returned to her apartment very well satisfied with her charitable visit.

By way of continuing a day so well commenced, she thought she could not do better than evince some little interest in the unfortunate Trémentin's widow. Madame Mornas had more or less acquaintance with all the personages of the tragedy which had occurred on the previous evening at Boulogne-sur-Seine. Dr. Aubrac, M. Gigondes' enemy, had formerly been the physician of Berthe's father, and, since her marriage, she had kept up an acquainta with Élise, whom she often met in society, chiefly at the Verda enos'. She would have seen her more frequently if her au-Madame Aubrac, had been less disagreeable ; but the grand and egregious vanity of the baroness annoyed her, and she limit herself to such relations as courtesy required. They had been o rather cool terms for some time, for Madame Mornas had n hesitated to express her disapproval of the marriage arrange' ' Madame Aubrac and Madame Verdalenc, and only accepted Élise after long resistance. M. Trémentin had not been one of Berthe's friends, although he had been very attentive to her, t such a point, indeed, that certain people pretended he was in 1. with her. But she had received his attentions with icy coldness and laughed at his pretensions to be a lady-killer. However, after the catastrophe which had suddenly put an end to this unfortunate marriage, there could no longer be any question of antipathies, and a visit of condolence was necessary.

It is true that Madame Mornas might have limited herself to writing, but she did not consider that sufficient ; and despite her husband's peculiar position in the matter, she resolved to leave her card in person at the house of Élise's aunt. M. Mornas had

taken the brougham to go to the Palais, but his wife could have ordered another equipage, for her stables contained four horses and three carriages. However, she thought a cab would be more suitable for the visit she was about to make, and she therefore ordered one from the nearest stand.

The Baroness Aubrac resided with her niece, at the corner of the Rue La Fayette in a handsome apartment, the windows of which looked out on the church of St. Vincent de Paul. Élise was to have left these rooms the previous evening to go and live with her husband in the Rue d'Hauteville; but it was doubtful if she had taken possession of her new home, and, moreover, Madame Mornas did not care to see her at such a moment. Accordingly she drove to Madame Aubrac's house, and was not a little surprised to meet her at the door. The baroness was returning on foot just as Berthe alighted from the cab, and she caught hold of both her hands, exclaiming: "I was sure that you would come. You, at least, have some heart, madame. You do not abandon us in our misfortune. You are not like those Verdalencs, who have not given a sign of life since yesterday."

Madame Mornas had not expected such an effusive greeting from a woman who had never been her friend; but she received it calmly, expressing her sympathy, excusing herself for coming a little too soon to inquire after Madame Trémentin, and declaring that she meant to retire as soon as she heard that the young widow's condition gave no cause for anxiety. But the baroness would not listen to this. "No," she said, still retaining Berthe's hands, "no, you shall not leave us so quickly, after coming to console us. Élise is with me, in a pitiable state, and it would do her good to see you. She would never pardon me if I let you go. You must see her; come up with me."

Madame Mornas, who did not like the idea very much, tried to excuse herself to Madame Aubrac; but the tenacious baroness was so demonstrative that her gestures and appeals began to attract the attention of the passers-by. Berthe preferred to yield, rather than to provoke a scene in the street, but it was against her will, and she already began to repent having come at all. The apartment was on the second floor, and much too large for a single woman. Dr. Aubrac had taken it because he had a great many patients in the neighbourhood, and at his death his sister-in-law, who loved display, had established herself there to watch over Élise and live luxuriously, in accordance with her tastes. With the twenty thousand francs a year left by the doctor, and her own modest income, she did not think it too much to keep four retainers. "Where is my niece?" she asked of the servant, who came to open the door in answer to her ring.

"In her room, madame; and I think that she is lying down."

"Very well; I will wake her myself. Leave us."

Berthe again tried to retreat, protesting that she did not wish to disturb Élise's sleep, but it was of no avail. She was forced to enter the drawing-room with the baroness, who, without giving her time to sit down, exclaimed : "Ah, madame ! how right you were to blame the choice my niece made. It appears a woman that M. Trémentin knew, paid some one to murder him."

"What ! Is she known then ?" exclaimed Madame Mornas, with a start of surprise.

"No, not yet ; but M. Verdalenc is determined to find her, for it is certain that a woman prompted the deed."

While the baroness was speaking, Madame Mornas stood near a window facing the church, on the steps of which she perceived a man whom she thought she recognized. This man was watching the house with singular attention, and one might have thought that he was expecting a signal. "The crime was inspired by jealousy," continued Madame Aubrac. "We have no enemies, and M. Trémentin was not rich enough for his heirs to covet his property. So it must have been some woman's revenge. He had abandoned her to marry, and she killed him, or rather had him killed."

"Do you think, madame, that a woman would allow herself to be so carried away by passion as to cause her lover's death ?" asked Berthe, without ceasing to observe the man who was watching the windows.

"Yes, I do think so. If my husband had betrayed me, I would never have suffered it."

"We poor women are made to suffer, however," said Berthe, who found the baroness most absurd and ridiculous. "And it seems to me that in such a case, if I wished for vengeance, I should rather revenge myself on my rival ; but after all I should not have the courage."

"And I would have killed them both," exclaimed Madame Aubrac. "It was a great mercy, by-the-way, that Élise was not struck. I myself had a lucky escape, since I was beside Trémentin. Verdalenc says he had noticed a difference in his cashier for a year past. He who was formerly so gay, appeared preoccupied. He would absent himself for hours from the office, and was never seen in the evening. He led a mysterious life it seems, and Verdalenc, who thought a great deal of him, conceived the idea of arranging a marriage for him, so as to break off a dangerous connection which he had with some woman or other."

"How do they know that ?"

"Verdalenc has no doubt of it, and he declares that he will soon be able to prove it."

"I confess, I have not much faith in M. Verdalenc's penetration."

"Well it seems that long ago, Trémentin confided in him, and acknowledged that, after some terrible scenes, he had broken with a woman who had ruled him with an iron rod. This woman, he added, would never pardon him for having deserted her, and he declared she was quite capable of killing him."

"It seems that he told everything except her name," remarked Madame Mornas. "I always had a poor opinion of M. Trémentin.

and what you tell me, my dear madame, shows me that I judged him rightly. He dared to boast of having abandoned a woman who loved him, in order to make an advantageous marriage."

"It appears he no longer cared for her."

"That is a fine excuse," said Berthe, "but if she still loved him, I can understand that his treachery wounded her to the heart ; I don't mean by that that I approve of what she did, if she killed him, as you think, which I strongly doubt."

"Who could have done it then ?"

"You ask me too much, my dear madame. I have married a magistrate, but he has not taught me how to discover criminals ; for myself I should be too much afraid of making a mistake."

"I can understand that. Remember. however, that M. Trémentin confided in his employer, and it is the latter's duty to enlighten justice."

"Perhaps. It seems to me, however, that he has undertaken a dangerous mission. Let us admit, if you like, that the murder was instigated by jealousy. But in that case, what would you say if they accused—that young man whom you received last year, and who made no effort to conceal the love with which Mademoiselle Aubrac had inspired him ?"

"Louis Marcuil ! a journalist ! a rhymer, who hasn't a farthing in the world ! I closed my door to him six months ago ; my niece first met him at the boarding-school where she was educated with his sister. When I went to see her there I sometimes met him in the waiting-room with his mother, a good sort of woman, who is reduced to work for a living, although she is the widow of an officer. Élise was very fond of the sister, and I think that the brother did not displease her. It was a foolish flirtation, like all young girls have, but nothing more ; and she no longer thought of him when she decided to marry M. Trémentin."

"Well he has not forgotten *her*, I'm sure. One of his friends told me that he lived for her, and that when he learnt she was about to marry, he became nearly insane. I have heard that he even tried to pick a quarrel with M. Trémentin, who refused to fight."

"A man doesn't fight on the eve of his marriage. Trémentin did quite right."

"Perhaps not ; for if he had been killed in a duel before the marriage Élise would not be a widow. And now that he has been killed at his wedding-dinner, suspicion may fall upon M. Mareuil."

"Oh ! that would be absurd !" exclaimed the baroness. "I know that this rhymer is liable to indulge in extravagant acts, but I don't think him capable of committing a murder."

"Do you remember him well enough to recognize him again ?"

"Certainly. He has one of those faces which are never forgotten, although he isn't handsome. But why do you ask me that, dear madame ?"

"Because—it seems to me—I am probably mistaken—but it seems to me that that man over there on the steps of the church is he."

Madame Aubrac darted to the window and looked in the direction indicated by Madame Mornas. The lace curtains of the window were partially drawn back. "Don't come too near; he will see you," said Berthe.

"Yes," murmured the baroness, in bewilderment; "it is he, the scamp! What can he be doing there? He has nicely chosen the day to come and gaze at our house."

"He doesn't limit himself to gazing. Just now he was making signs to some one, and I think he was answered, for he nodded his head, as if to say, Yes. He was not addressing us, however, for we have not stirred, and he hasn't seen us. Could it be Élise?"

"Her room is on the same side as this one, but I cannot believe that. No, it's impossible; she would not have the impudence to hold any communication from her window with that scamp. Besides the servant told us that she was asleep. Still I will make sure."

"It is useless," said Madame Mornas. "Look!"

"She herself!" cried the baroness. "She! crossing the street and going straight towards him while he comes to meet her! She is holding out her hand to him—he takes it in his! Great heavens! She is mad!"

"No; she loves him, that is all," replied Berthe.

"How did she manage to go out? She must have taken the servants' staircase. Ah! this is too much, and I won't allow her to compromise herself in this way."

But Madame Mornas checked the baroness by saying: "Take care, madame! If you made a scene in the street, it would compromise your niece much more seriously."

"What!" cried the baroness, "do you advise me to allow Élise to talk to that wretch, in a public place, on the day after her husband's death?"

"It is unfortunate; but if you interfered it would be dangerous," said Madame Mornas, in a tone which impressed Élise's aunt. "It is possible that no one has yet remarked them. But if you speak to them, you may attract the attention of certain people who are probably watching this house."

"What! do you think the police have been ordered—"

"I think that nothing will be neglected to arrive at the truth; and if it were known that Élise had an interview to-day with M. Louis Mareuil—who loves her madly, and yesterday loved her without hope—unfortunate deductions might be drawn. M. Verdalenc, if he knew of it, would acknowledge that he is mistaken, and that M. Trémontin was not assassinated by a woman."

"That's true; but, great heavens! what is to be done?"

"Nothing, dear madame, except to advise your niece to be more prudent in future. She does not seem to understand her situation. Show her what she exposes herself to by continuing to see this young man. If you don't warn her, passion will drag her into even more absurd actions than the present one. Just look, M.

Mareuil has both her hands in his, and their faces are close together."

"And I must bear this! After bringing up that silly girl in the strictest way! I must allow her to behave like a shop-girl who has met a clerk in the street! No, it's impossible! I must put an end to this scandal."

"You will provoke a greater one; and, besides, it is too late; the lovers are going away. See, they are walking side by side towards the street beside the church."

"This is the height of indecency! The knave must have bewitched her. Look; she is taking his arm now! The fool! she is lost! I will never see her again as long as I live!"

"That would be very wrong, my dear madame; for, after this escapade, she will need your advice more than ever. Only, it will be better for you not to run after her, for if you succeed in joining her, which I doubt, she won't listen to you. Believe me, dear madame, let her alone for the present, and when she returns make her realise how wrongly she has acted; she is sensible and won't let such a thing occur again."

"The mischief is done already. That Mareuil will abuse her confidence."

"Oh, you go too far! M. Mareuil is a gentleman. I'm convinced of it. He would have done better, both in Élise's interest and his own, to have kept away to-day; but he will do nothing to hurt her reputation. He wishes to marry her, you know."

"Marry her! That would be shameful! But there, he is taking her away; they are gone! Where is he taking her too, the wretch? To his own house? No; he would not dare to; he lives with his mother, and his sister, and they would not allow it."

"Question Élise when she returns. She won't refuse to tell you what she has done, and you can then advise her. If I could talk to her, I am sure she would tell me why she resigned herself to this marriage, when she loved some one else. Ah! those who forced her to marry M. Trémentin are very much to be blamed."

"Yes; the Verdalencs, Madame Verdalenc, especially. I have nothing to reproach myself with. I left my niece completely free, and I think that she would have persisted in her refusal; but seeing that things were not progressing, the Verdalencs had recourse to other means."

"What did they do?" asked Madame Mornas, quickly.

"Why, Élise received an anonymous letter which said that this M. Mareuil, who pretended to care so much for her, was trifling with her, for he only cared for her fortune, and was the lover of an actress with whom he would squander his wife's dowry. Well, I would bet that it was Madame Verdalenc who wrote that letter."

"That would be abominable. And did Élise believe in that calumny?"

"Not at first. She showed me the letter, and I advised her to reflect before making up her mind. But the next day, at the theatre—Verdalenc had offered us seats in his box, and his wife took care to show my niece M. Mareuil who was talking to the actress in question."

"He is a newspaper man remember, so he might know her without being her lover."

"Élise did not think of that. She told me that very evening that she did not care to see him again ; and as I did not like him, I approved her. From that time, she began to think more favourably of M. Trémentin, and when three months afterwards Madame Verdalenc came to ask her hand for him, she said yes at once."

"Poor child ! a trap was laid for her, and she allowed herself to be caught in it. It was a piece of folly which has cost her dear. Moreover if the authorities accused the young man she loves—for she has never ceased to love him, don't doubt it, madame—she would find herself in a horrible position. Such a misfortune must be prevented, and I will try to do so. I can tell you now what every one will know to-morrow. My husband has been selected to investigate this affair. He is now at the Palais de Justice."

"Indeed ! Oh, then, my niece has nothing to fear. But pray put M. Mornas on his guard against the foolish conjectures of M. Verdalenc who merely wants to give himself importance and would very likely lead justice astray. Yesterday when we were all upset by that terrible catastrophe, he followed the commissary of police wherever he went, and pretended to direct the investigations, although he had seen nothing—nothing more than the others at least. I went off very early with Élise, and, of course, I have not been this morning to the Verdalencs ; I had enough to do to console my niece and to arrange for poor Trémentin's funeral. I understood yesterday, however, that the shot was fired from a cabin opposite the restaurant, and that two of the guests saw the assassin running towards the Bois de Boulogne ; however, that is all I know."

"And I don't care to know more. That is my husband's affair, and not mine. I am only concerned in the defence of Élise. When you see her tell her that I am entirely devoted to her, and that if she will give me her confidence she will not repent it." And then, as the baroness was about to complain again of her niece's conduct, Madame Mornas added, taking leave : "Don't scold her too much. I hope she will marry M. Mareuil some day ; and if I can help her in any way, I will do so."

## III

THE Avenue Frochot ought to be called the Alley of Fine Arts, for it leads nowhere, and is only inhabited by artists. Painters, authors, and actors form a little colony there. Madame Mareuil, after her husband's death, had gone to live there, with her son and daughter. They occupied a pretty little house, surrounded by a garden. And yet Captain Mareuil, a gallant soldier, promoted for his bravery, had left his widow a very scanty pension, while her own private means merely consisted of three thousand francs a year which her father had made as a contractor for public works. It can easily be imagined how she had to economize, and how many sacrifices she had to make to educate her children. Her son Louis, who had literary aspirations, eventually embraced journalism ; Annette his sister, painted skilfully fans which sold for a high price, while their mother executed embroidery for a large establishment in the Rue des Jeûneurs. Union is strength. It is also happiness, and they were perfectly happy in their pleasant little home. The house had only one storey, and the garden was not as large as M. Verdalenc's drawing-room, but it was full of flowers tended by Annette herself, and the whole place was prim and neat.

On the morrow of the wedding-dinner at Cabassol's, the mother and daughter were sitting in the little garden ; but on this particular day they gave little thought to their embroidery and painting. Madame Mareuil, reclining upon a rustic bench, watched Annette as she wandered to and fro. They had both been crying ; but the mother had choked back her tears, and Annette even tried to smile as she spoke to Madame Mareuil, who shook her head sadly while she listened. The widow was about fifty and still a handsome woman, while Annette was a fresh and rosy brunette. "No, mother, I don't see any one coming," said the girl after going to the gate for, perhaps, the tenth time ; "but don't worry. Louis has been detained at the office, and, if necessary, I will go there."

"You won't find him," murmured Madame Mareuil. "The paper comes out in the evening, as you know ; and he left us yesterday afternoon. What has become of him ? Where has he gone ?"

"Perhaps he has been sent by the newspaper to report something. He may have been sent away to Lyons or Montceau about the strikes. He may have been obliged to leave at once, and he didn't have time to come and bid us good-bye ; we are so far away."

" He would have written to us."

" He will write from where he has gone. We shall receive a letter to-morrow, unless he sends us a telegram to-day. He must know that we are uneasy. Besides, mother, what do you fear? That some accident has happened to him? If that were the case, we should know it."

" I fear everything ; the poor boy is in despair ! "

" You exaggerate. He knew for some time that Élise was going to marry, and, although it caused him terrible suffering, he finally resigned himself to the inevitable."

" You don't know him. He is too proud to complain ; but his heart still bleeds. For the last two months he has only thought of her. You have noticed as well as I that he is a changed man. He was once so gay and talkative, and now he has become gloomy and silent. When I speak to him about his book and his hopes, he scarcely answers me. And, when he went away yesterday, he even forgot to kiss me."

" It has seemed to me lately that he was more sad and pre-occupied than usual, but—"

" Because the fatal day was approaching. Élise Aubrac was married yesterday, and yesterday he disappeared."

" You mean, he has not yet returned. But what connection do you see between his absence and Élise's marriage? He was not invited, and he would certainly never dream of going there to annoy her," answered Annette, assuming a jesting tone, although she was far from feeling gay. " Do you imagine he has left Paris for fear of meeting the bride's carriage ? "

" I have a presentiment that he wished to see Élise again for the last time," said Madame Mareuil, in a husky voice. " Ah ! it is she who has killed him by her cruelty. She had promised to be his wife, but she married that man, and Louis lacked the courage to bear it ; he is dead, I tell you."

" Then we have only to die as well, cursing Élise whom I loved so much—Élise, who loved me as if I had been her sister ! Listen, mother ; I don't know what she promised him—Louis did not tell me, and I have not seen much of her since she left school ; for her aunt thinks that a girl who works for her living, as I do, would be out of place in her drawing-room ; still I am sure, Élise isn't heart-less ; and if she has changed in her feelings towards my brother, it is because she has been made to believe that he no longer cared for her ; and Louis was wrong, perhaps, in not trying to justify him-self. But I think he is cured of his love, that he has never thought of suicide, and that his delay in returning will be explained quite naturally. Hark ! I hear some one coming up the street. It is he, perhaps."

Madame Mareuil rose, and Annette ran to the gate. " No," she cried ; " it isn't Louis. But dry your tears, mother. It is his friend, M. George Darès, who is coming to tell us about him. We shall know at last why he did not return last night."

Madame Mareuil hastened forward, so that when George Darès came up, he found them both at the gate. He saluted Madame Mareuil respectfully, smiled at the young girl, and said in a careless tone : " I came to see Louis. Isn't he up yet, the lazy fellow ? " Then, perceiving that they both turned pale : " What is the matter ? " he added, changing his manner. " Is Louis ill ? "

" We haven't seen him for twenty-four hours," answered Annette. " We hoped that you came with a message from him. He left us yesterday afternoon, much earlier than he usually goes to the office, and we have not seen him since."

" I am surprised at that," replied George. " Did he say anything to you when he went away ? "

" Nothing. He has been grave and preoccupied for several days."

Darès exchanged a glance with Mademoiselle Mareuil. They understood one another, and then the dramatist said to the widow : " Will you allow me to enter, madame ? I have something to say to you, and this is not the place to do it."

" Come in, sir," murmured Madame Mareuil, leaning on her daughter's arm. She could scarcely stand, and it was with a faltering step that she went and sat down on the garden bench.

" I can understand your anxiety, madame," said George, who had remained standing. " I will search for Louis, and I promise to bring him to you. But, first, I should like to know—"

" My son is dead ! " exclaimed the mother, with a burst of sobs.

" Dead ! No, indeed ; I saw him yesterday evening, between ten and eleven o'clock. If he had followed my advice, he would have returned straight home ; but he was not disposed to listen to reason, and I suppose he passed the night running about the streets like a madman. It is extremely unfortunate, for I have something serious to say to him, and I hoped that he would come to me this morning as I asked him to do, but, seeing that he did not come, I decided to try and find him, and as we are neighbours, I naturally came here first."

" Where did you meet him ? " asked Annette nervously.

" Where he ought not to have been, mademoiselle. You doubtless know that Mademoiselle Aubrac was married yesterday—"

" Ah ! I guess what you are going to tell us. My brother was no longer master of himself, he went to see Élise again, and then a scandal followed, perhaps."

" Well, I prefer to tell you the truth at once. M. Trémentin who married Mademoiselle Aubrac yesterday morning, was killed in the evening at his wedding-dinner."

" Killed ! That isn't possible ! "

" I was there. The dinner took place at Boulogne, in a room overlooking the street, and a shot was fired through the window."

" And he was killed ? Before his wife ! It is horrible ! But who did it ? "

" The murderer contrived to escape. I pursued him, but I could not catch him ; and when I returned I found—your brother, who told me he had come to Boulogne, impelled by I know not what sentiment—"

" By despair ! " murmured Madame Mareuil.

" Does he know that Élise is a widow ? " asked Annette.

"I told him so. I was not surprised to find that he did not regret M. Trémentin, but I fear that his behaviour was remarked, and that the people round about us overheard certain things he said. Remember that every one is aware that he was extremely in love with Mademoiselle Aubrac, that he is so still, and that the police are seeking the assassin."

" Do you think that they will accuse my son ? " cried Madame Mareuil rising to her feet.

"I fear they will suspect him," answered George Darès, after a moment's hesitation.

He thought it would be as well to warn the widow of the danger which threatened her son. "That would be infamous. and Louis would have no difficulty in proving his innocence," said Madame Mareuil, firmly.

"I hope so, madame ; but it is none the less true that he did very wrong to mingle with the crowd before the door of the restaurant. The commissary of police asked us our names, and what is still worse, M. Verdalenc was with the commissary."

" He hates Louis, it was he who arranged Élise's marriage and he only managed it, I am sure, by slandering Louis," said Annette.

" Then you will admit, mademoiselle, that Louis was guilty of great imprudence in showing himself, and that was not his only piece of folly. For instance, when Madame Trémentin went off with her aunt, Madame Aubrac, he had the extraordinary idea of following her carriage. I shouldn't wonder if he passed the night under her windows."

" Do you really think him guilty ? "

" No, mademoiselle. If it were proved to me, I would refuse to believe it. I would even deny the evidence, for I have as much esteem as friendship for your brother. But I may, at any moment, be called before the examining magistrate ; it is certain that I shall be summoned as a witness, and I don't wish to compromise Louis. He will be questioned, too, and so as to avoid any discrepancy in our testimony, I wish to talk with him beforehand."

" Are so many precautions necessary to protect an innocent man against a shocking accusation ? " asked Annette, with a searching look at George Darès, who abruptly lowered his eyes.

He was not speaking the truth ; for, since he had discovered that the leaves found in the cabin had been torn from a volume of poetry entitled "Songs of the Sea-shore," he felt certain that Louis Mareuil had fired the shot, but he loved the sister of the unhappy man too much to say what he thought before her. A man may write for the stage, and pass his evenings behind the scenes of a theatre, and yet none the less have a heart. Now that of George

Darès was very susceptible, and although he pretended to be *blasé* and sceptical he had not gazed indifferently on this young girl who in no respect resembled the damsels of the stage.    The very contrast was the thing which pleased him, and he had said to himself more than once that the man who married Annette Mareuil would be a lucky fellow.    He even wondered if he were not in love with her.    Still, he was in no hurry to marry, for he thoroughly enjoyed the life of a Parisian bachelor, which is the pleasantest in the world.    He met Louis Mareuil often enough, as the latter's position as a journalist brought him in contact with dramatic authors ; but he rarely saw his mother and sister.    Still the latter forgave him the infrequency of his visits, and whenever he chose to come, they received him as if they had parted from him only the evening before.    Annette even mischievously pretended not to notice his long absences, although she suffered from them more than she cared to let him know.    Two weeks had just elapsed since he had been at Madame Mareuil's when he met her son at Boulogne.    The meeting had at the very first awakened his suspicions, and the adventure had terminated with a discovery which left him no doubt as to Louis's guilt.    Darès had returned to Paris overwhelmed with consternation.    He had with him the strips of paper, part of which had been used by the murderer to load his gun, and he intended to burn them despite his declarations to the contrary.    But Caussade had seen them, and was prejudiced against the author of the " Songs of the Sea-shore."    Now Caussade would certainly be summoned as a witness, and he was not a man to remain silent, even though his friend Darès had begged him to say nothing of what had been found.    He had plainly declared, while they were returning to Paris by the tramway, that he meant to speak, and so poor George had passed a very miserable night.    If he threw those accusing leaves into the fire, the investigating magistrate would look upon such an action as a reason for not accepting his evidence. George also thought that if, by any possibility, the crime had been committed by another person these torn pages might some day, perhaps, serve to discover the real murderer.    So he finally concluded to keep them, and he intended to show them to Louis Mareuil for whom he had waited all the morning.    It was only after considerable hesitation that he decided to go to the Avenue Frochot.    It was absolutely necessary for him to see and question Louis, for if he obtained a confession from him, he meant to advise him to fly and to furnish him with the means of doing so.    He hoped that the mother and sister would not be present at the interview ; and he had no idea that he would find them alone, and quite as alarmed as himself, or that the situation of affairs would oblige him to tell them of the occurrence of the previous evening, and even to warn them of the danger Louis was in.    Still this was what he found it necessary to do.

Madame Mareuil listened in silence to his embarrassed explanations, but Annette who, was less overcome, plied him with questions which he did not dare to answer, for he could read in her eyes that she reproached him for doubting her brother's innocence.

"You are silent," she said, sadly.

"Mademoiselle," answered George, "I would give ten years of my life to be able to confound the persons who may accuse Louis. If I could only have an interview with him! He could easily prove his innocence, and then he would have no more ardent or zealous defender than myself. Why is he hiding himself? What has become of him since yesterday? And how can he leave you in such anxiety, knowing that you live only for him?"

"He is dead, I tell you," murmured Madame Mareuil.

Annette touched George on the arm, and moved away from the bench on which her mother was seated. George understood and followed her a few steps down the walk. "Why do you speak like that?" she asked him, in a low voice. "Don't you see that you are wounding me to the heart? I also am beginning to believe that my brother is dead; for I shall never think he is a cowardly murderer. His absence is incomprehensible. But if we are not to see him again, I don't wish my mother ever to know that he has killed himself. And I rely upon you to help me in concealing the manner of his death from her."

She spoke in a manner which touched George Darès deeply. Her eyes sparkled, and her sweet face expressed indomitable resolution. He had never seen her look so beautiful. "I hope that you do not doubt my devotion," he said, significantly. "I am ready to do anything to prove to you that you have no better friend than myself."

"Even if Louis is living, and if he is accused?"

"I swear it to you!"

"And I believe you. You will not forget like Élise forgot; and I shall always remember that you remained true to us in our misfortunes. Now I ask you to tell me what you think of doing in order to defend Louis? You will be examined, you say. What have you seen? Speak without fear. I do not lack courage. I can hear everything; however, speak low as my mother is there."

"I saw the murderer running away; I thought I told you that."

"Then, you must be sure he was not my brother."

"I saw him from a great distance, at nighttime, and in a driving rain; and I scarcely noticed his figure or dress. I lost sight of him at the entrance of the Bois de Boulogne, and an instant afterwards I heard a vehicle rolling towards Paris. He was in it without doubt."

"A vehicle. That was strange. He had premeditated his crime then. But while the vehicle bore him away, Louis, you tell me, was under the windows of the restaurant. That fact alone would be sufficient to prove that he is innocent."

"There are other matters," stammered George, "and magistrates are suspicious by nature. Louis will have to render an account of how he employed his time before, during and after the crime; yes, even afterwards, for he will be asked where he passed the night, and if it happens that he does not wish to answer—"

"We will ask him," cried Annette, joyously. "For here he is!"

At this cry, George, who stood with his back turned to the avenue, faced about and saw Louis Marcuil outside the gate. "It is indeed he!" murmured Darès, feeling relieved and uneasy at the same time; "but—he is not alone."

Annette had already gone to welcome her brother. Madame Marcuil, seated upon the bench, and overwhelmed in sorrow, was unconscious of what was taking place. George wondered how he could get Louis away from his family, and subject him to the necessary examination, and another cause of anxiety to him was the presence of a woman who accompanied Louis—a woman clothed in black and carefully veiled. He was afraid to guess who she was, and was so troubled that he did not dare to advance.

He was not left long in uncertainty, however; for the strange woman raised her veil and threw her arms about Annette; and he saw that she was none other than Élise Aubrac in mourning for her husband of a day. "They must both be mad," thought George, paralysed by astonishment.

However, Louis held out his hand, and Élise greeted him smilingly, precisely as they would have done before the fatal shot; and although he was not lacking in either coolness or assurance, the dramatic author hardly knew what to do. Fortunately Madame Marcuil interfered, and the scene took an unexpected turn. Instead of opening her arms to her son, she stopped him with a gesture and said severely: "Where do you come from? And what have you been doing while I was weeping? I believed you dead, and I now ask myself if I can rejoice to see you alive."

"Pardon me," faltered Louis. "I have made you suffer, but if you knew—"

"I know that M. Trémentin was murdered yesterday; that you have disappeared for twenty-four hours, and that you dare to reappear here in company with his widow." As Madame Marcuil spoke she gazed sternly at Élise, who did not lower her eyes.

"You have been told then," began Louis.

"That you were seen, immediately after the crime, near the house where it was committed. Yes; justify yourself."

"Justify myself! Am I accused then?"

"The facts accuse you. I refused to believe that my son could be suspected. But I fear now that he is guilty, and that he has pushed his audacity so far as to bring his accomplice to me."

"Madame," said Élise, with a firmness which increased George's astonishment, "it is for me to explain to you your son's conduct and my own. He was outrageously slandered, and I was weak enough to believe that he had deceived me, and to consent to a marriage I abhorred. I received an anonymous letter, and those who concocted it are the real murderers of my husband. It was he who deceived me; a woman with whom he carried on an intrigue has avenged herself because he abandoned her to marry me. This morning, a second letter apprised me of the truth, and informed me that I should be killed as well."

"Have you got that letter?" asked George Darès.

"No ; I burned it."

"You were very wrong to do so. It would have proved—"

"That my husband was killed by a woman he had forsaken? Who will doubt it? Those who knew him must know her also. I alone was in ignorance. She threatens me with death. But that will not prevent me from repairing the wrong I have done your friend. I have never ceased to love him, and, as he has been willing to forgive me, I shall marry him. He passed the night under my windows. I saw him, he called me, and I went down to him. He explained to me that we had been the victims of an infamous plot. We exchanged new vows, and our first thought was to sanctify our betrothal by obtaining the blessing of Louis' mother. I have lost mine. I was alone in the world. But I have a family now, for I will be your daughter, madame, and Annette shall be my sister."

Annette caught hold of her friend's hands, and held them in her own. She was won over to the cause which M. Trémentin's widow had pleaded with such simple eloquence ; but Madame Mareuil, although shaken, was not convinced. "You forget that your husband is not yet buried, and that your place is with Madame Aubrac, your aunt," she said coldly.

"The man who deceived me was never my husband," replied Élise, calmly ; "and I wish to separate from Madame Aubrac, who helped him to deceive me, and who has no control over me, since she is my aunt only by marriage. I shall avail myself of my liberty to live alone, until the day I marry Louis."

"There is nothing more to be said," thought George. "I must put the girl into a play ; but she will find herself mistaken, if she thinks that by acting in this way she is arranging her lover's affairs."

"Is it thus that you pretend to justify my son?" asked Madame Mareuil, with an emotion which her daughter began to share.

"But, mother," cried Louis, "there is no need of any justification, for I have nothing to reproach myself with. I don't hide that I went last evening to Boulogne, and that I remained for several hours pacing up and down before Madame Aubrac's house. I hide it so little that I am quite ready to tell it to the magistrate who is seeking for the murderer. I would go to him to-day, if I knew where he is."

"That's a good idea," said Darès. "It is much better not to wait until you are summoned before him. Let us go to the Palais together ; we can have a chat on the way."

Annette understood, and she thanked George with a grateful look. She knew that her brother had a sure friend in him, and she longed to be alone with her mother and Élise to talk over the situation. They were all five standing in the middle of the garden walk. Madame Mareuil did not appear disposed to relax in her severity, and no one could have told how the matter would have ended, when an unexpected event happened. The gate had remained open, and a strange gentleman, after looking for a moment at the number of the house, entered, coughing discreetly, to announce his presence. This visitor was well dressed and of good appearance ; George Darès left the group to ask him what he wished. "Have I the honour to speak to M. Mareuil?" asked the gentleman, bowing very politely, but watching the little group a short distance off out of the corner of his eye. "No," said George, "M. Mareuil is yonder, with his mother and sister, and—another lady. Do you wish me to call him?"

"It is needless, sir," replied the stranger ; "if I spoke to him in private, the ladies might be alarmed, and there is no reason why they shouldn't hear what I have to say to him." The gentleman now advanced, hat in hand, towards Louis Mareuil, and George had nothing to do but to follow him. Louis left the ladies on seeing this stranger, and asked somewhat abruptly, "Do you wish to see me, sir?"

"Yes, sir," replied the new-comer, "but I am sorry to disturb you. I beg you to allow me, first of all, to pay my respects to your mother." And he bowed politely to the ladies with the ease of a man of the world. Annette looked at him with uneasy curiosity, while Élise nodded disdainfully ; she longed to see the intruder leave. "Excuse me, madame," he said, smiling to Madame Mareuil, "excuse me for addressing you before being introduced. Unfortunately, I knew no one who could render me that favour, and as my business is pressing—"

"First of all, sir, who are you?" asked Madame Mareuil.

"My name, madame, would tell you nothing. I am an attaché of the Palais de Justice, and I have come to ask your son to go there with me."

This was a thunder-clap, and Madame Mareuil and her daughter turned as pale as death. Louis struggled against his emotion, but did not succeed in concealing it. Madame Trémontin kept a better countenance, and did not appear to suspect that her turn would come, and that her presence in Madame Mareuil's house on the day after the crime would be badly interpreted. As for George, he had understood the situation from the beginning, and he only thought of helping Annette's brother in the trials he would certainly have to undergo. "You arrive at the right time, sir," he said, in as careless a tone as he could assume. "Louis and I were just speaking of the lamentable event I witnessed last night at Boulogne, and I suppose you have come for my friend to give his evidence respecting it." The attaché bowed in the affirmative. "Well, when you came in, I was just proposing that we should go together to the Palais de Justice, and ask the magistrate who has charge of the matter to hear us. I saw the murderer and can give a description of him."

"You are, no doubt, M. Alfred Caussade, the painter?"

"No; Caussade was there also, but I am George Darès, a dramatist. I see you know all about the matter."

"Oh, very little. I happened to see the list of witnesses, and I read your name among them."

"Then, sir, I can no doubt accompany my friend Mareuil, who, without me, would have almost nothing to tell."

"Excuse me, the magistrate will no doubt summon you soon; but just now he merely has a little information, confidential information, to ask of M. Mareuil. I am not charged with summoning the witnesses, and I have simply been sent for M. Mareuil."

"Can you not ask me for this information here?" asked Louis, who thought the man's manner suspicious.

"No, indeed; for I am quite ignorant of what may be required of you. But if you fear to be detained too long, you need give yourself no uneasiness. The magistrate is waiting for you in his office, and he will certainly not keep you long. Ten minutes' interview, perhaps; but a private one." This was said with so much simplicity that Darès, who had his suspicions, took confidence again. "Besides," continued the courteous messenger, "I can tell you, to ease your anxiety, that the magistrate who wishes to see you must be known to you, for his name is M. Pierre Mornas."

Élise's face brightened; and George said to Louis, to whom the name of Mornas conveyed no idea: "You have often met Madame Mornas at Madame Aubrac's, and I myself have once or twice seen the husband at the Verdalencs'. I am delighted that he has charge of the investigation. He is an intelligent and impartial magistrate."

"Very well, sir," said Louis to the official. "Will you tell M. Mornas that I will be at his office within an hour?"

"In an hour M. Mornas will not be there. He begins the investigation to-morrow, and he has an appointment with the public prosecutor to-day, so he desires to see you immediately. He asked me to bring you, if I found you at home, and so I trust you will kindly come with me. I have left my carriage at the end of the avenue, and as I am familiar with the interior of the Palais de Justice, I can take you to M. Mornas at once. The ladies will excuse me for dragging you away, I hope," he added, graciously.

"Go, my son," said Madame Mareuil, with the gravity of a Roman mother. Annette pressed her brother's hand to show him that she agreed with her mother, and Élise encouraged him with a glance. She even said: "Return quickly. You will find me here."

"I am ready," said Louis, anxious to have the business over.

The magistrate's messenger did not wait any longer. He bowed to the ladies, and then took leave of George Darès, who accompanied his friend to the gate. "It is singular, though," thought the dramatist. "This attaché of the courts must be at least fifty. He is a long time entering the magistracy."

"I hope that you will remain with my mother until my return," said Louis Mareuil to his friend, pressing his hand.

" Yes, I promise to wait for you," replied George. " M. Mornas will probably not keep you long, and I have nothing to do to-day. Don't forget to tell him that I am at his orders whenever he wishes to see me, and tell him that my testimony will probably be the most important, for I saw what no one else saw. And, above all, be prudent," he added, in a whisper.

Louis reassured him with a gesture, and then joined the attaché, who had discreetly walked on. "What a charming man M. George Darès is !" said the attaché as soon as Louis was by his side ; " he has so much talent. I saw his last piece the other night, and I was never so much amused. You are very fortunate to know him. He is your neighbour, I believe ? "

" Yes ; he lives near here, in the Rue Condorcet," said Louis.

"And M. Caussade, the painter, lives in the Rue Duperré. You know him also, I think ? "

" Not nearly so well as I do George."

" Ah ! I thought you were very intimate with him. But you met him yesterday at that dinner which ended so tragically ? "

" I met him yesterday, but I was not invited to the dinner."

" Excuse me, I was told that you were a friend of Madame Aubrac's, who is, I think, the bride's aunt. What a frightful misfortune for the young woman, to become a widow on the very day of her marriage ! I once had the honour of seeing Madame Mornas, who is greatly interested in her, and who told me that she was charming. I pity her with all my heart."

Louis made no response to this speech ; and the attaché did not enlarge any further on the subject of Élise Aubrac. They reached the end of the avenue where the carriage was waiting—a roomy brougham drawn by a good though far from stylish horse. The coachman wore a frayed livery and dirty white cotton gloves, and plainly enough this was one of those equipages of the state, which are placed at the disposal of certain high functionaries as long as they remain in office, and then pass on to their successors. However, Louis Mareuil, busy with thoughts of love, paid no attention to these details, nor was he surprised to see a poorly dressed man approach to open the door of the vehicle. He thought the fellow was simply a beggar. Meanwhile, the attaché, taking no notice of this individual, courteously made way for Louis to enter the brougham. He then followed himself, and the shabby-looking man, after closing the door, sprang unperceived by Louis on to the box beside the coachman.

Young Mareuil was absorbed in dreaming of future happiness with Élise ; but his companion showed himself exceedinlgy loquacious and insisted upon talking. The horse had started off at a fast trot, and they rolled rapidly over the pavement. " At this pace," said the attaché, " we shall soon be at the Palais. But I am sorry to have disturbed your family party ; the ladies will be very angry with me." And as Louis did not say a word, he continued : " M. Darès was kind enough to point out your mother and sister to me, but I did not catch the name of the lady who was with them. She is remarkably beautiful, and, what is better still, has a very sympathetic face. Is she any relation of yours? But no, she was in deep mourning, and if she were your relative, you would be in mourning, too."

Louis, although surprised and indignant at this indiscreet question, was obliged to answer it, and he did not think of concealing the truth. "She is M. Trémentin's widow," he said, coldly.

"What!" cried the attaché, "the widow of the gentleman who was murdered yesterday! I can scarcely believe it. Her husband's tragic death is so recent. Excuse my astonishment—I did not reflect that Madame Trémentin is probably the friend—"

"Of my sister; yes, sir, her best friend."

"And she came for the consolation she needed. That is quite natural, and I spoke too quickly. Madame Mornas did not exaggerate. She is charming, and mourning is very becoming to her." However, Louis took no notice of this enthusiastic eulogy, and the attaché continued: "She shows great courage in controlling her sorrow to go to see a friend; her husband was killed before her eyes, and is not yet buried. Did she see him after the catastrophe? I suppose not; they must have taken her away, and, I presume, she passed the night at her aunt's, where she lived, I believe, before this unfortunate event." Louis continued to keep silent, but began to find his companion very annoying, and even something worse. His suspicions were aroused, and the man's singular words set him thinking. "Excuse me, sir," said the messenger; "I forget that you may be tired, and my questions probably weary you. Besides, we are nearly at the end of our journey, and in a few moments it will not be I whom you will have to answer."

The brougham had, in the meanwhile, followed the Rue Montmartre, crossed the Central Markets, and reached the Pont Neuf. Then turning on to the Quai de l'Horloge, it skirted the new buildings of the Palais de Justice, facing the former Place Dauphine, and finally described a semi-circle, passed under an arched gateway, and drew up in a courtyard. "Here we are," said the attaché, "and if you will be kind enough to get out, I will show you the way." At the same time he opened the door, near which the man who had been seated on the box now appeared.

Louis then noticed two police agents standing close by. He began to understand. "Where are you taking me, sir?" he cried.

But the attaché had already disappeared, after whispering a word or two to the coachman's comrade. "Get out, please. They are waiting for you," said the man at the door of the vehicle. Louis alighted, looked about him, and at once understood the whole matter. He was in a court full of policemen, and which looked very like the court of a prison. "Go on!" now said the man in the rear with a gesture of authority. Louis would have liked to catch him by the throat, but he controlled his anger, and walked in the direction indicated. He longed to have an explanation with the pretended attaché, who must be a commissary of police or an officer of the peace. Meanwhile the man followed him very closely. They passed various offices on the ground floor, and reached the foot of a winding staircase. "Go up !" said the man with a fresh gesture. Louis did so ; and on reaching the upper floor he found himself in a large ante-room where there were three clerks. The man who was following Louis now motioned him to a chair ; and in the meanwhile a policeman stationed himself at the top of the stairs, to prevent any attempt at flight. But Louis did not dream of escaping ; he only thought of defending himself. The agent had entered a second ante-chamber leading out of the first. He appeared again in a minute or two, and then motioned Louis to follow him. Louis asked nothing better. He did so, and after crossing a room in which there was nothing but shelves full of green pasteboard boxes, he entered an office where a man sat at a desk writing—a man whom he recognised immediately. It was the pretended attaché. "At last, sir," cried Louis, "you will tell me what this miserable joke means. You came to ask me to go and see M. Mornas, the investigating magistrate, who desired, so you told me, to obtain some information from me. Where is he ? "

"You shall see him presently," replied the official. "What is your name ? where do you live ? what is your occupation ? "

"My name, you know it ; and my place of abode also, since you came to my house to draw me into an infamous trap."

"Pray remember that you are speaking to a judicial functionary ; don't make your situation worse than it is."

"My situation ? Of what am I accused, then ? "

"You know that you are accused of murdering M. Trémentin."

"I ? That's absurd. I reached Boulogne just after the crime had been committed, and George Darès saw the murderer fly."

"You can tell that to the investigating magistrate, and M. Darès' testimony will also be taken. It is not my duty to examine you, but to enter your name upon the jail-book. If you refuse to give me the information I ask of you, I shall have to write it down of my own knowledge. I have no time to lose."

Louis turned very pale ; but he struggled against the emotion which filled his heart, and said in a firm voice : "Very well, sir. Give me materials to write to my mother."

"I regret that I am unable to grant your request. The investigating magistrate will decide whether you are to be kept in solitary confinement or not ; and until he has done so, it is impossible to allow you to communicate with any one whatsoever." And addressing the policeman on guard at the door, the chief of the detective service added : "Conduct the prisoner to the Dépôt."

Louis lowered his head and did not answer a word. Ten minutes afterwards the massive door of the jail closed upon him. It was all over with his dreams of happiness ; and the unfortunate man said to himself, thinking of Élise : "What if they should accuse her of being my accomplice ? "

## IV

M. MORNAS arrived at the Palais at half-past twelve. He had a short conversation with the public prosecutor, and he was already installed in his office when his wife was making her call on M. Gigondès. As she had foreseen, his honourable scruples had given way, and he had consented to take charge of the investigation. He had to clear up one of the most puzzling affairs that had been presented for a long time, and he had taken hold of it rather late, as sixteen hours had elapsed since the crime had been committed. But it was less important to proceed speedily than surely, and, moreover, the night and morning had not been badly employed.

The commissary of police at Boulogne had completed his inquiries, and the chief of the criminal investigation service had been occupied since early morning in collecting precise information as to M. Trémentin's friends and past life. M. Mornas found the chief's report on his desk, and naturally commenced by studying it before summoning the suburban magistrate who was awaiting his orders. The document was a model of clearness. Its author declared that M. Trémentin had been killed either by a woman who cared for him, or by a man who cared for Élise Aubrac. As regards the first supposition, the report called attention to the fact that M. Trémentin had had several intrigues with women in all ranks of life. One only of them was known at present, and the chief of police did not hesitate to mention her by name. This was Madame Verdalenc, whose former connection with her husband's clerk was almost of public notoriety; but this appeared to have come to an end some years before. An investigation must, therefore, be made into M. Trémentin's love-affairs, and an accomplice would probably have to be sought for, as a gun was not a weapon adapted to the use of women. On the other hand, Élise Aubrac had never had but one lover, M. Louis Mareuil, who had wished to marry her, although he had no fortune, and who hated his rival to such a degree that he had attempted to provoke him to a duel. But, said the report, M. Mareuil had held himself aloof for the last six months, and seemed to have renounced his pretensions. He, moreover, had excellent antecedents, he belonged to a very respectable family, and he lived a very regular life. If the second supposition were followed up, it would be necessary to inquire if Madame Trémentin, who had not been married entirely of her own free will, had not been acquainted

with the intentions of her rejected lover. An attentive perusal of
this document left the examining magistrate in a state of great per-
plexity. He remembered, however, what his wife had said when
she advised him to accept the mission, and, at first sight, it had
seemed to him impossible that a young girl, loved and esteemed by
his dear Berthe, could fall in love with a man capable of committing murder.

The report of the crime drawn up by the Boulogne commissary
was there beside the other one, and though it was detailed enough,
it was dry and lifeless. M. Mornas determined to question the commissary who had drawn it up, and then go with him, if necessary,
to inspect the scene of the crime. The commissary of Boulogne
proved to be a clever man, a little too convinced of his own importance, perhaps, but quite incapable of losing his head and exaggerat-
ing unimportant facts. He commenced by relating very succinctly
how he was summoned to the restaurant ten minutes after the
crime, and how he had found M. Trémentin dead, the bride in a fainting fit, the guests stupefied, and M. Verdalenc in a state of extraordinary excitement. The latter gentleman had overwhelmed him with
incoherent statements, and had almost insisted on assisting him in
his investigations. He had accompanied him everywhere, repeating
over and over again that the murder of his cashier should not go
unpunished, that he suspected some one, and would furnish important information. "This conduct must have appeared singular to
you," said M. Mornas, who had read Madame Verdalenc's name in the
report furnished by the chief of the criminal investigation service.

"Yes," replied the commissary ; "and I even wondered if M.
Verdalenc were not trying to lead me astray. It was not long,
however, before he formally accused a young man whom we met at
the door of Cabassol's restaurant. I did not at first attach much
importance to this, but later on I thought that M. Verdalenc might
perhaps be right."

"A young man, you say ?"

"Yes, a journalist named Louis Mareuil, and M. Verdalenc declares that this young man had asked for Mademoiselle Aubrac's
hand."

"That does not prove that he is guilty. I have here some precise information about him, and it gives him an excellent character.
I don't understand, it is true, how he happened to be in front of
the house where the crime was committed."

"That would not be a sufficient reason for accusing him, but
there are others. An inhabitant of Boulogne, a respectable tradesman, approached me and told me something Mareuil had said and
which he and two other persons had overheard. Mareuil was talking in the street with two gentlemen whom he knew, and who
formed part of the wedding-party. He asked them in a loud voice,
and no doubt advisedly, who had been killed. It is scarcely possible that he was ignorant of the facts ; for all the people about
were speaking of the occurrence. However, one of the gentlemen

whom he questioned answered, I don't know why, that the ball had struck Madame Trémentin, whereupon Mareuil exclaimed: 'Unhappy man that I am ! I thought that it was he ! ' "

" That's strange ; I can't understand what he meant."

" Nor did I, at first ; it was only after reflection that I thought those words might signify : 'I aimed at the husband, whom I hate, and I have killed the wife, whom I love. But this is only a conjecture on my part, for they might also mean : 'I knew that some one had been killed, and I thought it was the husband.' Three witnesses, all worthy of belief, will testify before you that he said those words to a person whom you will certainly question, M. George Darès, a dramatic author. M. Verdalenc introduced me to him, in the street, as well as to a M. Caussade, a painter, who was also among the guests. When the shot was fired, these two gentlemen rushed out of the room to pursue the murderer. They were the only ones who had any presence of mind. They followed him to the entrance of the Bois de Boulogne, it seems, and, on their return, they met Mareuil at the door of the restaurant ; at least, that is what M. Darès told me."

" Do you think that M. Darès didn't tell you the truth ?" asked M. Mornas.

" No, sir ; for we should then have to suppose that he was an accomplice of Mareuil's, whereas M. Verdalenc answers for him. Besides, I did not ask any explanation from him. I simply took his address and that of the journalist whom I already suspected."

" Do you think, then, that he is the person who fired the shot ? "

" The moral proofs are against him ; he mortally hated M. Trémentin, who had no other enemy, so M. Verdalenc assures me, and after having escaped into the Bois, he may have returned to Boulogne by another road, in order to establish an alibi. The tradesman who reported the compromising words he used, declares that he was outside Cabassol's only a minute or two before M. Darès accosted him."

M. Mornas reflected, and his face grew grave. He was beginning to fear that the second supposition of the chief of the criminal service was the right one, and that it might lead to the arrest of Élise as an accomplice. "That is an important point to verify," he said. " Does M. Verdalenc, who has so poor an opinion of this young man, go so far as to suppose that Madame Trémentin was implicated in the affair?"

" Oh, not at all. On the contrary, he spoke most warmly of her. She once had a sort of inclination for Mareuil ; but she has quite overcome it, and has not seen him for a long time. She was prostrated after by grief the death of her husband ; and moreover, she barely escaped being hit by the bullet which struck him, and, to express my personal opinion, I am not at all sure if that bullet was not intended for her."

The magistrate raised his head. He willingly accepted this idea which put Élise out of the question. Madame Mornas was interested in her, but she was not interested in Louis Mareuil ; and now it appeared that this unfortunate youth could be accused without exposing Élise to any suspicion. "Continue," he said. "How did you conduct the inquiry, and what have you discovered ?"

"I could do hardly anything last night. I had only two inspectors at my disposal—who had come from Paris on another matter, and who happened to be in my office when I was called for. It would have been quite useless to search the wood. I simply observed that, in order to fire, the murderer had posted himself in a hut exactly opposite the restaurant. He must have had the key of this hut, which was always locked up. The land on which it is built is common property, but the materials are of such little value that the owner abandoned them."

"The man who built the hut must be found."

"He died more than twenty years ago, and it is believed that he made a present of it to one of his workmen, who has never set foot there; at least, he has never since been seen at Boulogne, and no one remembers his name. It is not even sure that his master gave him the cabin. It was only a rumour, and I have not yet been able to verify it."

"But it is the first thing to find out. As the murderer was in possession of the key he can only be the owner of the cabin, or some one who knows him."

"You shall see the key, sir ; and you will observe that it is not new, and has not been used for a long time, for it is covered with rust."

"And you found nothing inside the cabin ?"

"Absolutely nothing, except some footmarks. It was raining very hard, and the ground round about the cabin was muddy. I could see that several persons had entered the place, for there were footmarks of different dimensions. Of course I took care that they were not effaced."

"The murderer was not alone, then ?"

"Yes ; I think he was. When he fled, he left the door open, and other people may have entered the hut, attracted by the catastrophe. However, I made an important discovery this morning when I returned to the place. While examining the window through which the shot was fired I found underneath it, between some stones, a fragment of paper which the assassin used as wadding for his gun. This paper is important, and so I have brought it to you." The commissary produced his memorandum-book, opened it, and took out a bit of paper blackened with powder. "This was undoubtedly used as wadding," he said, handing it to the magistrate, "and you will notice, sir, that there are some printed words upon it. The fragment was torn out of a book."

"Yes, beyond doubt ; and from a book of poetry too, for the words rhyme : ' cause,' ' pause,' ' beam,' ' seam.' You are right, this is an important discovery."

"All the more so, as Mareuil is a poet as well as a journalist.

M. Verdalenc told me so. He says the fellow passes his time in writing verses, instead of working, and that in order to have his books, which nobody reads, printed, he spends all the money his mother and sister make by hard toil. See ! this paper is new, and the impression quite fresh."

" If this young man is really the author of the book which the murderer tore to load his gun with, it will be a strong presumption against him. But there are here only some ends of lines, rhymes which occur in all poetry."

" You could summon Mareuil's publisher and printer. They will certainly recognise the paper and the type, and will even be able to tell the page on which the four verses we have, appear."

"I will send for them to-morrow. This is serious, very serious," concluded M. Mornas, rising, and pacing slowly up and down his office. This was a certain sign of preoccupation with him, and, indeed, he was in great embarrassment. The two proofs furnished by the commissary against Louis Mareuil, seemed overwhelming. The fragment of paper, especially, left almost no doubt as to his guilt. On the other hand, the information respecting his antecedents and his general conduct were favourable, and it was improbable that a man so highly spoken of in the report of the chief of the detective police should suddenly commit so audacious a murder. Still M. Mornas tought Mareuil's case a bad one, and resolved to do his duty, at the risk of causing pain to his wife. "You have told me," he said, stopping suddenly in his walk, " that, yesterday evening, you simply took M. Mareuil's address. But have you done nothing more this morning ?"

" After seeing the public prosecutor, I went to the office of the paper for which Mareuil writes. The editor was not there, but a clerk told me that Mareuil, contrary to his usual custom, had not put in an appearance on the previous evening."

" What do you conclude from that ? "

" That not a moment should be lost in setting a watch upon him. If he has returned home, which I doubt, he will certainly not sleep there to-night, for he must expect to be arrested. He will take a train for Brussels or London during the day."

" I agree with you that we must make haste, not to arrest him, but to examine him. He may be able to establish his innocence, and, in that case, I do not wish to have cause for regret by taking a premature measure. I will not detain you any longer. Will you be kind enough, as you go out, to ask the chief of the detective service to come up here ? Tell him that I wish to speak to him at once."

When M. Mornas was left alone, he felt more perplexed than ever. He began to think that Louis Mareuil's arrest was indispensable ; but he did not wish to issue a warrant before doing all that was possible to avoid such a step. He had full confidence in the intelligence of the chief of the criminal investigation service, and he wished to consult him first, to find out what he thought of the case, and to arrange with him so that Louis Mareuil might be arrested with as little scandal and publicity as possible. The chief was not long in appearing. He was a very different man from the commissary, far more clever and intelligent, but also more imaginative and accessible to prejudice. At the first words M. Mornas spoke to him, he interrupted him to inform him very politely that Louis Mareuil was already lodged in jail, and, as the magistrate uttered an exclamation : "I had special orders to act as I did," he continued, "and I thought, sir, that you had been informed of the matter. A warrant for arrest was handed to me to be executed immediately. The matter was urgent, for it was feared that he might try to leave the country, and, for that reason, the public prosecutor did not dare to wait."

"He might at least have informed me of his action. I was about to give the same order, but I had certain instructions to give also. The young man's family is an honourable one, and ought to be treated with respect."

" I did that, sir," replied the chief, and thereupon he recounted the circumstances of the arrest.

" How did Mareuil behave ?" asked M. Mornas.

" Very well, until he was brought into my office. Then he at first became very angry and insulted me ; but afterwards he calmed down and asked to be allowed to write to his mother. All this took place only ten minutes ago ; for I had only just sent him to the Dépôt when the Boulogne commissary came to tell me that you wished to speak to me."

" I see that you have acted intelligently as you always do. And now, what is your opinion in regard to this matter ? I have read your careful report. Tell me whether you believe M. Mareuil to be guilty."

"If I only take into account the facts I so far know, there can be no doubt of his guilt, for they are all against him."

"Do you think that the moral proofs are not ?"

" Not precisely. It is said that he had a great hatred of M. Trémentin. But I think that investigations should be made elsewhere also. Trémentin had more than one enemy. My impression is that there is a woman in the case."

" You think then that some woman, who had been abandoned by Trémentin, must have killed him."

" There are women on both sides," said the chief.

" What ! do you think that M. Trémentin's widow influenced Mareuil in murdering her husband ?"

" I don't go so far as that. But when I called at the prisoner's house, I found Madame Trémentin there."

" Impossible ! " cried M. Mornas, in consternation.

" It is quite true, sir ; and when I adroitly questioned Mareuil he said—as if it were the most natural thing in the world—that Madame Trémentin was his sister's best friend, and that she had called to see her."

"A few hours after her husband's murder! She has no feeling, then, and she is very audacious!"

"It is evident that Trémentin's death has not affected her much; but as for her being audacious I don't believe it. She is without feeling, but she has not strength enough to appear in public for the sole purpose of turning aside suspicion. If there had been an arrangement between herself and her former lover to get rid of her husband, she would have taken care not to show herself at her lover's house on the day after the crime; she would have waited until the excitement had subsided."

"Then, you think that she is not his accomplice?" asked M. Mernas, with a sigh of relief.

"I would almost swear it. If she were guilty, she would surpass in boldness the cleverest scoundrels I have ever known. But a woman of twenty doesn't play such a dangerous part with such superlative coolness."

"That is my opinion; but what can we think of this man Mareuil, who receives her at his house, although he knows well enough what took place at Boulogne last evening? He was there; he was seen there."

"Yes; the commissary told me that. I cannot say it was he who fired the shot, but if he did, I feel certain that Madame Trémentin knew nothing of it. As regards the actual facts of the crime, I should like to call your attention to M. Darès and M. Caussade, who saw more than anyone else. Their testimony will be important."

"I will hear them after the prisoner," replied M. Mornas, who although Louis Mareuil's arrest had greatly modified the state of affairs, did not yet despair of finding him innocent. He, indeed, hoped to discover the real criminal, and thus deserve both the advancement he coveted and the gratitude of his dear Berthe, who was interested in Élise. He longed to begin the battle, and so, having placed the paper which had served as wadding for the murderous gun in a drawer of his desk, he signed a printed formula, and rang for a messenger. This formula was an order to bring Louis Mareuil from the Dépôt to his office. "You will not take down the questions and answers until I tell you to do so," M. Mornas now said to his clerk. "At the outset, I may not formally examine the prisoner, and it is useless to record a simple conversation."

The clerk bowed. The fact is the magistrate did not intend, in the first place, to treat Louis Mareuil as a criminal. Despite the apparent proofs against him, M. Mornas still hoped that he would establish his innocence by proving an alibi, for instance; and if his explanations warranted an order for immediate release, he wished to spare him the annoyance of signing a report which would have to be recorded. The magistrate, therefore, meant to give the examination the appearance of a simple interview. He did not wait long. The messenger reappeared, received an order, and, instead of returning with a policeman escorting the prisoner, he ushered in Louis Mareuil as he might have ushered in a visitor. The poor fellow had not yet recovered from the blow he had received, and the treatment he had been subjected to had exasperated him. Still his features, which were contracted with anger, relaxed a little when he saw the magistrate come towards him and heard him say : "Don't be alarmed, sir."

For the last half hour, no one had addressed him as "sir." "To whom have I the honour of speaking?" Louis asked.

"I am M. Mornas, the investigating magistrate, and I have a few questions to ask you."

"I am ready to answer them, sir ; but permit me to tell you that your name has been strangely misused. A man, belonging to the police, presented himself at my house about an hour ago, and told me that you desired to speak to me. I consented to accompany him, but instead of taking me to your office, he had me thrown into jail. I ask you why this has been done?"

"A warrant had been issued for your arrest, and it is customary to take prisoners at first to the Dépôt."

"So I am accused of committing a murder?"

"It depends upon you to prove your innocence. I have sent for you to enable you to show that a mistake has been made. I am disposed to believe that you are innocent, and I shall have no doubt of it when you have frankly answered the questions I am about to put to you."

"I ask nothing better, as soon as we are alone," said Louis Mareuil, with a glance at the clerk, who was nonchalantly trimming his quill pen.

This sort of behaviour wounded M. Mornas. Kindly disposed as he was, he could not allow a prisoner to speak to him in this way, and he at once changed in manner. "An examining magistrate must be assisted by a clerk, in accordance with the law," he said, taking his place behind his desk. And he added, pointing to a cane-bottomed chair : "Sit down."

"This is an examination, then?" said Mareuil. "Very well ; I prefer that. I at least know where I stand."

It was fated that the young fellow should make mistake after mistake. M. Mornas understood the allusion, and was very angry at hearing his considerate action likened to the treacherous courtesy of the chief of the detective service. "Gervais, take down the questions and answers," he sternly said to his clerk. Mareuil had seated himself and was waiting. "You are called Louis Mareuil," began the magistrate, casting his eyes over the report he had read on first entering his office ; "you are twenty-five years old, and you live with your mother at No. 19 Avenue Frochot?"

"Yes, sir ; this is the third time within an hour that I have been asked all that," replied the young man, angrily.

"You are attached to a newspaper, I believe?"

"Yes ; but I also write on my own account. I published a volume of poetry three weeks ago. But may I know how these details, foreign to the matter in hand, can interest you?"

"It is for me to ask questions," replied M. Mornas, drily, "don't forget that. Do you follow, Gervais?" The clerk nodded in the affirmative, and the magistrate continued: "Now you were at Boulogne-sur-Seine yesterday evening. Several persons saw you and spoke to you in the street opposite Cabassol's restaurant. At what time did you reach Boulogne, and by what route?"

"At about ten o'clock, I think. I went by rail to Auteuil and then on foot along the Saint-Cloud road."

"And you went straight to Cabassol's?"

"Yes ; I asked where it was, and I had no difficulty in finding it. There was a crowd before the door."

"Why did you go to the restaurant where M. Trémentin's wedding-dinner was?"

"There is no need for me to tell that."

"I know that you once hoped to marry Mademoiselle Aubrac, and that you hated the honourable man she preferred to you. That doesn't explain why you went to Boulogne last evening. On the contrary, there was every reason why you should wish to be as far as possible from the place."

"I am not bound to explain to you the sentiment which influenced me ; and I shall not say a word whenever you speak of the lady whose name you have just mentioned."

M. Mornas involuntarily started. It seemed to him that Mareuil had guessed the delicate point of the case, and was determined not to have Madame Trémentin mixed up in the affair. "Take care," he said ; "you place yourself in a very bad position by refusing to answer. Do you acknowledge that you challenged M. Trémentin to fight a duel not long ago?"

"Yes ; that is a fact."

"M. Darès, who met you in front of the restaurant, just after the crime had been committed, told you, probably to try you, that the murderer had killed Madame Trémentin, and you exclaimed : 'I hoped that it was he.' What did those words mean?"

"I am not obliged to explain them."

"Well, tell me what you did from the time you mingled with the people in the street? I know already that you were accosted by one of your friends, M. Darès."

"And by a painter, M. Caussade, whom I do not know so well. A commissary of police came up, accompanied by M. Verdalenc, who employed M. Trémentin. This commissary asked my name and address of M. Darès, who gave them to him."

"What happened after that? Did you remain there?"

"I returned to Paris."

"And you went home?"

Mareuil, for the first time since the beginning of the examination, seemed visibly embarrassed. "No," he said, after hesitating for some little time.

"You were at home, however, when the chief of the detective service arrived?" said M. Mornas.

" I had just reached there."

" Then you passed the night elsewhere. How did you employ your time ? "

" In walking about."

"Till one o'clock the next afternoon ? That is very improbable." Mareuil remained silent. " When you received the chief of the detective service, you were not alone," resumed M. Mornas. " You were talking with your mother, your sister, your friend—"

" And Mademoiselle Aubrac," interrupted Mareuil. " That is what you mean, is it not? Well, the lady whom you call Madame Trémentin came to my mother's house, and she came there with me, and I went to fetch her. Question her if you wish to know why she came, and have her arrested if you dare."

" There is no question of that," faltered M. Mornas, taken aback by this unexpected reply. And he made a sign to his clerk, who understood that he did not wish the prisoner's violence to be recorded. The idea had suddenly struck him that by thus speaking of Élise, Mareuil hoped to embarrass and perhaps intimidate him ; the prisoner must be aware that Madame Mornas knew Élise Aubrac very well. Now the employment of such tactics shewed that he was guilty, and made it presumable that the young woman was not his accomplice. " Madame Trémentin is in no way implicated in the affair," said M. Mornas. " Return to the facts. Do you know how M. Trémentin was killed ? "

" With a gun, I was told. I have never owned a gun in my life, and if I did own one, I should hardly know how to use it."

The magistrate slowly opened the drawer of his desk, took out the paper he had placed there, and unfolded it, attentively looking at the prisoner. But Mareuil did not lower his eyes or change colour ; he did not seem to understand. " Do you know this ? " asked M. Mornas. " You see that it is a bit of blackened paper which has been torn from a book, and judging from the words which are still legible, the book was a volume of poetry. The lines rhyme."

" What is that to me ? " said the young man, with a shrug of his shoulders.

" I wish to know if these verses are yours," asked M. Mornas, coldly. The more exasperated the prisoner grew, the more icy the magistrate became.

" If there is nothing there but the ends of the lines, I cannot promise to inform you," replied Mareuil, ironically. " Still I can tell, perhaps, if the type is that used by my publisher."

" Then look at it," said M. Mornas, laying the paper on the table, without letting go of it. Mareuil had no difficulty in guessing why. "Yes," he said, "I recognise the grain of the paper and the Elzevir type ; I even recognize the rhymes ; they are common enough, and it will cost me nothing to confess they are mine. This fragment will be found at the top of page 99—the number is still there—of ' Songs of the Sea-shore,' the book I recently published."

" I warn you that your answer will be taken down."

" I expect that. What else have you to ask me ? "

" You will not make me believe that you don't understand the drift of my last question," said M. Mornas. "The paper I have shown you was used as wadding for a gun."

" Wadding ? " repeated Mareuil, without flinching. " I thought guns were loaded with cartridges."

" Not all of them : the one the murderer used was made in the old-fashioned way, for this bit of wadding was picked up in the street, under the windows of the Cabassol restaurant, and it was blackened with powder."

" I believe what you say. But I have already told you that I have no knowledge of the management of fire-arms."

" You served your time in the army, I suppose."

" Yes ; and I confess that I made a very bad soldier. I noticed, however, that the guns furnished to us did not require wadding, and as I have never been a sportsman, this is the first time I have seen what you just shewed me."

This was said in a careless, quizzical tone that astonished M. Mornas to the highest degree. He wondered if these airs of disdainful assurance sprang from the young man's certainty of innocence, or if he were playing a part which would be the height of impudence. "Then how do you explain," he asked, "that the man who murdered M. Trémentin used a page of your book to load his gun ? "

"I do not explain it at all," replied Mareuil, drily. "However, the copies of my book have not all remained on the shelves of my publisher. The first edition is almost exhausted, and has passed into a great many hands. A large number of copies have been sold, and I have given several away to my friends ; I have even given several to people who were merely acquaintances."

" So you assert that the murderer possessed the book in some way, and utilized it to load his gun ? That would be highly improbable, you must confess."

" Unless it were calculation on his part ; that is, if it were anyone's interest to turn suspicion on me, he has chosen the best way to effect his purpose."

"You insinuate, then, that he knew your peculiar situation respecting M. Trémentin, and foresaw that you would be accused?"

" Why not ? A great many people know that I had a quarrel with M. Trémentin, and that I proposed a duel, which he refused. Nothing more was wanted to charge me with a crime I did not commit. My arrest is proof of that. I will even add," continued Mareuil, " that if I were cowardly enough to murder anyone, I should not be so foolish as to load my gun with a bit of paper torn from a page of my book. I might as well have used my visiting card."

" Who are the persons," asked M. Mornas after a pause, " to whom you gave copies of your book ? "

" I did not keep a list," replied Mareuil, "and I don't perceive the reason of your question."

" Well, I admit that your position is a well-founded one—that the murderer may have imagined this abominable ruse, and have used a leaf of your book to ruin you. But I must draw two conclusions from this : first, that he had the book in his possession, and secondly, that he was well acquainted with you. So we must look for the scoundrel among those to whom you gave the volume. Please give me their names."

" In the first place, I don't remember them all ; and, if I did, I should take care not to mention some of them, for you might accuse another innocent person. It is quite enough that you accuse me—though I am sure of establishing my innocence, for I have no fear. But another person as guiltless as myself might become alarmed and not know how to defend himself. As for me you can keep me in prison, but I defy you to prove that I killed M. Trémentin. I hated him, I confess, but I never dreamed of murdering him."

M. Mornas made no rejoinder ; he reflected for a moment, and then, after writing a short note, he rang for a messenger, and spoke a few words to him in a low voice. Finally, turning to Louis Mareuil, he said : "I have nothing more to ask you here."

" Are you going to send me back to jail ? " asked the prisoner.

" No. I am about to send for M. Darès and M. Caussade. I have only one more question to ask you in this office. As you did not go to bed last night, you are still dressed as you were last evening at Boulogne ? "

" Yes ; I had just returned home when your agent arrested me, and I had no reason to change my clothes."

"Very well ; that is all that I wished to know. You can retire."

Louis was too proud to ask what was to be done with him. He followed the attendant who was waiting at the door, and left the room without saluting the magistrate. The police agent who had conducted him from the Dépôt was in the corridor. The attendant said a few words to this man, and then departed to deliver M. Mornas' note. The police agent then made Louis a sign to go on before, and followed close after him. They passed along several corridors and descended a narrow staircase, and when they reached the ground floor the police agent introduced the prisoner into a sort of guard-room, where two other police agents were smoking their pipes, and motioned him to sit down on a wooden bench. Mareuil did not take advantage of the permission, but stood, waiting to see what was to be done with him. At the end of twenty minutes he heard a vehicle stop before the door, and guessed that it was for him. This time it was not the official brougham, but a four wheel cab, with an agent on the box and two inside. He was obliged to get in, and he resigned himself to the inevitable. He asked no questions of the agents, and the cab drove out of the courtyard and rolled along the Quai des Orfèvres. At the same moment, on the other side of the Palais de Justice, the examining magistrate, the chief of the criminal investigation service, and the Boulogne commissary set out in the official brougham. "And so," said M. Mornas, in reply to a remark made by the chief, "you think that your secretary will find these gentlemen at home ?"

"As to Caussade the painter there is no doubt of it," responded the chief. "He passes all his time in his studio. It will take longer to find M. Darès, perhaps ; but I left my men on guard at the end of the Avenue Frochot, and one of them is very intelligent. If M. Darès has left Mareuil's house, this man will know where he is. I shouldn't be surprised if Darès had taken Madame Trémentin back to the Baroness Aubrac's."

"I must see him to-day. I particularly want him and his friend Caussade to explain to me, on the spot, the facts which followed the murder. I want to go with them over the road which they took in pursuing the man who fled, and to see the precise point where they lost sight of him."

"That is an important matter, it will enable us to tell if an alibi is possible," said the commissary of Boulogne.

"I will make him repeat on the spot what happened yesterday," said M. Mornas. "And while we are waiting for him we can visit the cabin. I believe that you have taken steps to prevent any one from entering it."

"Yes ; I stationed two gendarmes there. We shall find the footprints just as I saw them last night."

The conversation now took another turn, while the brougham rolled on towards Boulogne. At last the three functionaries alighted at the door of Cabassol's restaurant, and the commissary was at once joined by the inspectors who had assisted him on the previous evening. They told him that nothing fresh had happened, and that they had awaited his arrival to search the wood. "Let us first see the room where M. Trémentin was struck," said the magistrate.

The landlord of the establishment came forward, hat in hand, and conducted the officials to the first floor. The dining-table was cleared of the glass and crockery ; but where the bridegroom had sat, the table-cloth was spotted with blood, and the pane of glass, broken by the bullet, had not been replaced. The commissary called M. Mornas' attention to the fact that the window was just on a level with the window of the cabin and exactly opposite it. "Where was Madame Trémentin seated ?" asked the magistrate.

"Here, sir," replied the commissary, pointing to a chair. "The bullet must almost have grazed her hair. M. Trémentin was on the other side of the table, opposite his wife, and at the moment the shot was fired, he had risen to reply to a toast. He was struck in the heart, and so the bullet must have passed very little above Madame Trémentin's head."

The magistrate and the chief exchanged a look ; they both had the same idea, an idea which had already occurred to the commissary. " I would like to see exactly what were the positions occupied by the bride and bridegroom," said M. Mornas.

" That is very easy," replied the chief of the detective police. " I am not much taller than the bridegroom so I will stand in his place, and the commissary can take the seat occupied by the bride." This was done, and M. Mornas, by stooping down, saw that a direct line drawn from the broken window to the chief's breast would pass two or three inches above the commissary's head. "Was it a skilful shot or an awkward one ?" asked the chief ; " in other words, who was aimed at ? The whole matter rests upon that. If Madame Trémontin was aimed at, it was not the prisioner who fired the shot. He is in love with her, and he now hopes to marry her— that is when the ten months, stipulated by law are up. If, on the contrary, the bridegroom was aimed at, it may be that the prisoner is guilty, but even that wouldn't settle the question."

" That is also my opinion," said M. Mornas. " We must now visit the cabin. The prisoner will arrive while we are there, and if your men bring M. Darès and M. Caussade we shall obtain some information which will clear up important points."

The gentlemen left the restaurant and crossed the street, preceded by the two inspectors who were waiting for them. When they reached the door of the cabin, which was guarded by a gendarme, the commissary produced the key and opened the door. "Oh, oh !" cried the chief, "several people have been in here. We shall have great difficulty in finding out anything from all these footprints. But, no, it will be less difficult than I thought, for the marks are perfectly distinct." The chief of the criminal investigation service was very expert in solving problems of this kind. He knelt down to see the footprints closer, and after due examination and comparison, he rose, saying : " Four persons have been in here, one of whom was a woman who wore high-heeled shoes. See, the heels are clearly marked."

" That's true," muttered the magistrate.

" And her feet are remarkably small. The others are men's footmarks. Two men with light shoes seem to have entered together, for the steps are side by side ; but the other individual followed a less regular line, and wore much stouter boots."

" I must tell you," said the commissary, " that after the shot was fired the door remained open until my arrival. These footprints may be those of some people of Boulogne who entered after the catastrophe."

" You would have found them here when you came."

" I found no one, that's true ; but I entered myself."

" I know it. Here are your footprints. They are much larger than the others. And when I said four persons, I meant without counting you. You came in alone, didn't you ? "

" Yes ; I left M. Verdalenc and my men at the door. I understood at once that it was necessary not to efface those marks, and I took care where I stepped."

C

"You went to the window and returned straight to the door. Here are your footprints. I must say, however, that the others did the same. They only entered and went out again; they were no doubt in a hurry."

"But, come," said M. Mornas, who had attentively followed these interesting deductions, "you don't suppose that the murderer was with anyone when he fired."

"No, sir. That isn't possible. A man doesn't bring anyone with him when he is about to commit a murder. And yet, there is something here which I can't explain; but which the investigation will clear up. The window was open when you arrived, commissary?"

"Yes; I shut it myself."

"Well, I am going to open it again. We need more light."

One is never so well served as by one's own self, and the chief crossed the first room and entered the second one on tip-toes. When he had opened the shutters, the light streamed into the cabin. M. Mornas had remained on the threshold with the commissary; but they now joined the chief, who was again at work examining and counting the footprints. "This is peculiar," he said; "all the steps end at the window. But the two persons who entered together drew a little on one side before going out, whereas the woman's feet, and the feet with the heavy boots walked straight from the door to the window, and from the window to the door again."

"What do you conclude from that?" asked the magistrate.

"Nothing at present. But they are signs which may be useful later on. Ah! here is a vehicle, and I see my secretary. He has lost no time; he arrives before the prisoner, and he brings a gentleman who must be M. Caussade, for I don't recognise him, whereas I know M. Darès. I will tell him to wait."

"There is no need of that. I can question him here. And it is better to interview him at first in the absence of the prisoner."

It was indeed Caussade, who alighted from the vehicle with a very discontented air. He had been taken away from his studio, which did not please him, for he feared to accuse a man in whom his friend Darès was interested, and yet he was determined not to lie. The chief received him at the door of the cabin. "I am going to take you to the investigating magistrate," he said, "but step very carefully, so as not to efface those footmarks you see."

"Those footmarks!" exclaimed Caussade, "why, I made them myself."

"You came in here then?"

"Yes, last night, with M. Darès. We had just returned from giving chase to M. Trémentin's murderer."

"Come, sir, the magistrate must hear you."

Caussade, who already regretted having said so much, allowed himself to be conducted before M. Mornas. "We are already further advanced," said the chief, rubbing his hands. "This gentleman has recognised his footprints and those of M. Darès. Out of the four persons who have entered here, only two remain to be discovered."

" I sent for you, M. Caussade," said the magistrate, who desired to proceed more methodically, " to ask you for some information respecting the facts laid before me by the commissary of Boulogne. Now I beg you to tell me what you saw after the murder had taken place."

"I saw—a man running away. My friend Darès told that to the commissary, and I can only repeat to you what Darès said."

" Did you pursue this man ?"

" Yes, to the edge of the wood, where I slipped and fell. My friend helped me up, but meanwhile the man disappeared. We could do no more, and so we gave up the attempt, and returned to the restaurant immediately."

" When did you enter this cabin, then ?"

Caussade hesitated a little. He was afraid of casting suspicion on Louis Mareuil and he was not aware that the unfortunate young man had been arrested, for he had not seen Darès since the previous evening, and the chief's secretary had been discreet. " Why," he eventually said, "we came in here on our return from our fruitless chase. Darès thought that the shot had been fired from this window, and he prevailed on me to come up here. We found the door open and the cabin empty."

" Then you had been here when I spoke to you in the street ?" said the commissary. " Why didn't you tell me ?"

" Because you didn't ask me."

" You afterwards talked with a young man, named Louis Mareuil," said M. Mornas. " Were you not surprised to find him outside the restaurant ?"

"He explained to Darès that on passing at the end of the street he had heard some cries, and seen a crowd of people, and had then approached through curiosity."

" But did he explain to you why he had come to Boulogne ?"

" Here he is," exclaimed the chief, who was standing near the window ; " the cab has been rather slow, but it has come at last. What are your orders, sir ?"

" Tell your men to bring the prisoner here."

Caussade started : he understood that he was about to be confronted with Mareuil, who was certainly accused, and the prospect was far from pleasant. Louis Mareuil speedily appeared, escorted by two police agents. The chief received him at the door, and led him before the magistrate. Louis was pale, but he still retained his haughty demeanour. He nodded to Caussade, and waited. "Just step here," said the chief to him, " and place your foot on this mark."

Mareuil smiled disdainfully. "Oh, I see !" he exclaimed. "You wish to ascertain if my foot corresponds with that impression. But it would be waste of time. I willingly admit that I came in here."

" With M. Caussade and M. Darès, perhaps ? "

" No ; they met me in the street, a moment afterwards ; there was no one in this cabin."

" What did you come here for ? "

" I wanted to see what was taking place in the house opposite. So I looked out of that window, and only remained here for a moment."

Caussade gave a sigh of relief. Mareuil had not seen him. Mareuil did not know that he had hidden with Darès to watch him : and Mareuil acknowledged that he had entered the cabin. Nothing now obliged Caussade to testify against him. The magistrate glanced at the chief, and on reading on his face that he was struck, like himself, by the prisoner's clearness of language, he considered that the moment had now come to give another turn to the interrogatory. " You must have remarked the appearance and costume of the man you pursued," he began, addressing Caussade.

" I only saw him from a distance, and it was dark. All that I remarked was his figure. He was short and slim. I thought I also distinguished that he held a gun in his hand, and that he wore a low, felt hat."

" Like the prisoner," muttered the commissary.

"He escaped from you on the outskirts of the Bois de Boulogne?" asked M. Mornas.

" Yes ; he ran along a pathway which must lead to the race-course."

" Do you think that between the moment you lost sight of him and the moment you met M. Mareuil at the door of Cabassol's, the man whom you pursued would have had time to return ? "

" I couldn't say," responded Caussade, who understood the drift of this question. " However, I scarcely think so. He would have had to make a long detour so as not to meet us, and it is some distance from here to the wood."

" The distance will be carefully measured. How long did it take you to return from your pursuit ? "

" I couldn't say exactly. A quarter of an hour, perhaps ; but I must add, that just after we lost sight of the man, we heard a sound of wheels, and we both thought that a vehicle had been waiting to take him back to Paris."

" You are sure you heard a vehicle drive off ? " asked the chief.

"Perfectly sure ; and as it was raining very hard, probably no one was driving for pleasure in the Bois de Boulogne."

Louis Mareuil had listened with an impassive countenance to the above conversation ; and the chief now approached the magistrate, whispered a few words in his ear, and walked with him into the first room, leaving the prisoner in charge of the commissary. "Well," asked M. Mornas, "have you any opinion ? "

" I have a conviction that Mareuil speaks the truth. I believe myself that the culprit is a woman.'

"But it was a man who was seen running away with a gun in his hand."

"A woman in man's clothes. Unfortunately for herself, and fortunately for the prisoner, she retained her shoes, and her footprints in the cabin have betrayed her. It now only remains to find her, and I will do so."

"It seems to me that you are a little too confident," said the magistrate. "Footprints are not sufficient proofs."

"Will you consider, sir," rejoined the chief, "that M. Caussade and the prisoner himself have confirmed the opinion I gave on those footprints? Four persons came in here. We know three of them, by their own avowal. The fourth remains : and there is no doubt but that it was a woman."

"Granted ; but it is doubtful if she fired the shot. Remember that some woman among the crowd may have entered the hut out of curiosity ; and besides, the person whom M. Caussade pursued was a man."

"Well, sir, he told you that this person was short and slim. Now all women look little when they don masculine garments. This person also wore a low hat, and women, disguised as men, always wear that style of hat."

"And you think she disguised herself to come to Boulogne ? But this isn't carnival time, and it is forbidden to appear in public in the costume of the opposite sex."

"And so she took care not to come on foot."

"You think, then, that the noise heard by M. Caussade—"

"Was the rumble of a vehicle which was waiting in the wood for her, and which was conveying her home. This vehicle was probably a private one."

"Then you think the woman is rich ?"

"That is my opinion ; but I'm not sure as to her social status. She may be a lady or she may belong to the questionable classes. We must look for her in those circles, for she certainly was not a work-girl."

M. Mornas reflected, and his face clearly showed that these words had made a great impression upon him. "This woman," resumed the chief, "must be remarkably intelligent, and possess extraordinary energy. It is evident, moreover, that her position and conduct place her above suspicion. And she operated with so much audacity, because she knew that her reputation was spotless. Criminals of the lower classes don't act with such boldness and precision. We have only to discover how this woman procured the key of the cabin ; and to do that we must find the owner."

"The commissary of Boulogne made some inquiries on the point, and no one could give him the name of the man to whom this shanty belongs. It was built thirty years ago by a contractor, who has long since been dead."

"If I had charge of the matter, I should soon learn something "

" I beg of you to take it in hand ; but, meanwhile, tell me frankly what you think I had better do with this young man, Marcuil ? "

" Well, even supposing he is guilty, I don't think there would be any harm done by setting him at liberty, temporarily ; I should be able to watch him without his suspecting it, and if it were he who fired the shot, he would betray himself by some imprudent action sooner or later ; it was a mistake to precipitate matters."

" Well," said the magistrate, " I cannot give him absolute liberty ; but I can let him go home on bail with the knowledge that he is under police surveillance."

" That step would be an excellent one, it seems to me. Being forewarned, he will be upon his guard, still, I will do my best to arrive at a certainty. But he recomes my secretary with a person who is certainly not M. Darès."

The magistrate and the chief were in the outer room, near the door, before which a gendarme was on guard. In the inner room they had left Louis and Caussade, whom the presence of the Boulogne commissary condemned to silence, and who, besides, had nothing to say, for they knew each other very slightly, and had but little sympathy in common. The person whom the chief had noticed approaching was a man of about sixty, tall and stout, a little bent, but still firm upon his legs. He was dressed in black clothes, cut with no pretence to style, and, at first, he would have been taken for a workman, who had saved enough money to support himself comfortably. He saluted the officials without appearing embarrassed, and he had evidently come with the intention of speaking to them. " Excuse me, gentlemen," he said, without any further preamble, " for presenting myself before you without being summoned, but I am Jean Bigorneau, and I live at Boulogne, on the Quai du Quatre-Septembre. The commissary knows me very well. I have heard that you wanted to find out who owns this cabin, so I have come to tell you that I worked at one time for M. Fauvel, the contractor who built it. He died in '63, and though he was not very rich, he had saved a little money all the same."

" This cabin must belong to his heirs, then ? "

" He only left one daughter, who has never claimed it. And besides, he gave it, during his lifetime, to one of his workmen, who had been born a gentleman. People said that this fellow had been employed in some government school, and was discharged in disgrace. He certainly knew as much as an engineer, and he spoke like a professor ; and he was quite young too, twenty-five at the most, when old Fauvel died. He had worked for him eighteen months or so."

" Do you remember his name ? "

" Yes, indeed ; it was a queer name, Garnaroche, Pierre Garnaroche. He disappeared a long time ago. Before the war with Germany, he came here from time to time, and I met him here and there, sometimes in the finest *café* of the place, ordering the best of everything, and paying like a prince ; and sometimes I saw him in a blouse, in a low wine-shop. I must tell you that his education had done him little good ; it was money thrown away, and old Fauvel often said that he would come to a bad end. At one time, too, Garnaroche slept here as he had no money to hire a room. He squandered all the coin he made, and Fauvel gave him the cabin out of charity."

"But if it was in a bad state twenty years ago, why hasn't it fallen into ruins by now ?"

"Garnaroche had it repaired once, when he was in funds. He had his ups and downs."

"He continued to inhabit it, then ?"

"No, sir, but there were people who said that he received some women here. I forgot to say that he was a very handsome fellow, with a figure like a dragoon's and a face to turn any girl's head."

"And has anyone ever seen the women who came here ?" asked the chief, with a glance at M. Mornas.

"I don't think so. It was also said that Garnaroche was a smuggler, and hid the merchandise which had escaped duty here."

"And after the war he never turned up again ?"

"Never, sir. I have always had an idea that he was killed in Paris, during the Commune in 1871."

"Possibly ; but he must have left the key of this cabin with someone, for the place was entered yesterday—"

"I heard of that this morning, and I thought of Garnaroche at once."

"And you came to say that you believed him to be the murderer."

"No ; I am not at all sure of it. He may, as you say, have given the key to somebody."

At this reply the chief drew the magistrate a little on one side, and said to him in a low voice : "To my mind, sir, the affair is now as clear as daylight. This Garnaroche was a sort of adventurer, who made all the capital he could out of the education he had received, and his physical advantages. He may very well have been the lover of a woman in good society and have met her in this cabin. When the intrigue came to an end, the woman kept the key, and later on, she became acquainted with M. Trémentin. When she learned that, by a singular chance, the wedding-dinner was to be given opposite the abandoned cabin—which she could enter just as she liked—she took advantage of the opportunity to avenge herself."

"It is quite possible, still, we don't know who she is."

"We shall find her, I answer for it. If Garnaroche is living, I shall discover him, and he will be obliged to speak up, were it only to prove that he himself isn't the murderer. Even if he is dead, the contractor who employed him, and who took an interest in him, must have known the life he led—"

"But the contractor has been dead nearly twenty years, and a woman, intimate with Garnaroche in '63, must be old now."

"I am convinced that the one who killed Trémentin was not precisely young. A young woman would have been easily consoled for the loss. Moreover, the contractor Fauvel left a daughter, and M. Bigorneau, who evidently knows her, will tell us where she is."

"Well, it seems to me that Louis Mareuil hadn't the slightest connection either with this fellow Garnaroche or his employer."

"He was only a baby when they were working at Boulogne. Where could he have procured the key of this cabin? This key is old and rusty, so it could not have been made expressly from an impression taken from the lock. There are merely appearances against the prisoner, and before a jury the case would fail."

"I shall set him at liberty on bail, and I shall proportion the amount to the means of his mother, who isn't rich."

"She will be very happy to see her son again. I have nothing to do now, except to ask the address of Fauvel's daughter."

During this conversation Bigorneau, hat in hand, had quietly waited for permission to leave. "Your information is useful," the chief said to him. "But I must ask you one more question. Fauvel had a daughter who is still living, I think?"

"An only daughter, sir, who is now a widow. She married a poor officer—so poor that Fauvel wasn't very well pleased with the marriage—a sub-lieutenant named Mareuil, who was killed during the siege of Paris."

"Mareuil!" exclaimed M. Mornas. "You say that Fauvel's daughter is Madame Mareuil?"

"Yes, sir," replied Bigorneau, surprised by the effect which his words had produced. "I know her well, and she knows me very well too, although it is some time since she saw me. The last time I met her was two years ago, in the Rue Montmartre; I was going to see a friend, who lives near the markets. With what her father left her, she hasn't much to live on, for she has two children, a boy and a girl. Ah!" added the garrulous old fellow, "I remember seeing the boy when he was a little fellow; but when I worked for old Fauvel, the girl wasn't born. The mother told me, however, that her daughter made money by painting fans, and that her son wrote for the newspapers."

The magistrate looked at the chief, who appeared disconcerted enough. Bigorneau's ingenuous words had quite changed the aspect of affairs. "And so," said the chief, "you think that this lady will be able to tell us what has become of Pierre Garnaroche, who was in her father's employ?"

"As to that, gentlemen," replied Bigorneau, "I don't know. Madame Mareuil must have seen him in the old times, for her husband was in garrison in Paris the year that Fauvel died. But I don't think she would have liked Garnaroche much; Mareuil didn't, and it would surprise me if his widow had kept up the acquaintance. Still, all the same, she may know if he is living."

Doubt was no longer possible. Louis Mareuil was surely the grandson of the contractor, who had built this cabin and given it to one of his workmen. And so Louis Mareuil might have been able to procure the key. "I thank you, for the trouble you have taken," said the magistrate. "I shall make use of the information you have given me. Be careful not to talk to your friends of the persons you have mentioned. Silence is necessary, in order not to trammel the action of justice."

"I shall not speak, sir, I am not a gossip, and I would willingly give a hundred francs out of my own pocket to have the murderer discovered." With this praiseworthy declaration, Jean Bigorneau bowed and went off.

"I begin to think that I was on a false track," said the chief to the magistrate. "Will you authorise me to address a few questions to the prisoner, in your presence?"

"Willingly," replied the magistrate, and they passed into the second compartment of the cabin, where Caussade was walking nervously up and down, while Louis leant against the wall, with his arms crossed and his head erect. The commissary was standing before the open window, with his back turned to the curious crowd, which the arrival of the police had attracted into the street. "May I retire, sir?" asked Cussade.

"Yes, sir," replied M. Mornas, after a moment's reflection; "you will wait, however, outside, or in the restaurant, if you prefer it, until I have finished with the examination of the prisoner. I may have need of you again before returning to Paris."

Caussade left the cabin, grumbling to himself, and the chief then asked Louis Mareuil: "Do you know Garnaroche?"

Louis did not seem troubled by the question, but he made a gesture, which did not escape the chief. "I have spoken once or twice to a man who bears that name, but I know him very slightly. He was once a workman, employed by my grandfather, and he says he knew me when I was a child. He has taken advantage of this to address me in the street; but he has never been to my house."

"Your grandfather, M. Fauvel, the contractor, was greatly interested in this workman, and was very kind to him?"

"I did not know it."

"Well, when did you meet this Garnaroche last?"

"Some months ago; at the Palais Royal, I think."

"Do you know his address and occupation?"

"No. It seems to me, however, he was a steward or gamekeeper, somewhere not far from Paris, I don't remember where."

"It will doubtless come back to you. It is important, in your own interest, for you to remember."

Mareuil made no reply, and, upon a sign from M. Mornas, the chief called an inspector from outside. "Well," said the magistrate to the prisoner, "you are to be taken back to the Dépôt. I shall question you again to-morrow. Night brings counsel. I hope to find you better disposed to answer me."

Louis turned his back on M. Mornas without a word, and placed himself under the guard of the inspector, who had advanced to lead him back to the vehicle occupied by the police agents. "My dear colleague," said the chief to the commissary, "one of your townsmen has helped us out of our embarrassment. We now know the name of the contractor and that of his workman. And I should have known these names earlier, if you had gone at once to the tax-collector of Boulogne, and found out to whom the cabin belonged. It must figure on the tax-list, for someone pays the taxes; please find out, to-day, if the owner is a man named Garnaroche, and if his present residence is known."

"I won't fail to do so," muttered the commissary, rather confused at not having thought of this simple proceeding sooner.

"Well," said the magistrate, "I will put off the remaining investigations to be made here till another day. It is more urgent to find out through whose hands the key of this cabin has passed. Before we measure the road the assassin must have followed, if he returned here after running to the edge of the wood, will you search the bushes among which he may have thrown his gun, and keep me informed of whatever happens in your jurisdiction?"

The commissary went away, rather crestfallen and very much dissatisfied at not having been the first to receive Jean Bigorneau's testimony. After his departure the chief turned to M. Mornas and said: "I am, perhaps, mistaken again; but I have a presentiment that the prisoner did not obtain the key from Garnaroche. He didn't lose countenance when I spoke to him so suddenly about that fellow. I think it more likely that he found the key at his mother's house. The late M. Fauvel might have kept it, and it may have had a tag attached to it—' Key of the Boulogne cabin,' or something of the kind; and I should not be surprised if the finding of the key prompted the crime. There still remain the questions of the gun and the vehicle stationed in the wood, to be cleared up."

"And so," said the magistrate, "you abandon the other supposition? It was a likely one, however."

"It is so still, and I don't cast it aside entirely. However, the most important point now is to find this Garnaroche, and I will take care of that. If he is really a steward at some château the lady owner may have known Trémentin and then all would be explained. If it really were a woman who avenged herself, she must move in good society. Disreputable females don't murder a lover who leaves them."

M. Mornas made no answer to the chief. At heart, he was a little humiliated at having only played the second part in this difficult investigation. His advancement seemed less certain to him, and on all sides he perceived difficulties which he had never dreamed of. He gladly entered the carriage to return to Paris, for he desired to reach home and consult his wife.

# V.

Eight days had elapsed. Louis Mareuil has been transferred from the Dépôt to Mazas. His mother and sister spent their time weeping, and Darès went to see them constantly. Like the chief, he had become convinced that Louis had only been imprudent, and that M. Trémentin had been killed by some woman. And for this woman he was seeking. He hunted through society, and constantly visited the people whom the cashier had frequented, watching and listening without appearing to do so. Madame Mornas, whom he met at the Verdalencs', and who was warmly interested in Élise Aubrac, told him that her husband had found nothing conclusive against young Mareuil, and that the unfortunate affair would probably soon terminate by his being set at liberty. Then the dramatist was examined by the magistrate, and he came fairly well out of the trial. He could, without lying, refrain from speaking of the torn leaves he had found in the cabin, and which he had carefully preserved. He was convinced that the copy of the "Songs of the Sea-shore," a fragment of which the murderer had used to load the gun, had been purchased by some woman of good society, and he hoped that chance would enable him to discover the mutilated volume in some boudoir. It was a chimerical hope, however, for the woman who had used it, probably with due intention, must have burned what remained of the book.

Caussade was only half in Darès' confidence, and in fact he was angry with his friend for having mixed him up in an affair which had already caused him to lose considerable time. He had been obliged to go again to Boulogne, this time with Darès, whom the agents had missed on the occasion of the first visit to the place. Accompanied by the chief of the criminal investigation service, they had gone along the road from the restaurant to the wood, searched the bushes round about the Longchamp race-course, and the ground in the neighbourhood of the cabin where the assassin had lain in ambush. But no traces were found of the gun or of the vehicle, while as for the possibility of the individual who ran away having returned to Cabassol's, nothing positive could be established.

The widowed Élise had meanwhile broken off all connection with the Baroness Aubrac. After her escapade, she did not return to her aunt's home, and still less did she go to the apartment in the Rue d'Hauteville, which she was to have inhabited with her husband. She boldly suggested that she might live with Madame

Mareuil, and as the latter had the good sense to oppose this arrangement, she unhesitatingly placed herself under the protection of Darès, whom she scarcely knew, but who in her eyes had the merit of having taken Louis' part. And Darès engaged on her behalf some pretty furnished rooms in a very respectable house on the Boulevard Haussman. The result of this imprudent conduct might have been foreseen. The young woman was sent to Coventry by respectable people. The baroness turned her head away when anyone spoke of her. Madame Verdalene only pronounced her name with a modest blush. M. Verdalene consigned her to the fire and flames, and did not hesitate to insinuate that, if Mareuil were the murderer, Élise was probably his accomplice. Madame Mornas, alone, did not turn her back upon Madame Trémentin. She defended her, and almost approved of her conduct. She prevailed upon her husband not to summon Élise as a witness, and she even went to see her in spite of M. Mornas's advice ; without betraying her husband's secrets she let her understand that the innocence of Louis Mareuil would finally be established, and that he would not remain much longer in prison.

In point of fact, however, M. Mornas was very much perplexed. He waited for light which did not come. And he was obliged to confess with chagrin that he had fallen upon one of those criminal cases in which circumstantial evidence plays the chief part. Indeed, the moment seemed approaching when he would have to confess his powerlessness and give up the case. However, among the various judicial functionaries one man was not discouraged. The chief of the criminal investigation service sought unceasingly for a solution of the problem, without letting it be thought that he was doing so. In appearance, matters remained as they were after Jean Bigorneau's deposition, and the chief's final official act was to see the tax collector. This functionary declared that the taxes for the cabin had always been paid by the man named Pierre Garnaroche, but that they were two years in arrear, and that Garnaroche's present residence was unknown ; so that the cabin would be seized and sold as firewood for the profit of the state. As for the key the chief acquired the certainty that it had never been in possession of the prisoner's mother. Madame Mareuil, on being questioned as to her relations with Garnaroche, had replied with such clearness that there was no doubt as to her sincerity. She said that the man was a kind of vagabond whom her father had employed out of charity, and that he had never crossed her threshold since her father's death. She knew that he had accosted her son in the street and she had made Louis promise to "cut" him the first time he did so again. It had to be admitted, therefore, that if the prisoner had used the key, he had procured it by asking Garnaroche for it, and that an understanding existed between them. To decide this point it was necessary to find Garnaroche, and the chief spared no pains. His most skilful detectives were put on the track, and quietly searched both Paris and the provinces. The department of the Seine

was visited discreetly ; but neither in Paris nor at the various châ-
teaux in its vicinity could any sign of the man be found. It became
more and more evident that, in changing his status, Garnaroche
had also changed his name. Information must, therefore, be obtained as to the antecedents of the stewards and gamekeepers within a radius of fifteen leagues around the capital, and this would
take a long time.

Matters remained in this state when the evening arrived of the
first performance of a piece to which George Darès had greatly contributed, although his name only appeared third upon the programme. This piece was a kind of extravaganza, a sort of work
which Darès excelled in ; earning no little money by it, while waiting
till he was able to make a literary name with real comedies. In
other times, this first performance would have been an event for
him ; but his feelings caused him to forget his interests, and so as
not to abandon Madame Mareuil and her daughter in their distress,
he had left the task of superintending the rehearsals to his colleagues.
However, he was obliged to be present at the performance which
was to decide the fate of the work. Annette Mareuil herself had
urged him to do so, and so that the evening should not quite turn
him from the task he had in hand, he had sent boxes to Madame
Mornas and Madame Verdalenc, as well as a stall to the chief of
the detective service, who had graciously accepted it. Caussade also
had given himself a holiday, and had taken a seat in the stalls next
to Darès, who was glad to have some one to speak to. Only Élise
was absent ; and if the author had not offered her a box, it was because he did not wish her to carry her forgetfulness of propriety to
the point of showing herself at a theatre but a week or so after her
husband's death. The piece was to be performed at the theatre of
the Porte Saint-Martin, and it had a fair amount of plot and was
full of witty sayings. The house was crowded on the occasion of the
first performance. All the first-nighters had turned out in force :
critics, editors, and fashionable men about town, without counting
a sprinkling of prominent tradespeople. Darès and Alfred Caussade, ensconced in a corner of the stalls, carelessly watched the stir
and confusion occasioned by the spectators reaching their seats, and
exchanged comments every now and then. Darès had left his two
colleagues the care of watching the performance from behind the
scenes, and they were astonished at his thus deserting the battle-
field when the engagement was about to commence ; but they excused him, as they thought he was in love, in which they were not
mistaken : however, the woman he loved was not in the house,
and it was not to pay court to her that he had wished to retain his
liberty. Annette Mareuil was at home with her mother, and
George was now looking round the auditorium for some person who
might help him to save Louis. "Ah!" he said, nudging Caussade,
"there are the Verdalencs. I was sure they would take advantage
of my box."

"What a queer idea of yours to send one to them !" growled the painter. "The husband looks like a fool, and the wife resembles Beef-à-la-Mode. But who is that other matron who is taking her place in front of the box ? Eh ! by Jove ! it is that old fool, the Baroness Aubrac, Élise's aunt. I didn't know that she was so intimate with the Verdalencs."

"She has quarrelled with her niece, and as the Verdalencs dislike poor Élise very much, she has naturally been drawn towards them."

"It must be acknowledged, too, that Madame Trémentin did all she could to quarrel with her aunt, and with the world in general. I know that she didn't love her husband, but she wasn't forced to marry him."

"It was the Verdalencs who made the match, assisted by the aunt ; and Madame Verdalenc, little heart as she may have, must repent of having urged her former lover to contract this marriage ?"

"Is it quite true that he was her lover ?"

"My dear fellow, no one doubts it ; the chief of the detective police spoke of it again only the day before yesterday. I sent him a seat, by the way, and you can see him from here, in the same row as ourselves."

"Hum ! Why didn't you invite the examining magistrate as well ?"

"I did. That empty box opposite to us is his. But I doubt if he will come, though I hope to see his wife. She is on our side, that is, on Mareuil's side."

"Well, I think that this M. Mornas is a perfect fool. He has no opinion of his own, and your chief of the detective service leads him by the nose."

"So much the better. If we had a pig-headed magistrate to deal with, Louis would be sent to the Assize Court ; and Louis is innocent, I would stake my life on it !"

"Well, I wouldn't," said Caussade, with a shrug of the shoulders.

"Oh, suppose we talk of something else. Look ! the box-opener is pulling up the screen before a box in front. Two lovers must have come to see my piece in secret. Every seat is taken in the house. If the manager isn't satisfied, he must be hard to please."

"I see a woman behind the screen ; I can't distinguish her features, but I just espied the flash of her eyes. She doesn't wish to be seen, but she wishes to see. Upon my word, I half think that she is looking at us."

"At me, probably. Her admirer, who, no doubt, keeps himself in the background, has told her that I was the author of the play."

"You coxcomb ! But raise your eyes, and look at Madame Mornas entering the box you just pointed out to me. How superb she looks in her black dress. Good heavens ! what shoulders ! And her face is full of expression. But I should think she was thirty-six, at least."

" You are not far wrong. Why, she isn't alone, and it isn't M.
Mornas who accompanies her. Where the devil has she picked up
that escort ? He looks like a mummy ; and a badly preserved one,
too. This is the first time I have ever seen him. He surely isn't a
friend of her husband's."

" Well, he certainly won't compromise her. He's seventy-five,
if he is a day. By-the-bye, all the persons who figured in the
Boulogne affair seem to be here, to-night. Do you see that grey-
haired fellow in a seat under Madame Mornas's box, and who looks
so astonished at occupying such a good place ? "

" He is a workman in his Sunday clothes. This proves that he
has some taste, since he has paid to be present at the first performance of our piece. Those are the sort of spectators I like."

" My dear boy, you are mistaken," said Caussade ; " that man
is very well known to M. Mornas and the chief of the detective
police. The other day, while I was in the hut at Boulogne, he
came to tell them a lot of things which I didn't hear, as I was too far
off, but his talk must have been very interesting, for they listened
to him for twenty minutes."

" Then that explains to me why the chief asked me for a seat for
a gentleman whose name he did not mention."

" So your appreciative spectator is simply a police spy. I suspected it. But this isn't the time to talk. The orchestra is coming
in, and so we must turn our backs on the audience, and sit down to
appreciate your masterpiece."

George Darès did as his friend suggested, not without some regret,
for he had none of the emotion which the rising of the curtain causes
to new authors, and he felt that something interesting might happen
in the auditorium before the end of the evening. The orchestra
commenced playing a brilliant overture, and the audience had just
ceased coughing, when a tardy spectator appeared at the end of the
row of stalls, where the two friends were located, and tried to
reach a seat, beyond. " Halloo ! look out, will you ? " cried
Caussade, as the new comer trod on his toes.

" Keep your feet under the seat then," replied the tardy arrival,
continuing on his way.

Caussade was enraged. "What times these are !" he muttered
between his teeth. " A first night audience used to be composed of
well-bred people ; but now, we have boors, who stamp on your
feet, and don't even trouble themselves to apologise for their awk-
wardness."

" The fact is," said Darès, " that fellow comes from the
country ; you can see it by his appearance. I would bet that he
came to Paris on purpose to visit the theatre."

" He had better have stayed at home ! " growled Caussade.

The person whom he was so angry with seemed quite out of
place in the stalls ; not that he was exactly common-looking, for
he was a tall fellow, with a magnificent figure, and a face which
would not have passed unnoticed anywhere. He had a lion-like

head—crowned with an abundant crop of curly reddish hair—and a fine pair of restless blue eyes. However, his face bore marks of all kinds of dissipation. He might have been taken for an artist, had it not been for his odd dress : a kind of shooting jacket, buttoned up to the chin, very tight pantaloons, and a cap, which he did not take off until he was seated. "Don't bother about him any more," said Darès to Caussade, "and reserve your attention for my play."

The curtain rose upon a scene representing a vineyard, in which each kind of vine was personated by a pretty woman. The piece was entitled "The Diseased Vines," and the phylloxera played the principal part on it. A superb woman figured as the microscopic and devastating insect which seems bent upon destroying all the vineyards of France, and in the first scene she announced her wicked intentions in a song. She meant to surprise the poor vines while they were asleep, and prick them with a long gold needle, which she brandished in her hand. The phylloxera was a tall, handsome blonde, and the threatened vines were all of them pretty girls. The spectators were pleased, and a murmur of approbation sped through the auditorium. The occupants of the stalls brought their opera-glasses into play, and people in the boxes applauded discreetly. The Verdalencs and Baroness Aubrac were not the last to show their approval. "George Darès is certainly very witty," whispered Madame Verdalenc, from behind her fan, "and I have already forgotten that we ought not to be here this evening."

"Why not, my dear!" asked the banker gravely. "Poor Trémentin is only just buried, it's true, but he was no relation of ours, and it is perfectly proper for us to go to the theatre. The code of society is precise upon the point. I appeal to the baroness."

"Oh !" said Madame Aubrac, "I do as I like, and I don't trouble myself much about what people say. To be sure Trémentin became my nephew by marriage ; but my amiable niece has taken care to break the bonds which attached me to her ; and so I can allow myself to do what she herself would do, if she were not restrained by some slight sense of shame. Still, I am not quite sure that she hasn't come to the theatre this evening, in secret. The author of the piece is now her best friend."

"I don't understand Darès' conduct !" exclaimed M. Verdalenc. "It was no use for me to try to prove to him that Mareuil killed my cashier ; he wouldn't listen to me."

"Don't say anything against Darès, who has given us the best box in the house," murmured Madame Verdalenc. "It is said, that he is in love with Mademoiselle Mareuil himself, and I always excuse lovers."

"Then you ought to excuse my niece as well," exclaimed the baroness. "When I remember that we proved to her, as clear as day, that Mareuil was deceiving her with an actress ; and yet to think that he had the audacity to come under my windows and watch for Élise on the day after her husband's death ! She actually went to join him, and heaven only knows what he could have said to her to induce her to follow him ! Madame Mornas was at my house at the time ; and what surpasses everything is that she has taken my niece's part. She goes to see her ! "

" It is scandalous ! " exclaimed Verdalenc. " Her husband can have no authority over her. Indeed, he always impressed me as not amounting to much, and besides, the fortune is almost entirely on his wife's side. M. d'Arlempe, whom I knew very well, made a great deal of money, and left it all to his daughter."

" However, he scarcely brought her up properly," said Madame Verdalenc. " It is a miracle that she has not turned out badly. But she has always been accustomed to do what she chose, and I am sure she didn't ask Mornas's permission to spend the evening at the Porte Saint-Martin. By the way, I should like to know who that is with her ? "

" I can tell you," said the baroness. " That wretched old man is a kind of homeopathic quack, whom poor Aubrac, Élise's father, had a great quarrel with at the Academy. I believe that the old fellow is a tenant in Madame Mornas's house. She must have taken him as an escort, as he was close at hand."

" It was a singular idea of hers. He looks as bewildered as an owl."

These words were exchanged in a low voice, and did not prevent M. Verdalenc from examining the actress who represented the phylloxera through his opera-glass. " I thought I was not mistaken," he said ; " that is the creature we saw one evening talking to Mareuil in the stalls of this very theatre."

" So it is. I recognise her now," said the baroness. " I must tell Madame Mornas about it, so as to prove to her that Élise is Mareuil's dupe. Besides, I shall be delighted to tease her about her connection with my niece, and when that idiot of a Gigondès knows that I am the sister-in-law of his old enemy, he'll have a fit."

" Is the old fellow's name Gigondès ? " said Madame Verdalenc, laughing ; " but pray, dear baroness, let me listen to the song the Burgundy vine is singing. She's a pretty little thing, and she has a nice voice."

The conversation ceased, and was not renewed until after the act, which finished amidst loud applause. The spectators in the stalls and the pit now rose and faced the boxes, and several people soon recognised one another. " Don't you think, dear madame, that men are very ugly now-a-days ? " said the baroness, looking at different gentlemen in the stalls, who seemed to be posing for the benefit of the fair occupants of the grand tier.

" You are two severe, baroness," said Madame Verdalenc, scanning the crowd, below with her glass. " George Darès, for instance, is not so bad-looking."

" Bah ! he lacks distinction. His friend Caussade is better than he." .

"You know M. Caussade, don't you ? "

"Not very well ; but he was once intimate with my brother-in-law, who pretended he loved art and had a mania for having his portrait painted. He commissioned Caussade to paint his portrait and his daughter's also. I have the pictures at home, but they shall not remain there. I don't wish to see Élise again, even on canvas."

"I understand that ; but I think we are troubling ourselves too much about her. She is a disgraced woman, and we have nothing more to do with her. But you spoke just now about the ugliness of men. Well, I can point out one who doesn't resemble his neighbours. Look at that tall, bearded fellow in the middle of the stalls, in the same row as M. Darès and M. Caussade. He is looking this way. Do you see him ? He is very good-looking."

"Yes ; he has an original face, as original as his dress. But are you sure he is looking at us, dear madame ? "

"Don't you see that he is staring at this box ? "

"Or at some other," murmured the baroness, who was not so sure as Madame Verdalenc of the power of her charms.

"We shall know very soon," replied the banker's wife. "He is going towards the entrance, and he is coming up here, no doubt, or at all events to the first gallery, to see us nearer."

"It is, perhaps, your diamonds that attract him," insinuated the baroness, maliciously ; "and in your place, if I met him in the street, after dark, adorned as you are, I shouldn't feel very secure. He looks like a brigand."

"Really, ladies," now said M. Verdalenc, in his deep bass voice, "you do that fellow too much honour to remark him. He is some supernumerary from a minor theatre."

Madame Verdalenc shrugged her shoulders, and the baroness smiled as she thought of the conjugal misfortunes of the banker, who had made a great mistake in marrying a woman so sensible to manly beauty. An instant later what Madame Verdalenc had foreseen happened. The man she had noticed appeared at the entrance of a passage in the middle of the gallery, and stood there with his eyes obstinately fixed on the boxes on his right hand side. "He is better-looking than I thought, and not so young," murmured the baroness, who was as much of a connoisseur as her friend.

"Age is nothing. I never fancied boys," sighed Madame Verdalenc. And she began to dart languishing glances at the man stationed ten paces from her. He did not notice her at first, but his attention was before long attracted to her, for she was covered with diamonds, and sparkled like a jeweller's window. An exchange of glances took place, without M. Verdalenc, who was seated behind his wife, perceiving it. Others saw it, however, although seated much further off. Darès and Caussade, who were watching the ill-assorted couple, exchanged their impressions in a whisper. "Caussade," said George, "that awkward fellow who stepped on your foot is carrying on a flirtation with Madame Verdalenc."

"She has very bad taste," sneered Caussade. "He is dressed like a groom or a dog-keeper. By-the-way you ought to keep an eye on the fellow. Everything connected with the Verdalenes is of interest as regards your inquiry."

"Quite so, but come, you don't expect I shall find Trémentin's murderer here. And besides, that fellow can't be Garnaroche the owner of the cabin."

"Why not?"

"Well," said Darès, "if he were, the man from Boulogne, to whom I sent a seat, would have already recognised him. Where is that man, by-the-way? I don't see him any longer."

"He has, perhaps, recognised the fellow, and gone to wait for him in the passage. If I've made a good guess, they will soon meet, for the red-haired man is going to retire."

"Yes, he is either going into the lobby, or he means to wander about behind the Verdalenes' box. I wish I could tell the chief about all these manœuvres."

"You can do that after the next act. They are going to commence, and I hope that you will keep quiet. I have been bothered enough already, and if that brute tries to return to his place, now that everybody is seated, I will do my best to prevent his passing."

Caussade was not disturbed, however. The man in the shooting-jacket did not dream of descending to the stalls again. As Darès had foreseen, he was wandering about the corridor on the first tier; going from box to box, and applying his eyes to the little panes of glass in the doors. He was looking for someone, undoubtedly—someone whom he had perceived while he was standing at the entrance of the gallery, and whom he hoped to find again by examining the boxes one after the other. However, he had evidently neglected to count them beforehand, so that the numbers furnished him with no indication. Some of the little windows, through which he looked, were, moreover, masked by green curtains, but he pulled the latter aside without the least hesitation. At last, some of the box-openers noticed his strange goings-on, and one of them approached to ask what he wanted. Perhaps she hoped that he would give her a piece of silver for any information she might impart; however, he received her in a manner which made her draw back in alarm, and then imperturbably continued his inspection.

Meanwhile, there was laughter and applause in the auditorium. The spectators in the boxes were watching what was passing on the stage, and did not hear this inquisitive fellow as he drew aside the curtains. He had reached the seventh box, and stood with his face close to the little window, when someone clapped him on the shoulder. He turned round sharply and recoiled in surprise, on finding himself face to face with Jean Bigorneau, of Boulogne. "So it is really you, my lad," exclaimed the old workman. "I thought I recognised you just now, but I wasn't sure. I said to myself, 'That must be Garnaroche over there ; it's his face, and yet he doesn't usually dress like that.' So to see you closer, I left my seat."

"You had better have remained there," replied the red-haired fellow, with a surly air. "I don't run about after you ; and, if I had known I should meet you here—"

"You wouldn't have come ? Why so : weren't we always good friends ? It's a long time since we had a drink together, it's true ; but it isn't my fault if you never set foot in Boulogne. There are some folks there who said you were dead."

"Let them say it. I shall never go back again."

"I'm sorry to hear that. What are you doing now ?"

"I am living on my income."

"Indeed ! then I am no longer astonished to see that you live in Paris. Boulogne isn't lively, especially in the winter. But have you forgotten that you have some property there ? You ought to sell your cabin. It's of no use to you."

"What cabin ?"

"Come, don't pretend innocence. The one opposite Cabassol's restaurant. You used to live in it."

"I shall never use it again. But look here, Bigorneau, how long are you going to bother me with your chatter ?"

"Don't get angry, my lad. It is in your interest that I've come up here to speak to you. I thought that, perhaps, you didn't know you were being looked for."

"Who wants me ?"

"The commissary of police, of course ; and you know very well why."

"Indeed, I don't."

"Don't you read the papers then ? Well, if you did you would have seen that a gentleman was killed the other day at Cabassol's, and that the shot which killed him was fired from the cabin which our old employer, Faurel, gave you."

"Then the door must have been forced open, for it was locked."

"That's just the point ; and I'm glad that you answer me as you do, for I see that you have nothing on your conscience."

"Is there any chance of my being accused ?" asked Garnaroche, in quite another tone.

"Hum ! it might happen ; but I'll tell you how the matter stands. However, this isn't a very good place to talk ; there are detectives in the house."

"Well, come into the public lounge, there's no one there just now."

"Lead the way then, I don't know where it is."

Garnaroche started off at once towards the lounge, but not without a backward glance at the door of the box near which Bigorneau had surprised him. When they were alone in the lounge, the old workman resumed : "It's my fault if the police are after you, and I want to put you on your guard, for I believe now that you are not to blame in this matter, and, if I've done you a wrong, I must try and repair it. Now listen : the commissaries, the magistrate, and the whole outfit came to Boulogne on the day after the murder. The evening before, the cabin had been found open, with the key in the lock. Then the police inquired for the owner, and as I remembered Fauvel and you, I went to them and told them what I knew. I didn't think of injuring you, for I wasn't even sure that you were alive."

" What did you tell them about me ? " asked Garnaroche, with a frown.

" I said that you had disappeared since the war, but that before then you had sometimes came to the cabin and not always alone. Then they took it into their heads that it was a woman who had fired the shot."

" A woman ! " repeated Garnaroche, visibly impressed by this information.

" Yes. It seems they found her footprints in the hut, and they think you lent her the key. I thought so, too, and if it were true, it wouldn't prove that you were guilty, for you might have given it to a girl without knowing what she wanted it for."

" But who was killed ? "

" A gentleman who had been married in the morning, and who was giving his wedding-dinner at Cabassol's. So, you see, it was thought at once that he had abandoned some woman to take a wife, and that this woman had revenged herself. But you couldn't have been mixed up in it ; the gentleman had done nothing to you."

" What was his name ? "

" It was something like Trimoulin, or Tromatin ; I heard it said that he was a cashier in a banking house, and that the banker paid for the dinner."

" Trémentin, perhaps ? " asked Garnaroche, with strong signs of of emotion.

" I think that's it. But did you know him then ? "

" No, I've heard of him, that's all."

Garnaroche was now no longer the same man, and his trouble did not escape Bigorneau, who resumed : " Listen to me, my lad ; I have an idea that you know whom you gave the key to, and it doesn't need much penetration to guess that it was a woman. If it was she who did the deed, I'm sure she didn't consult you ; but that does not prevent you from being compromised. For that reason, if I were in your place, I should tell the truth to the magistrate, and let the woman get out of it the best way she could."

" You are mistaken," said Garnaroche, in an unsteady voice. " I didn't lend the key. I lost it a long time ago."

" The person who used it must have found it, then, and discovered that it belonged to the cabin. The police will never believe that. You had better get out of their way. By-the-bye, I've heard that they've arrested old Fauvel's grandson, Louis Marcuil. Perhaps the poor fellow knew the woman they are looking for. You must remember him, the little fellow who used to come to Boulogne sometimes with his grandfather."

" I saw him barely three months ago, and spoke to him in the garden of the Palais Royal."

" And did you meet his mother too ? "

" No ; I've never set foot in her house since Fauvel died ; she didn't like me."

" The magistrate thinks, perhaps, that you gave the key to Louis Mareuil. You know how that is, and if he's innocent, you can't let him be condemned when it's in your power to save him." Garnaroche made no reply. "Remember," continued Bigorneau, "that the police have a description of your person and will certainly nab you in the end. The chief of the criminal investigation service is in the stalls, and I shouldn't be surprised if it were he who sent me a seat. He probably thought that you might come to the theatre. He is aware that you are fond of amusement, and that I know you, and if he has seen me leave my seat—"

" Then why did you come to speak to me ? "

" Because I wanted to warn you ; and now I advise you to clear out, unless you want to tell him the name of the person who used the key." Garnaroche was in a state of extraordinary agitation. He evidently hesitated to follow Bigorneau's advice, and did not know what to do. " You would do wrong to allow yourself to be clapped into jail for the sake of a worthless woman," continued Bigorneau, " and it would be still worse to let others remain there. But, if you don't wish to tell the truth, get out, my lad ; you've no time to lose."

" Will you promise me not to say that you've seen me ? "

" No, I don't wish to lie. But if I'm asked what I think of the matter, I shall say that I believe you are innocent ; and, as for being caught, you can make your mind easy, as I don't know where you live."

" Good-bye, then, and thanks," said Garnaroche, hastening out of the lobby.

Bigorneau did not try to detain him. He preferred to let him escape, for he was sincerely convinced that his old companion was not guilty of this crime, whatever else he might have to reproach himself with ; and he excused him for not denouncing the woman. He was about to return to his seat when, in the very corridor where he had met Garnaroche, he was suddenly accosted by the chief of the criminal investigation service, who at once said to him : " Good evening, Monsieur Bigorneau. I was looking for you."

" You honour me greatly, sir ; I didn't think that you had seen me."

" Oh, yes ; I knew that you were here. I asked the author of the piece to send you a seat ; and as I wished to speak to you, I left my place when I saw you had left yours. I thought that you were tired of the play and were going away."

" There's no danger of that. I don't get a chance to go to the theatre very often, and I have never been so much amused as this evening."

"Really! One wouldn't think so; for you left your seat just as the second act was about to commence."

"It was so warm! I needed fresh air, and so I have been walking about the lobby."

"Alone?" asked the chief, eyeing Bigorneau, closely.

"No," answered the old workman, after a moment's hesitation. "I met a man I knew—"

"A tall fellow, with red hair and a cap. Ah! he was odd-looking enough, and he stood for ten minutes in the middle of the gallery. What have you done with him?"

"Nothing, sir, he has left the theatre, and he won't return, for he didn't care to meet you."

"Then he's that man Garnaroche?"

"Yes, sir; and I was very much surprised to see him here."

"So surprised that you let him get away instead of bringing him to me. But he can't be far."

"Excuse me; I don't think he stopped to hang round the door of the theatre, as I told him you were after him, and it was that which decided him to leave."

"Then you are right. He is already far away, and it is useless to send my agents after him," said the chief, coldly. "But do you know, Monsieur Bigorneau, you have placed yourself in a very bad position, and it only depends upon me to arrest you as being in collusion with a man implicated in a murder?"

"I've no fear of that," answered Bigorneau, calmly. "I was the first to tell you a week ago that the cabin belonged to Garnaroche; but I wasn't charged with arresting him."

"You need not have told him, however, that I was here."

"I questioned him, sir, and after he had answered me, I was sure that he had nothing to reproach himself with. He didn't even know that anyone had been killed at Cabassol's."

"So you undertook to inform him of it, eh? You mixed yourself up in what didn't concern you, and you will probably repent of it. I shall be obliged to report your conduct. But tell me exactly what transpired between you."

"In the first place, I spoke to him to see how he would behave. Well, he received me almost rudely, as I disturbed him, for he was eyeing the women in the boxes; then, when I told him the story of the murder, he listened to me quietly enough; it interested him, but it didn't trouble him. Then I spoke of the key; and he answered that he had lost it, and I guessed that he was lying."

"By Jove! he lent it to some woman, and he was her accomplice."

"If you had heard him, sir, you would think, as I do, that the woman didn't tell him what she wanted the key for. I could read on his face that he knew nothing, and that he was very angry with her. He must have met her, and given her the key, expecting that she would write and tell him when to meet her there."

The chief listened very attentively to Bigorneau's words, and while marvelling at his sagacity, he could only acknowledge that his ideas were logical. The old workman with his natural good sense had arrived at the same conclusion as the most skilful and experienced detective. "Well," said the chief, in a much milder tone, "if he wishes to reward the jade for the bad trick she has played him, he only has to denounce her."

"That is just what I advised him," replied Bigorneau, "and the suggestion threw him into a frightful state of agitation. He must still care for her, for he finally decided to get away, rather than reveal her name, although I told him that the grandson of our old employer was accused. He declared, however, that he had never set foot in Madame Marcuil's house since Fauvel's death."

" Did you ask him where he lived, and what he was doing ? "

" Yes ; he told me that he was living on his means, and I saw that I should draw nothing more from him ; but I have an idea, which is perhaps correct. Maybe the woman he gave the key to is here in one of the boxes, and that he came up to the gallery to see her more closely. At all events, when I met him in the corridor, he was standing close to the door of one of the boxes."

" Which one ? " asked the chief, quickly.

" I can't say ; for the doors are all alike, and I didn't notice the number. It was on this side, though."

At this moment the act ended, and several spectators came into the corridor. The chief had several more questions to ask Bigorneau, and he was about to draw him into a corner where he could talk to him quietly, when the door of a box close by was opened, and the Baroness Aubrac came out, accompanied by M. Verdalenc. The chief guessed at once that she was about to visit some one in a neighbouring box. He knew both the baroness and the banker by sight, and he was also acquainted with Madame Verdalenc; indeed, since he had been charged with making inquiries respecting Trémentin's friends, his discreet investigations had already apprised him of many curious things. He had noticed that the woman who was said to have once been in love with Trémentin, was in the theatre, and he had also remarked the glances she had exchanged with the tall fellow whose costume and appearance had attracted his attention. He now knew who this man was, and Bigorneau's clear replies only confirmed the suspicions he had previously formed. He wondered if Garnaroche had not been Trémentin's predecessor in the good graces of Madame Verdalenc, and if she had not in-. sured him a modest livelihood in the country. She might have asked him to give her the key of the cabin, without telling him what use she wished to make of it, and have confided that key to some unscrupulous dependent—a woman, most likely. People willing to commit a murder for money are to be found tolerably easily in Paris, and Madame Verdalenc was rich enough to pay a high price. The chief was so convinced that this was the correct solution of the problem, that he determined to question Madame Verdalenc's servants privately, and have her maid watched. She herself had been present at the wedding-dinner, and had even been seated beside Trémentin, and this fact did not agree very well with the chief's idea ; still he did not allow it to shake his views, for he was convinced that the bullet which struck Trémentin had been intended for Élise Aubrac. He said to himself that Madame Verdalenc must have been furious at seeing a man, whom she still loved, marry a young and pretty girl, and have sworn to avenge herself, not upon her faithless lover, but upon the rival she execrated.

Bigorneau knew nothing of all this ; he had not been able to indicate which box Garnaroche had been so much interested in, and he even seemed to think that it was not the one occupied by the Verdalencs. The chief now determined to examine all the other boxes, and, on seeing Madame Aubrac on the banker's arm, the idea suddenly came to him to follow them. They were evidently going to pay a visit to someone they knew ; for they were examining the numbers inscribed on the doors. To watch them, the chief had no need of Bigorneau, so he dismissed him, with a request not to leave the theatre until after the performance. The old workman went off, but without making any promise, for he guessed that the chief wished to make him an active auxiliary, and the idea did not please him at all.

The chief now mingled with the crowd, promenading about the corridor, and saw M. Verdalenc open the door of a box occupied by a lady and an old gentleman. After an exchange of courtesies, Madame Aubrac went in alone, and Verdalenc returned to join his wife. At this moment the chief was accosted by Darès, who had come up in hopes of meeting the man in the shooting-jacket, and who was not sorry to communicate his suspicions to the great detective. "Well, my dear sir," said Darès, "have you seen that man from Boulogne-sur-Seine to whom I sent a ticket ? When you left your seat, I thought you were going to join him."

"You guessed correctly, and we will talk about that presently ; but, please tell me, isn't that M. Verdalenc who just passed down the corridor with a lady ?"

"The Baroness Aubrac ? Yes, it's he ; and I'm very glad he didn't see me, for he is a perfect bore."

"Who occupies the box where he left the baroness ?"

"I don't know the old gentleman at all, but the lady in a black dress is Madame Mornas, the wife of the magistrate."

"Oh, indeed !" said the chief. "Well, did you notice that tall, queerly dressed fellow, who stood for a quarter of an hour at the entrance of the gallery ogling the women in the boxes ?"

"I should think I did ; he began by treading on Caussade's feet. Caussade is so furious with him that he pretends he must be the famous Garnaroche, the owner of the cabin."

"M. Caussade is not mistaken. It was Garnaroche himself. Unfortunately, he is far away by this time. I arrived too late, for Bigorneau, the man from Boulogne, spoke to him and let him get away. Instead of serving me, the old fool has injured me, for he told Garnaroche that I was looking for him, and related the story of the murder, so that now the rascal is on his guard. This will teach me not to depend upon people outside of the profession."

"Dear me ! I regret having sent him a seat."

"But, after all, I owe it to him if I now know Garnaroche's face. I have his description in my head, and the whole police force will have it to-morow. Besides, I'm almost sure he will turn up again, at the house of the woman who borrowed the key of the cabin."

"You will have to find out where she lives."

"I may know that this evening. She is probably here."

"Well, just now he was looking at Madame Verdalenc, and Caussade, who has altogether too much imagination, tried to persuade me that she might be the woman who used to go to the cabin."

"It is quite possible ; but will you render me a service ? "

"Very willingly."

"Are you acquainted with Madame Mornas well enough to present yourself at her box ? "

"I am not intimate with her, but I have often met her at the Verdalencs', and as she has done me the honour to accept the ticket I sent her, I can pay my respects to her."

"Then do so now while the Baroness Aubrac is with her. Lead the conversation round to the man who was looking at the boxes, and from the ladies' answers you will know if they noticed him. You can even mention Garnaroche's name, if you see fit."

"And then tell you my impressions ? The deuce ! "

"You don't desire to undertake a task, which properly belongs to my functions. I can understand that, and if it were not a question of proving the innocence of your friend, I shouldn't ask you to undertake it ; but you are interested in M. Mareuil, and—"

"You are right," said Darès ; "the end justifies the means. Where shall I find you again ? "

"In the public lounge, after the next act."

Darès was endowed with quite enough skill and tact to execute his instructions properly. He considered Madame Mornas to be a very intelligent woman, and a little conversation with her would not be wearisome. She knew how to set people at their ease, and he was aware that she had taken Élise Aubrac's part from the beginning. He could, therefore, be sure that she would give him all the information in her power. He proceeded at once to her box, and on entering it he found himself face to face with M. Gigondès, who had yielded his seat in front to Madame Aubrac, and who appeared plunged in profound meditation. The old man raised his head and looked at the visitor with a bewildered air. The baroness appeared astonished also, and not very well pleased ; but Madame Mornas received Darès with marked cordiality.

"How kind of you, to come and see me ! " she said. "Your piece is charming, and I don't know how to thank you enough for your kindness in sending me this box."

"It is my place to thank you, madame, for having accepted it," replied George. "I regret that M. Mornas has not come, but I can understand that he was not inclined to listen to the nonsense of a burlesque."

"Oh, it wasn't that: the piece is full of witty sayings which would have amused him greatly, but his work just now absorbs all his time. However, let me present you to the Baroness Aubrac, whom you have already met at Madame Verdalene's, and to M. Gigondès, a savant who resides in my house."

An exchange of salutations followed, and then a spell of silence. The baroness fanned herself diligently; M. Gigondès, who viewed her with no favour, on account of the name she bore, lowered his head and frowned, and Madame Mornas alone remained pleasant and gay. "Do you know," she said to Darès, "that Madame Verdalene will be very jealous if you don't go and pay her a visit when you leave us? Oh! when the next act is over, for I intend to keep you as long as possible."

"I mean to go and see her," said Darès, "and yet I fear that there is a coolness between us, since that sad event which threw so many people into mourning. One of my friends is accused of a crime. I have naturally defended him, and I know that M. Verdalene is very hostile to him. I hope, however, that we sha'n't quarrel, since he has done me the honour to use the box I placed at his disposal."

"You will be fast friends again when the mistake, which M. Mareuil is, the victim of has been acknowledged; and I think I can tell you that this will soon occur. Indeed, there is no serious proof against your friend, and he would already be free if certain mysterious points were cleared up."

"What, dear madame!" cried the baroness, "are you interested in the man who has caused all the extravagant conduct of my unfortunate niece?"

"I always take the part of lovers," said Madame Mornas, sweetly.

"But this fellow deceived Élise and made love to her solely on account of her fortune. Didn't I tell you that he was very intimate with an actress? Well, it's that very creature who represents the phylloxera; and, between ourselves, if M. Mornas summoned her, he would be edified as to Mareuil's habits and sentiments."

"Excuse me, madame," said Darès, quickly, "but I know the lady in question. She plays in all my pieces, and I can assure you that she is the wife of the first comedian of the troupe, and that she is greatly attached to him. The people who have spread the report that Louis Mareuil was her lover have slandered him, and perhaps intentionally."

The baroness drew herself up with an offended air, and addressing Madame Mornas, she said: "Excuse me, madame, for having disturbed you. I have the misfortune not to be of the same opinion as this gentleman, and I don't care to discuss the point with him. I will rejoin Madame Verdaleno."

"As you please, madame," rejoined Berthe, drily.

Madame Aubrac rose up, and George had to do the same so as to allow her to pass out ; wishing to be polite, he said : " Will you permit me, madame, to offer you my arm to your box ? We are not of the same opinion ; but I am none the less at your orders."

"Thank you, but the box is only a step or two away, and I can go very well alone." With this refusal, clearly articulated, Madame Aubrac executed an exit, such as one sees on the stage after a stormy scene.

" What a goose she is ! " exclaimed Madame Mornas, when the irascible baroness had closed the door behind her. " You were too good-natured, sir, to place yourself at her disposal. She and her friends, the Verdalenes, have sworn to ruin M. Mareuil, and I am not at all sorry to have broken with them. Perhaps that is what she wanted, for I can't imagine why she came here."

" She doubtless wished to be disagreeable to me," said Gigondès.

George did not understand, and Madame Mornas remarked with a laugh: "M. Gigondès once had some reason to complain of Élise's father, and the baroness, who knows of this, perhaps meant to annoy him ; for, before your arrival, she continually talked of the late Dr. Aubrac—"

"Ah ! I had a quarrel with him," interrupted the homeopathist, warmly ; " a furious quarrel, in which I was beaten, because my adversary made use of illegal weapons. He was the cause of the ruin of my great discovery."

"Come, come, let us talk of something else !" said Berthe, gaily. "Let us talk of less learned things. There is a box below there which greatly puzzles me, the one with the screen up. But look— someone is lowering the screen, and good heavens ! it is Élise ! "

" Madame Trémentin ! " muttered George. " No ; it is impossible, and yet—"

" I tell you it is she," said Madame Mornas, examining the box through her opera-glass. " She is at the back of the box, but I recognise her perfectly well, and I am sorry to see her here. This time, the impropriety is too great ; and her aunt will have good reason for complaining of her."

" If she has already forgotten her husband's death, she ought at least to remember that Louis Mareuil is still in prison," said Darès.

" I shall scold her soundly ; and if I listened to my own feelings, I should do so at once; but the baroness and the Verdalenes would comment on my absence, even if they have not already perceived Élise. You must go and tell her to leave."

" That would be still worse. Heaven knows what people would think ! And, besides, I shouldn't succeed, for she has come to see my piece and she will wish to remain to the end. I ought to have suspected this ; she asked me a multitude of questions about this first performance, but I did not guess their purport. As she didn't dare to ask me for a box, she has purchased one."

" To show you the interest which she took in the success of her lover's best friend and most devoted defender. Poor child! I have not the courage to blame her, but it is my duty to warn her that she is doing very wrong. I shall go and see her to-morrow."

"So shall I. The most vexatious thing about it is that the chief of the detective police, who arrested Louis Marcuil, is here, and he knows her. Ah! at last she has decided to raise the screen again."

"Well, I don't understand why she lowered it even for an instant, unless it was to brave public opinion."

George did not find the explanation a probable one, and remained silent. "She is the living portrait of her execrable father," muttered Gigondès, who had taken up an opera-glass. "I should like to try my discovery upon her—" Darès listened without understanding; but the vindictive old man now explained himself more clearly. "I acknowledge," he said, with a chuckle, "that just now, when I saw that woman who plays the part of the phylloxera brandishing her gold needle, I said to myself that I had only to dip its point in the blood of one of my poisoned rabbits, and lightly prick one of the girls on the stage, for her to fall down dead, and then the experiment would be decisive. Three thousand persons could bear witness that it had succeeded, and my colleagues wouldn't dare to deny the evidence."

"Well," said George, "I confess that this variation would create a striking effect, but a burlesque is not a melodrama, and then we should have some difficulty in recruiting the actresses."

"Suppose we change the subject," interrupted Madame Mornas. "You said just now that the chief of the criminal investigation service was in the house. My husband has spoken to me about him, and I was glad to learn that he believes in the innocence of your friend. Did he come to the theatre in the hope of discovering the real criminal?"

"Yes, madame; he hasn't concealed his plan from me, and just now he told me that he had a strong clue. You know, no doubt, that the great point is to discover the owner of the cabin, where the murderer hid, so as to fire upon M. Trémentin."

"Good heavens, no! My husband doesn't keep me posted as to the progress of the investigation, and I don't venture to question him. Then, did the owner of this cabin commit the crime?"

"Yes, or he lent the cabin key to some other person. Unfortunately, this man left Boulogne a long time ago, and no one knew what had become of him. However, an active search was instituted; a providential chance sent him here this evening; and an old inhabitant of Boulogne recognised him."

"Then he has been arrested?"

"Not yet. He learned that the police were after him, and he decamped. This proves that his conscience isn't clear. But he will be caught, for the authorities have a full description of his person. The chief saw him, I saw him myself, and you, perhaps, noticed him also?"

"I!" exclaimed Berthe Mornas; "why should I have noticed him? I don't know him."

" Because he was very queerly dressed, and didn't look like any-one else in the house. Imagine a tall fellow, bearded like a Merovingian king, and dressed like Robin Hood, not ugly, though, but rather with the head of a hero of romance. Caussade was tempted to sketch him in his note-book."

" You were seated near this mysterious person then ? "

" He sat in the stalls, in the same row as ourselves ; but he did not remain there long. After the first act, he stationed himself at the entrance of the gallery."

" Wasn't his hair red, and didn't he wear a cap ? " asked M. Gigondès.

" Exactly."

" Then it was he who stared in this direction for some minutes."

" I didn't notice him," said Berthe.

" Because your back was turned to him, dear madame ; but I faced him, and saw him perfectly, and the Verdalencs must have perceived him also, for he chiefly directed his attention to them."

" That is the opinion of the chief," said Darès. " And he be-lieves that Madame Verdalenc once had some kind of connection with the suspected man."

" But where could she have known an individual who certainly doesn't move in the same society as herself ? "

" He was once a gentleman, it is said, and he has sunk into an inferior position. When he was young, he must have been much better looking than M. Trémentin."

" Oh, I am indulgent ! " said Madame Mornas, repressing a smile, " and don't believe in scandal. Tell me, what is the name of this man whom the authorities suspect ? "

" Garnaroche."

" What an odd name ! "

" It suits him very well, for everything about him is odd—his looks, his dress, his presence at the theatre to-night, and his sudden disappearance. He must have paid a high price for his stall, and yet he left before seeing three acts."

" He made a great mistake," said Madame Mornas; " but I don't wish to detain you longer. Your friend is waiting for you in the stalls, and perhaps you will be able to find some way of making Élise understand that she ought not to be here."

" I despair of succeeding, but I would be sorry to bore you longer," replied Darès, a little surprised by his sudden dismissal. He rose, bowed, and left the box, no better informed than when he entered it. " This woman is most capricious," he thought ; " she appeared delighted to see me and disposed to keep me near her all the evening. The wind has changed abruptly. I would swear now that she wanted to be alone with that old poisoner ! "

MADAME MORNAS, while talking with Darès, had learned so many things of interest to herself that she no longer felt disposed to enjoy the wit of the burlesque, or to admire the beautiful scenery and costumes. She thought of Élise, of Madame Verdalenc, and of the chief of the detective police, who was, perhaps, watching them both, and she longed to see her husband, whom she had left at home, studying the papers of the Mareuil affair. She especially longed to know what he thought of the new incidents which had occurred, and of which he probably knew nothing as yet. So she made up her mind to return home, and scarcely had George Darès left the box, than she broached the question of departure to M. Gigondès. She told him that she felt tired, and should not wait till the end of the act, but as she did not wish to deprive him of the pleasure of seeing the play through, he might remain till the finish. Thereupon the old man replied that the piece interested him very little, and that he asked nothing better than to return home, where his rabbits were waiting for him. And he spoke the truth, for, to induce him to accompany her to the theatre, Madame Mornas had been obliged to exert all her influence over him. She had had to urge him a long time before he would consent to array himself in an old dress-suit he had not worn for years ; and he had then only yielded so as not to disoblige his benefactress, who, not caring to go alone to the theatre, had selected him as her escort.

As she now wished to leave without her departure being noticed, she took advantage of a moment when an amusing scene absorbed the attention of the audience. M. Gigondès, who still piqued himself upon his politeness, helped her to put on her cloak and offered her his arm. They met no one they knew in the passages or on the staircase ; and when they reached the boulevard, M. Gigondès hailed a cab. Madame Mornas had come in her brougham, but she had dismissed it, and the Rue de Turenne was too far off to think of walking. She, therefore, entered the cab with Gigondès, and they rolled towards the Boulevard du Temple without exchanging a word. The old doctor was no talker, except on the subject of his scientific works, and Madame Mornas was too pre-occupied to indulge in a trifling conversation. However, after some ten minutes' silence, she took pity on the old man, who did not dare to breathe a word, and said to him : "Do you know, my dear neighbour, that you alarmed M. Darès with your threats against poor Élise Aubrac ?"

"I didn't threaten her," muttered Gigondès, "I expressed a wish, that was all."

"A murderous wish. You declared that you would take great pleasure in pricking her with a poisoned pin. I know very well that you won't do so, but there is no use in saying such things. If an accident happened to that young woman, if she died very suddenly, and the doctors were unable to tell the cause of her death, Darès, who is her friend, might accuse you."

"He might accuse me, but he couldn't prove that I was guilty, even if I were so. My poison leaves no traces, as I told you when you came to see me. Ah! she or any one else might easily be killed with impunity, for on my table there is a certain blue glass vial—"

"Hush! what you are saying is abominable!" interrupted Madame Mornas, and nothing more was said until the vehicle stopped before the door in the Rue de Turenne. Gigondès alighted first, and gallantly offered his arm to Madame Mornas, who was not a little surprised, on getting out, to perceive a man standing beside the house door, and so close to the wall that he seemed to form part of it. It was very dark under the archway of the door, and M. Gigondès, still engaged in his scientific reveries, did not notice the individual hidden there. He had indeed stretched out his hand to ring the bell, when the man suddenly emerged from the shade. The old savant recoiled in alarm, and took refuge behind Madame Mornas, who did not appear nearly so frightened. The stranger was wrapped up in an ample cloak, with a hood drawn over his head, and although his attitude was not aggressive, the meeting was far from being a pleasant one. "What do you want with me?" asked the magistrate's wife, bravely.

"I want to speak to you," responded the mysterious stranger, placing himself so that the light of a street-lamp fell upon his features.

Madame Mornas did not flinch. She had doubtless recognised him, and expected this strange request. "Please pay the cabman and send him away," she said to Gigondès. And while the astonished homeopathist scoured his pockets for some money, she drew aside a few steps to speak to the stranger who followed her without a word. Gigondès did not understand the affair at all, but after he had sent the cab away, Madame Mornas approached him and said: "You are my friend, are you not? Can I rely upon your devotion and discretion?"

"Can you doubt it?" murmured Gigondès.

"No; and as I don't, I ask you to do me a service. I must have a private interview at once with the person I have just spoken to. The honour and perhaps the life of a woman is at stake. A woman who isn't my friend, but who doesn't deserve the fate with which she is threatened. I can't prolong the conversation which I have commenced in the street, nor can I continue it in my own apartments; so I ask you to lend me yours."

"Certainly, madame; but are you not afraid that the door-keeper—"

"He is half asleep, and he will think that this man is with you. If we meet any one on the staircase, say something to this fellow, and I will take care of the rest. Ring, please."

Gigondès obeyed without replying, and the door opened. The stranger knew what he had to do. He placed himself beside the old man, without removing the hood from his head. Madame Mornas went in first, and repaired straight to the room, where the doorkeeper was dozing in an arm-chair, near a good fire. He rose, on recognising his mistress, but she motioned to him to sit down again, and took care to pause for a moment before the window. When she moved away, after replying with a nod to the door-keeper's repeated bows, the stranger and Gigondès had passed by. They all three reached the fourth floor safely. Gigondès followed the instructions he had received, and kept close to the man with the cloak, but he was so alarmed that he did not dare to look at him. He lit a candle to illuminate his apartment, and Madame Mornas then exclaimed : "Now, my dear neighbour, I must ask you to leave me alone with this gentleman."

"I will go into my laboratory," said Gigondès.

"No ; we will go in there. I shall be obliged to you if you will wait for me here."

Gigondès would have preferred another arrangement, as he did not like to have the mysteries of his laboratory seen ; but he could not refuse anything to a woman who was his creditor for so many quarters of rent, and he understood that by borrowing his rooms she placed herself in such a position that she could never demand the money due to her. He, therefore, obediently did what she asked. He lighted the lamp on his desk, drew two chairs forward, and returned to the outer room, where the stranger stood waiting, motionless. "Thanks," said Madame Mornas to Gigondès, while motioning the stranger into the laboratory. He entered, and she followed him, taking care to turn the key in the lock. They were alone at last, and she knew that Gigondès would keep good watch in the outer room. The visitor threw the hood back off his head, and proved to be Garnaroche. He and Madame Mornas exchanged a long look before speaking a word. She was the first to begin. "Why have you left Apremont?" she asked coldly. "I forbade your doing so."

"I know it ; but I couldn't stay there any longer," replied Garnaroche. "I longed to see you."

"Indeed ! Well, how did you guess that I was at the theatre this evening?"

"I didn't guess it. I came to Paris in the hope of meeting you. But you will do me this justice that I did not try to compromise you by wandering about near your house. This evening I was passing along the boulevard just as you entered the Porte Saint-Martin. The opportunity was too good to be lost. I had great difficulty in procuring a ticket, but by paying a high price, I managed to obtain one. From the seat I occupied, I could see you in your box—"

"And you no doubt meant to accost me. I am glad that you did not have that audacity. But you have done still worse in coming to wait for me here."

"No ; for that old man who accompanied you is certainly not a friend of your husband's. Besides, I shouldn't have come at all if it hadn't been absolutely necessary for me to speak to you."

"Why, what have you to say to me ?"

"You know very well. You must know that you are in my power."

"What do you mean?" exclaimed Madame Mornas, pale with anger or emotion.

"Well, just now, at the theatre, in the passage behind the first tier of boxes, I met a man from Boulogne who told me what happened at the Cabassol restaurant a week ago."

"The husband of a young girl in whom I am still interested was murdered there. I know that ; but I can't guess what you mean."

"You astonish me ! I flattered myself that you hadn't forgotten the cabin where you used to come and see me once upon a time."

"We will admit that I remember it."

"The shot which killed that man was fired from there. And you knew the victim, I think."

"Very slightly. He was the cashier of M. Verdalenc, a banker, whose wife I often meet. I have seen him, but I have never received him at my house."

"And so," asked Garnaroche, slowly, "he was never your lover?"

"The question is an insult, and I will not lower myself to answer it."

"I was your lover, however."

"Ah ! you do well to reproach me with that ! "

"I don't reproach you ; but do you know who is accused of this murder ?"

"A young man named Louis Mareuil."

"The grandson of that good old fellow Fauvel, who gave me bread when I was driven out of your father's house. From the secretary I was, I became a common labourer. The fall was a terrible one ; but I have not forgotten that if it hadn't been for Fauvel I should, perhaps, have starved to death ; and I don't wish his daughter's son to be unjustly condemned, for he is innocent, is he not ? "

"I am convinced of it. But what connection is there between the crime committed at Boulogne and your conduct towards me ? "

"You don't know, then, that the police are looking for me, as the cabin where the murderer hid himself belongs to me."

"It would be easy to prove, I suppose, that you were at Apremont on the day the crime was committed ? "

"Yes ; but they will ask me what became of the key. Now, I left it with you when you ceased to come to the hut, and if I revealed the fact that it has been in your possession for the last fifteen years, you would be immediately arrested."

" Arrested !  I !  You are mad ! "

"You don't know, then, that the shot was fired by a woman.  I was told that by the man from Boulogne—Bigorneau, who worked with me in Fauvel's time, and he added that I must know this woman. He remembered that the cabin was often lighted up in the evening, and he didn't hide this circumstance from the people who questioned him.  The officials have concluded that the woman who came to see me had the key, and used it to enter the hut, where she concealed herself to fire.  Now *you* have that key."

" I had it, it's true ; but I haven't got it now.  Why should I have kept it?  I no longer had any need of it.  Besides, prove, if you can, that I ever had it.  Between your word and mine no one will hesitate."

" Do you think so ?  I warn you that if you haven't kept the key, I have kept at my place the letters written by Mademoiselle Berthe d'Arlempe.  I should only have to show them—"

" Now you threaten me again with betraying the weakness I once had for you.  Well, go to my husband, take him those letters you swore to burn—"

" I sha'n't give them to your husband, but to the chief of the detective police, if I am arrested."

" So it is the fear of arrest that makes you act like this ?  But it only depends on yourself never to be arrested.  You changed your name a long time ago, and if you think they are going to look for you at Apremont, you have only to cross the frontier.  I will furnish you with means to do so, and with sufficient money to enable you to live in a foreign land."

" Thanks ; I have had enough of your charity, and I have no fear for myself.  I ask for Louis Mareuil's freedom."

" He will be free to-morrow."

" How do you know ? "

Madame Mornas hesitated for an instant ; but the situation was such that she was forced to speak.  "My husband told me so," she murmured.  "He is charged with investigating the affair, and he is going to order the young man's release.  Are you satisfied now ? "

" No," answered Garnaroche.  "I must know what you did with the key."

" I threw it into the Seine."

" You wouldn't dare say that to a magistrate.  If you had thrown it into the river, it couldn't have been used to open the cabin door.  I might perhaps believe that you had lent it to some one."

" And suppose I did lend it to a woman who didn't wish to tell me what she wanted it for ?  Suppose one of my friends confided to me that she had a lover, and that she wanted a place to meet him.  Suppose that I then remembered the cabin at Boulogne, and that I had the key.  Suppose I was foolish enough to give it to her, and that, later on, I thought no more of my imprudence, until I learned that a crime had been committed, and that the investigation was in my husband's hands ; can you imagine what I must have suffered, and will you reproach me for not having denounced that woman ? "

" Yes ; since it was a question of saving an innocent man," replied Garnaroche.

" You forget that I could not denounce her without denouncing myself. I should have been obliged to say how I happened to have that key. I had only two courses to choose from : to be silent or kill myself."

" And you preferred to be silent."

" Yes ; because I intended to use my influence over my husband to effect Louis Mareuil's release. I have accomplished my object, but I can always kill myself. My fate is in your hands."

" It is not your death I wish," said Garnaroche, in a hollow · voice. " I wish you to be what you once were."

" You know very well that that is impossible ! " cried Madame Mornas.

" Why impossible ? " said Garnaroche. " Because you no longer love me ? Ah ! for fifteen years you have forgotten me, and I have suffered in solitude."

" What have you to complain of ? " interrupted Madame Mornas. " Did I ever abandon you ? Didn't I do for you all that I could ? "

" Ah ! you think that you are quits with me because you assured me an existence by putting me in charge of your property, ten leagues from Paris. I was your lover ; you have made a game-keeper of me."

" It was what you, yourself, asked of me."

" Because I loved you enough to sacrifice myself to your ambi-tion. I was your father's secretary when you fell in love with me. He drove me out of his house. I became a common labourer, but you still cared for me, and did not fear to meet me in that cabin, where you were able to come, thanks to the help of your maid. One day, however, you thought of marrying and getting rid of me. You prevailed on me to go and live in the woods, upon some pro-perty your mother had left you. I was fool enough to believe in your promises ; but ah ! I soon learnt that you had taken another lover, and that you hated the past."

" You are mistaken ; I have never loved anyone but you," ex-claimed Berthe.

" Why didn't you marry me, then ? I was as good as that magistrate you chose. I was better born and more intelligent than he. I was poor, it's true. But you could have raised me by be-coming my wife. You preferred to treat me like a lackey. You threw me a crust of bread to buy my silence. You never guessed that I was patient because I still hoped, and that at last my patience would fail me. Well, learn to know me now. I came as a sup-pliant ; I can now speak as a master, for you are at my mercy, and nothing will stop me."

"How do you know that I don't regret the resolution I once took? I have since appreciated the value of the love I had lost. But it was too late. I never dared to ask you if you still cared for me."

Garnaroche started and looked at Madame Mornas, fixedly. They were both standing near the table, on which M. Gigondès' papers and vials lay in confusion, and the lamp but feebly lighted the large room, all encumbered with books and chemical apparatus. They were some distance from the door, and they did not speak loud enough for the old man to hear them. "Prove to me that you are not lying," exclaimed Garnaroche, in a voice trembling with emotion.

"No," replied Madame Mornas; "if I yielded what would become of us? I could not see you without exposing you to dangers you could not escape from. If you prolonged your stay in Paris, you would certainly be arrested, and if I went to Apremont I should put the people who are looking for you upon your track. At the theatre, it may have been noticed that you were watching me, and who knows if I shall not be watched as well?"

"You are not so this evening, and I am certain that no one followed me. Nothing prevents you from leaving here with me. It is scarcely ten o'clock, and the play won't be over till after midnight. You can tell your husband that you remained till the end. That old man who occupies this apartment won't contradict you, I suppose."

"I am sure of his discretion, but—Where do you wish me to go?"

"To a house which I took a month ago. It stands on the Quai de Valmy, in front of Saint-Martin's Canal, and I alone have the key to it. If you consent, I will start to-night for Apremont, or for some foreign country, if you exact it, and then await your commands."

Madame Mornas's eyes wandered aimlessly over M. Gigondès' table. "Swear to me that you will leave France, and that you will not return until I summon you!" she said.

"I swear to obey you, Berthe, and from this moment I will be your slave as formerly."

"Come then, and not a word to the man in the next room. Let me speak to him." Berthe then raised her hand warningly, and added: "Go first, and cross the room without stopping."

Garnaroche opened the door softly, and Berthe turned and stretched out her hand as if she wished to extinguish the lamp. Garnaroche could no longer see her. The blue vial was there—the vial which contained the poison prepared by Gigondès. She took it up, concealed it in her left hand, and then entered the adjoining-room almost at the same time as her lover. Gigondès was asleep in an armchair. He woke up with a start and gazed with a bewildered look at Garnaroche, who was walking softly towards the door. "I have still another favour to ask of you," said Madame Mornas, approaching the old savant.

Gigondès, still half asleep, faltered out some protestations of devotion which Madame Mornas cut short by saying : " My husband won't come up here, and if he meets you, he won't question you ; but if you chance to speak to him, pray don't tell him that we were tired of the theatre, and came away before the end."

" I will be careful, madame," muttered the old man, taking up a candle to light Madame Mornas out. Garnaroche was already on the landing ; he had passed on like a shadow, and opened the door noiselessly.

" There is no need of a light," said Berthe to Gigondès. "Don't disturb yourself, and forget all that has happened this evening." She then in her turn glided out of the apartment. The gas was still lighted, and in descending the stairs it was necessary to pass the rooms where M. Mornas was studying his papers. If a servant had chanced to come out Berthe would have been embarrassed, not to explain that she had conducted M. Gigondès to the fourth floor, or to make it appear that she did not know the man in front of her, but because she would have needed a pretext for going out again at such an hour. However, she reached the ground floor without any kind of accident. Garnaroche took the lead, and rapped at the door of the house-porter's room, masking the window with his lofty stature, while Madame Mornas glided with lowered head towards the street door. The porter, still sleepy, pulled the cord, without even turning his head, and a moment later Berthe and Garnaroche were in the Rue de Turenne. There were few people in the street, as it was both cold and late. " We shall find a vehicle on the boulevard," said Garnaroche.

" I prefer to walk," answered Madame Mornas.

" But the Quai de Valmy is a good way off."

" We must take every precaution. If my husband knew I had gone out, he would perhaps institute an inquiry. All the police agents are at his disposal just now. The first idea would be to question the cabmen, and the one who drove me, either with you or back home afterwards, might be found."

" I must accompany you home again. Alone, you would be exposed to danger."

" Very well ; you shall accompany me to the corner of the Rue de Turenne. Give me your arm, please."

Garnaroche trembled at the touch of the woman he had loved so many years. This odd Bohemian had not lied when he said that his life of enforced exile had been spent in regretting her. Time had not calmed his passion. He still saw Berthe as she once was, and he had twenty times tried to speak to her in private, for he loved her too much to wish to compromise her ; but the opportunity had never presented itself. And so when he had heard Bigorneau's story at the theatre his only thought was to take advantage of the information to compel Madame Mornas to see him again. The story of the cabin had given him a new idea. He remembered perfectly well that the key had remained in Berthe's hands. He did not know whether she had really killed M. Trémentin, whose name he had learned by following him to his lodgings one evening long ago, when he had seen him in Madame Mornas's box at the Théâtre Français, but he knew that, guilty or not, her reputation would be ruined if he spoke out.

Madame Mornas, on her side now, hated Garnaroche quite as much as she had once loved him ; she felt that she was at his mercy, and her pride revolted at the thought that this man, whose silence she had paid for, could by a single word disgrace her, and cause her husband to drive her from the house. There was one sure way of avoiding the danger which threatened her. She meant to kill him, and she possessed the means of doing so. Gigondès' vial of poison had been before her eyes while Garnaroche was talking to her, and she had only had to stretch out her hand to take it. At the foot of the staircase, while Garnaroche was rousing the porter, she had uncorked the bottle, drawn a very sharp pin from her hair, dipped it in the murderous liquid, and left it there. When she placed her right hand upon Garnaroche's arm she held the vial and poisoned pin concealed in her left. " I will kill him when we reach the deserted quay which borders the canal," she thought.

They walked along side by side, he leading the way, and she saying to herself : " When the time comes I will disengage my arm on some pretext or other, and take the pin out of the vial. It will have had time to become impregnated with the poison, and then I will prick him in the hand." But she suddenly recalled the explanations which Gigondès had given her on the day she had gone to see him for the first time. According as the blood was in such or such a condition, to use the mad doctor's own words, it would kill a person on the spot or after a long interval. Now what was the strength of the poison in the vial ? If it were of the instantaneous kind, she could effect her object without running any risk, for she was sure of Gigondès' discretion, and no one would dream of accusing her of the death of a man whose corpse would be found in the street. But if, on the contrary, death only ensued after a long interval, the murder would be almost useless, for Garnaroche might be arrested at any moment. He had sworn to cross the frontier the next day, but Berthe knew that lovers' vows are no better kept than drunkards' promises. Now, even if Garnaroche did not speak, Berthe would none the less be lost, for it would be very soon discovered that the owner of the Boulogne cabin had become the manager of a small estate which belonged to Madame Mornas, the daughter of M. d'Arlempe, whose secretary this same Garnaroche had once been. No more would be needed for suspicion to fall upon her, and, moreover, she had no guarantee that Garnaroche would be silent to the end. He might, for instance, wish to avenge himself, for it would not be easy to prick him without his perceiving it, and he was clever enough to divine that the prick was an attempt at murder.

Berthe thought of all this as she walked along leaning on Garnaroche's arm. She considered that he had forfeited all claims to consideration, and her heart did not beat in the least degree more quickly at the thought of dealing him his death-blow with her own hand. Berthe was a woman of strong character, and Garnaroche was the only man in the world who knew her well. Her friends, her husband, and her father, had never suspected the amount of cold resolution and indomitable energy that existed in her nature. And just now Garnaroche was under the charm, and little suspected that he was playing with his life. He had never seen Berthe look more beautiful. Age had ripened her beauty without altering it ; her figure was superb, and her brow without a wrinkle. When they had reached the esplanade by which the canal is approached from the Place de la Bastille, Madame Mornas felt that the moment was approaching, and that it was time to prepare for the deed by diverting Garnaroche's attention. "I'm tired of this. I want to walk alone," she muttered, at the same time disengaging her hand. And, as Garnaroche paused in astonishment, she continued : "Oh ! for a few steps only. I'm not accustomed to take any one's arm."

"You never took mine before, my dear," replied Garnaroche, gaily. "I was always too poor to accompany Mademoiselle d'Arlempe in the street." This familiarity revolted her, and her last hesitation vanished. Anything rather than remain in the power of this man ! "We are nearly there, and if it were lighter, I could show you the house," resumed Garnaroche ; "but with the fog about here we can't see ten steps ahead. You had perhaps better take my arm again."

Berthe had now had the time to draw out the pin, cork the bottle again, and place it in the bosom of her dress. She pretended to arrange the lace scarf which covered her head. "You are right," she said ; "I can scarcely walk on this slippery pavement. Just let me fix this lace on my hair."

There was no one in sight, and a moment afterwards she held out her gloved hand to Garnaroche, who, in trying to take it, pricked himself so deeply that he uttered an exclamation almost akin to an oath. "Have I hurt you ?" asked Berthe. "Forgive me ; I forgot that I still held this wretched pin which I just took out of my hair." And she threw it away with an angry gesture.

"It's nothing," said Garnaroche, "and it was my fault. I have grown so rough, from living in the woods, that I don't know how to take hold of a woman's hand. I only got what I deserved. Come on."

Berthe, who had hoped to see him fall, obeyed like a condemned prisoner being led to the scaffold. Gigondès had lied. His poison did not kill like lightning. She was now at Garnaroche's mercy, and if she could have escaped from him, she would have thrown herself into the canal. But he held her fast and whispered tender words in her ear. How long did they walk on like this ? She never knew.

She had lost her head, and allowed him to lead her mechanically. But suddenly Garnarocho stopped. " This is odd !" he murmured, raising his hand to his forehead. "I feel dizzy. Oh ! it will go off. Here we are ! Do you see that wall ? The door's there, and—"

But he did not finish. His voice died away in an inarticulate rattle. He staggered and fell like a log upon the muddy pavement. Bertho bounded backwards to prevent him from dragging her down with him. He did not stir again, but she lacked the courage to lean over him to make sure that he was dead. She fled without looking behind her, and without knowing what road she took. Chance led her to the Place du Château d'Eau. There she recognised her surroundings, recovered her self-possession, and went straight home. She rang the bell, but the house-porter made her wait before pulling the cord. Still, at last, the door opened, and she was glad to see that the gas was extinguished. She knew the vestibule and the staircase well enough to reach her apartment without a light, and on seeing her maid, who had waited for her, she calmly asked, " Where is my husband ? "

" In the library, madame."

" Come and take off my dress. You can then tell him that I have returned." Bertho thought of everything. She did not wish her husband to perceive that she had been walking in the mud.

# VII.

ÉLISE AUBRAC was not crazy, as the baroness thought. Having ascertained how the latter had deceived her in conjunction with the Verdalencs, anent Louis Mareuil, she had decided to live independent, like a young girl of free America, and to wait calmly and confidently till her lover was restored to her, the lover she had first chosen and whom she never ceased to love. She had so arranged her life as to give no cause for slander. The furnished apartments which Darès had hired for her were on the first floor of a respectable house. They belonged to an English family who were passing the winter at Nice, and who, for economy's sake, let them for the time they were away. As a companion Élise had the old housekeeper called Victoire, who had brought her up, and who had not hesitated for a moment to leave the disagreeable baroness. The young widow received no visitors excepting Madame Mornas and Darès, who had constituted himself her protector and adviser, and she only went out to visit Madame Mareuil. She conceived great affection for Darès, who did not abandon his friends in their misfortune, and she dreamt of becoming his sister-in-law. She wished Annette and George to marry, and her plan seemed in a fair way to be realised. They loved each other, and if they had not mutually confessed it as yet, it was on account of the trouble in which the Mareuils found themselves.

Imprudently eager to witness the success of Darès' burlesque, Élise had taken Victoire with her. She went there closely veiled, and, at first, hid herself behind the screen of her box. But on seeing Darès with Madame Mornas, she had been unable to resist the temptation of smiling at the two friends, who alone had remained true to Louis' cause. The effect was deplorable, for others perceived her; and Darès did not fail to scold her on the morrow; but she cared little about the opinion of the Verdalencs, and in her present position it hardly mattered to her what the world thought. Moreover, George had brought her good news, for he had told her that the police were on the track of the real murderer; and he had promised to return on the following day.

It was noon, and seated at the window of her sitting-room, looking on to the Boulevard Haussmann, she awaited his arrival. With the success of his burlesque in her mind, she thought : "Annette will be happy and rich, richer than I ; and it is only right, for she is better than I am, but she will not be more loved. If Louis is willing, we will live together. We will take a house in the artists' quarter. His mother will live with us, too, and—" But her dream of happiness was, at this point, interrupted by a loud ring at the bell. "It is George," thought Elise, rising. And she listened while Victoire went to open the door.

But she did not hear Darès' ringing voice, and the door of the room was not opened. The housekeeper was, no doubt, speaking to some stranger, and Elise was about to return to the window, when Victoire appeared, carrying a small parcel. "A commissionaire has brought this for you, madame," she said, placing the package upon the table.

"That's singular ; I've bought nothing."

"I asked him who sent him, and he answered that the parcel was given to him in the street. I fancy it must have come from M. Darès or Mademoiselle Marcuil."

"Very well ; I'll see," said Elise, who remembered that Louis' sister had recently spoken to her of a fan she was painting, and which was to be a masterpiece. "Victoire's right," she thought. "It is a present from Annette, a surprise. And she untied the pink string which secured the paper. She was astonished, however, on taking off the paper to find a black morocco case inside. She opened it, and was yet more amazed to find it contained a necklace of a very peculiar kind. It was of gold and steel combined, with singular ornaments, pendants decorated with points, the whole worked and embossed in the style of the Italian Renaissance. "How singular, and yet how charming !" cried Elise. "Surely there isn't another like it in Paris. But who can have sent it to me ? Certainly not Annette. If she had possessed this strange piece of jewellery, she would have shown it to me before. Could it be George ? Yes ; he travelled last summer, through a lot of countries where no one ever goes. He must have bought it ; no one but a man of artistic feelings could have such taste, and as he can't make presents to Annette yet awhile, he thought of me." She drew the necklace from the case and examined it more closely. "The work is very delicate," she murmured, "and this combination of metals is most effective. He has sent me this necklace, as much as to say : Don't worry, but make yourself beautiful to receive Louis. Will _he_ come ? I don't dare to hope it, but George will come ; it's time already, and in a few moments he will be here. I should like him to see his present about my neck."

Approaching a mirror, she looked for the spring to open the necklace. But at first she did not find it ; the links seemed closely joined to each other, and the spring was probably a secret one. There was no other means of discovering it but to press successively upon each point where it might be hidden. In fact, the necklace seemed to be made of a single piece ; and Elise began to think that it was of no use except to place under a glass case as an ornament. Running it through her fingers, however, link by link, as a nun tells her rosary, she finally perceived an almost imperceptible catch, and on closer examination she discovered that this catch was surrounded by a circle of sharp diminutive points. This surprised her considerably, and she began to wonder what it meant. Was it intended to be something like a test imposed upon the person who received the present? However, Élise was not a woman to pause before a difficulty, and the question of pricking her fingers did not alarm her in the least. She longed to put on the necklace and see if it became her. She was indeed about to press upon the catch with one of her fingers, at the risk of hurting herself with the sharp points, when the door was suddenly opened. Turning at the sound, she uttered a cry of delight. George stood on the threshold with a beaming countenance. And as he read her thoughts on her face, he cried out : " Good news ! He will soon be free. His innocence is fully proved."

" What ! I can hope to see him to-day ? "

" That depends. The examining magistrate is very anxious to give him his liberty, but he is waiting for the chief of the detective service. I shouldn't be surprised if the real criminal were arrested this morning. She is a woman, I must tell you, and most likely of good standing in society. The chief told me so, without mentioning her name. It seems she has involuntarily betrayed herself. As I told you yesterday, the owner of the cabin was seen at the theatre on my ' first night,' but managed to get off. The chief almost despaired of finding him again, but, strange to say, a dead body was found on the Quai de Valmy yesterday morning, and its description tallied exactly with that of the man we had seen on the previous evening at the theatre. The body bore no wound ; but there's every reason to believe that the man didn't die a natural death, indeed, it is thought he was poisoned. The truth must be known by this time, for the autopsy took place this morning."

" Then was he an accomplice of the woman you spoke of ? Did she kill him to get rid of him ? That is very unlikely ! "

" On the contrary, it is very probable ; but the great point is, that in the man's pockets the police found some papers which will serve to discover the truth—an old passport in the name of Garnaroche, and a shooting-licence in another name, with an address at a little town near Chantilly. The chief went there at once, and the inquiries he made must have had important results. I shall see him to-day, and he certainly won't refuse to tell me how the matter stands."

" And you flatter yourself that he will inform you that the magistrate has recognised Louis' innocence ? Ah ! I should like to share your illusions, but I fear you are mistaken. I have been indulging in dreams myself ; I fancied that the necklace I just received was an omen of happiness."

" Has some one sent you a present then?" asked George, who did not understand what she meant.

" You know it very well, since it was you. I received it with delight, and I was admiring it when you came in ; look," added Élise, handing him the necklace. " You no doubt brought it back from your tour along the Adriatic. I guessed as much."

"I brought nothing at all, and I have sent you nothing. But allow me to examine this present. It's very curious, upon my word ; I saw nothing like it in the countries I visited last summer. And you say it was sent to you anonymously ? "

" There was no letter or card with it ; it was brought by a commissionaire."

" Be careful ! It's very compromising to accept a gift from unknown people," said George, gaily. " It's even dangerous sometimes. This necklace bristles with steel points. It looks like an instrument of torture."

" Yes, I had great difficulty in finding the catch, which must be pressed to open it ? "

" But you haven't opened it ? "

" No ; you interrupted me."

" Then I advise you not to try it," said George, earnestly, after examining the necklace closely. "This present looks very suspicious to me. The other night, in Madame Mornas' box, I heard an old idiot say he had invented a poison which kills people by a simple prick."

" I know him ; he's a physician, isn't he ? "

" Yes, a homœopathist, who once had a serious quarrel with your father and who bears you no good will. He declared in my presence that he would take great pleasure in trying the poison he has invented upon you."

" If he had any intention of doing so, he would not have said that."

" Possibly ; but, all the same, I implore you not to touch this necklace. I will put it back in the case, and I mean to try and find out where it came from. If you consent, I'll even give it to my friend the chief of police, who understands better than I do how to clear up a mystery."

" What's the use ? " sighed Élise. " It makes no difference to me who sent the necklace. I shall never wear it, since it does not come from you. I don't wish even to see it again," she added, closing the case which Darès had left open after placing the necklace inside it again.

At this moment Victoire entered the room, and whispered something to her mistress, who answered aloud : " You know very well that I am always at home to her." And then she said to George, " It is Madame Mornas."

The governess then ushered in the magistrate's wife, who advanced, with a smile on her lips, and kissed Élise on the forehead ; turning to Darès, she gave him her hand. " Well ! " she said, " M. Mareuil is saved. My husband signed the order for his release yesterday. He told me the good news this morning at breakfast, and I hastened here as soon as I could. I wanted to be the first to inform you of it."

"Thanks! oh, thanks!" faltered Élise, overwhelmed with joy and emotion. "I had a presentiment that I should owe my happiness to you."

"You don't owe it to me, dear child. The truth was bound to prevail, but the mistake lasted too long."

"It would still continue, if chance had not come to our help," muttered George.

"It is now proved, by unimpeachable witnesses, that M. Mareuil arrived at Boulogne ten minutes after the crime was committed, and that if he did not return to his mother's house it was because he passed the night wandering up and down the street under the windows of Madame Aubrac's apartments."

"But allow me to ask you," said Darès, with a certain amount of hesitation, "what about that roll of gun-wadding which was formed of scraps of Mareuil's poems?"

"My husband spoke to me of that. He at first took it as a serious proof against M. Mareuil, but he reflected that a great many copies of the book were sold by the publisher, or given by the author to his acquaintances. The real criminal was interested in turning suspicion upon a man whom Élise's marriage had driven to despair. So the imaginary proof against him has turned in his favour."

"And the real criminal, madame?" said Darès. "Your husband probably gave you information on this point. The chief of the detective service must by this time know the truth. No doubt it was after reading his report that M. Mornas decided to issue the order for Louis' release."

"I—I don't think so," said Madame Mornas, with a look of astonishment. "If my husband had seen the chief of the detective police yesterday, he would have told me about it this morning."

"But he, at least, spoke to you of the singular discovery the police have made."

"What discovery?"

"Well, do you remember that man who showed himself at the theatre on the night of the first performance of my piece, and who was discovered to be the owner of the cabin which the murderer entered?"

"I remember that you told me something of the sort in my box, but I didn't see the man."

"I saw him, though, and the chief of the detective service saw him as well. And do you know that the corpse of this fellow Garnaroche has been found on the banks of Saint Martin's Canal?"

Madame Mornas did not flinch. It is true that she had expected this revelation, and had had time to prepare herself. "Ah!" she said, coldly, "that is a singular coincidence. Do they know the cause of his death?"

"They didn't know it yesterday, but poison was vaguely spoken of."

" A man who has been poisoned doesn't go to the theatre," replied Berthe, with a forced smile.

" He might have been poisoned afterwards, and if that old fellow who was with you in your box can be believed, nothing is easier than to kill a man in a few seconds."

"I hope that you didn't take M. Gigondès' wanderings in earnest. He's half crazy, and he boasts incessantly of the discoveries he has made, but which only exist in his imagination."

" Well, I wouldn't trust him too far. He's vindictive, and he made my flesh creep when he threatened our friend here. Indeed, just now, a moment before your arrival, madame, I was wondering if the strange present which Mademoiselle Aubrac has received was not sent to her by that old idiot."

" A present ?" asked Berthe, with an air of astonishment.

" Yes," said Élise, " that necklace there was brought to me by a commissionaire who did not say who sent it. I thought at first that it came from M. Darès, but he denies it. Could it have been from you, dear madame ? "

"No, unfortunately, for it is really beautiful and of great artistic value," said Madame Mornas, taking the case which Élise offered her. "I confess that if I were in your place, I shouldn't bother myself about discovering the anonymous giver. I should keep it. What a charming ornament to wear with your mourning, neither any flashing gems nor bright new gold. It might have been made expressly for a widow. May I try it on ? "

" Don't do that, madame, I beg of you," exclaimed Darès. " I don't like the look of those steel points. Suppose M. Gigondès had dipped them in some venomous mixture ? "

" You are really too prudent, and, to reassure you, I'm going to try those points myself. They can't prick ; see they are round at the tips."

But it was fated that no one should experiment with the necklace, for just as Madame Mornas took it up, the housekeeper appeared and again whispered something to Élise. Élise looked at her and did not appear to understand. Neither did George, who was standing beside her, and Madame Mornas remained with the necklace in her hand without attempting to open it or replace it in the case. " Why didn't you ask the gentleman his name ? " inquired Élise.

" I did so, madame," answered Victoire, this time aloud, " but he says you don't know him, and that he has come to speak to Madame Mornas on a very important matter—"

" To me ! That's impossible ! " exclaimed the magistrate's wife. " How could anyone know I was here ? "

" It seems, madame, that the gentleman went to your house," said the housekeeper. " And he was told you had gone to Madame Trémentin's."

" What can this anonymous visitor want of me ? Is he really a gentleman ? "

"Yes, madame, I should say so ; he looks like one."

"Then we can admit him, can't we, my dear Élise ? I have no secrets from you, and we will ask him to explain the reason of his coming here after me."

"Excuse me, madame," said Victoire, timidly. "The gentleman impressed upon me that he wished to speak to you in private. He added that if madame refused to receive him here, he should wait for her at the foot of the stairs, and that madame would regret having forced him to choose such a place for an interview. What he has to say, madame, is pressing."

"Threats ! Turn him away, please. He is some beggar trying to intimidate me. I will show him that he has made a mistake ; he will obtain nothing from me by such proceedings."

"You would do right not to yield, if your conjectures are correct," said George ; "but who knows if this gentleman has not come with some news of Louis ? If that is the case, you would regret not having seen him." Élise said nothing, but she gave Madame Mornas a pleading look. "As for the private interview he asks for," continued George, "nothing is easier than to grant it. We can go into the next room where we shall be even better situated to receive other visits—for instance, Madame and Mademoiselle Mareuil, who are coming—"

"Then go, my dear child," said Madame Mornas. "I will join you when I have finished with this gentleman."

Élise thereupon followed George into the dining-room, while Madame Mornas, replacing the necklace in the case, told the housekeeper to admit the stranger. Berthe had lost none of her apparent coolness, though she was really beginning to feel uneasy. The visitor who entered was unknown to her, that is, she could not call him by his name ; but it seemed to her as if she had met him somewhere before. "You have asked to see me," she said. "What do you desire, sir ?"

"Madame," replied the visitor, bowing coldly, "I desire to speak to you respecting your former connection with Pierre Garnaroche."

Berthe turned horribly pale, but she did not lower her eyes. "I don't know what you mean," she replied.

"I will help your memory then. Pierre Garnaroche was the secretary of M. d'Arlempe, your father, who turned him out of his house for reasons which I need not recall to you. He then entered the service of a contractor, with whom he remained some years. Then his fortunes suddenly bettered, and—"

"Is it to give me this man's biography that you have intruded on my privacy ?"

"No ; on the contrary, it is to speak to you about his death. Yesterday morning his body was found on the Quai de Valmy."

"M. Darès has already informed me of that, but it has not the slightest interest for me."

"It will interest you perhaps when I tell you that the papers found upon Garnaroche's person fully acquainted the people who were looking for him with the name he had substituted for his own, with his recent place of residence, and also with the connection he had had with you."

"Ah ! Well ?" asked Madame Mornas, calmly making extraordinary efforts to control her emotion.

"He called himself Roland," continued the visitor, "and he lived at a shooting-box on the estate of Grandclos, near the village of Apremont. He lived there alone, on the income of this property, although he neither owned nor rented the place. You know better than any one whom it belongs to, as you placed it at his disposal gratuitously, without being authorised to do so by your husband, who leaves you the management of your fortune, but who would be greatly astonished to learn the use you have made of it."

"You no doubt propose to inform him of it ?" said Berthe, looking at the speaker fixedly. And as he answered by an affirmative sign, she continued : "Very well ; I understand. What is the price of your silence ? "

"It has no price. But if you reply frankly to certain questions I am about to put to you, I shall keep the information you give me to myself."

"What is it you wish to know ? "

"I wish to know who killed that man. You were the last person who saw him."

"That isn't true."

"Do you deny then, that on the night before last, after leaving the theatre, where you had spent a part of the evening, you joined Garnaroche who was waiting for you at a pre-arranged place ? "

"I deny it absolutely."

"But you were recognised on his arm, crossing the Boulevard du Temple, and two hours afterwards he was dead. And he had not died a natural death. He had been murdered."

"And it is I whom you accuse of this crime ? "

"He was not killed with a dagger or a pistol, but with just the weapon a woman might have used—a poisoned pin. Oh ! the nature of the poison and the way it was employed are known. We are even positive as to who prepared it."

"And what is your object in coming to me, sir ? "

"To obtain a sincere and complete confession from you. That is the only course left you ; but if you wish to avail yourself of it, you have not a minute to lose."

"Who are you, to speak to me in this fashion ? "

"I am the chief of the criminal investigation service, madame."

So far Berthe Mornas had made a brave fight. But when the visitor declared who he was, she realised that she was lost. "Have you seen my husband ? " she asked, with an effort.

"No, madame. M. Mornas doesn't know that I went to make inquiries at Grandclos ; he doesn't even know that Garnaroche is dead. The police agents who removed the dead body from the street are not aware that the man had any connection with the

Boulogne crime. I have said nothing, and I have assumed the responsibility of acting alone. On returning from Apremont I drove straight to the Rue de Turenne, for I wished to see you before speaking to any one. Indeed, I should like to prevent a shocking scandal—a scandal which will attract the attention of all Paris, and forever blacken the name of one of our most honoured magistrates."

"Well, admitting that I have deceived him, I know some of his colleagues who are in similar positions and who are none the less respected."

"None of their wives have committed two murders, with premeditation and aforethought ; none of them are connected with a woman who will pass before the Assize Court, and end on the scaffold or in prison."

"Two murders ! I ! You are mad. Whom have I murdered, if you please ? "

"On the night before last, you killed Garnaroche by pricking him in the hand with a poisoned pin. This poison you purloined from M. Gigondès, your tenant, who is still hunting for his vial. I know that Garnaroche entered his rooms with you ; that he left them with you, and that you killed him because he would have been able to say that when you broke off your connection with him, you kept the key of the hut from which a certain shot was fired."

"You don't suspect me, I suppose, of having fired that shot ? "

"I don't suspect you ; I am certain of it. Shall I tell you the number of the cab which you took on the Boulevard du Temple, and which conveyed you to the outskirts of the Longchamp Racecourse, where it waited for you to return to Paris ? The driver has told me that, on that particular evening, he was engaged by a lady who was veiled and wrapped in furs ; that, in the Bois de Boulogne, instead of a lady, he saw a boy get out ; that, at the end of three quarters of an hour, this boy returned out of breath and was driven to the Quai des Tuileries, at the corner of the Solferino Bridge ; that, then his "fare" was no longer a boy, but a woman—the same he had taken up on the Boulevard du Temple. She paid him well, and stepped on to the bridge with a package in her hand, a package which she threw into the Seine, and which contained her boy's clothes and—a gun, a pretty little gun, which was fished out this morning, and which was bought many years ago by M. d'Arlempe, for his daughter Berthe, who had a pronounced taste for masculine diversions. Am I well enough informed, madame, and need I enter into more circumstantial details ? Need I refer to your intrigue with M. Verdalenc's cashier ? Need I speak to you of the house communicating with two streets, which you entered on the one side, while M. Trémontin entered it on the other ? "

"No, no ; enough ! " gasped Madame Mornas, overwhelmed by this avalanche of proofs.

"Excuse me, madame ; it is not enough. I wish for a complete confession. M. Trémontin was your lover, and you killed him. Why did you kill him ? "

"Because his marriage was an infamous piece of treachery. He swore never to leave me, and yet he deceived me outrageously by marrying Élise Aubrac. Ah! I implored him on my knees; I wept; but he had no pity on me, and I had no pity on him!"

"You loved him, however?"

"Madly. I would have given my life to save his."

"Then it was not he you aimed at," said the chief, looking at Berthe. She trembled and made no answer. "You aimed at his wife, and your hand trembled; the bullet passed a little too high; it did not touch your rival's head, but it pierced your lover's heart?"

"Ah! you are the fiend himself," murmured Madame Mornas.

"I know also why you are here. You can't forgive Madame Trémentin for still being alive, and you long for her death. To be able to kill her with impunity, you have become intimate with her, by pretending to take the defence of the man she loves, by pleading Louis Mareuil's cause with your husband, after having committed the very crime which he was believed to be guilty of. With what did you intend to kill her? With a poisoned pin, as you killed Garnaroche?"

Berthe, who had covered her face with her hands, drew herself up at last, and said: "Let us make an end of this, sir. Nothing prevents you from denouncing me. Denounce, arrest me if you choose, but don't torture me."

"Then you advise me to go to M. Mornas, who knows nothing as yet, and say to him: Your wife is a twofold criminal; the murderer whom you are seeking is she herself; and you, a magistrate, have caused an innocent person to be imprisoned."

"But, whatever I say or do, you won't be silent."

"Yes; in one eventuality alone. I cannot point it out to you. I hoped you would understand me."

Berthe turned pale; she did understand. "You promise me that if I disappear, you will remain silent respecting me?"

"I can promise you that, since Louis Mareuil's innocence has been established. That is all I wish for, and I am of opinion that it is not indispensable for society to wreak punishment. The criminal always has a right to pay his debt himself, and, according to my ideas, it is better for him not to expiate his crime publicly; for, in such a case, his shame falls upon his family."

"I understand you, sir; and I can die without anyone suspecting me of suicide. Give me your word of honour that the word suicide shall not be pronounced when I am no longer in this world."

"I swear never to speak it myself, but I cannot answer for others."

"No one will dream of it, I am certain, if you don't betray me. My brougham is waiting at the door. I shall have time to reach the street and enter my carriage. When my coachman stops in the Rue de Turenne, he will find me dead, and the physicians will declare that I died of heart-disease." While speaking, Madame Mornas took up the necklace, which she had replaced in its case, and which the chief of police had not yet noticed. She took hold of it with both hands, looked for the spring, and when she had found it—"Farewell, sir," she said, in a firm voice. " Remember your promise."

" What are you going to do ?" cried the chief.

" It is done," rejoined Berthe, showing the thumb of her right hand, from the tip of which a drop of blood was oozing.

" What ! that necklace—"

" I hoped that it would kill Élise, and it has killed me. Lead me to my carriage, and help me to get in. I have only five minutes longer to live, and I don't wish to die here."

The chief could not help feeling a certain amount of emotion, but he did not let it appear, nor did he lose his head. He replaced the necklace in its case, and then pocketed the latter. Perhaps he still had some doubts as to the reality of the suicide committed before his eyes, for he said : " I am at your orders, madame, and I will accompany you all the more readily, as I don't wish anyone to learn that I have come here ; M. Darès knows me, and ought not to see me. I will, therefore, conduct you out and leave you at the door. Only allow me to say to you that we must not meet again, whatever happens. I have taken it upon myself to warn you ; I shall not repeat my warning, and to-morrow, I shall be obliged to do my duty."

" Have no fears," said Madame Mornas, bitterly. " The poison in my veins is sure and prompt. I shall never reach home alive. You have promised to be silent ; I rely upon your word."

" I again promise you to be silent, and to burn your letters to Garnaroche," rejoined the chief, looking as grave and sad as a judge who has just pronounced sentence of death. " Come, madame." He had learned, in the long practice of his delicate functions, that in some cases it is better, and even necessary, to depart from strict legality. He was conscious of having acted for the best, and yet, by giving this affair a secret epilogue, he certainly sacrificed his own pride ; for, if the case had come before the assizes, his skill and energy would undoubtedly have been highly praised. He was ready, however, to answer for his actions, and surely M. Mornas would never reproach him for having saved his name from the shame of a criminal trial. The condemned woman left the room the first, and she had the calmness to tell Élise's housekeeper that she had received some news which compelled her to go away without bidding her mistress good-bye. The chief, who followed her, could leave incognito, as he had come. Madame Mornas's coachman did not notice him, for she entered her brougham alone, while the functionary walked quietly down the street.

Some one saw them, however, some one who knew them both, and whom they did not perceive ; for he was on the opposite side of the way, gazing at the house in which Élise lived. Louis Mareuil, set at liberty that morning, had first hastened to his mother, and then, having with some difficulty obtained her consent to absent himself, he had repaired to the Rue Condorcet in search of George. He did not find him at home, but just as he raised his eyes to read the number of the house on the Boulevard Haussmann, he was delighted to see him standing at a first floor window. It can easily be believed that he did not tarry to watch Madame Mornas and the chief, whom he just noticed as they were separating. On the contrary he bounded up the stairs.

There are joys which cannot be depicted, transports which cannot be described. Élise hung on her lover's neck and kissed him over and over again. George was almost as moved as she was, and they all three spoke at once. After a quarter of an hour, however, when Élise had recovered her coolness a little, she said to Louis : " Come and thank Madame Mornas, who has so warmly undertaken your defence, and who has ended by gaining your cause with her husband."

" But she has gone away," replied Louis. " She got into her carriage just as I arrived."

" Gone ! without seeing me again," exclaimed Élise. " And to think I should have been so happy to present you to her ! "

" The gentleman who was so anxious to speak to her in private must have taken her away sooner than she wished," said Darès.

" If you mean the man who left this house at the same time as she did," said Louis, "I know him, and you know him as well. In fact, it was that miserable police agent who came to arrest me in my mother's garden, introducing himself as an attaché of the Palais de Justice. You were there, George, and you too, Élise."

" What ! the chief of the criminal investigation service ? " cried Darès. " It isn't possible ; you must be mistaken, my dear Louis. It is only natural he should have business with a magistrate, but what would he have to do with the magistrate's wife. The persistency with which he refused to give his name was most extraordinary. He did not wish us to know of his visit, then."

" He did not wish to be seen with Madame Mornas either, for he had scarcely left the house when he walked up the street without bowing to her."

" Stranger and stranger ! Why, he only returned last evening from an excursion which has certainly furnished him with positive information about the woman who murdered Trémentin. And yet, instead of going to see the magistrate at the Palais de Justice, he first went to the Rue de Turenne to ask for Madame Mornas, and then came here after her. He wouldn't have acted otherwise if she were guilty."

" Oh, George ! what an idea ! " murmured Élise.

" Another idea occurs to me about that necklace. Didn't I tell you that Madame Mornas was intimate with old Gigondès ? Who knows if it were not she who sent that necklace ? It is on the table

in the other room.   Come ; I want to look at it and give it to the
chief to be examined."   And, without waiting, George hurried into
the next room.

Élise and  Louis followed him.   The case and the necklace were
gone ; but on the white cashmere tablecloth there was a drop of
blood, still wet.   " She has hurt herself ! " cried Élise.

" No ; she has killed herself ! " said George Darès,  " and, in
doing so, she has paid the penalty for her crimes ! "

.          .          .          .          .          .          .

Yes, Berthe Mornas had paid her debt to justice.   She died in
her  brougham  on  her  way  home,  and  the  chief of  the  criminal
investigation service kept his word.   No one has ever known, or
will know, what was the real life of this woman, whom suspicion
had never sullied.   George alone had guessed the truth ; but Élise
and Louis had refused to believe him ; and besides, nowadays, they
all three only think of being happy.   In six weeks' time Annette
Mareuil will become Madame Darès, and ten months hence Louis
Mareuil will marry Élise Trèmentin, née Aubrac.   Gigondès might
speak ; but he is too much afraid of compromising himself.   So the
Boulogne crime is no longer discussed.   The affair is shelved, or
rather, forgotten.   As for M. Mornas, he sincerely mourns his wife,
and will be advanced in his profession.   So runs the world away.

THE END.

# CÉCILE'S FORTUNE.

## I.

IT is a dark night and a tempest sways the lofty pines of the Esterel forest. Two men are slowly climbing a wooded hill, through briers and over rocks, and beneath a canopy of dark foliage. At almost every step they pause to look around them, and listen. They remind one of hunted wolves. They strain their eyes to pierce the gloom, and listen as though to distinguish, amid the confused noises of the forest, some sound they dread. And when the storm, growling in the ravines, bursts upon them like a hurricane, or gives a plaintive human-like moan, they at once throw themselves face downward on the damp heather.

But it is neither the darkness nor the storm they fear. The darkness conceals, the storm protects them, and as soon as they recognise the loud voice of the mistral, they again begin ascending the wild height. They reach the summit at last, quite breathless, and lean against the trunk of an ancient oak. It is impossible to advance any further. An impassable precipice yawns at their feet.

"I told you so," muttered one of the fugitives. "We shall never get out of this accursed wood."

"I am not anxious to get out of it too soon," replied his companion. "Daylight will soon come, and after sunrise it will not be prudent for us to be seen on the highways."

"We shall be no safer here. The forest-keepers will assist the gendarmes in beating the woods. They must have begun by now, for the entire neighbourhood has been warned. Two cannons have been fired to announce that two convicts have succeeded in making their escape. The peasants know the signal, and they are aware that they will receive a handsome reward if they capture us as will no doubt be the case."

"If you are afraid, go back to Toulon ; you will, perhaps, get off with fifty lashes."

"I'm not afraid, but it is now thirty-six hours since we made our escape in a boat belonging to one of the hospital purveyors, and twenty-four hours have been spent wandering about the woods in a neighbourhood we know nothing of."

"You may not know this part of the country, but I do and we are going to the Château of Mérindol."

"Present ourselves at a château! You are mad."

"There is no one there to oppose our entrance. And we shall probably find a change of clothes there. The château used to be occupied."

"I begin to understand. We will dress ourselves afresh, burn our convict's clothes, and then we shall perhaps succeed in reaching the frontier, which is but a short distance off. Besides, we shall not want for money as I have our comrades' purse in my possession."

"The purse! Yes, we will talk about that presently," muttered the taller and stronger of the two convicts.

"Is it far to this château?" inquired the other.

"About three quarters of a league from here—to our right. I went there often enough in years past to find my way now with my eyes shut."

"Why did you not tell me so sooner?"

"Because you would have refused to follow me. You would have thought I was merely inventing a story to deceive you. I tell it you now, and that ought to be enough, Monsieur Mongeorge."

"It is enough," replied the convict whom his companion had addressed as "Monsieur Mongeorge," with an ironical emphasis upon the word "Monsieur." "Come, Ricœur, show me the way."

"That is not necessary," growled Ricœur. "I can enter the den without your assistance. You will remain here on guard, this is a good place to see anyone coming. I will bring you all you need as a change of clothes."

"Very well, I will remain then. But make haste. If daylight overtook us—"

"Don't be alarmed; I shall be back in an hour. But first of all we have an account to settle. You are carrying the purse our comrades intrusted to you. It is too heavy for you. Besides, we shall be obliged to separate. You wish to reach some foreign country, while I want to see Paris again; some misfortune may happen to one of us, while the other may escape. It isn't worth while to have all the money lost, so let us divide it."

"But I swore to deliver our comrades' money to an appointed person—to deliver it myself. Having confidence in me they mutually agreed to furnish me with the means of making my escape. You and I were chained together, you profited by the opportunity to make your escape as well. I am glad of it, but I can't do what you ask."

"But I tell you I want my share."

"Your share! You talk as if the money belonged to us. But you know that it is only a trust."

"Bosh! such talk might hoodwink judges, but it does not take with me. Give me half the money or—I shall take it from you by force."

"Take care, Ricœur. If you rob our comrades, they will be sure to have their revenge."

"I'm not afraid of them. I am going to change my skin, and enter a circle where they will never think of looking for me. Besides, all that is my affair. You need not trouble yourself about me. I do not ask what you intend to do."

"Oh, if I escape the gendarmes, I shall try to earn my living honestly. I have had enough of a convict's life, and have no desire to try it again."

"No more have I. But I have no foolish prejudices, and providing I make money I don't mind the means. You make me laugh with your scruples. An escaped convict who tries to live honestly, is sure to starve and to be recaptured sooner or later. I should like to know how you would manage to get a situation. People will be sure to ask you where you come from, and who you are. Shall you tell them that you were once a notary, and that you have just spent ten years at Toulon?"

"No," muttered Mongeorge, overcome by the pitiless logic of his companion, "I foresee that every door will be closed against me, but I know one person who will lend me a helping hand, and assist me in beginning life afresh."

"Don't rely on that. When a man is in trouble, his friends desert him; money's the only thing to help a chap along, and we should be fools not to divide the contents of your belt. Besides, I've made up my mind to make a fortune. With a title, some foreign decorations, and plenty of bounce, one can aspire to anything. But I must have a little money to start with, and you can supply it. Let us settle this matter now, once for all. Unfasten the belt under your blouse, count the cash it contains, and let us share the amount like two brothers."

"Never! I can give you a little of the money, and take a little for myself. Our comrades authorized me to draw on the deposit for our first expenses; but I promised to take the rest to—"

"To a thief who has become a banker, and invests convicts' money for them. And you pretend that you mean to be an honest man! How was this money you guard so carefully, obtained? It was stolen from the manager of the hospital, as you know very well. So, enough of those virtuous grimaces, old fellow! Give me half of the plunder, and do what you like with the rest."

"I shall give you nothing. You are quite capable of killing me no doubt, but I would rather die than betray the friends who helped me to make my escape. It is no question whether this money was stolen or not. I have received a deposit, I am determined to hand it to the proper party, and you sha'n't touch it."

"Say that you wish to keep it for yourself. Ah! you are not such a simpleton as I supposed. Well, we will say no more about it at present, and you had better accompany me to the Château de Mérindol. I have changed my mind. If we separate, we shall perhaps lose time. When our expedition has proved successful, we will resume the conversation, and I shall, perhaps, be able to convert you to my way of thinking."

"I fancy not ; but I am ready to accompany you."

The two convicts then started off along the edge of the precipice. The wind had fallen. The tempest was raging at a distance. The fugitives had scarcely taken a dozen steps, when Ricœur, suddenly springing upon his companion, caught him round the waist and hurled him into the abyss below. Mongeorge gave vent to a frightful shriek which the echoes of the forest repeated. That was all. The murderer leant over the precipice, but he did not hear the slightest sound. Ricœur was well acquainted with that part of the country, and he was aware that at a short distance ahead of him, he would find a path leading to the bottom of the ravine in which his victim was lying, in all probability dead. This path was very rough, and in the darkness, even dangerous ; but the murderer was sure-footed, and he reached the bottom of the cliff without any mishap.

Ricœur cautiously advanced, his hands outstretched, and his wolf-like eyes straining in the vain hope of penetrating the darkness that filled the abyss. The briers caught in his clothes. He trembled each time he found himself arrested by their thorns, or whenever a bird, awakened by his tread, flew by, touching his face.

However, he advanced, and in ten minutes or so, he stumbled over something on the ground. Mongeorge lay motionless upon the stony heather. Ricœur had almost trampled him under foot. The murderer soon recovered from his sudden terror and surprise ; he knelt down and placed his hand upon the chest of the prostrate man. Mongeorge's heart had not yet ceased to beat, but he was quite unconscious. Ricœur lifted his companion's blouse, and unfastened a broad leather belt which he wore next his body.

"That's all right," muttered the murderer. "There is enough here to start me in the circle I mean to live in." Then having thrust the belt in the pocket of his baggy, coarse linen trousers he added : "Still, there is something else I need, a change of clothes ; but I shall find what I want at the château, and it won't cost me a penny to dress myself in the latest style. Heaven grant that that fool of a Mérindol hasn't taken it into his head to spend the winter at his place. The fellow always was peculiar ; but at this season of the year he must be at Monaco, gambling away his last coppers ! Besides, if I find him in my way—well, so much the worse for him. I'll cure him of appetite for good !"

This soliloquy lasted until Ricœur regained the path by which he had descended into the ravine. He climbed it with difficulty, and just as he reached the top of the height, he fancied he heard a horse's tread. He turned in alarm, and at the other end of the gorge perceived a speck of light seemingly in motion. This light evidently came from a lantern, which was probably carried either by some belated traveller or a forest keeper making his round. Any meeting was to be dreaded, so Ricœur hastened at the top of his speed towards the Château of Mérindol which he wished to visit before sunrise.

Scarcely had he disappeared in the forest, than a rider, preceded by a man on foot, who carried a lantern in his hand, reached the entrance of the ravine. "Not that way, Monsieur Louis," said the pedestrian. "If you enter that gorge which we call the Bat's Hole your horse won't be able to get out of it. The road to Mérindol is to the right."

"I know that, Piganiou," replied the rider, "but we are in no hurry, and I want to know who gave the cry we heard just now. Perhaps someone has fallen into the ravine, and needs our assistance."

"Impossible, Monsieur Louis. In such weather and at this hour, there can be no one in the forest except ourselves. It must have been a fox."

"A fox? nonsense! It was a man, I tell you, a man who has fallen into the ravine. He must have lost his way; he was not familiar with the part, and did not see the precipice in the dark. Let us go on. We shall only have to retrace our steps."

The speaker was a tall young man, who sat his sorry-looking steed with an air of ease, and his companion was a squat elderly fellow, a trifle bent, who trudged on with his head lowered, like the peasant that he was.

"You were right, sir," suddenly exclaimed Piganiou, the peasant; "here is a fellow lying on his back. He looks as though he had fallen over the precipice."

"I was sure of it," cried the young man, springing nimbly to the ground; "if I had listened to you the poor fellow would have perished here for want of a helping hand."

"He is past all human aid, I think."

"We will see about that. Set your lantern down and help me to lift him up."

Piganiou immediately knelt down, and cast the light of his lantern on the prostrate body. "Good heavens," muttered the old peasant. "Look at this red blouse and green cap—the fellow's an escaped convict!"

"Yes," said his master, bending forward. "He was hiding in the forest, and tried to make his escape in the darkness, but the earth suddenly gave way beneath his feet."

"Ah, well, there is no great harm done. There is one rascal less in the world, that's all. But—no, look, he moves a little and puffs. However, he is as good as dead. It will be all over with him in an hour's time."

"Who knows? Perhaps he is only stunned. Help me to get him on my horse. I'm not going to leave him here."

"But he is a convict, sir."

"A convict is a man. I sha'n't leave him here to die when it will not take us more than half an hour to get him to Mérindol."

"To the château! under the roof of the deceased marquis, your father! Oh! Monsieur Louis, you surely won't do that?"

"That is exactly what *I am* going to do. And my father would have done the same under similar circumstances."

"But the gendarmes must certainly be looking for him ; and if he were found in the château—"

"He won't be found there. Come, come, take hold of him, under his arms. I will take him by the legs, and between us we will get him on to the saddle, and secure him with the straps that fasten my portmanteau. Besides, I'll support him. You can lead the horse, we shall have to go slowly, that's all."

"Ah ! Monsieur Louis, one has to do whatever you wish," sighed Piganiou. "But if any misfortune befalls you on this scoundrel's account, it won't be my fault, and you must remember that I advised you not to touch him."

"Oh ! certainly, certainly. Are you ready ? " asked the master, slipping his hands under the legs of the unconscious man.

The servant very reluctantly decided to obey, and the convict, lifted by the two strong men, was placed on the horse's back, face downward, and secured with a surcingle. The master held his head to prevent it swaying, and Piganiou, already provided with his lantern, was about to take hold of the bridle when the convict groaned :

"You have killed me, Ricœur—but God will punish you."

"Did you hear that, Monsieur Louis ? " cried Piganiou. "That name of Ricœur—it was that of the scoundrel who began your father's ruin."

"Ricœur ? " repeated the young man. "Yes, I recollect. A man of that name was a broker to whom my father intrusted certain business transactions, and who disappeared, taking part of our fortune with him."

"Which he obtained possession of by forgery," added the peasant. "Perhaps you don't know that he succeeded in escaping to Italy, where he squandered the money he had stolen from your family ; but he afterwards returned to France and began coining counterfeit money. He was then caught and sent to the galleys for life. He was still there last summer. I saw him at Toulon dragging a ball and chain about the arsenal wharf."

"The rascal only got what he deserved. But why do you tell me all this just now ? "

"Why, this Ricœur must have escaped in company with the man you are trying to save."

"Perhaps so—perhaps he flung his companion into the Bat's Hole. That exclamation just now was a charge of foul play. However, that is no reason why we should abandon this poor devil here."

"But Ricœur is capable of any crime, sir. If he really tried to kill this man, he can't be far off, and if he met us in the forest—"

"Well, we should be two to one."

"Oh ! he's as strong as four ordinary men. You must have seen him years ago ; but you no doubt don't recollect him, as you were still a child when he decamped with your father's money. But he knows you. Would you believe it, on the day I met him at

Toulon he recognised me instantly, and actually had the assurance to speak to me."

"Were you intimate with him in former years?"

"No, I always thought him a rascal, and I did not hesitate to say what I thought of him. But Monsieur le Marquis was too kind-hearted and credulous. He wouldn't listen to me, and his refusal cost him dear. I saw Ricœur at the château often enough, however, and when we met at Toulon the rascal inquired how my wife and children were getting on; strangest of all, he wanted to know what had become of you. He asked if you were rich, and if you spent the whole year at Mérindol. I did not tell him much, as you may suppose, Monsieur Louis, not liking to have your name brought into a conversation with a convict."

"I should think not," replied Louis de Mérindol, laughing. "However, I don't see that I have any reason to fear this scoundrel."

"But you forget that he is now at liberty, and that the idea of entering the château may occur to him. He knows that it is only a short distance from here, and that it is unoccupied."

"If he is so well informed, he must also know that he would find nothing worth stealing there. Mérindol is the abode of poverty, and I don't believe there is even a bottle of wine left in the cellar. I drank the last ones when I was here last summer with my two friends from Paris. Nice friends they were. They are not likely to repeat their visit. I have come down to my last resources, so my society will have no further charms for them."

"So much the better, Monsieur Louis; the Parisians have never done you anything but harm, and if you had never seen them you would still have enough left to rebuild Mérindol, and live there happily."

"Yes, if I had the courage to turn miller like you, but the will is lacking. I don't like the country, and I like solitude even less. I need the bustle and stir of Paris. I have lived there as the rich live. Now that I have nothing left, I shall lead there the life of those who toil, and I sha'n't be wretched on that account."

While this conversation was going on, the convict had begun to give fresh signs of life; such as sighs, moans, and convulsive movements. The jolting seemed to have aroused him from his lethargic condition. A considerable distance had already been covered. The ravine was a long way behind, and the wooded slope was expanding into a plateau. "Ah! Monsieur Louis," said Piganiou, "this idea of taking an escaped convict to your father's house is a very bad one. What do you mean to do with him?"

"Cure him first, and you shall assist me in doing so. You have not your equal as a nurse, as I have reason to know."

"It is true that I set you on your legs more than once when you had had a bad fall from your horse while galloping over roads where the fiend himself would break his neck. I have remedies of my own, which are better than doctor's stuff. But even if I set this

convict all right he would be no better off. What could you do
with him afterwards ?"

"I do not know yet, but I certainly sha'n't hand him over to the
gendarmes."

"But you cannot keep him at Mérindol."

"No, as I shall only remain there twenty-four hours to get some
papers and family relics which I don't wish to abandon. I must
intrust the task of saving this poor beggar to you. As soon as he
is able to walk, you must take him at night-time to your mill at
Reyran, dress him in your journeyman's clothes, and then go with
him to Fréjus, where you can take the train for Nice."

"Bless me ! Monsieur Louis, but this man would be recognised
as an escaped convict anywhere. The first gendarme we meet will
arrest him, and me with him."

"Then you can let him go alone. Your wife would be too
wretched if you were arrested. However, you certainly must
shelter this fellow until he can decamp with safety, and then you
must supply him with a disguise and such information as will prevent him from going astray."

"Ah ! Monsieur Louis, you are always the same. Your kind
heart will be the ruin of you."

"Very possibly ; but I can't help it. This man was no doubt guilty
of some ugly things in past years, but he has, perhaps, repented. Besides, I don't believe in chance, Piganiou. I believe that the hand
of Providence is apparent in everything, and if I happened to pass
near the Bat's Hole just as this poor devil was pitched headlong into
it, it was because Providence wishes me to save him."

"Upon my word, Monsieur Louis, you have a skilful way of
putting things. Ah ! you would have made a capital lawyer."

"That was my true vocation, perhaps ; but my father had very
decided opinions upon that point, as upon many others. He only
allowed me to enter the Polytechnic School on condition that I
would not accept any position under government afterwards. I
needed no urging to send in my resignation as an engineering cadet,
as I only wanted to amuse myself, and the result is that I find
myself, at the age of thirty, without money, and without a position
that would enable me to make any. Still, I have now decided to
work courageously—"

"That is a wise resolution, Monsieur Louis," sighed the miller,
"only you must allow me to say you begin foolishly. This runaway—"

"Silence, you stubborn fellow. It is too late to draw back now.
I can see the battlements of Mérindol rising above the pines. All
I possess in the world is that old pile, where I shall never set foot
again : having come to visit it for the last time I should like it to be
the scene of a charitable act."

A black mass indeed stood out against the sky on the outskirt of
the forest, where, on a kind of plateau, the ancestors of this im-
poverished young nobleman had, in days long past, built themselves
a feudal manor.

" Good heavens ! Monsieur Louis," Piganiou suddenly exclaimed,
" there is a light in the lower hall. That brigand, Ricœur, has
entered the château as I expected. He hurried there after getting
rid of his brother convict, and as he is still there, we shall have
trouble with him."

" I doubt it. If it is really Ricœur who has lighted the lamp or
candle we see burning there, he will take good care to decamp as
soon as he perceives your lantern."

" Taking everything he can lay his hands on away with him."

" Oh ! some worn-out shooting jackets and rusty old guns ? I
don't mind that. Let us make haste, and don't be afraid. If the
bird hasn't flown when we reach the château, I will make him take
flight."

Piganiou heaved a deep sigh, and raised his hands despairingly to
heaven, but he obeyed his young master, nevertheless. The storm
was over, the sky was clearing in the east, and the wind wafted the
sullen roar of the waves as they broke upon the rocks of Cape Roux.
The coast was only a short distance off, for the wooded hill, capped
by the Château of Mérindol, rose from the beach between the Bay
of St. Raphael and the Bay of La Napoule. It was one of the spurs
of Mont-Vinaigre. The two convicts, escaping from Toulon in a
stolen boat, had left the roads amid the height of a terrible tempest,
and after a perilous voyage, a westerly wind had driven them in the
middle of the night on to the sandy shore of the little Bay of Agay.
It seemed probable, therefore, that Ricœur had not formed his plan
till chance had landed him in a neighbourhood with which he was
familiar. The château in which he proposed to procure a change of
clothes looked well enough from a distance, with its square keep, its
two round towers and massive walls, behind which there was a
dwelling-house of less ancient date ; it had indeed been erected in
the reign of Louis XIII. However, the lordly warlike pile was now
crumbling to dust, and even the Louis XIII. dwelling-house only
contained three or four habitable rooms. There was but little
furniture left ; three or four dilapidated bedsteads, as many worm-
eaten wardrobes, a few unsteady tables, and a limited number of
ragged arm-chairs. Still, there were some cooking utensils and
some crockery ; and even art was represented by two large, broadly
painted portraits recalling Rigaud's style : one of them represented
an Admiral de Mérindol, who had been killed in an engagement in
the Indian Ocean when under the orders of the Bailli de Suffren,
and the other a Brigadier-General Mérindol of the time of Louis
XV., these being the most illustrious members of the family in
modern times.

Louis de Mérindol, the last of his race, had come to the château
for the express purpose of taking away these portraits, together
with his title-deeds, land grants, dating from the time of the
Crusades, genealogies carefully drawn up by d'Hozier, and other
parchments of a similar nature. He had left them at the old
château while he was leading the feverish wandering life of a

prodigal, but this life was now ended, and he did not wish to offend his ancestors by abandoning these mementos of a brilliant past.

They had been left too long already in this dilapidated mansion with no one to guard them, for Piganiou, the old family servant, resided at his mill near Reyran, at least twelve miles away. He kept the keys of the château, and visited it occasionally, but he seldom sojourned there. He was a married man, with two daughters. He had purchased the mill which his ancestors had managed for the lords of Mérindol for three hundred years, and he was now independent; but he was greatly attached to the son of his former master, and that very night he had given another proof of his disinterested devotion. Louis had dropped down upon the Piganiou household that evening in the most unexpected manner on his return from a disastrous trip to Homburg; and the faithful miller had complied with his request to guide him through the forest to the château, for Louis had but a poor recollection of the roads. It is true, that Piganiou had not foreseen the strange adventure that had since occurred, and perhaps he was now half inclined to regret that he had engaged in the undertaking.

"Look, Monsieur Louis," he remarked, again pausing, "the light is on the second floor now, in the room you occupied last summer."

"Yes, I see. It is very strange," murmured the young man. "Who can have taken the notion to trouble the bats and owls? See, there is a shadow moving across the window. I positively have a tenant. Ah! but now the light disappears. My tenant is leaving without having paid his rent. Ah, well! so much the better; we shall find the coast clear."

"And the house, too, probably. He only came to steal, of course," said Piganiou tugging at the bridle of the horse which soon reached the edge of the moat surrounding the castle—a moat, which was now dry, and perhaps had never been full of water, for in this land of Provence, rain seldom or never falls.

The drawbridge which had formerly spanned the moat was no longer in existence; but the parapets had so crumbled away, filling the cavity, that there was no difficulty in crossing. No trace of the portcullis or postern remained; and this once proud fortress, which had successfully resisted the assaults of the Huguenots and the attacks of the Spaniards when they invaded Provence under Charles V. could now be entered as easily as Piganiou's mill at Reyran. The battlemented gateway led into a narrow courtyard, at the end of which stood the house, a long tile-covered building, which looked much more like a barn than a nobleman's mansion. The light which had been seen on the first floor had now disappeared, and the only audible sound was the rustling of the pines in the forest near by. "Let us go in," said Louis de Mérindol, and seeing Piganiou hesitate, he went forward to the main entrance.

It was only necessary to push the door open, for the old lock had been broken, probably by a vigorous push. "What did I tell you?" exclaimed the miller. "The scoundrel forced the door!"

"It could not have cost him much of an effort," murmured Louis de Mérindol; "and I suppose he did not find it much more difficult to make his escape by scaling the north wall. Come on and hand me the lantern." Piganiou obeyed, though rather reluctantly. His master took the lantern, and entered the lower hall. "You are right," he exclaimed, "some one has been here. And our visitor felt the need of refreshment, it would seem. There is a bottle partially emptied and a glass on the table. I thought there was nothing left at Mérindol but water. No," he added, after smelling the glass. "It is rum. The last of the bottles I brought when I came here last summer. The rascal must be a sharp fellow to have succeeded in unearthing it. He probably did not confine his depredations to this. I am curious to see what he has taken; but first of all we must attend to our wounded man."

Mérindol and the miller between them succeeded in laying the convict on a camp-bedstead which stood in the apartment. The man groaned frightfully; but this was a good omen, as it showed that he was beginning to regain consciousness. At last Louis poured a few drops of rum into his mouth, and the convict then opened his eyes, and asked huskily : "Where am I?"

"You are with people who don't wish you any harm," replied Mérindol. "We found you in a ravine in the forest; and if we have taken the trouble to bring you here, it is certainly not to deliver you up to the gendarmes."

"The gendarmes," repeated the fugitive, trying to sit up, "then you know—"

"That you have escaped from Toulon? Unquestionably. You still wear your red blouse and green cap, and between you and me, you would not be able to go far in this garb. So it is very fortunate that you tumbled into the Bat's Hole as the ravine is called, especially as you have broken no limbs."

"No," muttered the injured man, stretching his arms, and moving his legs. "It is my head that struck the ground and my woollen cap broke the force of the fall. Ah! it would have been better if I had been killed!"

"Why? One should never regret being alive. If you were dead you would have no opportunity to atone for the past—a past that you regret, I am sure."

"Yes, indeed," sighed Mongeorge.

"Very well, that is all I care to know just now on that point, but tell me how this accident occurred?"

"It was not an accident. I was pushed over the precipice by—a man who—escaped with me."

"Ah! and why did he wish to get rid of you?"

The convict hesitated, but finally with an effort he replied : "To rob me."

"What! you had some money, then?"

Mongeorge did not reply. He covered his face with his hands, and began to weep. Piganiou muttered between his set teeth, and shrugged his shoulders impatiently ; but Louis de Mérindol pitied this man, bowed down beneath his burden of shame, and said gently : " Don't be afraid to confess the truth. I pledge you my word that whatever you tell me shall go no further."

" You give *me* your word of honour, me—a miserable, branded scamp. Ah, sir, I do not deserve it ! Whatever the consequences may be I will tell you all. I have been a convict for five years, chained to a man I loathed. I accepted my sentence to imprisonment for life as a just punishment for the crime I had been guilty of, and the idea of attempting to evade it never occurred to me. You don't know, perhaps, that convicts sometimes conspire to insure the escape of one of their number. Each has his chance, his day by turn, and when that day comes the others incur any risk in helping him. My turn had not yet come ; I had not dragged my ball and chain after me long enough, but something occurred which brought me into favourable notice. A robbery was committed in the office of the hospital manager—a large sum of money was taken from the safe and secreted in a spot only known to the parties who had stolen it."

" I heard something about that affair," exclaimed Piganiou. " All Toulon has been talking about it, and though all the convicts were soundly flogged, none ever revealed the whereabouts of the money."

" No ; it was effectually concealed," replied Mongeorge ; " but the thieves wished to place it where it would be safe beyond any possible doubt. They have an accomplice in Paris, a man who pretends to carry on an honourable business, but who is really the convicts' banker. They wished to send him the twenty-nine thousand francs they had stolen but not one of them had any confidence in his accomplices. I myself was but little acquainted with them ; they knew that I did not sympathize with them, and they had always ridiculed me unsparingly, still, it was upon me that their choice fell."

" Precisely ; because they knew that you did not resemble them. Such men have a wonderful gift for reading character. So they made proposals to you ? "

" They told me that if I would promise upon oath to take the stolen money to Paris, and deliver it into the keeping of an individual they would name, they would all unite in furnishing me with the means of escape."

" It was certainly a tempting offer."

" It ought not to have been one, for by accepting the custody of this money, I made myself their accomplice. God is my witness that I hesitated a long time, but I was finally coward enough to accept."

" I really can't blame you. When a man is condemned to imprisonment for life, he isn't likely to neglect any opportunity to regain his liberty."

" If it had been for my own sake alone, I think I should have refused ; but I had a reason for being extremely anxious to return to Paris—a reason I cannot explain to you, though I assure you it is one for which I have no cause to blush. I therefore consented to the proposal, and the same day I received a file, and was taught how to sever the chain which bound me to my companion. He was not to escape with me. The others distrusted him, but by chance we got off together. The chain was filed so that it would yield to the first strain brought upon it ; but it still held together well enough to deceive the eyes of our guards. I was to leave the arsenal the next morning, dressed like a naval surgeon. My disguise was ready, and a belt containing the stolen money was already secreted under my blouse. I had been at work all day with my squad near the shore. It was getting dark, and we were loading some stones which our companions had taken from a quarry, when suddenly a bank fell in, crushing three convicts and burying a superintendent. Everyone rushed forward to dig away the soil that covered him. A sailing boat was moored close by in charge of two sailors, who immediately sprang on shore to assist in the rescue, and in the confusion we were forgotten. ' Come,' said Ricœur to me."

" Ricœur, that was your companion's name, I suppose ! " said Mérindol.

" Yes. He dragged me along with him, and the leaders of the conspiracy did not try to hinder our flight, though they were not pleased to see Ricœur leave with me ; but if they had denounced him, it would have cost them their money, for I had it on my person, and I should have been searched. Well, the darkness enabled us to get out of the roads without being seen, and the westerly wind, which was blowing stiff, bore us swiftly on. Ricœur knew something about sailing, and he was familiar with the coast. We finished filing our fetters asunder, and I helped him in keeping the boat out at sea, for we feared being caught along the coast. After twenty-four hours' anxiety and peril, the tempest drove us upon a rocky shore, where our boat was shivered to pieces, while we managed to land."

" And then you plunged into the forest. Why on earth didn't your companion, who knew something of navigation, you say, try to reach Italy ? "

" That was what I wanted him to do ; but he pretended that it was impossible. I found out afterwards that he was very anxious to land here. He wished to visit a deserted château in this direction—the Château of Mérindol."

" That is where you are now. Chance has brought you to the very place your companion wanted to reach."

" Good heavens ! Then Ricœur is here ? The owner of the château is absent, isn't he ? "

" He has been away a long time."

" Ricœur knew it ; and it was this fact that induced him to come and steal some clothes."

"He may have found some, but he certainly did not stop to try them on. If he came here at all, he must be some distance off by this time, and if he should take it into his head to return, we will give him a warm reception. But please go on with your story. Do you know that you were lucky to escape being arrested by the coastguards."

"The storm probably compelled them to seek shelter. Besides, they could not suppose that smugglers would think of landing in a tempest violent enough to keep a ship of war in port. At all events, we saw no one, so we immediately began to ascend the wooded slopes that extend almost to the beach. I was nearly exhausted, and frightfully hungry, but Ricœur urged me on, telling me that before daybreak we should reach the cabin of a woodcutter of his acquaintance, and that this man would procure some food for us, and allow us to remain for a time in his hut. I knew nothing about this part of the country, and was entirely at Ricœur's mercy, so I followed him, until, after several hours' tramping, we reached the summit of a precipitous hill. I was fainting with fatigue, and Ricœur told me that I could stretch myself out on the ground and sleep, while he went to an unoccupied house to procure some clothes for us. I realised the necessity of changing our costume before we attempted to cross the frontier ; but Ricœur wanted something more ; he wanted me to give him half of the money his comrades had entrusted to my care. At first I tried to induce him to listen to reason. I explained to him that this money was a sacred trust, for we owed our liberty to those who had confided it to my keeping, and that if we betrayed the trust, they would certainly have their revenge on us sooner or later. But it was of no use. He ridiculed my scruples, and finally resorting to stratagem, he pretended he would not insist any further, and asked me to accompany him to Mérindol. I allowed myself to be deceived by his hypocritical airs, and managed to drag myself along beside him for a short distance. It was then that he sprang upon me when I least expected it, and, seizing me round the body, flung me into the ravine. In my fall I lost consciousness."

"But the brigand must have robbed you of your money after that ? Do you remember nothing about it ?"

"Nothing ; but the belt has certainly gone," murmured the convict.

"Of course. Ricœur took good care not to leave it in your possession."

"Oh, I have no hopes of recovering it. I did not regain consciousness until a long time after my fall ; in fact, not until I reached this château. The liquor revived me."

"Drink a glassful to complete the cure," said Piganiou, pouring out a bumper.

The convict just moistened his lips with the rum, and then stammered a few words of thanks which touched Mérindol deeply. "Come, come," said the kind-hearted young nobleman, "your limbs are not broken, and if your brain were injured, you could not talk so easily. It really seems hard to believe in such a miracle. Hold a light for me, Piganiou, and let me examine the effects of this remarkable fall more carefully."

The miller took up the lantern and raised it to the face of the injured man. His forehead was bloody, his cheeks badly bruised, there was a gash across his chin, while his eyes were so terribly swollen that they seemed to be bursting from their sockets. Thus disfigured, the face of the wounded man was frightful to look upon, and yet he had a kindly frank expression. "Come," said Mérindol, after examining him carefully, "I am sure now that your accident will have no serious consequences, and I see, with pleasure, that you have not a convict's face by any means. What was your trouble?"

"Forgery," said Mongeorge, huskily.

"The deuce! But it seems to me that the law does not usually punish forgery by hard labour for life."

"I was a notary, and I was accused of forging a will."

"You were unjustly accused, perhaps?" The fugitive hung his head and made no reply. "You are guilty, then?" inquired Mérindol, frowning.

"Yes, sir."

"It is better to admit it than to tell a falsehood."

"I was guilty, but if you only knew the strange circumstances that led me to commit such a crime; if you only knew my motive. I wished to repair an act of shameful injustice."

"Take care," interrupted Mérindol; "you will spoil all the good effect of your frankness. I am not your judge, but a man who thinks that all transgressions may be expiated, and who believes in your repentance. I have helped you out of a nasty predicament, and as I am naturally stubborn, I intend to save you altogether. This good man here will see to it out of regard for me. You will remain here until this evening—no one will think of looking for you here —and then you will go off with Piganiou, who will take you to his mill, a couple of leagues from here. There he will furnish you with a suitable disguise, and in a few days we shall find a way to get you safely out of France."

"Oh, sir, how can I ever prove my gratitude to you?"

"Very easily. You have only to earn an honest living. That is all I ask of you, and it certainly is not requiring too much. No oaths!" added Mérindol, checking the fugitive's protestations with a gesture. "Promises are of very little value, and I shall not be with you to see if you keep yours, for it is not likely that we shall ever meet again. So it is agreed. Not another word now respecting your past. But I have no objections to your telling me something more about the scoundrel who treated you so badly—about this Ricœur. He saw me years ago, when I was a child, and he came here often. Piganiou knows him. You say that he meant to come to Mérindol to-night to procure some clothes; and, indeed, he must have carried this project into execution, for on approaching the house we saw a light first on this floor, and afterwards on the one above. The light disappeared at last, and the scoundrel has undoubtedly decamped; but I should like to know what he has taken with him. Light me upstairs, Piganiou."

The miller, lantern in hand, preceded his young master up a winding staircase, and Mongeorge watched them go off with evident anxiety, for he feared that Ricœur would spring upon him from some hiding place and despatch him. An exclamation from the floor above soon turned his thoughts into another channel, however. "Ah! the scoundrel has taken the portraits!" cried Piganiou.

It was the truth. The portraits of the admiral and the briga-dier-general had both disappeared, but the empty frames were there. Mérindol was fairly stupefied. "Yes," he murmured at last, "the canvas has been cut out with some sharp instrument— probably with this razor—left here on the table. It must have been Ricœur who did it. But what on earth can he want with my family portraits?"

"Perhaps he intends to sell them," replied Piganiou.

"No one would buy them of him. No bric-à-brac dealer would give him fifteen francs for the smoky old pictures. The man must be mad."

"Not so mad, I think, as other articles seem to be missing. See the clothes which were hanging on the pegs there have gone."

"Yes; a shooting-suit of bottle-green velvet and a grey felt hat are missing. If Ricœur intends to travel in that costume he will not go far. Every one will take him for a brigand, and they will be right."

"Oh! he has money enough to purchase a new outfit in the first town he comes to."

"But all this does not explain why he took the portraits."

"Good heavens! that isn't all," exclaimed Piganiou. "Look, Monsieur Louis; he has broken open the escritoire."

Mérindol turned hastily, and perceived that the dilapidated article of furniture referred to had been literally hacked to pieces. The hatchet which had been used for the purpose was still lying on the floor beside it. "Oh, ho!" said the young man, "the rascal has appropriated my deeds and papers. He seems to be a collector of portraits and parchments. Perhaps he hoped to find something besides old paper though?"

"No, Monsieur Louis, he knew very well that there was no money here. The scoundrel wishes to pass himself off for you."

"He can't do that. In the first place, he must be fifteen or twenty years older than myself."

"That makes no difference. He does not intend to remain in France. He will go to some foreign country where you are not known, declare that he is the Marquis de Mérindol, and no one will be able to contradict him. He will take advantage of your name to commit new crimes.

"An agreeable prospect, truly! But what can I do to prevent it?"

"Why, we will go to Fréjus. The grey mare is tired, but she will go all the same when she has had a good feed. You can ride her. I will walk. I would willingly tramp forty miles to capture Ricœur. At Fréjus we will inform the gendarmes; the stationmaster will telegraph in every direction, and the scoundrel will soon be caught."

"Very good! But how about the other man? I told him that I would save him, and I cannot deliver him up."

"Then let him go wherever he likes. Besides, Monsieur Louis, you can't save this fellow, if you denounce his companion. The gendarmes have, of course, been warned of the escape of two convicts. If they capture one, they will want the other."

"I know it, and for that very reason, I have decided to denounce neither of them."

"Then you are willing that Ricœur should dishonour your name?"

"I don't think he will succeed in doing so. If he decides to remain in France, he won't be mistaken for a Mérindol. In the first place, I am very well known, and secondly, Ricœur couldn't pass himself off for a gentleman. If he thinks of operating in foreign parts, I can afford to laugh at him. He may swindle the inhabitants of the Argentine Republic, or marry a Chilian heiress by exhibiting the portraits of my ancestors, it matters little to me. I am anxious not to betray a poor devil who relies upon me to save him. Somehow or other, I fancy his crime was attended by extenuating circumstances. I will make him tell me his story presently."

"Well, sir, when he is once out of France, I trust you will do something to prevent Ricœur from using your papers. There mustn't be two Mérindols in the world, a true one and a false one?"

"There will never be but one, for if I ever happen to find the scamp passing himself off for me, I shall have no difficulty in making him surrender a name that does not belong to him; but in the meantime I shall not be a Mérindol. I only possess the six thousand francs I have in my pocket, and this château, which would not fetch a hundred louis, if I tried to sell it. When a man is reduced to such straits, he is no longer a marquis—no longer a Mérindol. There are two courses for me to pursue: either to blow out my brains, which would be an act of cowardice, or to endeavour to retrieve my fortunes by honest work, which I have determined to do. I am about to begin a new life. I have told the few friends I still possess of my speedy departure for New Zealand, they will soon forget me, and will never expect to see me again. They are right; Louis de Mérindol is dead, but Louis Bertin, the mining engineer, has just begun life, and will find some employment in England."

"You intend to leave your country and change your name? Ah, Monsieur Louis, if I need only sell my mill to save you from that—"

"Thanks, Piganiou; I know that you would give me all you possess, if I asked you for it, and I shall always be deeply grateful to you

for your devotion ; but my mind is made up. I shall soon be only
a toiler, and I shall not resume my name until I have made a fortune that will enable me to bear it with proper dignity."

"And I shall never more hear from you ? I sha'n't even know
where you are ?"

"Oh, yes ! I will write to you. But on condition, that you tell
nobody what has become of me. I wish people to suppose me dead.
Do not be alarmed. I have a presentiment that I shall be restored
to life again, and return to my country. Who knows ? Perhaps I
shall bring back money enough to rebuild the château."

"Heaven hear you, Monsieur Louis !" sighed the old servant,
shaking his head. "But all the same, I can't believe that you are
so easily reconciled to the loss of your family relics, especially as
you had just made this long journey for the express purpose of removing them."

"I might have saved myself the trouble," replied Mérindol,
laughing. "This will teach me not to indulge again in such weakness, for it certainly is a weakness to attach so much value to patents
of nobility when one has to renounce one's title and assume a new
name. But we are forgetting the man downstairs. He must be
dying of fear in the dark. I want to hear his confession, and this
evening you must oblige me by taking him to a place of safety. A
good action at the beginning of my new career will bring me good
luck."

When the master and servant returned to the hall below,
they found the convict standing. "So you are on your legs again,
I see," said Mérindol. "Now there will be no difficulty in getting
you safely out of the country. You can rely upon being on the
other side of the frontier to-morrow. But, before I do any more
for you, I must know the story of your life. Tell it me."

"My story," repeated the fugitive, hanging his head. "Ah, do
not ask me to relate that, sir !"

"Why not ?" replied Mérindol. "You just told me that you
were convicted of forgery. You will probably have nothing worse
than that to tell me, and perhaps your explanation will extenuate
your fault. What are you afraid of ? I have certainly shown myself
a lenient judge."

"Too lenient. I am not worthy of your compassion."

"Listen to me," said Mérindol, kindly. "I don't want you to be
sent back to the galleys. I am resolved that you shall have a chance
of becoming a different man. You don't look or talk like a hard-
ened villain, by any means. Whatever you may have to tell me,
I will assist you in making your escape, and perhaps I will do even
more for you. That will depend upon the confession you are about
to make to me. I wish it to be full and complete. Begin—but first
of all sit down and drink a glass of rum."

The convict declined the liquor with a gesture, but sank into an
old arm-chair that stood near by. Mérindol seated himself astride
a stool, and lighted a cigar, while Piganiou perched himself on the

edge of the table, and began to fill his pipe after extinguishing his lantern. The dawn was breaking, and all was now calm out-of-doors.

" I will tell you all, sir," began the convict, " since you desire it. My name is Jacques Mongeorge, and I am the son of a farmer who gave me a liberal education. He sent me to Paris to study law, afterwards he purchased a notary's practice for me in a small town of the Ardennes. I had lost my mother on coming into the world, and and my father died a year after I began practising. He left me a small estate, which I was obliged to sell to finish paying for my practice, but I managed to live very comfortably on my earnings. I had simple tastes, and liked my profession. But chance brought me misfortune. Near the town where I resided there was a château belonging to the Count de Porcien, an old man who had entirely re-nounced society after seeing a great deal of it. He was wealthy, but was not known to have any relatives ; he had resided in the neighbourhood for ten years or so, receiving no visitors, but he had brought with him a child who could hardly be his daughter, for she was only four years old, while he was over seventy. Her name was Cécile, and this was all that was known about her. When I began practising the child had grown into a charming young girl. She had been educated by an English governess, who accompanied her everywhere, and she never addressed a word to anyone when they went beyond the park, which rarely happened. I scarcely knew her by sight, but one day Monsieur de Porcien sent for me to draw up a lease he wished to renew with one of his farmers. This was the beginning of our intercourse. Subsequently I returned to the château, where at first he only consulted me about business matters, but gradually we began to discuss other subjects, and I soon dis-covered that Monsieur de Porcien was a man of varied and extensive acquirements, refined taste, and lofty ideas. He was a nobleman of the old school, perfected by contact with modern society ; con-sequently I felt both pleased and proud to be invited to play back-gammon with him of an evening."

" Mademoiselle Cécile was present, probably," remarked Mérindol with a smile.

" Yes, sir, and I fully appreciated her manifold charms both of mind and person. But she was a mere child, scarcely fourteen, and the affection I conceived for her was almost paternal, while she, in turn, manifested for me an almost filial love, which seemed even deeper than that which she felt for Monsieur de Porcien, though her manner towards her aged protector was always extremely affectionate and devoted."

" But you must have finally ascertained who she was?" remarked Mérindol, beginning to feel interested in the narrative.

" Never, sir ; and I don't think that she knew herself. The count told me she was an orphan, but that was all he did tell me, and I never ventured to question him on the subject. However, one day, about eighteen months afterwards, he informed me of his intention to bequeath the whole of his fortune to Cécile, and requested me to draw up a rough draft of a will. He wished to make her his sole legatee, with the reserve of a few trifling legacies which he indicated. His health had been severely tried during the winter, and he feared that death was not far off. I took him the draft that he asked for. He read it attentively, made two or three trifling changes, and then began copying it in my presence. I examined this copy carefully, and then pointed out several alterations which seemed to me advisable. He made a note of them, and told me he would give me the next day the duly-attested document, which would insure the transmission of his property to Mademoiselle Cécile. As she was mentioned in the will as the child of unknown parents, I concluded that the count had taken her from some foundling asylum. This idea agreed with several remarks he made in my presence respecting distant connections who were waiting to inherit his belongings. Two days elapsed, and then I was hastily summoned to the count's bedside. He had been taken very ill during the night, and felt that he was dying. Cécile was weeping alone at the bedside. He dismissed her with a gesture, and handed me a paper which he took from under his pillow. 'This is my will,' he faltered, though not without a terrible effort. 'Fortunately, I have had time to recopy the one I wrote in your presence. It is correct in every respect, and I depend upon you to see that my last wishes are carried out. It will perhaps be contested. I have evil-hearted relatives who will never forgive me for disappointing them, but you must protect Cécile's interests, and watch over her ; I entrust her to your care.' He could say no more. His voice failed him, and he gasped for breath. The priest whom Cécile had sent for entered the room. I lacked the courage to witness the death struggle, so I left the house and hastened back to the village. But when I looked at the document the count had handed me, I uttered a cry of despair. The count had made a terrible mistake. He had given me his rough copy, which, being neither dated nor signed, was of no value whatever."

"That was a fatality," exclaimed Mérindol. "What! had the count mistaken one paper for the other ?"

"Yes, sir," Mongeorge sadly answered. "I realised the consequences of this unfortunate mistake, but I flattered myself that it was not irreparable. I hastened back to the château, in hopes Monsieur de Porcien might still be alive, but, on arriving there, I learned that he had just breathed his last. I said to myself that the count had made a mistake in giving me this paper, but that the real will must be in existence—that it would be found under his pillow. But that same evening I learned that there were no grounds for this hope. The priest, whom I questioned, assured me that Monsieur de Porcien had left nothing in writing, and it seemed as if the deceased had burnt the real will, thinking that he was destroying the scrawl he afterwards gave to me. The next day the count's valet came to inform me that two of Monsieur de Porcien's cousins had arrived from Paris. It was impossible to say who had informed them of their relative's sudden death, but they had already taken possession of the château, and their first act had been to drive away the poor child whom the count had protected and cherished for so many years. Cécile was homeless and starving. Her governess had deserted her. She did not know where to go, and the valet, who was a kind-hearted fellow, had advised her to take refuge with me. He informed me that he would bring her to my house in an hour if I would consent to receive her."

"You did not refuse, I trust?"

"No," replied the poor fugitive, with a grateful glance at Mérindol, "no, I did not refuse. I knew that I should compromise myself, that slander would not spare me; but that made no difference. The house in which I lived was separated by a small garden from a pavilion, which I had furnished for the use of a friend who often spent his vacations with me. There I installed Cécile, who scarcely thanked me, so greatly was she overwhelmed by her grief. What should I do with this child? I could not think of marrying her. I did not love her in that sense, and yet I knew that her age would authorise the most malevolent suspicions. I shut myself up in my house to reflect. Under my very eyes there was the fatal paper, which needed only a date and signature to insure Cécile's happiness. I read it over and over again, cursing the mistake that had defrauded the orphan; and the more I examined the document, the more certain I became that only the stroke of a pen was necessary to make it valid. And I said to myself, that if I added the date and signature, I should repair an injustice, fulfil the last wishes of the Count de Porcien, and prevent this fortune, which he intended for his ward, from falling into the hands of relatives he detested. These relatives, who had driven Cécile from her home, were rich, while she was penniless. By restoring her the wealth of which a fatal oversight deprived her, I should be taking the part of Providence, which protects the weak. No doubt Providence would pardon me."

At this point, Mongeorge, who had gradually become extremely excited, paused. "Need I tell you the rest?" he asked, lowering his voice.

"You imitated Monsieur de Porcien's signature, then," exclaimed Mérindol.

"It was a very easy task, unfortunately, as I had in my possession several documents to which his name was affixed. I copied his signature below the will, and added the date, trying to imitate the handwriting of the testator."

There came a spell of silence. Mérindol was deeply touched, and even Piganiou seemed affected. The confession had been made so frankly that it was impossible to doubt the convict's sincerity, and to deny that there certainly were extenuating circumstances. "Proceed, sir," said Mérindol, at last.

"I can tell you nothing you have not already guessed," muttered Mongeorge. "I sent the will to the judge of the local court, and perhaps its validity would not have been questioned, if I had not been unpopular in the neighbourhood; but as I lived a retired life I was considered proud. Besides, it was known that the count's ward was in my house, and this gave rise to scandal. Three days did not elapse before I was arrested, at the instigation of the count's legal heirs. I barely tried to defend myself. What could I have said ? No one but Mademoiselle Cécile had seen the count give me the will which he supposed valid: nor had any one heard his recommendations to me. Besides, even had I succeeded in proving that Monsieur de Porcien intended to bequeath his property to the orphan, I should still have been guilty in the eyes of the law, for I had committed forgery. I confessed everything the first time the investigating magistrate examined me, and I was sent before the assizes for trial."

"And the jury found you guilty ? " exclaimed Mérindol.

"Alas, yes, I defended myself very badly, and the judges were prejudiced against a man whom no one supported. The fact that I was a notary, made my crime appear exceptionally grave. Moreover, the poor child for whom I had sacrificed my honour could not testify in my favour, for the grief and excitement she had undergone, had made her seriously ill. Only her written deposition, which no one believed, could be read, and she very narrowly escaped being accused as my accomplice. I was convicted, and sentenced to the highest penalty."

"And what became of the young girl ? "

"I think she is dead, though I am by no means sure. She was taken to a hospital—yes, to a hospital. Monsieur de Porcien's heirs treated her like an *intrigante* who had tried to defraud them of their relative's fortune."

"What were the names of these scamps ? "

"I have forgotten them—willingly forgotten them ; I was afraid I might be tempted to revenge myself, and God bids us pardon our enemies."

As Mongeorge spoke, he seemed transfigured. His eyes met Mérindol's unflinchingly, and his expression so plainly revealed his loyal feelings, that the young marquis took hold of his hand and pressed it. "I am only a convict," murmured the ex-notary.

"But you are going to become an honest man again ; you *are* one already ! " exclaimed Mérindol. "What do you propose doing when you are out of France ? "

"Earn my living honestly, by manual labour, if necessary."

"And you intend to make no attempt to find the girl you spoke of ? "

"I should not succeed ; even if she were still alive, it would be better for her never to see a runaway convict like me."

"But, if I found her, if I sent you news of her ? "

"Would you really do that ? " exclaimed Mongeorge.

"Yes, on conditions that you persevere in your resolution to atone for your fault by leading an exemplary life. I will see that you reach Italy in safety, and before leaving you, I will give you a small sum of money—enough for you to live on until you can find something to do. You must change your name, and write once a month to Piganiou, who will help you to escape this evening, and who will forward your letters to me. I promise to answer them promptly, and to give you any information I can about the orphan. You can give me the necessary particulars this evening when the hour comes for us to separate. In the meantime, you must rest. There is a bed upstairs. You need to recover your strength. Piganiou will show you your room, and bring you something to eat, and a bottle of wine. You can sleep at your ease. We will wake you up when it is time to start."

"How kind you are!" faltered Mongeorge, "how can I ever repay you?"

"By leading an honest life as I said to you before," interrupted Mérindol. "Now go."

The poor fellow did not venture to say any more, but followed Piganiou who now willingly guided him, for the story of this man who had become a criminal from very kindness of heart, had touched the old miller, though his was by no means a susceptible nature.

While the other two were ascending the staircase together, Mérindol opened a door which led to a broad terrace. "The other fellow must have escaped this way," he said to himself. "He is probably a long way off by this time, and I hope that I shall never meet him. The air of Paris is not likely to agree with him, and he will go elsewhere to be hanged; but even if he should take it into his head to return to his former haunts, he will not recognize the son of the man he once robbed, for Louis de Mérindol has ceased to exist. There is only Louis Bertin left."

## II

THE plain which stretches to the north of Paris is peculiarly unattractive. Here and there rise some dirty old buildings, while on all sides factory chimneys project upward towards the smoky sky. Near St. Ouen the scenery is less barren owing to the close proximity of the Siene, the banks of which are lined with factories, and workshops flanked by dwelling houses, standing in gardens where the foliage is of a dusty green. These abodes have been called into being by the fancies of rich manufacturers who find it both convenient and pleasant to imagine that they are enjoying the pleasures of country life while attending to their business.

Some three years after Louis de Mérindol's last visit to his ancestral manor, the largest and most imposing of these residences was unquestionably that occupied by M. Nalot, a metallurgist, who dealt mainly in brazier's ware and ironmongery. It had been erected for the express accommodation of his wife and daughter, who no doubt cared very little for society, for they seldom left their villa, where he himself spent three days of the week; during the rest of his time he was detained in Paris by business. He discounted bills promoted companions, and everything he undertook seemed to succeed wonderfully well. He was a man of about fifty, tall, and powerfully built, with a pleasant face. His manners were agreeable; he talked well, and though he exhibited great firmness when occasion required, he was very amiable in every-day life. All those he dealt with spoke of him in the highest terms, and his numerous workmen adored him.

Madame Nalot was at least twenty years younger than her husband, and still very handsome. She led a very secluded life, and had the reputation of being very kind-hearted and charitable, and though M. Nalot paid much more attention to his business than to her, she conducted herself in an irreproachable manner. Her tastes were elegant, but she was not coquettish, and seemed to like the solitude in which she lived, her visits to Paris being extremely rare, while at St. Ouen she had no society whatever. In summer time she took long drives about the surrounding country, and in the winter she devoted a deal of time to music, possessing great skill as a pianist, and a very pretty voice. These were the only diversions that Mademoiselle Gabrielle, M. Nalot's daughter by a former marriage, usually enjoyed with her step-mother, who treated her as if she were her own child.

However, this pleasant, if monotonous, existence had undergone a slight change within the last six months. A young engineer had assumed direction of the factory early in the winter. He had just spent two years in England, where he had attracted notice by the skill he had displayed in working an iron mine in Wales, belonging to one of M. Nalot's business acquaintances. The latter had praised the young engineer so highly, that the manufacturer of St. Ouen had thought it well worth his while to secure his services. He had made M. Louis Bertin a liberal offer, and the latter had certainly had no cause to regret his return to France. His new position was above his hopes, and M. Nalot held him in high esteem, as he proved by admitting him to his family circle. As Louis was an excellent musician, his employer's wife and daughter became fond of his society. A capital conversationalist, moreover, a first-rate amateur artist, and a good rider, he had every quality likely to please two women living in retirement. M. Nalot seemed to approve of the intimate footing upon which his valuable assistant was received in the family, and he himself remained oftener than formerly to spend his evenings at the villa, for he greatly enjoyed the conversation of the young engineer, who seemed to be well informed upon almost every topic.

And yet M. Louis Bertin had, as Louis de Mérindol, been an idle, reckless waif. When the awakening came, when he had squandered the last remnant of the ancestral fortune, an old college chum, who had remained his friend in adversity, had recommended him to an English mining company under the name of Louis Bertin. He had wished to begin his new life out of France. He wanted to be forgotten, and he had succeeded beyond his hopes. Paris is a city where ruined men soon pass from mind, and in six months Mérindol's whilom companions had ceased to remember his existence. Moreover, he had never sojourned there for any length of time. He was oftener met at Homburg, Baden, or Florence, than on the Boulevard des Italiens. Moreover, his fortune, though he spent it royally while it lasted, had been too small to enable him to hold a prominent place in what is called high life. He had ruined himself quietly ; his downfall had not been one of those that create a sensation, and so, after two and a half years' exile, he had concluded that he could return to Paris without fear of past memories. Moreover, St. Ouen is not exactly Paris, and Louis mentally resolved to visit the city but seldom. This wise resolve cost him little, as he had acquired a genuine love for his profession, without losing aught of his natural refinement, rough as his duties seemed to be. It appeared, moreover, as if, in renouncing his idle and luxurious life, he had renewed his youth. So he was not long in the society of a charming girl like Gabrielle Nalot without falling in love with her. But he was too proud to allow any one to detect his feelings, and though six months had elapsed since he had entered upon his new duties, nobody suspected the truth.

The time had passed by very rapidly since Louis Bertin had taken possession of the first floor of a pavilion which rose at the end of M. Nalot's grounds. It was an evening early in May, the air was mild and balmy, and Louis, after a hard day's work, had gone to stroll in the garden. He often met his employer's wife and daughter there. Madame Nalot was fond of reading English novels under the leafy branches, and Gabrielle came there to gather flowers. That evening, Louis strolled on smoking a cigar and reflecting over the strange vicissitudes of his life. Memories of the past crowded upon his mind, and he especially remembered his last visit to Mérindol, and the singular adventure which had marked it. He could still hear Piganiou's expostulations, and see the convict lying unconscious at the bottom of the Bat's Hole, the light shining from the window of the deserted manor, and the empty picture frames in the room which the thief had pillaged. He thought of all the actors in this scene which had occurred three years before. Piganiou was still residing at his mill. His business had prospered, and he still wrote frequently to Louis. But for nearly a year the latter had heard nothing of the unfortunate man he had saved. Guided by Piganiou, Mongeorge had reached Italian territory, where he was fortunate enough to obtain employment of a Genoese merchant, who made no inquiries as to his antecedents. At first the ex-convict had kept up a constant correspondence with his benefactor. His letters were most touching, and he solemnly promised to persevere in his honest endeavours. If he seemed to recollect the past, it was only as far as it was connected with the inquiries his generous protector had volunteered to make for him. Louis had not forgotten his spontaneous promise. On the contrary, before his departure for England, he made a trip to the department of the Ardennes, for the express purpose of obtaining some information concerning the Count de Porcien's unfortunate ward. The story as told him by the country folks was very unfavourable to Mongeorge : every one suspecting that he had desired to enrich the orphan girl and marry her afterwards. However, Louis persisted in believing that the fugitive had told him the truth when he asserted that he had been led astray by a feeling of unwise generosity. The young marquis did not succeed in learning the fate of the friendless orphan. He only heard that she had not died at the hospital, but that as soon as she had recovered, she had left the neighbourhood ; no one could tell him what had become of her although the general impression was that she had taken refuge in Paris. There were even persons who pretended having seen her driving through the Champs Elysées, in a handsome carriage, and who asserted she was leading a gay life. Mérindol had not the heart to repeat this gossip to Mongeorge, so he confined himself to informing him of Cécile's disappearance, and advising him to think no more about her.

The Count de Porcien's château in the Ardennes had been sold, and the heirs had returned to Paris. The governess, too, had gone back to England, and as for the unfortunate notary who had left neither friends nor relatives behind him, many people supposed that he had died at Toulon, or had been sent to New Caledonia, which had just been made a penal colony.

Morgeorge's reply was resigned in language, and everything seemed to indicate that he now only thought of establishing himself comfortably in his foreign home. Gradually his letters became less and less frequent, and finally they ceased altogether. Mérindol then began to think that the former convict was dead ; and, finally, he almost forgot him. As for Ricœur, the scamp who had stolen his papers and family portraits, he had probably gone to seek his fortune beyond the seas, for nothing had since been heard of him ; and one might hope that he had met with the fate he so richly deserved.

As these memories recurred to the young man's mind, while he wandered about the garden, the past seemed to him more than ever like a dream, and not a very pleasant one, so he was trying to bring his thoughts back to the present, when, at a turn in the path, he found himself face to face with Madame Nalot. He was about to throw away his cigar, but she exclaimed, laughing : " No, no ; I will not deprive you of a pleasure. Pray, finish your cigar. I wish it were allowable for me to smoke as well."

" Do you really mean it ? "

" Yes, I confess that I regret the prejudice that forbids us such an innocent recreation. You men have all the privileges, and it is particularly unjust in this case, for if I am not very much mistaken, smoking and dreaming go remarkably well together, and we are much more inclined to indulge in reveries than your sex is."

" Do you think so ? " said the young fellow, smiling.

" You must admit that if I did not like a quiet life, I should be terribly bored here."

" I cannot disparage what I myself am fond of. I have never been so happy as since I have been here."

" Is that intended as a compliment ? " asked Madame Nalot, with a searching glance of her large black eyes.

" I only said what I thought," stammered Louis. " Both you and Mademoiselle Nalot have treated me as one would treat a friend, and scarcely a day passes in which you do not kindly allow me to see you."

" That is certainly a compliment, but I suspect that you would much rather live in Paris than spend all your time on the quiet banks of the Seine."

" You are mistaken, I assure you ; and if Monsieur Nalot offered me a position in his Paris establishment, I should beg of him to leave me here."

" Your tastes are rural ones, I see. Have you never had any others ? "

" Yes, I have ; but one changes as one grows older."

" Why, you are but thirty, while my husband is fifty, and he is in no way partial to country life."

"Monsieur Nalot has an absorbing passion for business."

"A passion I should not advise you to cultivate ; we women can't understand it. We live only to love."

"Do you think that men never love ?"

"You say that as if you were in love, yourself."

This remark, which seemed very like a question, took Louis de Mérindol by surprise. Madame Nalot was usually reserved, and he was thunderstruck that she should question him point-blank about his private feelings. On the other hand he had noted how her eyes sparkled at times, how deep flushes spread over her creamy cheeks, and how her expression changed as if with constrained excitement. Her language and manner were refined ; she seemed to accept uncomplainingly the secluded existence that her husband imposed upon her ; and yet, Mérindol somehow fancied she had a spirit of rebellion that was only waiting for an opportunity to burst forth. He knew nothing about her past ; but he had often wondered what could have induced her to marry a rather vulgar man, who was by no means attentive to her despite her beauty. If Louis had been at all conceited, he might have flattered himself that Madame Nalot was making advances to him. When a pretty woman asks a young man if he is in love, he certainly has a right to reply with a declaration. But this idea did not occur to Louis, who was trying to devise some escape from his embarrassing position.

"In love !" he exclaimed, gaily. "I thought I was once, and perhaps I was ; but I am quite sure that such is not the case with me now."

"So you have no idea of marrying ?" persisted Madame Nalot.

"How foolish it would be if I had ! No one would have me."

"How do you know ?" The words were accompanied by a glance which furnished the young engineer with abundant food for reflection.

"Oh, ho !" he said to himself, "what can be her aim ? She evidently does not refer to herself, as she is already married. Does she intend to make me confess that I am in love with her step-daughter ?" Thereupon he added aloud : "We live in an age, madame, when one cannot marry without money, and I have none."

"But you have something better than wealth : youth, intelligence, and energy. With such attributes a man is always rich. You might leave my husband to-morrow without the slightest risk. Did you not secure an excellent situation in Wales ? You could do still better in America, if you chose to exile yourself as you did before."

"Perhaps so ; but now I am anxious to remain in France."

"I only mentioned America because I was born in South Carolina."

"Indeed ! I was not aware that Monsieur Nalot had ever resided in the United States."

"He ! he never crossed the French frontier in his life. It was in Paris that I met him. My mother brought me to Europe when she became a widow, six years ago. I had the misfortune to lose her shortly afterwards, and finding myself alone in the world, I married for motives of—reason."

Mérindol bowed without replying. He did not know exactly what to say, and he thought it better to be silent than to run any risk.

"I feel a little tired," resumed the charming creole. "Will you sit down for a moment in the conservatory? I am in the habit of taking refuge there in the evening when I find the air a little cool."

"I have spent many very delightful hours there," said Mérindol, who had been received in the conservatory by Madame and Mademoiselle Nalot only the evening before.

"You will not enjoy yourself so much this evening, for Gabrielle is not coming. She has not felt as well as usual to-day. Oh! it is a mere trifle," said the step-mother, as she entered the conservatory. "Hers is a very nervous temperament, and the slightest thing gives her the headache. Come, let us sit down near the azaleas."

The conservatory was furnished with divans which made it a comfortable spot for conversation, and Madame Nalot having motioned Louis to a seat opposite her, exclaimed without any further preliminaries: "What do you think of Gabrielle?"

The young man started at this unexpected question, and stammered out a few complimentary words. "Why are you so embarrassed?" inquired Madame Nalot. "Is it because you are not indifferent to the dear girl's charms?"

This was rather too much for Louis, who was not inclined to betray his secret. "You cannot suppose that, madame," he replied coldly. "I fully appreciate Mademoiselle Nalot's merits, but I do not dream of impossible happiness. She is rich, I am poor; and I have just told you my ideas on the subject of marriage."

"They are not mine, as I told you before. But if my step-daughter had no fortune, would you think of marrying her?"

"You must admit, madame, that you are asking me a question to which it is very difficult for me to reply. I have never asked myself what I should do in such a case. One does not make plans on a mere supposition."

"So you have never thought seriously of Gabrielle?"

"Never," replied Louis.

Madame Nalot blushed, and the young man failed to understand why. "You are right," she said, after a short pause; "marriage is a very stupid invention. Real happiness lies in independence, and I don't understand how a young man can consent to relinquish his liberty—especially at your age. I every day regret having relinquished mine." A reply to this last remark would have been too embarrassing, so Louis maintained a prudent silence. "However," resumed Madame Nalot with an easy air, "I am not in question, and I beg your pardon for having questioned you as to your private feelings. To atone for my indiscretion, I am going to be perfectly frank with you. I fancied I saw in you an inclination to cultivate the society of a certain young lady. You were so assiduous in your efforts to divert our solitude this past winter, that I somehow fancied that you were in love with my step-daughter."

"I certainly have done nothing to justify such a supposition," interposed Mérindol, quickly.

"Certainly not. It was mere conjecture on my part. We women see love everywhere. But I am very glad to find that I was mistaken, as I like you very much, and should be sorry to tell you anything that would make you unhappy, for if you loved Gabrielle you would be sorely grieved to learn that her father has certain designs in regard to her—"

"I naturally supposed she would marry."

"Yes ; you know perfectly well that a girl is not likely to began old maid when she is pretty and has a father worth several millions ; but you are probably not aware that my husband has already promised the dear child's hand."

"What ! she is about—"

"To marry a gentleman selected by Monsieur Nalot. It is decided. But how pale you are, what is the matter with you ?"

"Nothing, madame. I—"

"Ah !" exclaimed Madame Nalot, springing to her feet, "I knew that you loved her. Do not try to deny it ; your pallor betrays you."

Madame Nalot was even paler than Louis, however. She crumpled the lace of her dress in her clinched hand, and her eyes flashed fire. She looked superb. Louis would have admired her had he himself been less troubled in mind. Why had she dealt him this blow ? He began to divine the truth and it overwhelmed him with consternation. He expected she would give full vent to her feelings for she seemed to have lost all self-control. But he did not know her yet. She became calm as quickly as she had become excited. A smile parted her lips, and she said quietly : "Forgive me, my dear sir. I only wished to try you—a whim which suddenly occurred to me. See what idleness leads to. One desires diversion, and one grieves a friend."

"Do I indeed look grieved ?" inquired Mérindol. "I am surprised, perhaps, but why should the announcement of Mademoiselle Nalot's marriage affect me ?"

"Why, indeed ?" replied Madame Nalot laughing. "You assured me that you did not care for her, and you would not tell an untruth. But don't be angry with me. It is true there has been some talk of finding a husband for my step-daughter, but nothing is settled. I think there is one person who would have some chance if he pleased Gabrielle, but I doubt his success, although he is rich and of good standing. He is rather too old for her, however, as M. Nalot himself admits. So the matter is by no means settled. The fact that he he has not yet been introduced to me is proof of this.

But I don't know why I dwell so long upon a subject that interests you so little. Let us return to the garden and talk of something else."

She rose to leave the conservatory. Mérindol followed her, trying to invent some excuse for taking leave of her, for he longed to be alone to reflect upon the singular conversation which had just taken place. Madame Nalot however seemed bent upon keeping up the talk, and she was again reverting to love-matters when Mademoiselle Gabrielle was seen approaching. The young girl blushed deeply on catching sight of Louis. "Come and let me scold you, my dear," cried Madame Nalot. "I begged you to come down to the garden with me, and here you have kept me waiting more than an hour. Fortunately Monsieur Bertin has been charitable enough to keep me company."

"I beg your pardon," murmured Gabrielle, "but I sat down to the piano to look over the score of the 'Magic Flute' that we received this morning, and the time passed so quickly—"

"Gabrielle, my child, take care. I am afraid that Mozart's music will turn your head. I believe you like it better than anything in the world."

"I like flowers, too," said the girl, glancing at Mérindol.

"Heliotrope especially," replied Madame Nalot. "You have a bunch of it in your bosom and another in your hair, and you show your good taste. The perfume is delicious. But where did you get it? There isn't enough here to make a presentable bouquet."

"These came from St. Denis, I believe," replied Gabrielle, rather embarrassed.

"Oh, I am not reproaching you. Only when you send for them again get some for me. I like everything you like, my dear. You know, too, that your father is fond of seeing us dressed alike. When he brings us bouquets he always procures two similar ones. And by-the-way, speaking of your father, have you seen him? He told me that he would be here to-day."

"He returned a little while ago and went into the factory, so his valet told me ; I don't think he will remain here this evening, for the brougham is still waiting for him."

"Ah," said Madame Nalot, in a tone which indicated that her husband's frequent absences affected her but little.

Louis thought this a good opportunity to make his escape. "Monsieur Nalot must have some directions to give me before he returns to Paris, and if you will excuse me I will go to him," he remarked.

"I will allow you to do so on condition you return," replied Madame Nalot. "And, to be more sure of it, we will accompany you to the factory. What do you say, Gabrielle?"

"I think it will be a delightful walk," said the girl, looking down. She was evidently divided between a desire to detain the young engineer and some other sentiment which Louis could not fathom.

The factory was not far from the house, being reached part-way by following the path which skirted the Seine and then by crossing some waste land which extended to the road to St. Denis. The main entrance faced that highway. However it was written that Louis, Gabrielle and Madame Nalot, should not take their proposed stroll together. They had just reached the garden gate when they found themselves face to face with the manufacturer, who had apparently come from the factory on foot.

" We were just going in search of you," said his wife.

" Have you anything especial to say to me ?" he inquired, without even shaking hands with his wife or daughter.

Although Mérindol was accustomed to his employer's manner, he was struck by the coldness with which he greeted these two attractive women who were bound to him by the closest of ties. " Nothing," replied Madame Nalot, drily. " It is a lovely evening, and we thought we should enjoy a short walk. The garden is delightful, of course, but I know it by heart, and thought I should like a little variety in my promenade."

" You are right, my dear Marie, and I am perfectly willing you should go as far as you please with Gabrielle ; but this evening you must dispense with your escort, for I wish to speak to Monsieur Bertin on important matters, and must detain him."

" Very well, we will go alone then," replied the manufacturer's wife, " we are accustomed to it."

She passed by her husband without even honouring him with a glance. Gabrielle followed her, though she perhaps felt no desire to do so, and Louis was left with M. Nalot, who said to him, " I want to talk with you, my dear fellow. Come with me to the end of the garden."

Mérindol, rather surprised, followed him without a word.

When they reached a path where no one could see or hear them, the manufacturer suddenly paused, and said, with an easy air : " Would you object to marry ?"

Mérindol did not lack coolness and presence of mind, but his employer's question was so unexpected that it disconcerted him.

" Marry ! I have never thought of it," he stammered.

" I can understand that," said M. Nalot. " You are young, you have plenty of time to think of it, and you probably fancy that you can marry more advantageously when you have made a fortune. That is the reasoning of a sensible man."

" I do not deserve your praise, as I have **never** reasoned on the subject."

" Then you have made no plans, and have contracted no engagement ?"

" No, sir."

" I don't ask you this, my dear Bertin, from any desire to meddle with your private affairs, but in case you are free, I should like to know if you would feel inclined to marry a young lady handsomely dowered both by nature and her parents."

" Yes, certainly ; if she pleased me.'

"That assurance satisfies me, for I am certain that the young lady I refer to could not fail to please you. The time for a positive proposal has not yet arrived, however, so now that I know your views, let us give our attention to more pressing matters."

Mérindol bowed without replying. He hardly knew what to say, for surprises had followed one another with startling rapidity that evening. "One could swear that the husband and wife had both agreed to broach the subject of marriage to me," he said to himself. "What can they be after? It is not at all likely that they intend to throw their daughter into my arms, and yet the wife, who spoke more plainly than her husband, mentioned Gabrielle's name."

"My dear fellow," resumed the manufacturer, "our connection is not of very long standing, but I have had plenty of time to appreciate your worth, and I trust that we shall not separate. I charge myself with your future, which will be a brilliant one."

"I am very well satisfied with my position, sir; I am not ambitious."

"That is a mistake. All men of ability ought to be ambitious. It is the only way to succeed. I want you to be able to take my place one of these days. I am engaged in several enterprises, though until now you have only been acquainted with one of them—the least important of all."

"But the only one in which I can be of any real assistance to you. I am an engineer; nothing more."

"You are too modest. When a man can manage a large factory as you do, he is competent to do anything. It is not more difficult to manage a banking-house or conduct a stock exchange speculation."

"Excuse me, sir, but I know my abilities, and I assure you that I was not born to make a fortune in business. I managed my own affairs very badly; and I should not like to undertake to manage the affairs of others—"

"You mean that you squandered your own fortune. What does that prove? That you have to make another, and that you will certainly succeed in doing so. Economy is a very doubtful virtue, and an intelligent spendthrift has a better chance of making a position than a fool who contents himself with his income. Come, you must let me initiate you into my financial enterprises before making you a partner in them."

"If my services can really be useful to you, I will not refuse them, but I doubt their utility."

"This is the point in question. I have established near the Central Markets in Paris, a very prosperous concern. I deal in metals there, and do a good deal of bill discounting. Personally, I am too busy with large financial speculations to manage this establishment myself, so I have entrusted it to a very capable and honest man. But he is getting old, he is anxious to retire, and I am looking for some one to take his place. Now, I think you are the right man."

"On the contrary, I know nothing about commercial matters, nothing about bill discounting."

" You will have nothing to do with the discounting—that is in charge of a subordinate ; but your studies on metallurgy has taught you all that is necessary for you to know to buy and sell metals. You are most competent in such a matter.  On all questions of detail, old Dolizy, whom you will supersede, will give you information. At present everything here is so well organized, thanks to you, that the factory can dispense with your presence."

" What ! you intend to send me——? "

" To Paris, but only temporarily, to serve a sort of apprenticeship, which will be a stepping-stone to the future I dream of for you. You will remain nominally with the position you now hold, and you will resume your duties here as soon as you have completed your business education, or whenever you please ; for, if the experiment I propose proves distasteful to you, I won't insist upon your pursuing it.   Under such conditions, I trust you will not refuse to make the experiment."

" I should not like to disoblige you, sir, so if you insist—"

" Yes, I do insist, and on your own account.   Take my advice, Bertin.   Wealth will be the result of this experiment—wealth and happiness.   I spoke to you of marriage a moment ago ; I had my reasons for it. "

Mérindol blushed.   M. Nalot's meaning seemed sufficiently plain. What marriage could he allude to if not to one which would gratify the young engineer's dearest wishes ?

" I don't send you into exile, remember," added M. Nalot.   " The ladies would never forgive me for depriving them of your society. Paris is not far off, and you can come to St. Ouen every evening, if you like.   The matter is decided, is it not ?   You consent ?"

" Yes, and I am very grateful for the interest you take in me," replied Mérindol.   " When am I to enter upon my new duties ?"

" To-morrow, I will introduce you to Dolizy, and will personally install you in your new position, as well as in the suite of rooms intended for your use in Paris.   Of course your old quarters here will remain at your disposal, but you need not trouble about the factory. Corraille understands how it is managed, and he can superintend it for a time."

" Corraille, the overseer you engaged last month ?"

" Yes.   He is a rather surly-looking fellow, but he is energetic and industrious, and understands his business, as he proved in California."

" I have not yet had an opportunity of testing his ability, but he does not inspire me with much confidence."

" Indeed ?   What have you to reproach him with ? "

" Oh ! nothing—but he has a bad look, and suspicious manners. He often disappears suddenly, especially during night work, and the other workmen seem to have taken a strong dislike to him."

" Because he is strict with them, no doubt.   However, Corraille was recommended to me by a person whom I highly esteem, so don't be uneasy, my dear fellow. All will go well in your absence, and on your return, everything will go still better."

Mérindol interpreted these last words in a sense favourable to his fondest hopes, and his face brightened. "I shall be quite at your service to-morrow, sir," he answered.

"To-morrow !" repeated M. Nalot. "Now I think of it, I must return to Paris this evening, and I should like to install you in your new quarters as soon as possible. Suppose I take you with me ? My brougham is waiting for me, and I will drive you to our Paris establishment. You need not sleep there unless you like, providing you will meet me there early to-morrow morning."

"As you please, sir ; I think the ladies expected me to join them this evening but—"

"They must do without you for this once, my dear fellow. You can see them again to-morrow. Let us start."

Mérindol followed M. Nalot to the brougham. It was no slight sacrifice for him to leave St. Ouen so abruptly ; but he carried flattering hopes away with him, and he contented himself with glancing as he passed along at a window decked with clematis, on the second floor of his employer's house. It was the window of Mademoiselle Gabrielle's room.

## III

M. NALOT's brougham drawn by a pair of fleet horses rolled over the Avenue de St. Ouen, entered Paris, and at the expiration of three quarters of an hour drew up in front of an old building at the corner of the Rue de la Grande-Truanderie and the Rue Mondétour, two antique looking streets which the improvers of the French capital have respected. The building in question had certainly been first erected in the middle ages but it had been repeatedly repaired and partially rebuilt. The walls were six feet thick, the windows were little better than loopholes, and the drains were secured to a battlemented roof, but the entrance plainly dated from the seventeenth century, and the interior arrangements were those of present times. The door flew noiselessly open as if by enchantment, and M. Nalot's carriage, after passing under an archway, paused anew in a large, gas-lighted court-yard. A man in office-livery stepped forward at once to open the door and to assist the occupants of the vehicle in alighting. As Louis set foot on the ground, he glanced hastily around this strange court-yard which strongly resembled that of a prison. Stone walls pierced with windows, bristling with iron bars, rose up on all sides. Piles of metal of every kind were spread upon the pavement—piglead in pyramids, steel rails, sheets of copper and old iron of all descriptions. And they were nothing compared with the stock which the store-houses of the basement must contain.

"You probably did not imagine that we had such a large stock," remarked M. Nalot smiling.

"No, I confess it," muttered Mérindol. "All the copper I receive at St. Ouen is sent by a firm—"

"Dolizy & Co. Dolizy, whose place you will take, is my partner; I have my reasons for not wishing my name to appear. Perhaps the style of the firm will soon be Louis Bertin & Co."

"I do not deserve such an honour."

"You have mentioned your scruples before, but I trust I shall be able to overcome them. Come, and let me show you the rooms I intend for you."

Louis followed his employer up a wide stone staircase, and ahead of them went a tall office attendant who looked as imposing as a beadle. On the first floor one found the offices, the storey above being divided into suites of apartments of different sizes, all of which had apparently been recently furnished. The largest had been reserved for the use of the manager of the establishment, and it did not appear to have ever been occupied, for various needful articles were lacking. There was a superb clock on the mantelshelf, but no curtains at the windows, and no mattresses on the four-post bedstead.

M. Nalot frowned, and asked the servant why the room had not been prepared. The orders had been received too late, so the man replied. "I see that I have disturbed you uselessly, my dear Bertin," said M. Nalot. "It will be impossible for you to sleep here, so you will have to spend the night at a hotel. You would, doubtless, have preferred to remain at the villa, and enjoy Mozart's music, with my wife and daughter : but I should advise you not to return to St. Ouen to-night, as you must be here to-morrow morning at seven o'clock. You will find me in my private room as I shall spend the night here investigating an important buisness matter. Meanwhile you are quite at liberty. I shall not require your assistance this evening."

Mérindol was surprised, but certainly not annoyed, by this change in the programme, for he wished to have time for reflection, so he took leave of M. Nalot without asking for the slightest explanation, though his employer's conduct seemed a little singular. The manufacturer evidently wished to test Mérindol's ability in a new branch of business, and his attentions were most flattering ; but why had he decided to take him from St. Ouen so suddenly, especially when he must have known that the apartments were not yet ready ? All this seemed so incomprehensible to Mérindol that he finally ceased racking his brain to invent an explanation. He had plenty of other matters to think about. After leaving the establishment he wandered aimlessly through the streets, hardly knowing where he was going. He was thinking of the little room where Gabrielle Nalot usually spent her evenings, and where she must, at that very moment, be wondering at his strange disappearance. For he had left the villa without telling anyone where he was going. The servants had not even seen him enter the brougham. "I am half inclined to return to St. Ouen," he said to himself. "It is not yet nine o'clock. By taking a cab I can reach the station in twenty minutes, and I can return to Paris by the last train."

But it occurred to him that the gates of the villa were always closed by ten o'clock, so that it would be necessary to ring the servants up ; besides, if he saw Madame Nalot, she might question him, in which case he would hardly know what to reply. It would be better for him to postpone his visit, and he decided to do so. While musing, he had walked on, and he now found himself on the Quai de la Mégisserie, near the Pont-Neuf. He was asking himself what he should do till bedtime, when he perceived a steamboat approaching the quay, and the idea of going aboard occurred to him ; however, had he foreseen the result of his excursion, he certainly would not have made it. The boat was going down the Seine, making its last trip for the day ; but it would have been all the same had it been ascending the river, for Mérindol left his course entirely to chance, having no other desire than to muse upon his love affairs. For Mérindol was in love—more deeply in love than he was willing to admit—and he was now beginning to see a possibility of eventually marrying the girl he adored. M. Nalot, who never spoke rashly, had just given him an assurance, the meaning of which was sufficiently plain. It is true that he had not mentioned Gabrielle's name, but it was allowable to believe that he had referred to her, and Madame Nalot's language had been most precise. She had doubtless been apprised of her husband's plans, though she did not seem to approve of them. As for Mademoiselle Gabrielle, Louis knew what to think of her sentiments, although no vows had ever been exchanged between them. But her eyes had spoken unmistakably, and Mérindol had virtually made a declaration of love by means of flowers.

He had each night laid upon Gabrielle's window-sill a bouquet of heliotrope, to do which he was obliged to scale the wall of the villa like a cat, with the help of a trellis which M. Nalot had certainly not placed there for that purpose. Each morning the bunch of heliotrope had bloomed on the bosom of Gabrielle, who wore it all day ; and this preference for the fragrant flower had that very evening drawn a sarcastic remark from her stepmother. As Mérindol leaned over the railing of the boat, he said sadly to himself : "To-morrow, she will open her window and find nothing."

Then, to console himself, he reflected that he would soon be able to exonerate himself of any charge of neglect, as he should certainly see her on the morrow. While he was thus reflecting, the little steamer drew near the Pont de la Concorde, and Mérindol decided to land. He did not care to show himself on the boulevards, where he was likely to meet former acquaintances, but he fancied he would not run any risk by ascending the Champs Elysées on the left hand side, where, as a rule, but few people are found, most of the concerts and other places of public resort being situated across the avenue. However, the path he selected was not so deserted as he thought ; and he soon met a number of people bound for an open-air concert, where the orchestra was in full swing. Farther on he met a party emerging from a restaurant, and to crown his ill luck, he finally jostled a group of people gathered on the side walk.

"Why, it's he," said a woman who formed part of the little gathering.

"Impossible. He is in Australia or Kamtchatka," replied a man.

Louis, fearing recognition, was about to cross the avenue, when the woman added : "I am sure of it," and looking the young engineer full in the face, she said, "are you not Monsieur de Mérindol ?"

"Excuse me, madame," stammered Louis. "I have not the honour of your acquaintance."

"You don't know me ? Well, that is good. Must I tell you my

name to refresh your memory ?  Don't you remember Delphine—Delphine de Guibray, formerly of the Gymnase Theatre, and for the time being without an engagement ? "

" Why, Mérindol, is it indeed you ? " exclaimed the actress's escort.  " Where have you come from, my dear fellow ? "

Louis saw that further prevarication would be useless.  An unfortunate chance had brought him face to face with a young actress who had rendered him some slight assistance in spending his fortune, and with one of his former comrades, Jean d'Autry.  They were not alone.  The two gentlemen who had been chatting with them now approached, and two exclamations resounded at the same time, for they also had known Mérindol in the days gone by, and he recognized them at a glance.  Thus he found himself again in the midst of the very associations he was trying to forget, and nothing remained for him but to make the best of the matter.

" Well, yes, it is I," he exclaimed, as gaily as he could.  " How do you do, all of you ?  How are you getting on, my friends ? "

" How goes it with yourself ?  What have you been doing since your disappearance ? " asked Jean d'Autry.

" Oh ! I have been knocking about the world."

" After a position, eh ?  Have you found one ? "

" Not yet, but I'm still searching.  I'm only in Paris for a few days."

" That is no reason for shunning old acquaintances who have often regretted you.  Usually, when a fellow has spent his last penny, people say : ' Another good man gone wrong,' and think no more about him, while you were talked about for six months or so.  Remember that you were always a great favourite with us, and now we have found you again, we shall not let you go.  You must come to Delphine's and take tea with us."

" Impossible !  I leave this evening."

" For California ?  Don't try that dodge with us."

" No, for St. Germain, where a friend has granted me hospitality for a few days."

" Your friend must do without you until to-morrow.  We are going to have a good time of it.  Delphine has invited some friends, and there will be a game of baccarat with a gentleman who never stakes less than fifty thousand francs as banker."

" It is long since I played at baccarat."

" Yes, I understand ; for want of ammunition.  No matter, you can watch the others."

" Thanks ; but I am not yet sufficiently sure of myself to put myself in the way of temptation."

" Oh ! in any case, you will get off with the loss of a few louis, and I will lend you some if you like.  A man always wins when he has gone several years without touching a card.  I should be delighted to see you win five hundred louis from that rascal Porcien who has drained us all dry."

" Porcien ! " repeated Mérindol.  " What ! is the gentleman named Porcien ? "

"Yes," said Jean d'Autry, "this redoubtable player is called Porcien, in fact the Count de Porcien. Do you know him?"

"No, no, not at all," stammered Mérindol. "But it seems to me I have heard the name before."

"It isn't a pretty name, by any means, but the owner of it is worth three or four millions."

"And he is very agreeable, I am sure, whatever d'Autry may say to the contrary," added Delphine. "And, my dear Louis, I should like to introduce him to you. You will come, won't you?"

Mérindol did not say, "Yes," but he was in no haste to say "No." This Count de Porcien must be the cousin and the heir of the old nobleman who had protected that poor orphan, the innocent cause of Mongeorge's ruin. Mérindol had not forgotten the sad story, and he said to himself that the man who had despoiled Cécile might, perhaps, be able to tell him what had become of her.

"It's agreed. We carry you off," said Jean d'Autry. "Delphine's landau is close by; she never comes to dine at the Pavillon d'Armenonville without it; and it will hold us all very comfortably."

"No, I shall crowd you."

"Nonsense! you are as slender as ever. Besides, my dear fellow, I insist in your own interest. Porcien will bring with him to-night one of his friends who has made an immense fortune in America; he owns a silver mine somewhere in the Rocky Mountains, I think. You were an engineer, I believe, once?"

"And I am one still."

"Then you can talk with this gentleman, and he will perhaps offer you a splendid position."

The future Mérindol dreamed of was at St. Ouen, and he had no desire to cross the seas, but a feeling of curiosity impelled him to accept the invitation. He was a trifle superstitious, and he had a presentiment that he would learn something of importance respecting M. de Porcien. There was nothing, moreover, to prevent him from spending the night as he chose, for M. Nalot would not expect to see him before seven o'clock the next morning, and it would be pleasanter to spend the time among old acquaintances than in bed, at a hotel where he would probably not close his eyes. These considerations flitted across his mind, and he came to a decision. "I don't want to be accused of shunning my old friends, so I am at your service," he said.

"That's right!" the others shouted in chorus.

"It is really very kind of you," added Delphine. "I should never have forgiven you for not coming. In ten minutes' time we shall be there. I have the finest trotters in Paris."

The carriage, a superbly appointed equipage, was waiting a short distance off, the party climbed in, and the horses started off in the direction of the Rue de Téhéran, where Delphine, like a popular and well-paid actress, occupied a stylish flat on the first floor. By the time that the house was reached the whole party was in the most exuberant spirits, and shouts of delight arose when the maid answered that several friends of madame's had already arrived. "Monsieur de Porcien, too, is here," added the girl.

"Then I will take the liberty of introducing Mérindol to him, while you change your dress," said Jean.

"That is a good idea," replied Delphine de Guibray. "I sha'n't be long," and she hurried towards her room.

"Am I acquainted with any of the other people?" said Louis to D'Autry.

"No. I think not. Three years work many changes in our circle, as you well know."

"Then I must ask you all not to introduce me under my real name. Mérindol disappeared some years ago, and I don't care for any one to know that he has returned. Besides, this Monsieur de Porcien may have heard of me."

"I think not. He formerly resided in the country, and seldom visited Paris while you were here. But that makes no difference, we will call you whatever you like."

"Any name will do—Bertin, for instance."

"Here goes for Bertin! If your creditors heard of a Monsieur Bertin, they would never suspect it was you."

"I have no creditors; but—"

"You have a reason for maintaining your incognito. I don't ask what it is. But to prevent any blunder, I shall call you Louis." So saying, D'Autry took Mérindol's arm and led him into the drawing-room.

They there found half-a-dozen pretty women of the theatrical profession, but momentarily "on leave," who greeted them with exclamations of delight. The game of baccarat had not yet begun, as the gentleman who was to hold the bank did not appear inclined to waste his time upon members of the fair sex.

This capitalist was leaning against the mantelshelf, and showed no disposition to imitate the ladies, who darted forward to meet the new arrivals. But Mérindol had eyes for him alone; and this was only natural, as his principal motive in accepting Delphine's invitation had been to make M. de Porcien's acquaintance. The count might have been about fifty years of age, though he looked a trifle younger. He was tall and thin. His angular face was clean shaven, and his olive complexion indicated a southern origin, unless indeed he had merely been sunburnt by a prolonged sojourn in tropical climes. His whole appearance was certainly far from pleasing; and Mérindol's feeling on beholding him was one of repulsion.

"He looks like a man capable of obtaining possession of property by fraud, and of driving the rightful owner away," Louis said to himself. "I shouldn't be surprised if he found the will and threw it into the fire."

Mérindol now felt no desire to be brought into intimate relations with this man; but Jean d'Autry led him forward almost perforce, and said: "Permit me, count, to introduce to you one of my particular friends, a distinguished engineer, whom I can warmly recommend to you. If the American millionaire of whom I have heard you speak, needs a manager for his mines, he could not find a more competent person."

"Excuse me," interposed Mérindol, hastily, "but I did not ask you—"

"Ah, so the gentleman is an engineer?" interrupted M. de Porcien, gruffishly. "I am glad to hear it, and it is probable that my friend would be glad to avail himself of his talents. I will speak to him on the matter."

"This evening, eh?"

"No; he won't be here this evening; but I shall see him to-morrow. Your name, sir, if you please?" added the count, addressing Mérindol, who drily replied: "My name is Louis Bertin; but I assure you that I haven't the slightest desire to go to America."

"Louis Bertin!" repeated M. de Porcien. "Oh, I understand that you don't need to cross the seas to secure a situation. You have one already."

"How do you know that?"

"Are you not employed at a manufacturing establishment at St. Ouen?"

"Possibly," stammered Louis, thoroughly disconcerted. "But—"

"You need not blush," said M. de Porcien, looking at him intently. "I know your employer, and he has often spoken to me of you in the most complimentary terms. But I did not expect to meet you here."

"Why not, if you please?"

"Because Monsieur Nalot told me that you were a very steady and industrious young man. These gentlemen lead a fast life, as they have a perfect right to do, as they are rich, while you—"

"But Louis was rich once," exclaimed D'Autry. "He did wrong to run through his fortune so quickly, perhaps; but he certainly has a right to amuse himself for once in a way if he chooses."

"I don't object, I'm sure. I am not Monsieur Nalot's partner."

"You have no right to criticise my actions, sir," said Louis, hotly, "and your remarks are very much out of place."

"Oh, don't get angry, young man. I am not in the habit of concealing what I think; but I had no intention of giving offence."

"Come, Louis, what is the matter with you?" interposed Jean d'Autry. "We came here to enjoy ourselves, not to quarrel. Monsieur de Porcien is going to act as banker. Wait until you have lost some money before you lose your temper."

"You know very well that I don't play."

"That is to say you have given up playing, for there was a time when you did not deprive yourself of the pleasure. You were a very daring and brilliant player in your day."

"What I was is not in question, but I have no business here, and I am going off."

"What! what! you are going?" exclaimed Delphine, who had just entered the drawing-room in evening dress. "You shall do nothing of the kind. I object most decidedly. You promised to stay, and I shall keep you. The Count de Porcien would never forgive me if I let you go off like that."

" I beg you will not take my words seriously, sir," said the count in an entirely different tone. " I thought my age authorised a little freedom on my part ; but if I have wounded you, I sincerely beg your pardon, and I assure you that you will disappoint me very much if you refuse us the pleasure of your company. Madame de Guibray's friends are mine, and when I meet a well-bred man at her house, I am always anxious to retain him."

Mérindol replied to this courteous speech by a rather cold and haughty bow, but he refrained from giving any other sign of displeasure. He recollected that this was an ill-chosen place for any scene, and that his precipitate departure would make him appear ridiculous. It would be better for him to hold his tongue than to supply food for gossip. He meant, moreover, to take time by the forelock, and to acquaint M. Nalot with his adventure the next morning, for he thought it best to speak to his employer about the Count de Porcien, before the latter had an opportunity of seeing the manufacturer. Otherwise, M. Nalot might comment unfavourably on his conduct and his associates. It was almost certain also that M. de Porcien would learn Mérindol's right name sooner or later through Delphine, and it was equally probable that he would then tell M. Nalot that Louis Bertin was really Louis de Mérindol. The latter had no cause to be ashamed of his past life, nor had he any intention of retaining his incognito indefinitely. He realised that it would be necessary to resume his identity some day or other, and since M. Nalot had made him those matrimonial overtures, he had more than once asked himself if the time for revealing the truth had not already arrived.

At this point Delphine de Guibray interrupted his reflections. " Come, my dear fellow," she said, taking his arm, " the table is ready in the smoking-room, and the count is going to give us a nice game of baccarat. You certainly won't insult me by deserting us just as the fun is about to begin."

The count seconded her words by a smile and a gracious gesture, and the whole party wended their way to the smoking-room, where M. de Porcien took a seat at the table with the ease of a man who is in the habit of acting as banker. The others divided into two groups—all the women of the party instinctively congregating on one side, that on which the banker bestows least attention, as the money staked there is usually small in amount. Mérindol also stationed himself there, as he intended to risk merely a few louis ; and he placed himself between the mistress of the house and a pretty woman who would certainly have attracted his attention in days gone by, but whom he now scarcely condescended to notice. The count had produced a bundle of bank notes and two or three rolls of gold, and he was now engaged in opening the packs of cards he intended to use. He did this gravely, almost solemnly, with the care and

F

precision of a Monaco croupier. It was evident that card-playing was a serious matter, not a mere amusement, with him.

Jean d'Autry began the attack with a five hundred franc note, and his pocket-book plainly contained several others. He was a gay fellow of position, whom Mérindol had well known some years before, and he still seemed to have plenty of money. The women unanimously adopted one louis as the amount of their stakes, and Mérindol, who had scarcely a dozen about him, thought it advisable to follow their example. Baccarat is a most uncertain game. Sometimes luck shows itself on one side from the very beginning, sometimes nothing like a "run" is to be had. On this particular evening, however, the group on the right hand side of the banker—the gentlemen—lost persistently, while the ladies, on the contrary, were wonderfully fortunate. In less than a quarter of an hour two players had lost every penny in their pockets. One of those was Jean d'Autry, who staked like a madman, and several others near him were seriously crippled, while a glittering heap of coin had accumulated in front of each of the women. Mérindol had, of course, profited by the good luck of his feminine neighbours, and though he had played on the whole with moderation, he had now and then risked a few bold strokes, which had proved marvellously successful. In fact, he had already won some sixty louis, and everything seemed to indicate that this very respectable sum would be still further increased. However, his success did not elate him in the least. He did not care to lose, of course, but he was by no means anxious to win. He well remembered the time when a card had made his heart throb almost to suffocation, but now his thoughts were elsewhere than in the game. It was a beautiful young girl who had wrought this miracle.

"I'm stumped," exclaimed Jean d'Autry at last. "Can I play upon parole?"

"You? yes," replied M. de Porcien. There was no mistaking the meaning of this answer, which signified, "I am perfectly willing to give credit to Monsieur Jean d'Autry, who is rich enough to pay his debts, but I shall only deal in cash with the other players."

The count was not so much to blame for making this distinction, for there were several persons of doubtful credit present; and yet, this word *you*, addressed to Jean d'Autry in exclusion of the rest of the party, offended Mérindol deeply. Besides, the more he studied M. de Porcien's face and manners, the more he disliked him. He behaved well enough, he expressed himself correctly, and yet there was something artificial about it all. One divined that his elegant manners were acquired, and when he spoke it seemed as if he were reciting a lesson. Mérindol wondered how M. Nalot had happened to make this singular person's acquaintance; and he resolved to ask Delphine de Guibray some questions about him later on.

Meanwhile Jean d'Autry hastily scribbled a number of I O U's of five hundred francs each. M. de Porcien dealt the cards again, and the playing was resumed.　The stakes had increased in amount, the losers trying hard to retrieve their fortunes, and the winners becoming gradually bolder and bolder.　However, the ill luck of the masculine players persisted, and the good luck of the women became still more noticeable.

Jean d'Autry lost two I O U's of five hundred francs each, his neighbours even more ; and while their money helped to swell the pile in front of M. de Porcien, Delphine de Guibray won five louis, and Mérindol ten.　Finally came the utter rout of the players on the right, and a series of triumphs for those seated on the left. When the cards were exhausted, Jean d'Autry and his friends declared they had had enough of it.　The women, delighted with their good fortune, wished to continue ; but the count, probably considering it not worth his while to contend against such opponents, rose from his seat, and glancing at the notes given him by Jean d'Autry, remarked : " You owe me five hundred louis."

Mérindol had won a hundred.　He was glad that the game had come to an end, for gambling had certainly ceased to amuse him. He even resolved to take himself off as soon as possible, having to see M. Nalot early in the morning.　Delphine had just returned to the drawing-room, where the tea, which had served as a pretext for this card-party, was to be served, and thither the other women followed her, chattering like magpies.　Several of the gentlemen were discussing their defeat, as wounded veterans discuss the battles in which they have lost a limb.　Jean d'Autry, the most unlucky of them all, was brooding over his losses, and lighting a cigar to console himself.　."Your evening's amusement certainly cost you dear," Mérindol said to him in a low tone.　" What need had you to come here to play against this Monsieur de Porcien, for whom none of you are a match ? "

" He has such luck.　It's always the same.　I am fourteen thousand francs out of pocket this evening.　I had four thousand with me when I came, and the remaining ten thousand must be paid before noon to-morrow.　Monsieur de Porcien allows no delay."

" I never regretted my poverty so much before," said Louis. " But I was on the winning side this evening, and I made a hundred louis.　Will you take them ? "

" Thanks," replied Jean d'Autry, pressing his friend's hand cordially.　" I see that you are still always ready to oblige your friends. But I sha'n't take advantage of your kindness.　I know where I can raise some money.　A worthy usurer of my acquaintance will lend me what I want at twenty-five per cent. interest."

" I see that you also have not changed.　But as you bear your misfortunes so lightly, I may perhaps venture to inquire who this Count de Porcien is who always come off the winner ? "

" My acquaintance with him is not of long standing," replied Jean, " but I will gladly tell you all I know about him.　About a year ago Delphine, one of your old flames, by-the-way, was in very bad circumstances.　She had been ill ; she had no engagement ;

an execution had been put in; her horses were starving in the stables. None of her tradesmen would trust her for a penny; her companions were beginning to cut her, and she was seriously thinking of joining an operetta troupe which was about to start for Cairo."

"That wasn't such a bad idea," muttered Mérindol.

"No; but it is hard to make up one's mind to leave Paris. Delphine was spared this humiliation, however. On the day of the Grand Prix, when people had nearly forgotten all about her, we saw her at Longchamp, covered with diamonds, and prettier and more elegant than ever. Her turn-out, too, was magnificent. The surprise was intense, and there was a crowd round her carriage all day, for everybody wanted to know the origin of this change of fortune. But Delphine is shrewd. She told some of her friends that she had met an Australian nabob who was rolling in the gold of his inexhaustible mines, and who scattered nuggets broadcast. And she informed others that she had just inherited the property of an uncle, as if she had any wealthy uncles! Her father was a doorkeeper, and her mother went out doing housework by the day. People believed what they pleased; but though they watched her closely, no one was ever able to discover the real source of her wealth."

"I did not know she was so prudent. She used to proclaim her affairs everywhere."

"That is true; but some women are capable of anything, even of keeping a secret. At all events, early this winter, she began to give teas twice a week, entertaining the old set, and later on she invited several wealthy foreigners. Men liked to go to her house because they enjoyed themselves there. She gave the most delightful little supper parties, and an enjoyable game of baccarat always followed. At last, one fine day, or rather one fine evening, she introduced to us this Count de Porcien who just won my fourteen thousand francs. She introduced him as she would have introduced any other stranger, and as we did not find him a very congenial companion, we gave him rather the cold shoulder. But soon he began to hold banks of ten and twenty thousand francs, and as he had the good sense to begin by losing, we formed a rather better opinion of him. Besides, he was a count, or at least he said he was."

"I should like to see his family parchments. From what part of the country does he come?"

"I have heard him mention an estate he owns in the Ardennes."

"In the Ardennes! it is the same man then!" exclaimed Mérindol.

"Do you know him?"

"No, but I have heard that a Count de Porcien resided in that department. What does this one do in Paris?"

"Nothing that I know of. His principal occupation seems to be card-playing."

"But has he no friends or relatives?"

"Probably he has ; but I know nothing about them."

"That's strange. Does he go about with Delphine ?"

"Never, though he is evidently the source of her prosperity. When he is here, he acts as if he were the master of the house, but when we question Delphine on the subject, she always replies evasively. In fact it's strange, and I have often felt inquisitive and suspicious about this man."

"Do you suspect him of cheating at cards ?"

"Oh! no ; we have watched him carefully, and not one of us has ever been able to detect the slightest unfairness in his playing ; but the mystery about him naturally excites our suspicions."

"Still you all seem to be on the best of terms with him ?"

"Men who risk fifty thousand francs at a sitting are becoming extremely rare, my dear fellow. When you were a gambler you would have done the same ; you would have sought his company in the hope of winning money from him. And you succeeded, this evening, strange to say. However, you gathered up your money with superb disdain. You must have retrieved your fortunes since you left us."

"I have succeeded in earning a living," replied Mérindol, somewhat embarrassed.

"You must be earning a handsome one, as a windfall of one hundred louis affords you but little pleasure. You have a very lucrative position at that factory at St. Ouen, probably ?"

"I am content with it."

"Confess that you were trying to deceive me when I met you in the Champs-Elysées a little while ago. You were only passing through Paris, you told me ; you were going to St. Germain, to spend a few days with a friend. Why did you tell me all those crams ? Were you afraid to trust me ?"

"Not you, but your companions ; and even now, I do not feel entirely safe, so far as they are concerned. I can't imagine how this Count de Porcien can know the manufacturer who employs me. If Porcien should find out that my real name is Louis de Mérindol, he would perhaps inform my patron that I had entered his employ under an assumed name. Delphine has promised to be silent, but some thoughtless word may escape her in conversation, and so I am going. Not seeing me she will soon forget me. And, by-the-way, this is a good chance to make my escape. All the gentlemen have gone into the drawing-room. Will you show me the way out, without summoning any one?"

"Certainly, my dear fellow, but on conditions you allow me to see you again. I am living at the same place. You haven't forgotten my address ?"

"No, certainly not, and you may depend upon a visit from me soon."

"Then come this way," said Jean, opening a door that led into the ante-chamber. "Fly away, virtuous youth ! I will explain your sudden disappearance. I only warn you that if you fail to keep your promise, I shall go to your factory in search of you. I shall have no trouble in ascertaining where it is; I have only to ask the Count de Porcien."

"You won't do that, I am sure," replied Louis, putting on his hat and overcoat. And, after exchanging a cordial hand-shake with his old friend, he hastened down-stairs and out into the street.

Glancing at his watch, he found that he still had plenty of time for a walk before looking for a hotel, and as the evening was delightful, he decided to remain a little while in the open air, for he was not sleepy, and he felt that a little exercise was necessary to quiet his nerves. He walked slowly down the Boulevard Malesherbes towards the Madeleine. The thoroughfare was deserted, and he paced along with his head lowered, trying to decide what course he should pursue as regards his change of name. Was it best to reveal the truth to M. Nalot at once, or to wait—till the manufacturer learnt the truth by chance?

The first course was certainly the most honourable one, but it wounded Mérindol to be obliged to confess that he had denied his ancestry in order to earn a living more easily. Moreover, if he decided to reappear in his true character, he was in no condition to prove that his name and title rightfully belonged to him, for he no longer possessed the family papers which would have served to establish his identity. Ricœur had stolen them. This would not be an insurmountable difficulty of course, as Louis could obtain plenty of conclusive evidence from former acquaintances and friends—Jean d'Autry, Delphine, Piganiou, and the peasants of the Esterel—but he did not like the idea of resorting to such extreme measures, and asking M. Nalot to wait for proof of his identity until he could have proper certificates drawn up.

While thus reflecting, he reached the esplanade on the left hand side of the Madeleine church. There were several benches under the trees, and as Louis did not care to venture upon the main boulevards, the idea of sitting down here to rest occurred to him. Nearly all the seats were occupied by people of shady appearance, and Mérindol, not caring for such promiscuous society, walked on till he found a bench where only one man was resting, with his elbows on his knees, and his face supported by his hands. Mérindol sat down, paying but little attention to this solitary dreamer, who was plainly, though respectably, dressed in a black frock-coat and a silk hat. Like Louis, he was evidently in a meditative mood, from which the young engineer's appearance speedily aroused him. Turning partially round and resting one arm on the back of the seat, he began scanning Louis' face by the light of a street lamp near by. Mérindol's features probably awakened some vague recollection in his mind, for he soon drew a little closer, as if to see his companion more distinctly.

Mérindol soon became aware of this manœuvre, and his first impulse was to rise and go off, thus curtailing the stranger's scrutiny. But on returning his gaze, he, on his side, seemed to recollect having seen this man before ; and so they sat looking at each other, each of them thinking he recognised the other, yet fearing a mistake. The man in black was the first to speak. " Excuse me, sir," he said, timidly, "but may I venture to inquire if you did not once reside in the department of the Var ?"

" Reside, no," replied Mérindol, greatly astonished, " but I was born there, and I spent the first years of my life there. But why do you ask that question ? "

" Because I met there, some three years ago, a person who strongly resembled you."

" I was there at that time, but I only remained there a few days."

" In an old château near the forest of the Estérel, a château that belongs to you ? "

" Quite so. As you are so well informed you can, perhaps, tell me my name."

" The name by which you were formerly known or the one you have since assumed ? "

" You know that I have changed my name then ? "

" I have changed mine also," said the man, eagerly, " and my face, too, must have changed, as you don't recognise me."

" It seems to me that we have met before ; but where, I can't tell."

" Then you have forgotten that you saved my life ? "

Mérindol hesitated for a moment, and then the truth flashed upon him. " The convict of the Bat's Hole ! " he exclaimed.

" Yes, the convict, the poor wretch whom you brought up, nearly dead, from the bottom of a ravine, and who, thanks to you, succeeded in reaching Italy. Ah ! I knew that I could not be mistaken ! You are the Marquis de Mérindol, my preserver and benefactor—that is, I know that you now call yourself Louis Bertin ; at least, you signed that name to the letters you sent me while I was at Genoa."

" Letters which you ceased to answer after a little time, so I concluded that you were dead, and I, too, stopped writing. Explain your silence, and how it happens that I meet you again in Paris ? Don't you know the danger to which you expose yourself by returning to France ? "

" I do know it, sir, and I assure you that I should never have returned if I had not a duty to perform. I have sworn to find the orphan—"

" Ah ! the orphan for whose sake you committed a crime ! But I wrote to you that I myself had paid a visit to the Ardennes, and that no one could tell me what had become of the child. How can you hope to find her, and what can you do for her ? "

" Very little, alas ! I am not in a position to claim her. The ban that rests upon me has compelled me to assume another name. In any case, God forbid that I should link my fate with that of Cécile. But she may be poor, reduced to toil for her daily bread, and if so, I should like to assist her, to raise her from her poverty."

" You ! and how ?  Have you made a fortune then ?"

" A fortune, no ; but by industry and economy I have saved a little money, and the banker of Genoa, who employed me, bequeathed me a small amount.  I have almost enough to live upon with economy, and I have now but one aim in life : that is to repair, so far as lies in my power, the shameful injustice of which this young girl was the innocent victim.  I quite recently became satisfied, beyond a doubt, that Cécile was in Paris, and I am now looking for her.  I arrived here a week ago."

" With false papers, of course ?"

" They are false in the sense that they are made out in the name of Guiseppe Casaldi, but they were delivered to me by the authorities at Ancona, where I have recently resided, managing a branch house of my deceased employer's bank.  He himself sent me there, and his heirs have given me an interest in the business. Indeed, I hope that I shall some day become their partner.  I have done all I could to deserve this good fortune by practising the strictest probity."

" Oh ! I never thought you a dishonest man.  Had I thought that, I should have contented myself with assisting you to escape from France, and should have taken no interest in you afterwards. One can excuse a great fault or even a crime, but no one protects a rascal.  I am at a loss to understand, however, how you can have acquired this new position in so short a space of time."

" Oh! I learnt the language very quickly, and now speak it well enough for the Italians to think me one of their compatriots, though my employer and his family of course know that I am a Frenchman. They took me for a political refugee when I first applied for a situation, and I did not undeceive them.  Afterwards when my employer sent me to Ancona, he himself advised me to take the name I now bear."

" It seems, then, that you secured an excellent position ; and I am surprised that you should have abandoned it, and have come here, at the risk of recapture, to attempt to discover a girl who disappeared so many years ago.  It is a foolish undertaking, and you did very wrong to give up the position you held."

" I did not give it up, sir.  I asked for a two months' leave of absence, and obtained it.  When it expires, I shall, of course, return to Ancona."

" I am glad to hear that ; but you are greatly mistaken if you think you will be able to lay your hands on Mademoiselle Cécile in a few weeks.  If, by any miracle, you should meet her, you would not recognize her, nor would she recognize you."

" She may have forgotten me, but I am sure, that if I saw her—"

" Excuse me, but how long did you remain at Toulon ?"

" Ten years," replied Mongcorgo hanging his head.

" And three more years have elapsed since you succeeded in making your escape.  How old was the child at the time of your conviction?"

" She was fourteen."

" Fourteen years and thirteen make twenty-seven years. She must be twenty-seven now, and a woman changes wonderfully between the ages of fourteen and twenty-seven. Besides even if she is still living—"

" She is living, I am sure of it."

" Perhaps so ; but think of what may have happened to her during thirteen years ! She is married, perhaps ; possibly she is prematurely aged by want and toil, or by leading a gay life as was suggested to me in the Ardennes."

" That is impossible."

" But what else could you expect of a poor orphan, left homeless and friendless in a great city, where vice is ever on the watch for victims ? "

" The information I have obtained leads me to believe that Cécile has resisted all the temptations that surrounded her, and has earned an honest living in the humblest way."

" The information you have received, you say ? How did you manage to obtain any information ? "

" The firm I represent at Ancona has numerous correspondents in France. I wrote to all those residing in the north and north-east, requesting them to try and ascertain the whereabouts of Cécile, who, I told them, was entitled to a large sum of money bequeathed to her by a relative at Ancona. For a long time all their efforts proved fruitless ; but at last I received a letter from one of them stating that a person of Vouziers, near which town the deceased Count de Porcien resided, could give me some information about the orphan. It seems that after my trial, the poor child was taken to the hospital of Vouziers, where she lay ill for a long time. But one day, soon after her recovery, she disappeared, and it was ultimately discovered that she had started on foot for Paris, without money or references of any kind."

" I learned as much when I went to the Ardennes ; but the people there could tell me nothing more."

" Well, one day some years afterwards, this person of Vouziers met Cécile in Paris, recognized her, and spoke to her. He had often seen her at the château, being a timber merchant who had bought the cuts in the Count de Porcien's woods."

" In what situation did he find the poor creature ? "

" She was a waitress in a little restaurant near the Palais Royal. On my arrival here I had no difficulty in finding it, but Cécile was no longer there. She had gone away some six months before, stating that she had secured a position as cashier in a mercantile establishment."

" You must admit that this second disappearance was rather strange. Did she give the name of her new employer ? "

" Unfortunately, no."

" That looks bad. When a woman has no intention of doing anything wrong, she does not take so much pains to conceal her whereabouts. You have abandoned all hope of finding her now I suppose ? "

"Not yet, sir ; but my only hope now is that I may meet or hear of her, by chance. So I spend my time in walking about Paris."

"Take care that you do not find yourself face to face, not with her, but with some one who may have known you at Toulon. Who knows but what the very man who tried to kill you in the forest of the Estérel is here ? Paris is full of such people."

"Heaven grant that I may never meet Ricœur again ! " murmured Mongeorge. "I am almost sure, though, that he believes me dead."

"That is probable. He can hardly think you survived your fall into the Bat's Hole. Have you ever heard anything of him since that adventure ? "

"Never, sir."

"Still he must have succeeded in getting safely out of the country. Had he been recaptured, I should have heard of it, for I remained in the neighbourhood several days after your departure. He was certainly a shrewd rascal, and he had the money he stole from you to begin life afresh with. He had some valuable papers, too, those he took from my desk. Thus armed and equipped, a man can accomplish a good deal."

"Especially in Paris, and Ricœur often told me that a man of his stamp could live nowhere else."

"That's true. But as he had formerly resided here I doubt if he has ventured to return. Fear of recognition must have deterred him. If I come in contact with him, I shall send him back to the galleys, for he contributed not a little to my father's financial ruin."

"Oh ! if he returned to Toulon his former comrades would kill him, for having stolen the money they had intrusted to me."

"Excuse me, but I fancy you are the person who might incur danger in that respect. You were the convicts' cashier, and they would acuse you of having betrayed your trust ; all the more so, as they don't know that Ricœur stole the money from you, and that you nearly lost your life in your efforts to save it from his clutches."

"Yes," replied Mongeorge, bitterly, "I am considered a dishonest man even among convicts ; and yet, I assure you that if I had been able to do so I should have already refunded the twenty-seven thousand francs which Ricœur appropriated."

"I don't think you are called upon to do that ; besides, to whom would you refund the money, supposing you possessed it ? "

"I could obtain the amount from my employers, for my interest in the business is worth more than that, and I should hand it to the convicts' banker could I only find him."

"Who is this strange individual who makes a speciality of investing stolen moneys ? "

"He is a former convict."

"I thought so. What figure can a man who engages in this honourable calling cut in Paris ? I hardly suppose that he has a current account with the Bank of France."

"He may have one, for he has very large sums of money at his disposal. All the criminals in France are in correspondence with him. He is both their agent and banker. He protects them, too ; and his assistance is not to be despised, for he has, they say, an extensive acquaintance in all classes of society."

" What is his ostensible business ? "

" He changes it very often. When I escaped three years ago, he was a provision dealer in the Popincourt district ; but I don't know what he is doing now."

" Did you go to the address which had been given you, then ? "

" Yes, and I ran no risk in doing so, for I was not obliged to give my name, or to enter into any explanation whatever. I was simply to utter a certain phrase, and in case I received a certain reply to hand over the money. I was warned that I need expect no receipt."

"Thieves dealing on parole ! That's capital ! "

" However, on going to the address I had, I found the premises occupied by a carpenter, who plainly had no idea whatever of the meaning of my words. He informed me, however, that the previous tenant of the place had failed and absconded."

" Taking the convicts' money with him, eh ? These interesting capitalists seem to be unlucky."

"Not as unlucky as you think, sir. The sudden disappearances of their treasurer are periodical, and the object of them is to throw the police off the scent. The authorities have a vague suspicion that this treasure exists, but they can never lay their hands on the delinquents. Every two or three years the cashier moves, and probably changes his ostensible occupation as well. Due notice of this change is immediately sent to all the prisons and places of confinement in a sure but mysterious way."

" Well, as you have had no connection with penitentiaries for the last three years the notice hasn't reached you. So much the better, you are spared a dangerous undertaking."

" I have given up all idea of it. I now only think of finding Cécile."

" Well, if I can be of any service to you in that matter, I shall be glad to lend you my help."

"You will allow me to see you again, then?" inquired Mongeorge, with emotion.

" Why not ? I entertained you in my father's house when you wore a red blouse and green cap, and I can certainly keep up an acquaintance with you now. Where are you staying ? "

" At a quiet hotel in the Rue Trouchet—only a few steps from here."

" A quiet hotel you say ? That will suit me exactly."

"What do you mean, sir?" inquired Mongeorge, greatly surprised.

" I will explain myself. I usually reside at the factory I have charge of at St. Ouen. But this evening, the gentleman who employs me brought me with him to Paris, where I shall probably be obliged to remain some little time, to my regret. He wishes to give me the management of a concern he has started near the Central Markets, and I begin my duties to-morrow. However, I find myself houseless for to-night, as the room which I am to occupy at our place of business is not ready. I was thinking of looking for a hotel when you spoke to me. "Will you take me to the place where you are stopping?"

"What! you would not object—"

"To spending the night under the same roof as Guiseppe Castaldi? No, certainly not. You will even do me a favour by taking me to a suitable hotel. I shall call to see you occasionally as long as I remain in Paris. And who knows, I may perhaps be able to give you news of the girl you are looking for, for I shall have to deal with a number of merchants. If I should chance to hear any of them speak of a charming employée named Cécile I will certainly let you know."

"You are far too kind, sir," murmured Mongeorge, gratefully, with his eyes full of tears.

Mérindol now rose up, and he did not disdain to take the arm of the unfortunate man whom three years of commendable efforts had vindicated far more effectually than any legal decision could have done.

## IV

Louis de Mérindol had formerly been an idle, dilatory fellow, but since his conversion there had been a radical change in his habits. After spending the night at Mongeorge's hotel he rose with the sun, dressed himself with wonderful alacrity, and started for the Rue Mondétour, where he was to meet M. Nalot at seven o'clock precisely. The walk was not at all a short one, but Louis did not find it tiresome. Indeed, after his three years' absence from Paris it afforded him great pleasure to walk leisurely through the streets, and note the morning aspect of the city. Perhaps, by reason of his conversation with M. Nalot the night before, and the hopes it had stirred within him, everything now appeared delightful. The dingy old houses that rise up near the grand old church of St. Eustache seemed to him almost cheerful in their aspect; and he thought all the women who passed him charming. This was a delusion due to his state of mind, however, for the majority of those he met were huckster-women or cooks on their way home from market. But on reaching the end of the Rue Montmartre, he suddenly found himself face to face with a young woman who had just come from the Rue Montorgueil, and who was certainly worthy of admiration.

She was very plainly but neatly dressed, wearing a brown, tight-fitting jacket, a little hat she must have made herself, together with low-heeled boots and kid gloves which looked quite new. She was very beautiful. Her complexion was creamy; she had large, dark eyes, shining with soft brilliancy under arched brows; lips as red as pomegranate blossom; and, best of all, an intelligent, animated expression that gave one an irresistible longing to hear her speak. Her figure was perfect, and her hands and feet were of aristocratic delicacy. Mérindol, who was a connoisseur, noted all this at a single glance, and wondered who this charming creature could be. He had no idea of starting a flirtation, but from force of habit he could not help classifying the women he met, just as an agriculturist can't help distinguishing wheat from rye in the fields he crosses. To what social category did this young woman belong? She was not a shop-girl. Shop-girls go without gloves in order to purchase high-heeled shoes; and this young woman wore low-heeled ones. Nor was she a lady's-maid. Lady's-maids wear the cast-off garments of their mistresses; and this young woman's toilet had an unmistakeable air of individuality. Mérindol at last felt inclined to take her for a teacher, who was going to give some lessons, an excellent reason for being out so early in the morning.

The matter would not have engrossed his attention for long had he not seen that this young person was going in precisely the same direction as himself : in fact, to reach M. Nalot's establishment, he had only to follow her. He did so, but at a little distance, and he soon saw her pass the markets, and turn to the left into the Rue Mondétour. As she was about to enter this narrow, gloomy street, she was accosted by an old beggar-woman, and paused to give her alms. Moreover, Mérindol noticed that instead of contenting herself with giving some coppers, she entered into conversation with the poor woman; and as he drew nearer he perceived her drawing some bread and soup tickets from her pocket. As a rule, young and pretty Parisiennes are not so well prepared to perform deeds of charity in the street; and Mérindol decided that this one must be as good as she was beautiful.

He did not pause or slacken his pace, for fear of annoying her, but walked straight on to M. Nalot's establishment, at the corner of the Rue de la Grande Truanderie. He had only seen the building at night, and it now seemed to him even more gloomy and uninviting. The door was as massive as the gate of a prison. It would have successfully withstood a siege; and the metal M. Nalot had stored in this ancient abode was certainly safe from thieves. Moreover, Mérindol was unable to discover any bell. There was a knocker, or rather a make believe one, but it was securely riveted to one of the panels of the door.

"Press the little knob under the copper plate on the left-hand side," said a voice behind Mérindol, who was trying his best to lift the knocker.

The voice was wonderfully sweet and musical. Mérindol, greatly surprised, turned round and found himself face to face with the fair stranger whom he had met at the corner of the Rue Montorgueil. She now seemed even prettier, but she did not look quite so young. "What, madame, is it you?" Mérindol unguardedly exclaimed, in his astonishment.

"Do you happen to know me, sir?" inquired the young woman, evidently much surprised by his remark.

"I haven't the honour; only five minutes ago I saw you for the first time," replied the young man, smiling.

"I did not notice you. You have business with Monsieur Nalot, probably. I doubt if he has arrived yet."

"I have an appointment with him for seven o'clock this morning."

"In that case, you will be sure to find him in his office."

"I think so. But, excuse the question, madame, do you also wish to see him? I ask you this because I will wait, of course, till you have finished your business with him."

"I am obliged to you, but there is nothing I wish to say to Monsieur Nalot just now."

"But you have come here. Do you reside in the house?"

"I am employed here, sir."

"Indeed! So am I."

"You, sir! That is strange. I never saw you before."

"I came here for the first time yesterday evening."

"Then it was you who came in the carriage with Monsieur Nalot."

"Yes, madame; or should I say mademoiselle?"

"I am not married, sir."

"Well then, mademoiselle, I am the manager of Monsieur Nalot's factory at St. Ouen. Temporarily, however, I shall reside here. You just told me that you were in Monsieur Nalot's employ. May I ask your occupation?"

"I keep an account of all the goods received and sent away."

"Then I shall sometimes have the pleasure of meeting you, as I shall take Monsieur Nalot's place for a while."

"Then you will occupy his private office, on the first floor in the left wing, while my work is in the store-rooms in the basement. But I beg your pardon, sir," said the young woman, placing her finger on the copper button which served as a bell-knob, "it is getting late, and I must be at my post."

There were still many things that Mérindol wished to say to her, but the door flew open, and the young woman hastily entered the court-yard. Louis followed her, and found himself face to face with a strange-looking individual wearing a dark livery. He was a little, stunted, old humpback—a sort of Caliban or Quasimodo, and he, no doubt, seldom went outside for fear of being hooted by the street arabs. He darted a suspicious glance at the young woman who was crossing the court-yard, and who was already some little distance off, bowed to Louis Bertin with a surly air, and hastily closed the door which the latter had left open when he entered.

"Has Monsieur Nalot come yet?" inquired Louis repressing his inclination to laugh.

"Yes, as he slept here," replied the gnome, sulkily. "And he has been waiting for you for an hour or more."

"Ah!" replied Mérindol, drily, "he told me to be here at seven o'clock precisely, and it is five minutes to."

"Then go up the left staircase at the end of the court-yard."

"I shall find someone to announce me, I suppose?"

"I will warn the office attendant," growled the hunchback, giving two pulls at a bell-rope hanging from the wall. Mérindol turned his back on the doorkeeper and walked towards the same stairs he had ascended the evening before. On the first landing he met the office attendant who looked like a beadle, and he was immediately conducted to M. Nalot's private room. He found his employer seated behind a large writing table covered with papers, in a luxuriously furnished office. M. Nalot rose on seeing the young engineer, and advanced to meet him with outstretched hands. "Good morning, my young friend," he exclaimed, in a most affable tone. "You are punctuality itself, and I am glad of it, for I have a deal of business to attend to to-day. Pray sit down. You stayed at a hotel last night, no doubt."

"Yes, sir," replied Mérindol, a little surprised at the interest M. Nalot seemed to take in his slightest actions, for the manufacturer was not in the habit of displaying so much solicitude concerning his subordinates.

"And perhaps you were not sorry of an opportunity to amuse yourself a little. One always likes to renew one's acquaintance with Parisian pleasures when one has been deprived of them for some time."

"I care very little for them, I assure you, sir."

"I know that you only think of your work. Still, you are young, and you formerly lived in Paris, I believe ? "

"Yes ; but I am not at all anxious to reside here now."

"Not as a bachelor, perhaps, but if you were married, you would no doubt change your mind."

"I don't think so ; besides, I am not in a position to marry."

"You are not in a position to marry a dowerless bride, of course, though you are well able to earn your living. But I have great plans for you, and expect to see you at the head of a very handsome establishment before long."

"I am infinitely obliged to you, sir," said Mérindol, astonished by this overture, which was even more direct than those made the evening before. "The future you speak of would be very gratifying ; still, I should not like to pledge myself lightly."

"Oh ! it is understood that you will only marry an intelligent, pretty, and virtuous girl. You certainly have a right to exact all these attributes in the woman of your choice, and I shall soon ask you if you do not find them all in a certain person of my acquaintance." This time M. Nalot's meaning seemed so apparent that Mérindol did not know what to say. "I will insist no further just now," continued Gabrielle's father ; "I should merely like to know if, in case you came into possession of a large fortune, you would have any objection to investing it in business."

"I certainly could not invest it to better advantage, especially if it was in a branch of business in which I could utilise my practical knowledge."

"As, for instance, in the business you are managing so admirably for me ? " inquired M. Nalot.

"I should be only too happy to devote to it my time, energies, and—money, if I possessed any," replied Mérindol. "We are fast coming to the point," he thought. "He wishes to know if I should leave him in case he enriched me by a marriage. And yet I dare not hope that he really thinks of giving me his daughter."

"That is all I care to know," replied M. Nalot. "I am in a hurry, and I must explain as briefly as possible what you will have to do here for the next few days. The first thing will be to look over some accounts for me. There is a young woman here who keeps an account of the goods that come in and go out, and I should like to know if her books are correctly kept."

"She is not only a young, but a pretty woman, if I am not mistaken."

"What, are you acquainted with her?"

"I feel sure that I just met her, for on my reaching the gateway, and stopping to look for the bell, a young woman who came up, and saw my dilemma, pointed out the bell knob to me. We exchanged a few words. I told her who I was, and she remarked that she kept the stock account here."

"That is correct. You are probably surprised that I have intrusted a task of such importance to a woman."

"Especially to so young a woman."

"She is not as young as she looks. She is over twenty-five, and past that age, you know, a woman is considered to be an old maid; it is a great pity, for this young person is very attractive, clever, and industrious. She has but one fault, in fact. She is so very bashful, which is a failing with a girl who ought to be looking for a husband. I hope, however, that she will some day meet a man worthy of her. Besides, it is quite possible that she will come into possession of a very handsome fortune later on. She has an uncle in America—an uncle who has made a great deal of money in California. It is true that he has never written to her since he left this country fifteen years ago; but perhaps he will forget to make his will before he dies, and in that case my pretty clerk will prove a very desirable wife. But all that has nothing to do with the matter in hand. What I desire of you is this: the young woman performs her duties very well, and I don't think there is the slightest reason to doubt her honesty; still, the position she holds is one of such importance that I should like you, not to watch her—there is no need of that—but to superintend her work a little. As I should not like to wound her feelings, I intrust the task to you, instead of an ordinary employé, who would make her feel his authority. Your education, manners, and disposition make you the very person to fulfil this delicate mission."

"Which, I trust, will be a short one, sir, for it is not at all in my line."

"Oh, ten days or a fortnight will suffice for you to collect the necessary materials for the report, which you will make to me—verbally, of course—for I have no intention of making this little inquiry an important matter; and in the meantime, I don't wish you to confine yourself too closely here. I hope you will come occasionally to see how affairs progress at the factory. I never feel quite easy unless you are there. Besides, my wife and daughter would reproach me if you absented yourself entirely from St. Ouen."

"You are very kind, sir, and I will do my best to satisfy you," said Mérindol, reassured as to his employer's intentions by his concluding words.

"And now," resumed the manufacturer, glancing at his watch, "I will leave you to your new duties. My carriage must be waiting for me, and I have a deal to do this morning."

" Excuse me, sir, you speak of my new duties, but I do not very clearly understand of what they consist."

"Yes, I have neglected to enter into particulars, and now I haven't time to explain the organization of the establishment. But see Séranon, who is my cashier and factotum ; he will tell you all you want to know. The attendant will show you the way to his office. Still, as Séranon might bore you, I should advise you for the present to go down and have a talk with Mademoiselle Clémence ; let her explain her work and try to see for yourself how things are conducted. We will resume our conversation to-morrow morning, when you will understand much better what I desire of you. So, till to-morrow, my dear Bertin. Have you any commissions for St. Ouen ? I shall dine there this evening."

" Pray remember me to Madame and Mademoiselle Nalot."

" Rest assured that I will not forget your request ; if I did, the ladies would not fail to inquire after you."

Mérindol, delighted, bowed to his employer, and left the office, which had two doors, one of them being reserved for the private use of the manufacturer. The liveried giant in the ante-chamber offered to show Louis to the rooms which had been prepared for him ; but the young fellow asked to be conducted to M. Séranon's office.

The cashier occupied a sort of glass cage at the end of a room in which several clerks were at work ; a cage with a small window which was opened whenever anyone tapped upon the pane. Mérindol's guide rapped, and in the aperture there appeared a head bristling with stiff, grey hair. Beneath a pair of shaggy eye-brows gleamed two round tiger-like eyes ; betwixt them protruded a prodigious nose, fiery red, and a mouth stretched almost from ear to ear, revealing two rows of pointed, yellow teeth. The cashier's appearance was indeed so repulsive that Louis almost recoiled, but recovering himself, he said as politely as he could : "I was sent, sir, by Monsieur Nalot to arrange with you about—"

" I know," interrupted the cashier ; " you manage the factory at St. Ouen and you have come here to see if the accounts of that girl downstairs are all right. Well, how does that concern me ?"

" You don't seem to understand that Monsieur Nalot, our em-ployer, has sent me—"

" He can send you where he pleases ; I don't care, but I have no time to waste in chattering."

" That means, of course, that you refuse to give me the informa-tion I need."

" Certainly it does. Good-day !" said the cashier, abruptly clos-ing the window.

" Go to the deuce, you impertinent scamp," said Mérindol out of patience.

" Don't mind him, sir. He has such attacks, at times," whispered the guide.

" I will have nothing more to do with the ill-bred fellow,"

growled Louis, and turning away, he walked towards a staircase, which led, he imagined, to the store-rooms below. He felt a desire to behold a more pleasing countenance.

But he had made a mistake, for this staircase conducted him to a little court-yard he had not yet seen. This yard was not only small and damp, but it was surrounded by high, gloomy walls which made it look like a well. These walls were covered with green moss, and weeds had sprung up between the paving stones. All around there was not a single window but there were several doors, some large enough to admit a loaded dray, others of medium size which did not seem to be often used, and smaller ones having a rather mysterious aspect. Mérindol, surprised, began to examine the spot inquisitively. He was beginning to think that this mercantile establishment was very strange. The cashier acted very much as if he would like to devour any one who spoke to him, and the court-yards resembled those of penitentiaries. As Louis was not at all anxious to catch rheumatism by remaining in this sort of cistern, he turned to remount the stairs, and he had already set one foot on the lowest step when the noise of a big key turning in a rusty lock made him look round. One of the small mysterious looking doors of the courtyard partially opened, and almost instantly closed upon a man who paused and blinked like an owl disconcerted by daylight. However, the new-comer promptly recovered himself and walked towards the stairs at the bottom of which Louis de Mérindol was standing. Suddenly two exclamations of surprise resounded, and Mérindol cried out : "What ! is it you ?" He had recognised the new-comer, as his friend Jean d'Autry whom he had left at midnight in Delphine de Guibray's drawing-room. "What the deuce are you doing here ?" he asked.

"And what the deuce are you doing here ?" retorted Jean, who seemed quite stupefied. Then before Mérindol could reply Jean burst into a hearty laugh and added : "What an idiot I am to ask you such a question ! You are here for the same purpose as myself of course. You need some money although you won a hundred louis last night, and so you have come here to get it, just as I have."

"Nothing of the kind, I assure you."

"Oh I don't try to conceal it. There is nothing dishonourable about the matter, though the rate of interest here is rather high ; besides, I sha'n't go and tell your employer that you patronize the same usurer as myself."

"A usurer ?"

"Yes ; that beast, Séranon. You have already seen him, I suppose, though I fancied I should be the first customer here this morning, for I did not go to bed at all. The entertainment at Delphine's lasted till daybreak. I scarcely took time to dress afterwards and here I am."

"But how did you get in ?"

"In the usual way. You need not pretend innocence ; you

know old Rognas, who sells leeches in the Rue de la Grande-Truanderie, as well as I do?"

"Old Rognas!" repeated Mérindol, in amazement.

"What! you pretend you don't know him? Have you already forgotten that one enters his shop whistling the air of *Marlborough is off to the wars*, and that at this signal a hideous face rises from behind a cask which must be full of rattlesnakes. It is the face of Rognas, that vile old wretch who spends his time among reptiles. You tell him you have come to purchase some leeches, having been recommended to him by an acquaintance at Reims. He asks your name and how many of the lovely creatures you want, and you answer : five, ten, or twenty, according as you need, five, ten or twenty thousand francs, for each leech represents a thousand franc note. He then leaves you alone in his den, locking you up for fear you might try to make your escape. Ten minutes later he reappears, and either tells you he has no leeches on hand, or else that what you want awaits you at the *dépôt* as he puts it. But the *dépôt* is of course Séranon's office."

"Oh! I've seen Séranon, but I don't know Rognas."

"I thought as much, but you must have dealt with another intermediary—and have come in here by a different way. You were not taken down into a cellar, I presume?"

"No, indeed."

"A cellar connected with a subterranean passage which leads into this court-yard. Rognas accompanied me as usual to the door yonder and opened it for me. But the most astonishing thing is finding you here. This is not the first time I have been here, but I never before met any one but a man-servant who looks like a drum-major. It's he who conducts me to Séranon's office and I'm surprised he is not here. Perhaps he is still in bed."

"So you came here to borrow money of a usurer?" inquired the young engineer, greatly troubled by this strange narrative.

"You certainly don't suppose I came to bring him money."

"Do you think that the usurer is the owner of this establishment?"

"I know nothing about it, but Séranon must be rich enough to have a house of his own. But pray tell me about yourself ; if you haven't come to borrow coin why are you here?"

Mérindol was greatly embarrassed. He realized the necessity of explaining his presence, but, on the other hand, he did not care to confess that the manufacturer who employed him was the proprietor of this establishment. He flattered himself that there must be some mistake, that Séranon probably did business on his own account, and that M. Nalot was not aware of his cashier's disreputable transactions. "The fact is," he replied, "my employer sent me here to make inquiries about some copper he thinks of buying."

"Oh, yes. Séranon must deal in all sorts of metals. So you did not come in through the leech-shop. The establishment probably has two entrances."

"I only know of one, in the Rue Mondétour, and—"

"Why, there's a woman !" suddenly exclaimed Jean d'Autry.

On hearing this exclamation Mérindol turned, and at the further end of the court-yard he perceived a woman whom he did not at first recognize.

She wore over her gown a long olive-tinted smockfrock, much like the blouses worn in a sculptor's studio, and she had entered the little yard by a door which must have communicated with the larger court. The long garment which enveloped her did not disguise her to such an extent as to prevent Mérindol from recognizing her after he had recovered a little from his surprise. It was Mademoiselle Clémence in working garb. She carried a bunch of keys in her hand, and she had already advanced some little distance into the court-yard before she perceived the young engineer standing at the foot of the staircase with a gentleman whom she had never seen before. She stopped short ; and then, after a few seconds' hesitation, retreated to the door by which she had just arrived and waited, evidently for the stranger to go. At least Mérindol thought so, and his friend Jean must have been of the same opinion, for he remarked in an undertone : "I understand now why you are hanging about this cellar, and why Delphine de Guibray's little entertainments have lost their charm for you. So this is what you call purchasing copper. Well, as I haven't the slightest desire to interfere with your love affairs, I will leave you, especially as old Rognas must long since have announced my coming to Séranon, who is probably getting impatient ; so good luck to you till we meet again." Jean thereupon flew up the stairs, three steps at a time, and disappeared.

Meanwhile Mademoiselle Clémence still remained at the door. She was evidently waiting for Mérindol to approach and speak to her, and, as he asked nothing better, he hastened across the court-yard and approached his charming subordinate, hat in hand. "I am very glad to meet you here, mademoiselle," he said, courteously : "in fact, I was looking for you, but I made a mistake in the staircase, which is not so surprising, as the arrangements of this establishment are certainly very intricate."

"So intricate that though I have been working here for a long time I do not yet know the place thoroughly."

"Do you live in the building ?"

"No, sir. I reside in the Rue Montorgueil. I merely spend the day here. Have you seen our employer ?"

"Yes, mademoiselle, and he spoke of you in the highest terms, telling me that he thoroughly appreciates the valuable services you render him."

"I am greatly obliged to him for his good opinion, but I don't understand why he should think it necessary to make me a subject of conversation."

"It was indispensable as we seem to be destined to come into daily contact while I remain here. Monsieur Nalot wishes to initiate me into all the different branches of business in which he is engaged ; as regards his establishment here I have everything to learn, and can only do so by asking information of the persons familiar with the working of the place.  He told me, it is true, that Monsieur Séranon would initiate me into everything ; but I have just made an unsuccessful attempt in that direction, and don't feel inclined to repeat it.  Monsieur Séranon received me very ungraciously, so I decided to address myself to you."

"'Then you wish me to show you what my daily work consists of?'"

" Yes, mademoiselle ; but I would not like to cause you any inconvenience.  I will accompany you, but pray, proceed with your duties as if I were not present."

" I will try, though I shall be obliged to give you some explanations—explanations which you probably would not think of asking ; for instance, as regards the arrangements of the house.  This is the first time you have been here, but you are probably already aware of the ingenious manner in which our employer has utilized these old buildings."

" I have only noticed that there must be two entrances.  One in the Rue Mondétour, and—"

"The other in the Rue de la Grande-Truanderie.  I use the first one when I come in the morning, and leave by the other in the evening."

" You have to pass through this court-yard, then ? "

"No, indeed, I never set foot here.  If you find me here now it is because while I was looking over some merchandise stored in a vault which ends at this door, I heard voices in a spot where I thought no one ever came.  I had the key of the door, so I opened it to see that nothing irregular was going on.  If this yard is ever used at all I really do not know for what purpose."

This declaration afforded Mérindol considerable satisfaction, for it proved that Clémence was ignorant of the suspicious practices of Séranon and his accomplice the dealer in leeches.

" Come, now, sir," added Clémence, in her musical voice, "and I will show you the store-rooms, and what I do there."

As she spoke she stepped aside to allow Mérindol to pass, and as soon as he had crossed the threshold she closed and locked the door. The corridor into which she had ushered the young man led to a kind of rotunda having a zinc roof, and divided into compartments by partitions of sheet iron.  Each compartment was devoted to a particular use.  One contained iron rails, symmetrically arranged ; another, sheets of copper, laid one above the other; another, pig lead, in pyramidal piles.  Others, moreover, were filled with heterogeneous articles, thrown in pell-mell—battered saucepans, old iron pots, cracked boilers, rusty bolts and hinges, indeed, piles of old household utensils. A dray which had been run over iron rails, was standing in the middle of the rotunda, and four men were engaged in unloading it.  Mademoiselle Clémence drew a note-book from her pocket and made some entries in it.  "Who are these men ? " asked Mérindol.  " Their looks are by no means pleasant.  Where does our employer pick up such faces, I wonder ? "

"You had better ask him, if you really wish to know," said Clémence, "I can't say ; and I should not presume to question Monsieur Nalot. They are certainly not the kind of men I should care to meet in a lonely spot after dark ; but I only see them here. They bring me merchandise, coming in by a gate which you have not yet seen, and which is reserved for their special use. Near this gate there is a weighing-machine. I have the dray weighed, and take a note of the gross weight ; then the goods being unloaded before me, I have them weighed separately, and due allowance being made for the weight of the dray I know exactly how many tons of goods I have received. In the same way I keep an account of the output, and every evening I send a report to Monsieur Nalot."

"And is that all?"

"Oh, sir ! it is quite enough, for drays arrive and leave constantly, and I am kept busy from morning until night."

"You must be tired by the end of the day, unquestionably. It seems strange to me that our employer has not intrusted this fatiguing and difficult task to a man. I admit, though, that it is a question of confidence, for a dishonest person might conspire with the draymen to defraud Monsieur Nalot. However, he can rely upon your integrity and discretion, as you know all about his dealings in metals, where he obtains his merchandise and to whom he sells it."

"No, sir, I know nothing whatever about that."

"What ! the goods are brought here and taken away without your knowing where they come from or where they go ?"

"It may seem strange, but such is the case."

"But you certainly don't receive goods from anybody, and deliver them to anybody ?"

"I receive a paper every morning containing my instructions for the day, the loads I am to receive and deliver, and a list of the drays which will come, with their numbers. Only one comes at a time, and I am warned of its arrival by a bell in my office. To get here I have to follow a long corridor, and cross the court-yard on the other side of the rotunda. The driver gives me a number corresponding with one of those on my sheet of instructions. As I have the keys of the rotunda, I admit him and wait until the dray has been emptied or loaded. When it is all over, I return to my office to repeat the operation twenty minutes afterwards, perhaps."

"And apart from the work you never have occasion to enter into conversation with any of these draymen ?"

"No, sir ; and I assure you I have no desire to talk with them. Besides, they have unquestionably received precise instructions, for they never say a word to me, nor do they even speak with each other."

"That's strange," replied Mérindol. "In the factory at St. Ouen I often talk with my workmen."

"But there is nothing to hinder you from questioning these men if you like, sir. I am a woman, and I don't dare."

"That is true. I ought to have done that, instead of wearying you with my questions. But it's not too late."

The young engineer now advanced toward the draymen, who went on with their work without evincing any consciousness of his presence. There were four of them, all old and ugly; and Mérindol, who was in the habit of superintending young and intelligent workmen, wondered where these hideous scamps, who looked brutified by drink, could have been picked up. The youngest was at least fifty years of age.

"Where have you come from, my good fellows?" he inquired.

There was one who raised his head and shrugged his shoulders, but the others did not even look up. "Are you deaf?" asked Mérindol, and receiving no response he caught hold of the man nearest him by the arm and shook him vigorously. "It's you I'm speaking to!" he cried, angrily this time.

"I can hear," growled the man. "Well, what then?"

"I ask you who has sent us this old lead."

"It isn't my business to tell you. Apply to the governor."

"You are insolent, eh? Get out of here, or I'll thrash you."

"Don't try it," retorted the scamp, drawing from his pocket a long pointed knife, which he opened.

"I beg of you, sir—" began the young woman.

On hearing her voice Mérindol regained the calmness he had momentarily lost. "You are right, mademoiselle," he said. "I will have this rascal dismissed, but I must not compromise myself with him. I will speak to you by-and-by."

And he did not open his lips again until after the dray was unloaded. Clémence, more troubled, perhaps, than she was willing to admit, made the necessary entries in her note-book; and when the strange fellows had finished their work, she allowed them to go off without a word. The dray was dragged out into the court-yard, and then one of the men whistled. A gate communicating with a narrow street flew open, and a strong horse was seen held by a man as repulsive in appearance as the four others. Then the gate closed upon the party as if by enchantment, just like the door through which Jean d'Autry had so unexpectedly appeared. "Well, sir, you must now understand the nature of my duties," remarked Clémence. "Would you like to see my books now?"

"No, no," replied Mérindol. "I have seen quite enough to be convinced that extraordinary things go on here. What do you think about it, mademoiselle?"

"I will not venture to express an opinion."

"But you must certainly have one. It is impossible that you should not have asked yourself—as I am doing at this moment—if the goods received here have not been stolen."

"Oh! I can't believe that Monsieur Nalot is dishonest."

"But his attention may be so engrossed by more important enterprises that he is ignorant of what is done by certain dishonest subordinates, such as his cashier, that Séranon who looks very like the leader of a band of thieves. I am satisfied that the rascal practices usury. The young man you saw with me just now told me so. Moreover, there is an air of mystery about everything here ; and I don't like the way in which the business seems to be conducted. I must have an explanation with Monsieur Nalot, this evening, even if I am obliged to go to St. Ouen to find him. But first, mademoiselle, I beg that you will tell me all you know. You barely know me, and you distrust me, perhaps ; but I assure you that I am an honourable man, and that if I had any doubt of Monsieur Nalot's integrity, I should not remain in his employ."

" I believe you, sir ; and I will not hide from you that I have more than once thought of leaving his establishment, though I have earned a very comfortable living here for six months past."

" Six months past ! " repeated Merindol, struck by a sudden recollection.

" Yes, sir," replied the young woman. " I came here last November, and after seeing Monsieur Nalot I was intrusted with my present duties by Monsieur Séranon on the very first day."

" You knew Monsieur Nalot previously, I presume ? "

" No, sir. I had never even seen him before."

" May I venture to ask you who first recommended you to his notice ? "

" A person in his employ with whom I was but slightly acquainted, but if you would like to know the particulars I will tell you how everything happened. I am not ashamed of my past, and besides, I feel confidence in you."

" You do right to trust me, mademoiselle, as I hope to prove to you by-and-by. So you met a gentleman who was employed in this house ? "

" No, not in this house, though I believe Monsieur Nalot employed him elsewhere—at the factory, perhaps. At all events, I have never seen him working here. He is called Corraille."

" What ! Corraille, the new overseer Monsieur Nalot hired recently at St. Ouen—a man whom I heartily dislike, and who looks quite as villainous as the draymen with whom you have to deal every day ? "

" His looks are not in his favour certainly. However, rather more than six months ago he began to take his meals at a little restaurant where—where I served as a waitress."

" You, mademoiselle ; you were— "

" A servant in a little restaurant near the Palais Royal ? "

" Indeed," cried Mérindol, as a sudden light broke upon him. " But, pray, proceed with your story. So you saw this man every day— "

" Yes, and he seemed to take an interest in my lot, which was certainly hard enough just then. I had only accepted the situation for want of a better one. However, my employers were kind-hearted people, who understood that I was born for something better than the menial position to which unexpected misfortunes had reduced me. They ventured to tell Monsieur Corraille that, after having served a long time as under-teacher in a boarding-school, I had preferred to earn my living by manual work, rather than misconduct myself."

"Under-teacher in a boarding-school!" repeated Mérindol, becoming more and more surprised.

"Yes ; I served in that capacity twelve years. I am now twenty-seven, and I was only fifteen when I was first given a home by the worthy woman who kept the school. She brought me up as if I had been her own daughter. I was soon able to assist her in teaching the children intrusted to her ; and I should never have left her had she not died last year. I then found myself almost without money or friends, for I had led a very secluded life. The girls who attended the school were of modest position, and could not render me assistance in securing a position as governess ; however, the mother of one of them offered to take me into her employ, and I was only too glad to accept her offer. Later on, she strongly urged me not to refuse Corraille's offer to find me a more suitable and lucrative position. I accepted it, and you know the rest."

Mérindol had listened to this narrative with unconcealed emotion, and after a brief pause he abruptly asked : "Did you ever know a person called Mongeorge ?"

"Mongeorge," murmured Clémence, with a changed expression. "Yes, that name—"

"Is that of a man who was your devoted friend, and who paid dearly for his devotion."

"Who can have told you that ?"

"I know everything. I know that your name is Cécile, that your childhood was spent in a château in the Ardennes—a château which belonged to the Count de Porcien."

"My benefactor ! Ah, how I have wept his loss, and prayed for him ! "

"Driven away by Monsieur de Porcien's relatives, you were sheltered by a worthy man whose sense of justice revolted against such iniquity—by a notary who had charge of the count's will—a will which made you his sole legatee. And this unfortunate man, Mongeorge, led astray by his affection for you, committed a crime and the law showed him no mercy."

"I would have given my life to save him ; but what could I do ? I was a child when I was told he had been sent to Toulon—"

"Where he remained ten years."

"Is he dead?" the young woman asked, in a husky voice.

"No ; he is alive and at liberty."

"Thank God ! He was pardoned, then ?"

"No ; he succeeded in making his escape, and I know that he has atoned for his fault by the most irreproachable conduct. He succeeded in reaching a foreign country, and has since resided there ; but he has never ceased to think of you."

"Do you suppose that I have forgotten him ?" exclaimed Cécile.

"Well he has returned to France at the risk of recapture, for if he were recognised, he would be sent back to the galleys to end his days there. If he has run such a terrible risk it is because he is looking for you."

"Does he know that I am still living, then?"

"He has only been aware of it a short time. All trace of you was lost after the Count de Porcien's death. I myself went to the Ardennes, several years afterwards, to make inquiries about you, for I had promised Mongeorge to try and find you."

"I had taken refuge in Paris. I came on foot, and should have died here, had not Providence led me to the little boarding-school where I was so kindly sheltered."

"And it must be Providence that has brought about our meeting so soon after my seeing Mongeorge, whom I left only a few hours ago. He told me that a man from the Ardennes had seen you in an eating-house near the Palais Royal, and as soon as you began to relate your story, the truth flashed upon me. But why did the people of the restaurant refuse to tell Mongeorge where you had gone on leaving them?"

"I had begged them to keep my whereabouts secret. They told me that a gentleman had been there to inquire about me, and I thanked them for their refusal to give him any information. I thought the man was an enemy—that is, the same person who came into possession of the fortune which the Count de Porcien intended to bequeath to me."

"The Count de Porcien's heir?" exclaimed Mérindol. "Does he know where you are?"

"I think not," replied Cécile, "but I am sure that he has been looking for me a long time. It was because I believed that he hated me so intensely, that I fled shortly after my benefactor's death. My impression always was that this man, fearing that the count's real will might be discovered, wanted to find me to put me out of the way. I trusted, however, that if I disappeared he would imagine me to be dead, and then abandon his pursuit."

"It was for this reason, I suppose, that you changed your name."

"Yes; my real name is Cécile, and I took that of Clémence."

"Had you no other name?"

"No, sir, I never knew my parents," replied the young woman, blushing.

"Excuse me, mademoiselle, I did not intend to wound you. I had entirely forgotten what Mongeorge told me about you."

"I always thought," said Mademoiselle Cécile, as we shall henceforth call her, "that the Count de Porcien must have taken me under his protection but a short time after my birth. I remember no other face but his, and that of my nurse—a peasant woman of Brie, at whose house he used to visit me; and I was only three years old when he took me to the château where I remained until his death."

"Excuse me," said Mérindol after a brief silence; "but did the

count ever give you to understand either directly or indirectly that
you were his daughter or grand-daughter ?"

"No, sir," replied Cécile. "He treated me like his own child,
but I do not think I was, for in that case, understanding his character and feelings as I do now, I am sure that he would have
acknowledged me."

"You are mistaken, perhaps, not as regards his generosity of
heart, but as regards the law in such matters. You are probably
not aware that an illegitimate child, even duly acknowledged, in-
herits but a fourth part of his or her father's property ; whereas the
father, having no legitimate issue, is at liberty to leave all he
possesses to a stranger should he choose. The count may have
thought that it was to your advantage not to be acknowledged."

"He knew very well that I should have preferred the honour of
bearing his name to the advantage of possessing his fortune," replied
Cécile, firmly.

"I don't doubt it, mademoiselle," said Mérindol, struck by these
proud words. "But if, by an unexpected stroke of good fortune,
the real will should be found, it would be your duty to accept the
count's legacy, if only out of respect for his memory."

"I do not know what I should do in that case, but I hope it will
never happen. The heirs-at-law would certainly kill me."

"You would not lack defenders."

"There is certainly one upon whose devotion I could rely implicitly, but he is not in a position to render me effectual aid."

"Mongeorge! You are very much mistaken, mademoiselle. If
you would consent to accompany him to a foreign land, he would
gladly provide for your future. Would you object to seeing him
before he leaves Paris ?"

"I should be happy to have an opportunity of thanking him, and
telling him that I have never ceased to think of him."

"Very well, mademoiselle, I promise you that I will bring you
together in a few days' time. Not here, however. This place
seems very suspicious to me, although I only arrived a couple of
hours ago. I presume that you do not care to remain here."

"Oh ! I say to myself every evening that I will not return on the
morrow ; but I have so far lacked the courage to carry out my purpose. I should leave unhesitatingly, however, if I had an opportunity of earning an honest living, for I have undergone perfect
persecution here. Would you believe it, ever since I accepted this
situation I have had to submit to the most persistent and unwelcome
attentions on the part of certain employés. Monsieur Corraille,
who was the means of my coming here, informed me at the expiration of the first week that he should be glad to marry me. He told
me he was well-off, and that if we married, Monsieur Nalot would
give both of us very lucrative positions. Annoyed beyond endurance,
I wrote to Monsieur Nalot, making a complaint. He did not answer
my letter, but the scoundrel ceased to torment me. However, other
suitors came forward. I soon received the visit of a clerk who had

been appointed to superintend my work. He was a young man and less repulsive than Corraille, but I disliked him almost as much. He proposed to me ; I refused his offer, and after persevering for a few days, he also disappeared, another man taking his place."

" As a superintendent ? "

" Yes, and as a suitor also. The result was the same, and I thought I was finally rid of superintendents when—"

" When I presented myself," interrupted Mérindol, laughing.

" Oh, you don't resemble the others in the least."

" I shall at least have the merit of not presenting myself as a suitor for your hand, although Monsieur Nalot advised me to do so."

" Is it possible ? What, you as well ? "

" I did not at first understand the meaning of his words, or rather I misunderstood them ; but I see clearly now what he meant. It was to you he alluded, and I wonder what can be his object in making you marry—"

" I, myself, am quite ignorant on that point," replied Cécile, who, at this moment, was interrupted by the sound of a bell. " A dray is coming," she added, hastily, whereupon Mérindol rejoined :

" It isn't worth while that the draymen should see me. I am going, and shall return to deliver you. By to-morrow I shall have seen both Mongoorge and Monsieur Nalot. I want to clear up all this mystery."

## V

THE day seemed very long to Mérindol, for he spent almost the whole of it in running about after people he could not find. On repairing to the little hotel in the Rue Trouchet, he learnt that Mongeorge had already gone out, and would not return until late in the evening. Jean d'Autry, from whom Louis hoped to obtain some further information respecting the Count de Porcien, was also away from home, and his servant did not know when he would be back. In former years Jean had been in the habit of breakfasting at the Café de la Paix, where Mérindol next repaired ; but though he waited some time, his friend failed to put in an appearance. Even Delphine de Guibray had gone out and was not to be found ; and the attempts which Louis made to obtain M. de Porcien's address from her maid proved altogether unsuccessful. Although he offered the girl a louis for some information about the count, she feigned ignorance like a well-trained maid, and Mérindol finally relinquished his efforts. He whiled away the rest of the afternoon in the Champs Elysées hoping to espy Delphine's carriage among the crowd of equipages ; and this last venture yielding no better result than the others he finally resolved upon a decisive step.

The time had come for a full explanation with M. Nalot. Mérindol, since entering his employ, had never thought of inquiring into the manufacturer's antecedents, connections, or affairs. He had taken him for precisely what he appeared to be, an intelligent man of the middle classes, devoted to his business, and very proud of his fortune—more occupied with his speculations than with his family, but withal a kind husband and father. However, during the past few hours Mérindol had seen and heard so many strange things that he was beginning to doubt the integrity of this M. Nalot who had a usurer for his Paris factotum, and who employed such degraded-looking men. This doubt was very painful for Louis, for M. Nalot was Gabrielle's father. Mérindol still believed that the shameful goings on, he had just discovered, took place without the manufacturer's knowledge, but he felt it his duty to inform M. Nalot on the point without delay, and he was also determined to solve at any cost the mystery that surrounded his employer's intentions with regard to Cécile. Was it he who had organized a sort of conspiracy to compel her to marry even against her will ? Everything seemed to indicate it, but then what could be the manufacturer's object ? Was it an interested one ? The remarks he had made that morning seemed to show that he hoped to share with Cécile's husband, some fortune which was likely to fall to her. The talk about the Californian uncle was all humbug. Cécile had no relatives; though she might be acknowledged as the Count de Porcien's legatee in the event of the missing will being found.

The result of Mérindol's meditations was that, after dining near the Madeleine, he took a cab to St. Ouen intending to interview M. Nalot that very night. The pavilion he had formerly occupied was merely separated from the villa by the length of the garden; but it had a separate gateway, so that Mérindol could go in without being seen, and dress before appearing in the presence of the ladies. His windows overlooked the garden, and as he proceeded with his toilet, he glanced out occasionally in the hope of seeing Madame Nalot and her daughter taking a stroll, as they were in the habit of doing every evening in summer. However, he only perceived some of the servants. who, to his great surprise, were in full livery, and evinced great excitement as if some distinguished visitors were expected. The verandah was moreover profusely decorated with flowers, and all the drawing-room windows were open. It really seemed as if some kind of *soirée* was to be given, and Louis finally asked himself whether it would not be advisable to postpone his conversation with M. Nalot, after all.

He had almost made up his mind to defer the explanation, when he saw the garden gate, near the river, open to admit Corraille, the overseer, who was dressed in his Sunday best, with a silk hat and black kid gloves. Mérindol had a very poor opinion of this fellow, and, surprised by his appearance at such an hour, he remained on the watch. The overseer stealthily proceeded as far as the conservatory, and then hastily retracing his steps he sat down on a garden bench as if waiting for somebody's arrival. A few minutes later, Louis, more and more surprised, saw M. Nalot emerge from the house, and walk towards the overseer, who rose up with servile eagerness, and advanced with uncovered head.

The pair then walked down the path together, and although Mérindol could not hear a word of what they said, he watched them closely. M. Nalot's gestures were frequent and imperious. He was evidently giving orders, or perhaps reproaching his subordinate, who bowed humbly after each remark addressed to him. This went on during several minutes, and finally Corraille took his leave, bowing to the ground.

M. Nalot left alone, then lighted a cigar, and walked in the direction of the conservatory which was but a short distance from Mérindol's pavilion. Louis decided that this was a good time to show himself, and accordingly he hurried down into the garden.

Although M. Nalot frowned slightly on perceiving him, he quickly recovered himself, and his greeting was as cordial as usual. " I did not expect the pleasure of seeing you here this evening," he said, offering Louis his hand ; " but you are none the less welcome."

"I availed myself of the kind permission you gave me to come here. My presence in Paris did not seem necessary, and I felt that I owed Madame Nalot an apology for my unceremonious departure yesterday."

"My wife and Gabrielle did not expect to see you so soon, but your coming will be an agreeable surprise," replied M. Nalot. "We dined alone to-day, and the ladies are now dressing, for we expect a visitor—a person they have never met before. However, we are on sufficiently intimate terms for me to introduce you to all my friends, and besides, we can have a quiet chat until our visitor arrives. What have you been doing to-day? Are you pleased with your new position?"

"I wished to speak to you about it, and I must frankly confess that I have not yet been able to discover in what my duties consist. I went to Monsieur Séranon's office, but I could obtain no information from him. In fact, he received me in a very insulting manner."

"I can't understand that. Perhaps you saw him when he was engaged with other persons. Cashiers don't like to be taken from their duties, mine especially."

"Excuse me, sir, but he was alone. I began by saying that you had sent me to him, and he replied that he was not employed to teach me my business, and that he had no time to waste. When I ventured to insist, he shut his window in my face."

"Indeed! Séranon is an excellent accountant, very useful in all respects, but he lacks politeness and he has a very bad temper. There are days when no one can approach him, and at such times I myself carefully avoid him. I ought to have found out what mood he was in before sending you to him."

"Oh, I attach little importance to his reception, but I shall not expose myself to such affronts in future."

"Oh! I shall take him in hand to-morrow, and when you meet him again you will find him quite mealy mouthed; I know how to bring him to his senses. But let us speak of the other matter I intrusted to you. Did you see Mademoiselle Clémence?"

"Yes, sir," replied Mérindol, who then gave his employer an account of the incidents which had taken place in the rotunda, duly mentioning his altercation with the drayman who had threatened him with a knife. M. Nalot expressed his astonishment, and remarked that the carters were perfect brutes, almost always the worse for liquor. "Has Mademoiselle Clémence ever had any difficulty with them before?" he added.

"No," answered Mérindol, "she never speaks to them."

"Yes, I understand," rejoined M. Nalot, "she is proud; and she is quite right in being so. In fact, she is above her modest position. I feel convinced that she would insure the happiness of any man who did not attach too much importance to certain things one can dispense with. Her greatest misfortune is her ignorance if her parentage."

"She is an orphan, is she not?" asked Mérindol, diplomatically.

"The fact is she was a foundling, and in some people's eyes that is a disgrace. Would it be an insuperable objection to you?"

"To me!" repeated Mérindol in pretended astonishment, although he rightly guessed what the manufacturer was aiming at. "I really don't see what I have to do with the matter."

"I think you could easily win her if you chose. The question is whether she pleases you."

"Why, I have never seen beauty comparable with hers, and she is as wel.-bred and refined as if she were the child of wealthy parents; but—"

"But she has no fortune, nor have you. This would be a serious objection, but although this young woman will bring no dowry to her husband, she will bring him what are called expectations—very brilliant expectations."

"You mentioned an uncle residing in California, I believe."

"Yes, but I did not tell you all. I have good reason to believe that this uncle will leave her his entire fortune; and I know he is very ill. In fact, it is more than likely that he is dead by now."

"That alters the situation," murmured Mérindol, skilfully playing the part of a man captivated by brilliant prospects.

"That is to say, our dear Clémence will become a splendid catch," exclaimed M. Nalot. "What a chance you have! She does not suspect the good fortune awaiting her, and would feel only too happy to become the wife of a clever, young engineer who will soon be my partner. So, my dear fellow, you have only to marry her if you are so disposed. A little courting and the matter will be settled."

Mérindol pretended to reflect, and his attitude and silence seemed to indicate that he found the proposal a tempting one, and only hesitated for appearance 'sake. "Well, what do you say?" inquired Nalot. "Shall I ask the hand of the young lady for you? I think it would be better for you to plead your cause in person; but if it embarrasses you—"

"Excuse me, sir," interrupted Mérindol, "but you just told me that Clémence knew nothing whatever about her parentage. How does it happen, then, that she has an uncle? Foundlings have no relatives."

Nalot bit his lips. He realised that he had made a blunder; but he was not easily disconcerted. "Provided she gets the money, what difference does it make whether it comes from an uncle or a stranger?" he asked. "I only mentioned an uncle because I did not think the time had come to enter into particulars. The fact is, Mademoiselle Clémence is the illegitimate child of a rich man, who intends to leave her all his property when he dies."

"Indeed! why hasn't he ever paid any attention to her before? He must know that she is living as he proposes making a will in her favour. He is rather tardy in showing his interest in her, it seems to me."

G

"Better late than never," laconically replied M. Nalot, who did not seem inclined to enter into further particulars."

"All this seems the stranger to me," remarked Louis, "as Mademoiselle Clémence told me the story of her life—"

"Indeed ! May I ask what she said to you ?"

"I have no desire to conceal it. She informed me that she had formerly served as a waitress in a restaurant, frequented by that man Corraille, the overseer."

"Yes ; it was Corraille who recommended her to me. He had been struck by her gracefulness and intelligence, and could not bear to see her reduced to such a menial position."

"I asked her how she came to accept such a position, and she told me all her misfortunes," said Mérindol, who then briefly recapitulated Mademoiselle Cécile's statements. He was prudent enough not to allude to Mongeorge's escape from Toulon, but carried away by a sudden impulse he could not help adding : "And to think that the author of this poor girl's misfortunes is now living a gay life in Paris."

"Did she tell you so ?" inquired M. Nalot, eagerly.

"No, sir ; but by a strange chance I met the present Count de Porcien yesterday evening."

"Would it offend you if I asked you where ?"

"In a rather disreputable place, I confess. Some old friends took me, rather against my will, to the house of an actress who seems to be on the best of terms with this Count de Porcien. I met him at her house, where he goes to play cards. What surprised me was, that on hearing my name, he spoke of you. He knew that I was connected with your factory at St. Ouen."

"That surprises me even more than it did you," exclaimed M. Nalot. "I know the man's worth very well ; but he knows very little about me. I cannot imagine how he obtained this information. However, you have told me that you are aware that this Porcien inherited his cousin's property. The old count had made a will—which he unfortunately neglected to sign. And but for this oversight, Cécile would have been his sole legatee."

"There seems to be no doubt of that."

"Ah, well, my dear Bertin, I can now speak to you without the slightest reticence, concerning the plan I have formed to insure your happiness. I now know your character as well as if I had spent my life with you. You are one of those persons whose worth is apparent at once. I often asked myself what I could do for you. I first thought of increasing your salary, but I felt that this would be an inadequate reward for your services—"

"I am greatly flattered by your good opinion of me," interrupted Mérindol, "but I am amply paid already."

"You are too modest. You are not made for a subordinate. You have that practical knowledge of our business which neither I, nor the majority of those who own similar establishments, possess. What is needed is to place you at the head of an immense concern of this kind. But one thing—money."

"Money however is everything. It is impossible to succeed in any career without it."

"Granted ; and I first thought of giving you an interest in my enterprises, but I afterwards decided that it would be better to begin by insuring your independence by a marriage, which would enable you to choose your position yourself. Chance having put me in possession of an important secret, I resolved to take advantage of it to enrich you."

"And this secret is connected with Mademoiselle Cécile's inheritance, I suppose. Will you allow me to inquire how and when you learned it ? "

"About six months ago ; and I then turned my attention to improving Mademoiselle Cécile's position. As for telling you how the secret came into my possession, I cannot do that yet, for reasons that I will explain later on and which you will understand perfectly well. I do not even mean to disclose the good news to Cécile until all obstacles have been successfully removed."

"The person who is now in possession of the Porcien property will naturally not relinquish it without a struggle."

"Oh, there will be a lawsuit, of course, but he will lose his case. The authenticity of the late count's will is incontestable. It will suffice to compare the handwriting to prove that it was written by the late count, and opportunities for comparison will not be wanting, as there are at least twenty letters of his in the custody of the clerk of the court by which that notary was tried—"

"But the person in possession may have spent all, or part of the money, and as he honestly believed himself the rightful owner, he cannot be compelled to make restitution."

"You need have no fears on that score. By far the greater part of the property is land which the Porcien you saw yesterday still possesses and which he will have to give up—"

"If the missing will is produced. It is still in existence then ? Have you seen it ? "

M. Nalot hesitated for an instant, and then answered, evasively : "I know where it is."

"Excuse me, sir, for insisting ; but really, all this is so very extraordinary—"

"Oh, I can readily understand that you wish to obtain all possible information before coming to a decision, and I consent to tell you that the will is in the hands of a man who found it on the day following the Count de Porcien's death. This man is a rather disreputable character ; and though I am not at liberty to disclose his name, I can tell you that he was working at the château when he found the will."

"He must be a scoundrel, for he had only to produce the original will to repair an act of shameful injustice."

"No doubt, but being unscrupulous, he wished to derive some profit by his discovery. He makes no secret of that. He even boasts of having offered to sell the document to the deceased count's

heir ; but he probably set too high a price on it, for they did not
come to an agreement. Thereupon the man changed his tactics,
and devised a rather clever scheme. Cécile was then only fourteen,
but she would soon reach a marriageable age—"

"And the scamp flattered himself that he could then induce her
to marry him, I suppose ? "

" Yes, that was his plan. Although rather old and not at all
handsome, he relied upon her inexperience and poverty to persuade
her to marry him, and he intended to lay claim to the property in
his wife's name. However, her sudden disappearance from Vouviers
upset his plans. After seeking her on all sides during thirteen years,
a strange chance brought him face to face with her. He questioned
her adroitly, and as soon as all his doubts, as to her identity, were
dispelled, he again tried his old plan. Finding, however, that the
girl would never consent to become his wife, he came to me and
unblushingly told me his story, and inquired if I knew of any one
competent to obtain Mademoiselle Cécile's hand and willing to sign
an agreement to pay a handsome sum for the production of the
missing will. My first impulse was to turn the scoundrel out of
my office ; but when I threatened to denounce him for this attempt
at blackmailing, he coolly replied that if the authorities were set
upon his track he would burn the will, and thus ruin the orphan girl
for ever. It was the height of impudence I admit, and yet, his
words made me pause and reflect. I said to myself that if I refused
to help him, he would find plenty of less scrupulous persons, and
that Cécile might be induced to marry some good-looking but
unprincipled man introduced to her by this scoundrel. So would it
not be better for me to select a worthy man for her, and allow him
to negotiate with the finder of the will ? First of all, as I wished to
test her character, I offered her employment which she accepted.
I am quite sure of her integrity, and I can fearlessly propose her as
a wife to a man whom I highly esteem."

Mérindol started on hearing these concluding words, though he
was not unprepared for them. He was by no means in love with
Cécile, having bestowed his heart on another, but he said to himself
that she must not be prevented from securing possession of the property which her benefactor had bequeathed to her. Thus, it was
of the utmost importance to ascertain who held the will, and to
obtain information on that point it was advisable to feign indecision.
In such a case a little diplomacy was certainly no crime. "I am
deeply grateful, sir," said Louis, "for the interest you take in my
welfare, and the offer you make me. I don't reject it, by any
means, but pray remember that the consent of Mademoiselle Cécile
is indispensable, and that she has not yet been consulted."

"You shall consult her yourself, my dear fellow ; and I am sure
that you will succeed in gaining her consent."

"But I must know the exact conditions on which this man will
agree to give up the will, for it must be delivered to her."

"Yes, certainly, when the proper time comes ; but he doesn't wish to treat with her. He insists upon having the written promise of her future husband. You might pledge yourself to share with him the fortune which the document bequeaths to your wife. The money would not be payable until she came into possession. As Cécile would certainly not think of having it settled personally on herself—and besides she could not do so as you would already be married—you would be able to dispose of it."

"Then she is not to be told of her unexpected good fortune until after her marriage ?"

"No, that would not be advisable. I am satisfied that she would marry you just the same ; but it is as well to guard against a woman's fickleness."

This time Mérindol could hardly restrain his indignation ; still playing his part, however, he replied : "It is also necessary, sir, for me to take some precautions against this man, for if I married without satisfying myself of the existence and validity of this will, I should run a great risk of being disappointed. Can you show me the document, and allow me to examine it ?"

The thrust was direct ; but the manufacturer received it without wincing. "No," he replied, "the will is not in my possession, and the finder certainly won't consent to trust me with it."

"Then I must ask you to arrange an interview between him and me."

M. Nalot reflected for a moment, and then answered : "As matters now stand, my dear Bertin, I feel sure that I can trust you implicitly, so I will not conceal from you that the man who holds Cécile's future in his hand is our new overseer—Corraille."

"Corraille !" exclaimed Mérindol ; "I was right, then, when I told you that he was a villain ! "

"You are too severe," replied M. Nalot. "Corraille is hardly an honourable man, but remember he never had your training. He was formerly a poor devil of a locksmith and barely earned his living. A missing document, the importance of which he understood, for he is a shrewd fellow, came into his possession, and he determined to derive profit from it. This idea, which would never have occurred to you or me, seemed perfectly natural to him. He had found a will, and he wanted to sell it exactly as he would have sold any object he might have picked up in the street. Oh ! I don't approve of such principles, I assure you ; still it is true that Corraille, solely by his industry, managed to acquire technical knowledge and become overseer in a large factory at Reims. It was there that I found him, and his employer recommended him to me in the highest terms."

"That is more than I could do."

"Yes, I know that you were not satisfied with him, and I just gave him a good lecture for the want of punctuality you mentioned to me. He has promised to behave better in future. I almost forgive him for his apparent neglect, because I know that he is so anxious about his great scheme. I did not positively tell him I had thought of you, but he half guessed it when he learnt that you were going to work at our Paris establishment. He feels certain that you can win the heiress, if you choose, and he counts upon making a satisfactory bargain with you. And now, my dear Bertin, decide as you think best. I felt that I should render you a service by offering you this chance, and I am a little interested in the matter as we could unite our capital, and engage in some large enterprises. But my chief desire is to insure your happiness, and that of a charming young woman. So I hope you will decide to negotiate with the possessor of the will; you can, of course, break off all connection with him after the matter is settled, which will not take long. Think it over. There is no hurry. We can resume the conversation at some other time for I now see my wife and daughter approaching. Let us go and meet them."

The ladies came forward. Gabrielle's cheeks were rosy, but she did not smile; and Louis detected sadness, or rather anxiety in her blue eyes. Madame Nalot, however, was absolutely radiant, and her beauty had never seemed more striking. She had looked so different the evening before that Mérindol wondered what was the cause of the transformation. "My dear," said M. Nalot, addressing his wife, "our friend Bertin has felt so bored in Paris during the last twenty-four hours that he could endure it no longer. He missed us, and so here he is."

"Monsieur Bertin's coming is very opportune," replied the creole. "We shall not be alone this evening, as you expect a—a friend who will be very happy to make his acquaintance. Besides," she continued, while Louis bowed, "I am sure that Monsieur Bertin takes a great interest in Gabrielle's welfare, and I am glad to be able to tell him that her happiness is now assured. Yes, indeed, the dear girl will now soon be married."

Both Mérindol and Gabrielle turned pale.

"Yes," exclaimed M. Nalot, "I shall be able to introduce you to my prospective son-in-law this evening; he bears one of the noblest names in France."

"This evening!" exclaimed Mérindol.

"I am surprised that he has not already arrived. True, St. Ouen is a long distance from the Champs Elysées, but he has superb horses—a pair of Russian trotters worth as least ten thousand francs. Are you a connoisseur in horse-flesh?"

"By no means, sir," stammered Mérindol, stunned by the dreadful news. How was it that a wealthy nobleman was willing to marry a manufacturer's daughter? He could not be in love with her, for where could he have ever seen her?—she and her stepmother having led such a secluded life at St. Ouen. While Louis was reflecting M. Nalot resumed: "Ah! here he comes. I hear the sound of carriage-wheels. Let us go indoors. It is best for the reception to take place in the drawing-room. Come, Bertin."

The engineer would willingly have fled to escape the misery of meeting his more fortunate rival; but a glance from Gabrielle, an entreating glance which seemed to say, "Do not desert me," made him resolve to submit to the ordeal. He therefore accompanied the trio to the villa, and remarked that although Madame Nalot walked on by her husband's side, chatting gaily, she never once took her eyes off her step-daughter. "That woman hates Gabrielle," said Louis to himself, "and it seems to me she takes a strange pleasure in making me as wretched as possible. It is probably on account of the conversation I had with her yesterday."

At the foot of the steps, the manufacturer's wife paused to give an order to a servant. M. Nalot had gone forward, and his daughter, before entering the house, was able to whisper hastily to the young engineer : "I must speak to you. Meet me to night at two o'clock in the garden." Then she passed on.

Her father was already in the drawing-room, adjusting his cravat, and trying to assume a majestic attitude for the reception of his future son-in-law. Madame Nalot had scarcely had time to seat herself on the sofa, and Gabrielle was proceeding towards the piano to conceal her embarrassment, when the folding doors were thrown wide open, and a liveried lackey announced in a loud voice : "The Marquis de Mérindol ! "

Had a thunderbolt fallen at the young engineer's feet he would not have been more astonished. He could not believe his ears, and he gazed with all his eyes at the person who had so audaciously appropriated his name and title. The new comer was on the wrong side of fifty and he had an angular face, a squat figure and broad shoulders. His whole appearance suggested that of a street porter. However, M. Nalot welcomed him right cordially, and led him to Madame Nalot, who greeted him with her most gracious smile. Then came the turn of Gabrielle, who was as pale as death, and unable to utter a word in response to the fulsome compliments bestowed upon her by this clown rigged out as a nobleman. Finally, to complete the strangeness of the scene, M. Nalot introduced Louis by the name of Bertin ; and Louis allowed him to do so. He had not quite regained his presence of mind, and was still in doubt as to the course he should pursue. "Monsieur Bertin manages my factory with remarkable ability," remarked the manufacturer, "and I beg that you will treat him, not as my subordinate, but as my partner, for such I trust he will be before the end of the year."

"Are you a civil engineer, sir ?" inquired the false marquis, drawing himself up.

"Not exactly," replied the real one, "I studied at the Polytechnic School."

"I can't congratulate you on that. America has no institution of the kind, but she has the best engineers in the world. I have just returned from that part."

"That can be seen. Plenty of ill-bred people are met there."

"Oh ! oh ! You don't bandy words, young man."

"I do what I please and give but little concern to your opinion," replied Louis, turning his back on the visitor.

M. Nalot, greatly annoyed by this passage of arms, was too well acquainted with the young engineer's proud disposition to interfere, so he took his guest by the arm and led him out on to the verandah, under pretext of showing him the garden, leaving Louis tête-à-tête with his wife. Gabrielle had taken refuge at the piano at the other end of the room. "My dear child, you ought to give us a little music," remarked Madame Nalot.

The young girl required no urging, but immediately attacked a very difficult and noisy composition which she executed with a sort of fury, as if to conceal her emotion. Her step-mother at once took advantage of the uproar to say to Louis: "It seems to me that my husband's future son-in-law doesn't please you. Perhaps he was not as polite as he should have been, but confess that his impoliteness was not the only cause of the anger you displayed. You would like to marry my step-daughter yourself?"

"Mademoiselle Nalot is at liberty to marry as she pleases."

"Do you think this gentleman will please her?"

"I really don't know, madame; and I am surprised you should ask me such a question."

"I should ask you several others which would astonish you even more if we were not here. Do you intend to return to Paris this evening?"

"I meant to remain here, but I may change my mind."

"Will you promise not to leave without seeing me? I *must* talk with you, and in your own interest."

"I am very grateful to you, madame, for the interest you seem to take in my welfare; but I do not know whether—"

"Don't refuse. Here comes my husband. We will resume this conversation presently, when we are alone."

Just then M. Nalot entered, smiling, and followed by the pretended marquis. "My dear friend," said the manufacturer to Louis, "the marquis regrets having wounded you, and wishes to be reconciled. Come and take a turn in the garden. The ladies will excuse you for a moment."

Louis, although somewhat surprised by this proposal, readily consented, for he wished to discover why this stranger who was sporting an assumed name should have stolen his in preference to any other. Scarcely had the two reached the steps than the pretended marquis began his apologies. "Excuse me, sir," he began, "for having expressed myself rather curtly. I have never had a very high opinion of government schools; but I now know your value. My friend Nalot has just told me what services you have rendered him. It seems probable that we shall often meet, since I am to marry his daughter, and you are to become his partner, so we ought to be on friendly terms, and I shall do my best to ensure such a desideratum."

"And Bertin will do the same," exclaimed M. Nalot. "Indeed, you ought to be the best of friends, for if he has no handle to his name, he is nevertheless a nobleman by his principles and conduct.

Everybody cannot trace his ancestry back to the time of the Crusades."

"I attach so little value to mine that I did not hesitate to leave the province where our name has been illustrious for centuries, to engage in business."

"You allude to Provence, I presume," said the young engineer, without appearing to attach any importance to the question.

"Yes, sir, Provence," replied the marquis, a little surprised to meet a young man who seemed so well informed respecting his family origin. "Do you belong to that part of the country?"

"I have spent most of my life in Paris," Louis replied, evasively; "it was there that I met, several years ago, a young man who bore your name."

"And you lost sight of him long ago, eh?"

"About three years ago."

"Yes, it was about that time that the young fellow decided to join me in America. He had squandered his fortune and led rather a fast life; still I gave him a very cordial welcome. In fact, I was anxious to reform him, and make him my heir, for I then had no idea of marrying; but unfortunately he died three months after his arrival."

"Ah! he died?"

"Yes, and the poor boy left me no other legacy than two family portraits which he had refused to part with, even in his direst poverty."

"Two family portraits!" exclaimed Louis.

"A strange idea that of your nephew's in taking them with him to America," said M. Nalot, laughing.

"Ah!" replied the false marquis, "the boy had been carefully taught by his father to revere the name he bore, and he could not part with the portraits of two men who had made that name illustrious in past centuries."

"Portraits of an admiral and a brigadier-general, were they not?" inquired Louis Bertin.

"How do you know that?" hastily inquired the pretended marquis.

"I saw the pictures at the young man's château in Provence, where I spent several days with him."

"Indeed! Why, then, we are old acquaintances almost, since you have been on intimate terms with my poor nephew Louis. You must have heard him speak of me?"

"Never, sir."

"Indeed! Well the fact is, he was so terribly proud that he did not like to admit that he had an uncle who was engaged in business. He thought I had degraded myself."

"Well, he certainly proved that he was not so proud as he joined you in America."

"Oh! he was then at the end of his tether. Hunger drives the wolf out of the woods."

"It's strange!" exclaimed Louis, as if a thought had suddenly struck him. "But I remember now, that a few days before our separation, and on the eve of my departure for England, where I remained several years, Louis de Mérindol told me that all his family papers and the portraits of his great-uncles had been stolen from him."

"I don't understand what could have been his object in inventing such a story, for it was a pure fabrication, I assure you. I can easily prove the truth of what I say if you will call on me at the hotel where I am temporarily stopping. I have the portraits there."

"I should be delighted to admire them."

"Very well, then, Monsieur Nalot must bring you to see me some day. We shall be able to talk about your friend, my unfortunate nephew, whose loss I sincerely regret."

This was too much, and Mérindol, exasperated by such impudence, was about to unmask the impostor and tell him that he lied, when a servant hurriedly approached the verandah and exclaimed: "A gentleman who has just arrived from Paris wishes to see Monsieur Bertin."

Louis, turned round, surprised and somewhat annoyed at being diverted from his purpose. "Did this gentleman give his name?" he asked.

"No, sir; but his business seems to be urgent. He is in a cab near the pavilion, and he insisted strongly upon seeing Monsieur Bertin."

"Go and see who it is, my dear fellow," exclaimed M. Nalot, "and return to us when you have got rid of your visitor. Now that the ice between you and the marquis is broken, we shall spend a delightful evening, I am sure."

Mérindol hesitated for a instant, but concluding that he would soon find a better opportunity to reveal himself in his true character, he decided to absent himself for a few moments. Something told him that a man who came to St. Ouen expressly to see him at nine o'clock in the evening must have something important to communicate. He even suspected that his visitor was Mongeorge.

On reaching the road he perceived a cab, near which a tall man, wearing a very broad-brimmed felt hat, was walking impatiently up and down. Louis went forward, thinking there must be some mistake, when the owner of the strange looking hat bounded towards him and joyfully exclaimed: "Ah! thank heaven, I have found you at last."

"Piganiou!" rejoined Mérindol. "What, you have made such a journey at your age and without warning me of your coming! Why didn't you write to me?"

"Because I knew you would object to my leaving the mill, so I thought it best not to inform you beforehand."

"In any case I am very glad to see you. But tell me, has any misfortune befallen you or yours?"

"No, Monsieur Louis, my wife and children are quite well. They wanted to keep me at home, but I wouldn't listen to them.

Just think of it, Monsieur Louis; it is now nearly four years since I last saw you—four years come next November. Do you remember your last visit to the château ? "

" Yes, I recollect what occurred then, and really it is Providence that has sent you here to-night. Come, come with me." And Mérindol dragged Piganiou into M. Nalot's grounds almost perforce.

The worthy man, although surprised by this reception, offered no resistance. Louis bade him be silent and walk as quietly as possible, and then led him along a dark walk, to within some ten yards of the villa. Through the open windows they could distinctly see all that was going on in the brilliantly lighted drawing-room. "Look at the man who stands facing us," whispered Mérindol. "Do you know him ? "

Piganiou hesitated but an instant, and then murmured : "By the Blessed Virgin, it is the convict who stole your portraits and papers ! It is Ricœur ! "

" I was sure of it, but without your help, I could do nothing against the scoundrel. Let us go now. The time for action has not yet arrived, but it may come to-morrow, or perhaps even to-night."

## VI

MÉRINDOL was not a little excited by this unexpected adventure. Entering the pavilion he conducted Piganiou to a room overlooking the road, for he did not wish any light to be seen from the garden of the villa. He wanted to consult the old retainer of his family, and cared but little what M. or Madame Nalot thought about his abrupt departure. A man willing to marry his daughter to an escaped convict must be a villain of the deepest dye, and his wife, who favoured the plan, could be no better than he was. Mérindol concluded to let them think that he had returned to Paris; besides, he hoped that their attention would be too much engrossed by other matters that evening for them to trouble themselves any further about him. There was but one person who had any right to complain of his absence—poor Gabrielle, who was left a defenceless prey to the unwelcome attentions of a villainous suitor, and the machinations of an unprincipled father and step-mother. Mérindol did not wish to abandon her though he now felt less inclined to marry her. his recent discoveries had made him reflect.

A long conversation now ensued between Louis and Piganiou. The young marquis related what had occurred that evening, and the old miller strongly advised him to have Ricœur arrested. Louis was quite willing to do so, but for Gabrielle's sake he felt disposed to spare Nalot, who, so he rightly or wrongly conjectured, must have been the escaped convict's accomplice in various dark deeds. "Yes," said Mérindol, "I can at least spare Mademoiselle Gabrielle the disgrace of seeing her father sent to the galleys. I can tell her what is going on."

"So that she may warn these brigands!" rejoined Piganiou. "You certainly don't think of doing that?"

"I not only think of it, but I shall do it this very night, and I shall merely denounce Ricœur to the police when Nalot has had time to make his escape, if he has any serious cause for uneasiness, as I fear he has. I shall know for certain, however, when I have seen this unfortunate girl, for she told me that she would be in the garden at two o'clock to-night."

"And you will meet her there?" asked Piganiou.

"Yes, certainly. You can return to Paris if you prefer."

"Oh, no, I sha'n't leave you, Monsieur Louis."

"But I don't need you here, my good friend. On the contrary, you will rather be in my way."

"You may put me in a corner, and I will not stir from it ; but don't tell me to leave you, especially when you are about to run into danger, for I shall do nothing of the kind."

"What danger ?"

"Danger of being killed. How do you know that Ricœur did not recognize you ? He saw you often when you were a child. You have changed a great deal since then, it is true ; but he is sharp, terribly sharp, and he will take steps to suppress you."

"No doubt ; but not to-night. I have time to take my precautions ; and I assure you that I will be ready for him."

"Take care, Monsieur Louis, don't be over sure."

"Listen to me. You can remain ; but as I want the inmates of the villa to think I am alone, you must re-enter your cab, drive a short distance, then alight, pay the driver in advance for all the night, and tell him to wait for you. If he makes any objection, promise him twenty francs gratuity and he will consent, never fear. A sure means of returning to Paris must be at our disposal."

"Am I to come back here after doing that ?"

"Yes ; tap three times softly on the door, and I will admit you. If you ring, the servants will hear you, and I am anxious to prevent that. After your return you can go to sleep if you like. Shortly before two o'clock I will take a turn in the garden. Oh, the interview won't last long, and as soon as it is ended we will start for Paris together."

"Your plan suits me very well, Monsieur Louis—that is, if you will promise to call me in case you need me."

"Of course I will. So now go and make your arrangements with the driver and return as quickly as possible."

Piganiou needed no urging ; and Mérindol, after extinguishing the light, sat down, by the window to wait for him. In about twenty minutes the miller returned. The driver won over by his fare's generosity, was waiting on the road, at some little distance from the house, and could be relied upon. Mérindol now reflected that Mademoiselle Nalot might not keep the appointment she had made if she did not see him before she left the drawing-room; but on the other hand he was extremely anxious to avoid another meeting that evening with the pretended marquis ; so fearing that M. Nalot might send to ascertain what had become of him, he rang for one of his employer's servants—the pavilion was connected with the villa by an electric bell—and bade the man tell his master that having been taken with a violent headache he wished to be excused and was going to bed. He next tried to devise some way to let Gabrielle know that his pretended illness was only a pretext for not returning to the villa, and finally decided upon the following plan : Half an hour afterwards he went softly into the garden, and stealthily approached an open window at the end of the drawing-room—the same window to which he had previously conducted Piganiou. Stationing himself in the shadow of a tree so that he could see without being seen, he noticed that M. and Madame

Nalot and the pretended marquis were seated with their backs to the garden, listening to a piece of music which Gabrielle, who faced the window, was playing. Mérindol waited until the piece was concluded ; and then, just as the young girl was rising from the instrument, he suddenly stepped out into the light streaming from the window. Gabrielle saw him, but had sufficient self-control not to betray her surprise ; so he held up two fingers as much as to say : "I will come at two o'clock ;" and by a slight inclination of the head she let him see that she understood him.

Louis then rejoined Piganiou, who was almost asleep. "Lie down on my bed and rest," said Mérindol. "You are tired out."

The old man tried to protest ; but he was finally obliged to confess that he could not keep awake any longer, and consented to lie down with his clothes on, however not until Mérindol had promised to wake him up when the eventful moment arrived. Allowing Piganiou to snore on undisturbed, Louis went to the window overlooking the garden, and soon the heavy rumble of carriage wheels apprised him that the pretended marquis was on his way back to Paris. A quarter of an hour afterwards the lights in the drawing-room were extinguished and the shutters closed.

Two hours remained before the time fixed for the interview with Gabrielle, and Mérindol fell into a long reverie. His had been a delightful dream ; but the awakening had come suddenly, and the future which had been tinged with such roseate tints for a few months past, was again obscured by dark and threatening clouds. What was the situation? A hopeless love, a lost position, three years of arduous toil, ending in bitter disappointment. "I really believe it would have been better for me to have lived like an owl in my old ruined dungeon," he murmured. "I should have died of starvation, perhaps, but I should, at least, have escaped contact with the runaway convicts I now encounter at each step. I have a great mind to go back to Provence, and turn miller like Piganiou."

These reflections, and others of a similar nature, engrossed his mind until about a quarter of two o'clock. Piganiou was still sleeping so peacefully that Mérindol went out alone, contenting himself with leaving the door open so that he might call his faithful friend, if necessary. The young fellow proceeded towards the villa and stationed himself under a spreading sycamore, which would serve to conceal him in case an alarm was given. Not a light was visible anywhere in the house ; but the night was sufficiently clear to enable one to distinguish objects some little distance off. Mérindol could distinctly see the front of the villa, which was covered with ivy and clematis like an English cottage. In some places, however, the growth was not sufficiently dense to conceal the white wall, and against one of these bare patches there stood out a black line which Mérindol had never before noticed.

On looking at it more attentively he perceived that it extended from the ground to a window on the second floor, which he fancied was partially open. As all this seemed very strange to him. He softly approached the wall ; but he was utterly unprepared for the discovery which he made on stretching out his hand.

The black line was a strong, knotted rope, like those used by plumbers, firemen, and sometimes also by thieves. Had Gabrielle fastened it there with the intention of using it, to leave the house ? Mérindol could hardly believe that she was capable of performing such a gymnastic feat, and asked himself a little anxiously if some one had not surreptitiously entered the villa.

Just then a sharp cry broke upon the stillness of the night. It seemed to come from the second floor of the house, and the young engineer involuntarily looked up to see if the person who had shrieked was not visible at the window. But he saw only the creepers swaying in the early breeze, and all the inmates of the villa were probably sound asleep, for the silence which had been momentarily disturbed now seemed more profound than ever. Still the cry re-echoed dismally in Mérindol's heart. It was a woman's cry, or at least so it had seemed to him, and he anxiously asked himself if some one had not discovered Mademoiselle Nalot stealthily descending to the garden, and if the girl had not fainted in terror after uttering that wild cry. " She must think that I am here," thought Mérindol. " Who knows but she may have uttered that cry to summon me to her aid ? "

The supposition was absurd ; but lovers do not pride themselves on logic, and Louis was not in a condition to reason calmly, for this knotted rope, dangling from the window, had alarmed him greatly. He was still indulging in all sorts of surmises when a slight stir made him raise his head. To his infinite surprise he saw a man lean out of the window, seize hold of the rope, and begin to descend slowly and methodically like a person accustomed to this kind of exercise.

Mérindol rapidly drew a revolver from his pocket and cocked it, then, emerging from his hiding-place, he so stationed himself as to be able to attack the man in the rear. The fellow was evidently a burglar. " If you move or cry out, you are a dead man ! " exclaimed Louis with his weapon near the stranger's ear, and at the same time by twisting a scarf the fellow wore he almost choked him. This scarf concealed the lower half of the man's face, and a soft felt hat was, moreover, pulled down over his eyes in such a way that only the end of his nose was visible. Thus Mérindol was unable to say whom he had captured ; but this was not the moment for surmises, action was needful of all things. " March ! " said Louis to his prisoner, emphasizing the injunction with a vigorous kick ; " march, or I will break your head."

The scoundrel replied by a smothered groan and obeyed. Mérindol, without relaxing his hold or lowering his revolver, dragged him to the pavilion door, which he had taken the precaution to leave open. To close this door, he had momentarily to release his prisoner and for fear of an attempt at escape he gave him a vigorous push which stretched him on the floor.  He then at once slipped the bolt, and called Piganiou in Provençal dialect.  The miller sprung out of bed, and hastening to the spot with a lighted candle, exclaimed : " What is the matter ? "

" I have just caught a thief in the act," replied Mérindol.  And revolver in hand, he walked straight up to the man, who having scrambled to his feet was manœuvring to reach the door.  " Take his hat off," cried Mérindol to Piganiou, who sprang forward and executed the order with such dexterity that the prisoner's head was bare before he could make any resistance.  Prevented from concealing his face, he uttered a cry of rage, and dipped his hand into his pocket, as if to draw a knife.

" Keep still or I will send a bullet through you," said Mérindol, taking a step forward, and as he did so he recognized Corraille, the overseer.  " What ! " he exclaimed, " so you are the rascal who climbs into the villa at night to rob your employer ? "

" It's false," growled the wretch.  " I have stolen nothing ! " He was livid, his teeth chattered, and he looked wildly around him like a wild beast caught in a trap.

" We will soon see about that," replied Mérindol.  " Set down your candle, Piganiou ; and take off your leather belt and fasten this rascal's hands behind his back with it."

" Don't come near me," said Corraille, in a husky voice.

" No resistance, or I will kill you like a dog," rejoined Mérindol. " It is the last time I shall warn you."

" Come, give me your paws," said the miller, whereupon Corraille allowed himself to be bound without making any resistance. He was evidently much frightened, and Mérindol was surprised that the mere sight of a revolver should have such an effect upon a man who looked like a determined bandit.

" Now we will have an explanation," said Louis, " though it is hardly necessary, as you must know what awaits you."

" You are not going to murder me, I hope."

" Ah ! we do not care to soil our hands by touching you.  It is the gendarmes that you will have to deal with."

" You certainly won't have me arrested ? " said the scoundrel trembling.

" You cannot be fool enough to suppose that I shall set you at liberty.  Monsieur Nalot would never forgive me if I did."

" Nalot ! " repeated Corraille, shrugging his shoulders.  " I don't care a fig for Nalot."

" We will see if you talk in the same strain when you are in his presence ! "

" Yes, I shall," retorted the overseer.

" Then I will try the experiment to-morrow morning, but in the meantime, pray tell me why you entered Monsieur Nalot's house by the window, at two o'clock in the morning ? "

" In the first place, I did not enter the house by the window. I merely used the rope to get out.  I had been in the kitchen talking with the servants and fell asleep there. They thought it would be a good joke not to wake me, and when I opened my eyes I found that they had all gone upstairs and that I was locked in the house. Being unable to get out by the door and having a bit of rope about me I went upstairs myself so as to get out by one of the windows."

"That's nonsense! You concealed yourself somewhere in the villa, and when everybody was asleep you left your hiding-place to steal the plate or Madame Nalot's diamonds."

"I am not such a fool as to take them. You can search me, if you like. You will find nothing in my hands, or in my pockets."

"We will see about that presently. Perhaps you tried to break open a cupboard or secretary, but the lock resisted your efforts, and while you were at work, you were surprised by some one who gave the shriek I heard."

"The shriek!" repeated Corraille, turning still paler; "you are mistaken. There was no shriek."

"You lie! I heard a cry of pain—a woman's cry." Corraille started, and hung his head. "It was the cry of a woman, who detected you in the act, and whom you perhaps killed," added Louis.

"That's false! You can see that there is no blood on me. It happened like this. I met the cook on the stairs, and as I had no light she took me for a thief and gave a shriek, but I whispered my name, and as she knew why I was still in the house she didn't say anything more."

"But, if the cook saw you, you could have had the door opened, so why did you leave the house by the window?"

"Because I was afraid that her cry might have woke up the master or the missus, and I didn't want to be caught in the house. So, having my rope all ready—"

"Then you persist in declaring that you have stolen nothing?"

"I have given you permission to search me. You will merely find in my pockets my tobacco-box, my pipe, and some papers for a light."

"Papers!" repeated Mérindol, hastily. He had so far quite forgotten the story of the Count de Porcien's will; but he now remembered that the rascal who had possession of this will was at his mercy. "There are papers which are even more valuable than diamonds," he retorted, looking searchingly at Corraille, "a will for instance."

"I don't understand what you mean," stammered Corraille.

"Do you remember the Count de Porcien," asked Mérindol, "at whose château you worked as a locksmith thirteen years ago?"

"I'm not a locksmith, and I was never employed at any château."

"But you certainly stole something there—a will which you intended to sell. Come don't deny it, I know everything."

"Ah, you know everything," said the rascal, suddenly changing his tone. "Who told you, pray?"

"It was Monsieur Nalot."

"The scoundrel! I suspected as much. Well, as he has denounced me, I may as well speak out. Yes, there was a will not stolen but *found*, years ago in the Ardennes, and I am the person who found it. That rascal Nalot stole it from me—yes *stole* it. I should have returned it to the heiress, but Nalot took it from me to sell it to the man who marries her—to you, if she accepts you. So now you understand why he wished to employ you at his Paris establishment."

Mérindol could not doubt the accuracy of the charge. He had previously suspected that Corraille was only his employer's tool, and everything went to show that M. Nalot was simply a scoundrel. This thought filled Louis with grief and consternation, for M. Nalot was Gabrielle's father. But Corraille was certainly no better than his master, and he was at least his accomplice. A light suddenly flashed upon Mérindol's mind. He now understood why Corraille had scaled the wall of the villa. "He went there to recover the will," Louis said to himself. "The question is to find out if he succeeded." And turning to Piganiou the young engineer added aloud: "Search that man."

"Do not touch me," cried Corraille in a husky voice.

"Ah, so you refuse to be searched, now?" replied Mérindol. "A few minutes ago, you thought I should pay no attention to any papers found upon you. You did not imagine I knew all about the will which you stole back from Nalot a little while ago. Admit that that was your object in breaking into your employer's house at two o'clock in the morning?"

"Well, yes, it was; but if you denounce me, you will be sorry for it."

"Come search him, Piganiou," said Mérindol, shrugging his shoulders scornfully.

Piganiou complied, and speedily extracted from Corraille's coat pocket a paper, yellow with time. The prisoner offered no resistance.

Mérindol took up the candle which had been set on the stairs, glanced at the paper and saw that it was indeed the will. Cécile's inheritance was recovered. "And so," said Louis, "I was right, it seems. You had stolen the will. What did you mean to do with it?"

"I intended to sell it to the Count de Porcien," replied Corraille with unblushing effrontery. "I have been negotiating with him for three months past, for I never placed much reliance in old Nalot's plans, and Porcien was willing to pay me a handsome sum. Unfortunately, however, I hadn't got the document, and was only able to put my hand on it to-night. If I had known I was working for you, I shouldn't have taken so much trouble."

"You have spoken about me to the Count de Porcien, haven't you?"

"Well, yes, he made some inquiries of me respecting Nalot and the people about him, and I answered them. Porcien took an interest in the matter as he knew that Nalot could ruin him, if he chose. However, it's I who am ruined as it happens, for you have secured the will ; but I shall make the best of it, and as you will gain nothing by detaining me, I hope that you will release me at once."

" Release you ! I am going to hand you over to the gendarmes."

" They are all asleep at this hour," muttered Corraille.

" It will be easy to wake them up. We have a vehicle waiting, and we will take you straight to St. Denis."

" You certainly won't do that ! Hand me over to Nalot, if you like ; but don't have me arrested—or if you do the police will learn a lot of nasty things about Nalot, and that won't be very pleasant for you, as you have been in his employ for a year."

" What has Monsieur Nalot done, then ? " inquired Mérindol, secretly alarmed by this unexpected threat.

" Oh, nothing of consequence. He only practises usury, and acts as receiver to all the thieves in Paris. If you didn't guess that when you inspected his establishment, you can't be very sharp." Mérindol turned pale. Gabrielle was evidently the daughter of a dishonest man. "Nor is that all," continued Corraille, complacently noting the effect of his revelations, " the authorities may worry me a bit, but I shall get off easily enough, while Nalot will have twenty years' hard labour at the least. He had robbed and coined counterfeit money, and besides he's the convicts' banker, the man the police have 'wanted' for fifteen years or more. You don't seem to believe me, but it's true. You imagine that Nalot's an honest man, simply because his name is down in the Directory. Perhaps you also take Madame Nalot for a virtuous woman—a good-for-nothing creature who was obliged to fly from an English colony, where she was suspected of having poisoned her husband. She isn't Nalot's real wife ; he wouldn't marry her, for she would have put arsenic in his soup to get hold of his money. As for his daughter—"

" Silence, you scoundrel ! I forbid any mention of Mademoiselle Nalot's name."

" Oh, I know nothing bad against the girl herself, but I would advise you to ask Nalot to show you a certificate of her birth. You will find that she's a natural child. It isn't her fault, of course, and if Nalot is willing to dower her handsomely, the man who marries her won't do so bad."

" Silence ! " cried Mérindol once more.

" Oh, I'm not anxious to give you any further information ; but you will do as well to profit by that already furnished. Yes ; Nalot is the convicts' banker ; and although he has so far managed to escape detection, he will end his days at the galleys, all the same, and I'll send him there."

" What ! you intend to denounce your employer ? "

" I should be a great fool not to do so. You mean to hand me over to the gendarmes, you say. I can't prevent it, as I'm in your power, but I advise you to look out for yourself, for the police will

certainly make a raid on the factory and the place in the Rue
Mondétour.  You will be arrested just like every one else ; you will
go to the dépôt, and the Count de Porcien's heiress will go to St.
Lazare."

Mérindol turned pale.  He realised that Corraille was right.  If
the rascal denounced M. Nalot, both Cécile and the young engineer
would be involved in a terrible scandal.  No doubt they would be
able to justify themselves, but odium always clings in some degree
or other to persons arrested on suspicion.  Corraille saw that his
last blow had told, so he continued : "Of course I shall only do
this in self-defence, as I know very well that you were ignorant of
the real facts of the case ; I will even be silent, if you wish it.  You
have merely to let me go, and I assure you that the police will learn
nothing from me."

His meaning was clear.  He offered to sell his silence, and much
as Mérindol disliked bargaining with such a rascal, he felt that it
was probably the wisest course to pursue.  After all, Corraille had
only stolen a will—a will that Mérindol had succeeded in wresting
from him ; so would it not be as well to send the scoundrel off to be
hanged elsewhere ?  "What shall you do if I set you free ?" inquired Louis.

"I shall leave France never to return again.  It won't be a safe
place for me now."

"Well, answer one more question.  It shall be the last.  Do you
know the man whom your employer entertained this evening ?"

"The man who is to marry Mademoiselle Gabrielle ?  No, I never
laid eyes on him before, but I am sure that he hasn't been long out
of prison.  All Nalot's acquaintances are of that stamp."

Mérindol, after reflecting a moment, turned to Piganiou and said,
"Unbind him and let him go ; " and the miller, although still completely mystified, did as he was bid.  Corraille promptly availed
himself of the permission to decamp, and ten minutes later, Mérindol
and Piganiou entered the cab which was waiting, and started for
Paris together.

## VII

ON the second morning following the night on which Mérindol had left St. Ouen for good, Piganiou was breakfasting with his young master in a private room at a restaurant in the neighbourhood of the Central Markets of Paris. They had spent part of the previous day together, but Mérindol had found time to see both Cécile and Mongeorge separately ; and without telling them what had occurred, he had requested them to hold themselves in readiness to join him whenever he sent for them. Cécile, for whom he waited outside the establishment in the Rue Mondétour, had been only too glad to return home, as she did not at all care to remain in M. Nalot's employ. Mongeorge, warned that his preserver had a surprise in store for him, had promised not to stir from the hotel in the Rue Tronchet, so that Mérindol, who had quartered himself on Piganiou, felt sure of seeing both of them appear at the first summons.

Louis had greatly suffered, for Corraille's revelations had destroyed his fondest hopes. His only course now was to forget Gabrielle Nalot, the innocent child of an infamous father ; and he had resolved to leave Paris forever, and seek some quiet spot where he could live and die in peace. Before disappearing, however, he wished to make two people happy. Piganiou, who did not fully understand the situation, had a much simpler plan. He meant to try and persuade Mérindol to return to Provence, and reside either at the mill or in the old manor house. He had profited by the opportunity afforded by their tête-à-tête breakfast to make some suggestions of this kind ; but Mérindol had turned a deaf ear to his talk, and the meal came to an end without any important question being decided.

" What course do you advise as regards Ricœur ? " asked Mérindol, suddenly. " Don't you think I had better not trouble myself about him ? I am disgusted with all these knaves, but what good will it do to unmask them ? I shall never see them again, as I have made up my mind to leave France for good. What difference does it make if this scoundrel Ricœur has assumed a name which I shall never bear again ? "

" He will dishonour it," said Piganiou ; " he will commit some new crime, and then—"

" Then, my friend, everyone who knows me will rise up to defend me and confound the impostor. I have lived long enough in Paris and am sufficiently well known for the fraud to be speedily detected. I even doubt if he will dare to continue sporting my name and title which he assumed, I fancy, merely to deceive Monsieur Nalot. Mademoiselle Nalot knows the truth by this time, for I wrote to her yesterday morning. She will inform her father, and Ricœur will soon disappear."

Piganiou was about to make some fresh objection, but just then a waiter opened the door and ushered Mongeorge into the room. "Your letter was just handed to me," said the new-comer, gazing in astonishment at the old miller, who on his side evinced some surprise ; "and when I learned that you were waiting for me here, I made as much haste as possible, for I fancied you wished to see me respecting the terrible catastrophe which has occurred at Monsieur Nalot's villa."

"What catastrophe ?" inquired Mérindol.

"What ! haven't you seen the papers this morning ?" exclaimed Mongeorge, who seemed to be greatly excited.

"I must confess that I have paid no attention to the papers for a couple of days past, my dear Mongeorge."

"Mongeorge ! is your name Mongeorge, sir ?" cried Piganiou, springing to his feet.

"This is a good time to remind you both that you met each other some three years ago," said Mérindol.

The old miller now cordially offered his hand to the ex-notary, and quite an affecting scene ensued. Mongeorge had to recount afresh the various incidents of his sojourn in Italy, and Piganiou congratulated him on the success of his efforts. "However," he added, "it is dangerous for a man to return to France when he has escaped from Toulon. Judges have excellent memories, and the gendarmes also ; besides, there is the danger of meeting old and disreputable acquaintances, like that scoundrel who tried to murder you, for instance."

"Ricœur !" replied Mongeorge.

"Yes ; he is in Paris," replied Mérindol. "I have seen him, and so has Piganiou. And guess what he has done ! You, perhaps, recollect that he stole my papers and portraits on the same night that he attempted to murder you? Well, with them to support his statements, he now calls himself the Marquis de Mérindol, and was positively introduced to me under my own name."

"But you certainly did not tolerate such an outrage ? You cast his past in his teeth, of course ?" exclaimed Mongeorge.

"I said nothing—for several reasons—one of which was that you were in Paris. I did not care to initiate an investigation which would bring your escape to mind again."

"And for my sake you would allow this scoundrel to escape ? But no, it shall not be. I know what I must do—"

"You certainly cannot think of denouncing him yourself, for such a step would be your ruin."

"What of that ? I shall have done my duty."

Mérindol started. Again he realised that a truly noble, generous heart beat in the breast of this unfortunate man who had worn a convict's blouse during so many years. "My dear Mongeorge," he said, affectionately, "I will tell you in a few moments why you must not think of sacrificing yourself in such a manner. But you spoke of a catastrophe. What has happened at St. Ouen, then? A robbery has been committed, perhaps, and a missing employé has been accused of it?"

"Oh! it is far worse than that! Mademoiselle Nalot has been murdered."

"Murdered!" cried Mérindol, wildly.

"Yes, on the night before last. The papers state that yesterday morning the servants of Monsieur Nalot, a wealthy manufacturer, residing at St. Ouen, found their employer's daughter dead at the foot of the stairs. She had been strangled, for her throat still bore the marks of the murderer's fingers."

"It was Corraille!" exclaimed Mérindol.

"Ah, the scoundrel!" muttered Piganiou. "That is why he was in such a hurry to get away, and so afraid that we might hand him over to the gendarmes. I told you, Monsieur Louis, that we ought not to let him go."

"Well, the papers say that the police are on the murderer's track," interrupted Mongeorge. "His object in entering the house was evidently robbery, for a secretary had been broken open, and it is supposed that he was seen by the unfortunate young girl just as he was about to make his escape, and that he killed her to prevent her from alarming the other members of the household. Monsieur Nalot, it appears, lost no time in entering a complaint; and he seems to think that the murderer was a stranger. He clearly states that he does not suspect any of the members of his household or any of his employés."

"The scoundrel lies!" muttered Mérindol. "He knows very well that Corraille was the murderer, for he must have discovered that the will is missing, and Corraille is the only person who could have had any interest in securing it."

"The will!" said Mongeorge, failing to understand.

"Yes, the will of the Count de Porcien, the real will, which he signed and dated, while he only gave the rough draft to you. The villain who killed Mademoiselle Nalot found it in a desk which he was repairing at the count's chateau, where he was employed for a few days. He kept it in the hope of turning it to advantage afterwards. He wanted to marry Cécile. Monsieur Nalot was his accomplice, and the will was in his possession. Corraille entered the villa to steal it in order to sell it to the present Count de Porcien, who would have destroyed it, undoubtedly—and Corraille evidently killed Mademoiselle Nalot, who must have surprised him in the house."

"How terrible!" murmured Mongeorge. "But if this man Corraille tried to marry Cécile, as you tell me, he must know where she is."

"It was through him that she obtained a situation in Monsieur

Nalot's establishment. For she is found and I have seen her. But don't interrupt me. Nalot wanted to marry her to any subordinate who would consent to share the Count de Porcien's legacy with him. He thought me capable of consenting to such an infamous bargain, and so he sent me to his Paris house in order to acquaint me with the poor girl. I was fortunate enough to gain her confidence, and she told me her story. Need I say that she spoke of you, and that I told her you were in Paris, and that you had been trying to find her for years."

"Then she knows that I escaped from the galleys?" said Mongeorge who was greatly moved.

"Yes, and she assured me, with tears in her eyes, that she longed to have an opportunity of thanking the generous friend who had suffered so much for her sake."

"So she consents to see me?"

"I am expecting her every minute, and indeed here she comes, now," said Mérindol, hearing the sound of approaching footsteps in the passage outside.

The next moment the door opened and Cécile, escorted by a waiter, appeared before them. Piganiou, who had not previously seen her, was quite dazzled by her beauty, and looked at Louis as if to ask him why this lovely young woman had come there.

In the meanwhile, Mongeorge sank back on his chair, overcome with emotion. Mérindol took Cécile by the hand, and when the waiter had gone, he led her to the man who had devoted his life and honour to her. "Embrace her," he said to Mongeorge; and Cécile, giving a cry of joy, threw her arms around her old friend's neck. "I have united you. My task is accomplished," added Louis de Mérindol, with an emotion he did not attempt to conceal.

Cécile sobbed convulsively, and Mongeorge was unable to utter a word; delight all but stifled him. Piganiou, quite disconcerted at first, now began to understand the situation.

"We shall not be separated again. You will promise me that, will you not?" said Cécile at last.

"Alas!" murmured Mongeorge, "I shall be obliged to spend my life in exile."

"I know it, and I will gladly accompany you wherever you may go."

"What! you would consent to do that? No, I cannot allow such a sacrifice on your part."

"It will be no sacrifice. What is there to keep me in Paris? Are you not my only friend?"

"You have not yet heard that you are rich, mademoiselle?" said Mérindol.

"Rich! why I have not even a livelihood now. Even if I had desired to remain at Monsieur Nalot's, I could not do so, for when I went to the Rue Mondétour this morning to give notice that I should not return again, I found a crowd assembled at the gate and heard several persons say that Monsieur Nalot had absconded, and that several of his employés had carried off all they could during the night—"

"Ah, I understand!" interrupted Mérindol. "Nalot realized that he would be a ruined man if any attempt was made to investigate his affairs. The detectives summoned to his villa at St. Ouen might pay a visit to the Rue Mondétour, and he did not deem it advisable to wait for that. Corraille, by murdering Mademoiselle Gabrielle, compelled Nalot to disappear; and to-morrow, people will discover that this prominent manufacturer was simply the convicts' banker."

"The convicts' banker!" exclaimed Mongeorge.

"Yes, my friend, the provision dealer whom you sought in vain in the Popincourt district, has been conducting an entirely different business, under an entirely different name. He has been practising usury with the help of a scamp named Rognas, who pretended to deal in leeches, in the Rue de la Grande-Truanderie."

"I just heard that Rognas had also absconded," said Cécile.

"Like all the members of the band, of course. Ah! in a few hours, all Paris will know the story of the man by whom I was employed, and whom you, mademoiselle, also served. Don't you think, therefore, that the very best thing we can now do, is to leave France, and at once?"

"Now that I have found Monsieur Mongeorge," said Cécile, "I know that I am going to Italy."

"We will all go there," said Mérindol, "that is excepting Piganiou who can't leave his family. But he will accompany us as far as Marseilles. As for myself I will not remain a day longer in this accursed city."

"You, mademoiselle," continued Louis, turning to Cécile, "must return here when the excitement caused by Nalot's hasty flight has abated, for you will have to assert your claims to the late Count de Porcien's property. Here is his will, which makes you his sole legatee."

"What! you have found it?" exclaimed Cécile.

"I took it by force from the scoundrel who had stolen it. You are rich, now, mademoiselle. You will have to bring an action, of course, to recover the property; but you will win the suit unquestionably."

"But to gain it I shall be obliged to explain how this will came into my possession, thirteen years after my benefactor's death, reveal all I owe to you—inform the authorities that you were the superintendent of Monsieur Nalot's factory, and that I, myself, was employed at the establishment in the Rue Mondétour, the den of a band of thieves!"

"You will have no difficulty in proving that you were ignorant of what was really going on there, and I shall be able to vindicate my own character, if I am suspected of having abetted that rascal Nalot."

"Do you think, sir, that wealth will compensate me for the sacrifice of my peace of mind ?" inquired Cécile, looking Mérindol full in the face. "I can live happily and peacefully with those I love. Do you think I should be the gainer by the change ?"

"What ! you would leave the scamp who defrauded you in undisputed possession of a fortune that does not belong to him ?"

"No matter, I don't know him and don't wish to know him."

"Ah ! if you did, you would speak differently ; believe me, mademoiselle, he deserves punishment. He is a confirmed gambler, and leads a life of dissipation. Moreover, he knows that this will is in existence, and that he has no right to his cousin's property. Corraille offered to sell him the will, and this would certainly have been effected, had not Providence placed Corraille in my power. I wrested the stolen document from him, mademoiselle, and I now hand it to you, in order that you may be able to assert your rights in a court of law."

Cécile took the paper and tore it in pieces without even unfolding it.

"What are you doing ?" exclaimed Mongeorge.

"You can see for yourself, my friend," Cécile replied. "I prefer to remain poor, for now I am sure that you will allow me to accompany you to Italy, and I am also sure that no one will marry me for my fortune."

"Dash it !" cried Piganiou, "there's spirit for you."

Mongeorge and Mérindol exchanged glances. "When shall we start ?" inquired the young engineer.

"This evening, if you like " replied Mongeorge.

"And I am to accompany you, am I not ?" asked Cécile.

"And so am I," chimed in Piganiou. "You can certainly stop for a few days at my mill at Reyran. I will afterwards take you as far as Nice, and you can go along the Riviera to Genoa."

"Why not ?" said Mérindol. "Our friend Mongeorge has become Signor Giuseppe Casaldi, a resident of Ancona, and no one in our province knows him. People will take mademoiselle for his wife."

"For his daughter," interrupted Cécile.

"Yes, that will seem more probable," muttered Mongeorge.

"There is one slight change I should like to propose, however," continued Mérindol. "Instead of deferring our departure until this evening, why can't we start at once ? There must be a day train for Marseilles or Lyons. It is best not to lose a minute. What do you say ?"

"I am ready," said Cécile.

"My luggage won't be an impediment. I merely brought a valise," remarked Piganiou.

"I settled my bill at the hotel this morning," observed Mongeorge in his turn, "and I have all my money about me."

"And I have, in my pocket, enough to defray the expenses of

all of us," exclaimed Mérindol. "Let us be off, my friends. I don't care to remain any longer in this Paris, where a scoundrel can creep into an honest man's skin by assuming his name. If Ricœur is ever convicted under mine, I will return and expose him."

*     *     *     *     *     *     *

Twenty years have elapsed, and Paris has long since forgotten the celebrated trial which engrossed its attention for a month, and which the papers styled "The affair of the Rue Mondétour." Seventeen persons appeared before the Assize Court of the Seine, and among them Monsieur Nalot, who was proved to be the leader of a band of thieves and receivers of stolen goods. The St. Ouen crime only figured incidentally in the case, Corraille having succeeded in escaping to England, and thence to America. The scoundrel was never captured, so that Gabrielle's death remained unavenged, unless her murderer was hanged elsewhere for other crimes. A long and careful investigation revealed, however, all the knavery of the man whose daughter she had been, unfortunately for herself. Nalot, denounced by a letter from Corraille, who had hoped that Louis Bertin would be compromised in the affair, made no confessions, but his guilt was fully proved, and he was sentenced to fifteen years' hard labour ; he ended his days in New Caledonia, where his cashier, Séranon, is living still. Ricœur, warned in time, had fled, and thus escaped the ruin which overtook his prospective father-in-law. These two scoundrels had no suspicions of each other's real character, however. Each had tried to deceive the other. Ricœur had merely presented himself as the Marquis de Mérindol to dazzle a man whom he supposed to be a wealthy capitalist ; so he speedily renounced the title, and decamped, after burning the portraits which he had stolen from the old château. He returned to California, where he was eventually killed in a gambling-den which he opened at San Francisco. The self-styled Madame Nalot was not troubled by the authorities. She took to a dissolute life, more in accordance with her tastes than the quiet existence she had led at St. Ouen, and, some ten years afterwards, she perished miserably.

On the other hand Providence fittingly rewarded the deserving Mongeorge, who, after becoming the head of a large banking-house, died about a year ago, happy and honoured. No one in Italy was aware that this worthy man had ever been a convicted criminal ; and even if the fact had been known, public opinion would still have upheld him, for he had amply atoned for his one error by a long life of industry and integrity. Louis and Cécile closed his eyes after nursing him through his illness.

Is it necessary to add that the orphan married Mérindol six months after their departure from Paris ? The marriage, which Nalot had striven so hard to effect, thus became an accomplished fact ; but he was unable to reap any profit from it. Mérindol had certainly loved poor Gabrielle, but he had not loved her long, and his heart soon opened to a deeper and more sensible affection. Cécile shared this love, which was disinterested on either side, for she and Louis were both poor.

Wealth came at last, however; for the Marquis de Mérindol, as an engineer, won both fame and riches in the country of his adoption. He has just re-purchased the land that formerly belonged to his ancestors, and he is having the old château restored. Piganiou, who has become an octogenarian, is hale and hearty yet, and superintends the repairs with untiring zeal. He hopes to live long enough to receive his master next autumn, and he has quite ceased to regret the assistance he rendered to the escaped convict in the Bat's Hole. Besides, such adventures are no longer to be met with in the forest of the Estérel. The penal establishment of Toulon has long since been suppressed, and only the old folks of the district remember the red blouses and green caps which made the convicts so conspicuous.

THE END

S. Cowan & Co., Strathmore Printing Works, Perth.

www.ingramcontent.com/pod-product-compliance
Lightning Source LLC
Chambersburg PA
CBHW030127030726
47498CB00007B/2587